Praise for *The Tiger's D*

"K Arsenault Rivera turns many of the standard conventions of fantasy on their heads. . . . A love letter . . . thoughtfully rendered and palpably felt."
—*The Washington Post*

"Rivera's immense imagination and finely detailed world-building have produced a series introduction of mammoth scope."
—*Publishers Weekly* (starred review)

"*The Tiger's Daughter* sinks its claws into a reader and refuses to let them go until the very last page. . . . [There's something] mythical about this book."
—*Culturess*

"Rivera's debut novel kicks off an epic fantasy trilogy that pairs gorgeous prose with captivating female protagonists. You'll be enthralled with her story of two warriors journeying through a dangerous world, and you'll be clamoring for the next book by the final page."
—*Paste* magazine

"First in a series, this novel embraces its strong female protagonists and forbidden love. Both romance and fantasy readers alike will find this title unforgettable."
Booklist

"Rich, expansive, and grounded in human truth. It is a story of star-crossed loves, of fate and power and passion, and it is simply exquisite."
—V. E. Schwab, *New York Times* bestselling author of the Shades of Magic series

"The epistolary tale at the heart of *The Tiger's Daughter* unfolds with deceptive elegance, leading the reader to a conclusion at once unexpected, touching, and apt."
—Jacqueline Carey, author of the bestselling Kushiel's Legacy series

BY K ARSENAULT RIVERA

The Tiger's Daughter

The Phoenix Empress

The Warrior Moon (forthcoming)

Sixteen Swords (forthcoming)

THE
PHOENIX
EMPRESS

K ARSENAULT RIVERA

TOR

A TOM DOHERTY ASSOCIATES BOOK

NEW YORK

THE PHOENIX EMPRESS

Edited by Miriam Weinberg

A Tor Book
Published by Tom Doherty Associates
175 Fifth Avenue
New York, NY 10010

www.tor-forge.com

Tor® is a registered trademark of
Macmillan Publishing Group, LLC.

The Library of Congress Cataloging-in-Publication Data
is available upon request.

ISBN 978-0-7653-9257-2 (trade paperback)
ISBN 978-0-7653-9256-5 (ebook)

Our books may be purchased in bulk for promotional,
educational, or business use. Please contact your local
bookseller or the Macmillan Corporate and Premium
Sales Department at 1-800-221-7945, extension 5442, or by
email at MacmillanSpecialMarkets@macmillan.com.

First Edition: October 2018

Printed in the United States of America

0 9 8 7 6 5 4 3 2 1

For those who must keep fighting

The Empire of HOKKARO and all her Children

LEGEND

Battle
O-Shizuka's March
Road
Border
Plum Tree

DAO DOAN

HANJEON

XIAN-LAI

Father's

Lazy R.

Kosei-ri
Hanjeon Palace
Three Kings Road
Sodol
Lazy R.
Nodaira
Kunomi
Shinno
Churi
Xian-Lun
Xian-Ru Grand Temple
Road of Broken Oaths
Ban-diam
Jade R.
Bronze Palace (Xian-Lai City)
Xian-Qin
Crimson River
Peizhi Lake
Xuan Vu...
Ruby Palace (Dao Doan City)

Copyright 2019 by Tim Paul

THE PHOENIX EMPRESS

BARSALAI SHEFALI

ONE

It is an hour into Sixth Bell on the third of Nishen. Playful zephyrs swing through the narrow streets of Fujino. Outside the teahouses, girls in soft greens and pinks call to the passersby. They play their shamisens despite raw red fingers, conjuring songs about tea leaves and marital fortunes. Cooks standing behind stalls wave meat on skewers. Down the alley, two men are arguing over the proper price for coal.

When Barsalai Shefali was younger, she imagined this city was the busiest place in the world. This city's closer to the steppes than it is to Salom, where the cities are piled atop one another like a Hokkaran lady's robes. It's not so imposing as Alaraas, either; the castles in Ikhtar's capital are like teeth on the horizon. Here only the Jade Palace looms—and it can hardly be said to be looming when its shape is so pleasing to the eye. In the earliest hours of the morning, when the fog settles around the palace, the whole city is a hymn of green.

How she's missed this. Strange—she never imagined she would.

With any luck, Shizuka's finished with whatever it is that called her away. Shefali does not have a head for it. Listening to supplicants? Settling tax disputes?

Shefali imagines the Empress of Hokkaro sitting in front of her desk, her dress slipping off her shoulders. Her slender neck and graceful wrists. The way she'd look over her shoulder with that knowing smirk.

No matter how awful the day has been thus far, her wife is less than an hour's ride away.

The people of Fujino give Shefali a wide berth as she rides through the streets. An army walking six men abreast would have less space to itself. That is fine with Shefali. The more space, the better. This way she can afford to look up at the sky and hum the Bandit King's song without fear of veering into a crowd.

Come to think of it—aren't there fewer people here? Yes, there are the singing girls; yes, there are guards; yes, there are merchants and messengers and wives running errands with their babies on their backs—but there are fewer of them. The cacophony she hated as a child has dimmed to a dull roar.

The palace itself is surrounded on all sides by a wall. Just past the wall are the Imperial Hunting Grounds, with tall evergreens like aggressive strokes of paint. Anyone attempting to lobby the Imperial Family for assistance must make their way through the hunting grounds. The rich hire guides.

Shefali has never had need of a guide. The steppes raised her as much as her mother and aunts and uncles. If some starving animal should come across her, they will hunt together for food. That is all. She finds herself almost hoping to see one of the famed beasts of Fujino—it would be a relief to hunt the proper way again. To once more string her bow.

All the hunting she did in the East involved fangs and claws.

But that time is behind her now—she is sure of it. As the stables rise up ahead of her, she feels the tension slide off her back like water.

The hostler knows better than to offer to take Alsha. Shefali respects him for it. Once, when she and Shizuka were children, this man caught them holding hands. Back then, he chided them. His silence now is growth.

She allows herself a moment with Alsha, with her oldest friend aside from Shizuka. Shefali slips her gray mare a sweet. In the slow thunder of her heart, the steady winds of her breathing, Shefali feels the steppes.

Home. She's finally home.

Or she will be, when she's back in Shizuka's arms. Somewhere in the palace is Shefali's wife, and she means to find her.

BEFORE, SHEFALI NEVER bothered to learn the layout of the Jade Palace. To this day, she does not know which way leads to the gardens, or the library, or the barracks. Whenever she needed to find one of these places as a child, O-Shizuru and O-Itsuki sent guards with her. O-Shizuru often sent her along with an apology for having to put up with the place.

But now Shefali has her nose. Every few steps, she sniffs the air and searches for a trace of her wife's scent. The downside? She also picks up the scents of guards and servants and courtiers. Brief flashes of their lives play out in front of her. Some are ordinary—preparing tea, tucking in children. Some are . . .

Well, now she knows which of Shizuka's servants work for Ren.

The closer she comes to Shizuka's room, the more ghosts there are. They stand along the hallway as faded images of their former selves. Many bear wounds. A woman stands with her own severed head in her hands; a man on his knees scrambles to shove his ghastly entrails back into his body. One plucks ants from her ears, pinches them between her fingertips, and eats the remains.

Shefali pays them no mind. That is the trick of it. The moment you acknowledge a ghost, it latches on to you.

I am Barsalai Shefali, and I have earned that name twice over, she thinks to herself. Over and over she thinks this; over and over she pictures her hand in her mind. These are her fingers; these are the poems written in their webbing; this is the half-moon scar of her childhood promise. This is her hand. She will not allow it to change.

As she nears the next turn—why are there so many? As if an army would be waylaid by bad architecture—Shefali kneads her palm with her thumb and forefinger. Yes. This is *her* hand. A small victory for the day, then, that she did not lose control.

The door is before her now. Two guards in red enamel armor bow to her.

"Empress Wolf," they say to her.

Is that what they are going to call her here? So many names she's borne—what's one more? Yet "Empress" has never been Shefali's title, and to wear it now would be to wear robes over her deel.

"Barsalai," she corrects them, and as they slide open the door, Shefali's heart leaps up, her soul singing the song her wife once wrote for them.

But when the door closes again, there is only silence.

Silence, and the treasures of an Empress who no longer values material comforts as she did in her youth. Amidst the less-loved representations of wealth, in the corner of the room is a screen where Minami Shizuru—the Queen of Crows, Shizuka's beloved mother—stares at the viewer. The tattoo on her arm is both plainly visible and reproduced accurately.

Silence, and the altar to the parents Shizuka has lost. There, up on a shelf where the sunlight can find it in the mornings: a misshapen lump of bronze that was once a war mask; a scroll of beautiful writing Shefali cannot read, but knows to be the words of O-Itsuki, the Poet Prince. Shizuka's father, Shizuru's husband. Dust has settled on most of Shizuka's possessions like the first snow of winter—but there is no dust on the altar.

Looking back toward the doors, Shefali yet finds only silence, though her eye falls on the instruments that could break it. A zither inlaid with pearl and gold next to her writing desk; a shamisen with a phoenix's head for a neck. These, too, have been recently used, even as the stack of papers on Shizuka's writing desk grows taller than a small child.

Only silence and these *things;* only silence, and not Shefali's wife.

It should not hurt. Of course Shizuka is busy. It is nearly Seventh Bell, but she is the Empress now—there is much that demands her attention, much Shefali cannot fathom about her duties.

But it is that—precisely that—which is the arrow in her throat.

Barsalai Shefali journeyed for eight years through the desert and the mountains to return to her wife. For eight years, the focus of her life has been narrow and sharply rendered; a blade against her suffering. Nothing mattered except the feather. Nothing mattered except returning home to Minami Shizuka, to her wife, to the girl who laughs like a popping fire.

And now that she is here—what are all these *things?* From whence came this statue of Shizuka cloaked in a phoenix's wings? Where is the room they'd shared as children, where is the bed Shefali sneaked into over and over? She does not recognize the massive one in front of her, circular and raised up off the ground, the sheets embroidered with peacock feathers. These papers on her desk—Shefali runs her hands over them. Why are there so many? Why is Shizuka's writing desk so dusty when it was one of her prized possessions? The ink bowl is missing—why is the ink bowl missing?

Eight years she's spent trying to return to Shizuka—and she returned to the Empress instead. A woman whose habits she does not know.

Eight years she's spent trying to return to Fujino—and she's found the streets empty instead. A city she recognizes only in the vaguest sense, like a friend she met once when they were both children.

Of course, nothing is the same. She was a fool to assume otherwise. This journey has never been about her—and still she *made* it about herself. On their way back from the Womb, Shefali did not even bother to visit her own family. That, too, eats away at her. What has become of the Qorin since the Toad lost his throne? She tries to tell herself that they must be doing better than she remembers. If Shizuka is Empress, then surely she's granted the Qorin their freedom; surely she's granted Shefali's mother her proper title.

Surely.

But then—

SHEFALI THOUGHT SHIZUKA would be home by now.

And she expected to see more people in Fujino; she expected to see more happy faces. Shizuka swore she'd look after her people. That is why she stayed. That was the whole point of her staying.

And if she didn't . . .

What use are any of that girl's promises? She does not know the weight of an oath. She is not a proper ruler.

Strange. Shefali is used to the voices that call to her. After eight years of dealing with them, she knows each one as well as her own cousins.

But this voice—this man's voice—is new.

Shefali pushes aside the thought. A spasm it was, no more. Indulging it will lead nowhere good.

So Barsalai Shefali alone breaks the silence with a sigh. In her deel is a small piece of near-black Surian wood. Before they went into the Womb, she'd started whittling away at it to pass the time. Debelo did not share her sense of urgency, after all, and she could not find the place without him. So she waited, and she whittled.

The piece remained untouched after they emerged.

She takes it from her deel now. A vague snout, two rough-hewn legs, the rest of the body still trapped in the wood. Once, she dreamed that this would be a wolf.

Shefali holds her knife in her hand. She lets herself feel the weight of it and, more important, the stiffness of her fingers around it. Whittling requires fine control—another reason she's given it up. Some days she can hardly close her fingers together.

It is the third of Nishen. Today, she can close her fingers together. Today, she can whittle.

And so the wolf begins to take shape.

SHEFALI DOESN'T HEAR her wife coming—it's Last Bell, and the criers are wandering the halls, reading from the Divine Mandates: "A flower blooms only when nurtured. It is the Hour of the Daughter."

The lead crier starts the chant. By the third syllable, his junior begins, and then his junior, and so on, so that a simple phrase becomes an echoing cacophony. Shefali doesn't understand the practice. Labeling hours is an affront to Grandmother Sky to begin with— she will tell you what time it is with the changing of her cloak, with her two great eyes. Labeling your hours with needless racket when everyone who can sleep *should* be sleeping, all for the sake of some supposed spiritual edification—there is nothing more Hokkaran to Shefali.

Except, perhaps, her wife.

Shizuka is approaching, finally. Shefali can smell her: peonies and chrysanthemums, sharp metal and sweet wine. It is the wine that most concerns her. That smell has clung to Shizuka like her innermost set of robes for as long as Shefali's been in Fujino. At first she said nothing, for who would begrudge the Empress a drink? Who would say to her: *No, you cannot celebrate the return of your wife?*

But it has been three days.

And Shizuka has returned to the room later and later each day, today at Last Bell, today fumbling with even the flimsy paper door between them, today tripping over her eight robes as she crosses the threshold.

Shefali is there to catch her. She has always been there to catch her; tonight is different only in that it is at last physical again. For eight years, she dreamed of this: her wife in her arms, the smell of her, the weight of her, the sound of her laughter. And she is laughing now, as she nuzzles against Shefali.

But her face is painted white, her teeth are painted black; she has shaved off her eyebrows, and she wears the full eight layers of a Hokkaran Empress of years past. Her amber eyes have gone glassy, her laugh is . . .

Well, she might be laughing at anything.

"Are you all right?" Shefali asks her, though she knows what the real answer is. She scoops Shizuka up into her arms. She hardly weighs anything at all, even in all those layers.

Shizuka reaches up for Shefali's cheek. She pinches it, as she used to when they were younger, though there is no longer any fat there to pinch. Only skin and muscle. Shefali indulges her—Shizuka's touch fills her with warm joy, even when her new habits confuse.

"I," says Shizuka, and she makes the word last several heartbeats, "have *never* felt better."

"Never?" says Shefali. She finds herself smiling in spite of the situation, in spite of the drunkenness. So much of her is happy just to be with Shizuka again. She kisses her wife's forehead. If the white paint smears onto her lips, she hardly cares. "Not once in all our time together?"

"Hmmm," says Shizuka. She shifts in Shefali's arms, laying her head against Shefali's heart. "Well. You're right. Maybe I *have* felt a little better than this."

"Only a little?" Shefali says. She sets her down on the bed she does not recognize. Shizuka holds on to her deel and tries to pull her in.

Shefali wants to join her. Truly, she does. This teasing they're doing is as natural to her as firing a bow, as natural as steering her horse. She does it without thinking—just as she helps Shizuka out of her outermost robes.

But as she sheds each robe, she comes closer and closer to her unadorned wife. As Shizuka drunkenly wipes her makeup off on a proffered cloth, as her scar is revealed, Shefali comes closer and closer to the woman she left behind.

And it gets harder to reconcile her with the woman who has lost her ink bowl, with the woman who leaves important papers unattended, with the woman who comes home later and later and drunker and drunker.

"Only a little," says Shizuka, her face now bare, tugging insistently at Shefali's deel. There is hunger in those glassy eyes. "Perhaps you can come and make your arguments, if you feel differently. . . ."

Gnawing at her heart. The core of her soul wants nothing more than Shizuka—nothing more than the feel of her skin against Shefali's, her impossible warmth; nothing more than to let herself consume and be consumed by her.

But she wants *Shizuka*. And this woman before her is not quite her.

Shefali kisses her forehead. She holds Shizuka's face in her hands, running her thumb over the raised skin of her scar.

"Maybe another night," she says.

And it is as if she's struck Shizuka—her warm skin goes as pale as the makeup she's now shed, and she takes Shefali's hand with startling urgency.

"Are *you* all right?" she says. Her voice is clearer now; the worry sops up her drunkenness like a sponge. She tries to sit up and only flops back down.

Shefali catches her and kisses her on the forehead again.

"I am," she says.

Shizuka wrinkles her nose. Her scar pinches at her skin. Shefali winces; she should have known better than to lie to Shizuka.

"Something's wrong," says Shizuka. She's slurring a little, but the clarity's returning to her eyes. "Shefali, what's wrong? Have I done . . . I've done something, haven't I?"

Shefali watches her cover her face with her hands, hears her take a deep, sharp breath. She presses her lips together.

"We can talk about it tomorrow," says Shefali. "When you've rested."

"It's my fault, isn't it?"

"Tomorrow," says Shefali. Again she kisses her cheeks, her forehead, both eyes in turn. Even as her soul aches—it's *her* fault, she's upset Shizuka—she forces herself to hold together. In the morning they can speak of all this at length, in the morning they can—

A small thought, a whisper she does not consciously hear: *What use is it to talk to her about any of it? Four months of peace. You wanted four months of peace.*

The man's voice again.

Shame's wave swallows her. Is it better to let the matter lie? What did she intend to say? *I wish you would stop drinking, you're not yourself anymore?* What did she think that would accomplish? Is it worth it to hurt Shizuka if it means . . . If it means getting her back?

Anything is worth it to return to who they were. She'd promised to slay gods with Shizuka—and how is she meant to do that when the woman can hardly function? How can they be like two pine needles when they spent eight years so far apart?

Shefali opens her mouth once, and then twice. The words live in her heart somewhere, if only she can summon them.

I want to be with you. Really be with you, when you can remember that I'm here.

I want to know who you've become.

I want to know what's happened to this place, to this Empire, to my people.

But the words are stubborn, and not inclined to leave their ger in the middle of the night.

Tomorrow. She said tomorrow.

Perhaps that answer satisfies Shizuka's worries, or perhaps she resigns herself to it; perhaps the drink has finally caught up with her, or perhaps it is the crown that saps away her strength. The result is the same: in the time it takes Shefali to come to her realization, Shizuka falls asleep in her lap.

Seeing her like this—yes, it is for this she traveled. For the calm on her wife's face, for the way she curls up against Shefali, for her curtain of black hair and her skin soft as the morning clouds.

Four months of this—yes. That is what she wanted.

Shefali walks her fingertips across the bridge of Shizuka's nose. Tomorrow. Will Shizuka remember in the morning? And if she does—where will Shefali start?

In the quiet, in the dark, she makes her oath.

"Four months of peace," she says, "four months with you."

SHIZUKA BEGINS TO shift in her sleep. At first only a little—she takes her thumb out of her mouth and rolls, burying her face deeper into Shefali's lap. At first it is only this, and though Shefali can smell the cherry-sweet fear coming off her, she soothes her by smoothing her hair, by caressing her face and whispering to her.

But it is getting worse.

A low moan leaves her, going higher and higher until she is near screaming. Her rolling turns to thrashing. When Shefali tries to hold her—tries to keep her safe from whatever is making her so terrified, she smells *so sweet*—the thrashing only gets worse. Shizuka shoves her, hard. Shefali backs away—she wants space? She's asleep, this must be another nightmare; should she stop it? Should she wake her when she doesn't want to be touched?

Now Shizuka is screaming, now she is curling up into a ball, now she tears at her own hair, and Shefali's heart drops into her stomach. The sanvaartains say that if you wake someone during a nightmare, part of them will always be trapped within it—you must overcome the dream yourself if you are to be free of it. Shefali cannot count how many times she was awakened in the middle of the night by one of her cousins screaming just like this.

"Leave them to it," her cousin Otgar always mumbled. "It'll make them stronger."

But confronted with this sight, Shefali knows nothing about it will make Shizuka stronger. She doesn't need to be stronger, anyway, with all that she's been through.

And so Shefali scoops her up into her arms, in spite of how she thrashes; and so Shefali wraps her arms around her wife and holds her close, so close.

"Shizuka," she says, smoothing her hair. "You're safe. You're only dreaming."

She is gasping now, she is gulping in breath as if it were water and she has been wandering through the desert for years. But she is not awake.

"Shizuka," she says. "Please. I'm here. Listen to me, listen to my voice. I'm here, and you're safe."

Still—she's growing more still. Her heart isn't, of course; Shefali feels it like a hummingbird against her chest. Shizuka herself, though—the tension is falling away. She's starting to slump against Shefali now, and as Shefali keeps repeating that she is safe, her breathing begins to slow. Each breath—each slow breath—is a victory.

For long moments, Shizuka remains slumped against her. At some point she must have woken, for she's returning Shefali's embrace, but it seems she cannot yet bring herself to speak. That is all right. Shefali well knows the value of silence—and she can smell the fear, the guilt, the shame coming off her wife already.

"Take whatever time you need," Shefali says to her. "I'll be here."

The clock tick, tick, ticks the seconds—but it is a liar. That sort of time has no meaning here, not anymore. There are eternities between each tick: lifetimes and generations. As far as Shefali is concerned, the rest of the Empire—the rest of the world—can hold its breath until Shizuka says it can breathe again.

She rocks the two of them back and forth slowly, slowly. Her aunts used to do this when her cousins awoke, frightened conquerors of their own imaginations. There was a song, wasn't there? A song that they would sing? Shefali never heard it clearly—Burqila Alshara sang for no one—but she'd heard the melody. She wakes the memory of it now, hums it as she rocks Shizuka back and forth, back and forth.

"I missed your singing," Shizuka whispers. Soft and precious, that sound; Shefali squeezes her tighter.

"I'm here now," she says. "I'll sing whatever you want."

Shizuka half laughs, half smiles, laying her hand flat against Shefali's chest. "Careful now," she says. "Don't make promises you can't keep."

"Songs are easier to find than phoenix feathers," Shefali says.

"So they are," says Shizuka. She sighs, balls her fist, taps it against Shefali's chest. "I . . . My love, I'm sorry. I thought—"

"Shh," says Shefali. She kisses the top of her head. "When you're ready."

"I thought I was ready!" Shizuka answers. "I thought . . . I always thought that when you returned, I'd be better. That I wouldn't . . . That I could sleep, that I wouldn't want to drink, that I'd stop being so afraid. When you left, I felt so—"

"I'm here now," Shefali says. Being apart from her was a wound she'd stitched together, but hearing all this is tearing it open anew.

"I know," says Shizuka. She lays her head against Shefali's shoulder. "And I thought that would help. Shefali, I thought that would help, but I'm . . . I'm not getting better."

As porcelain under a hammer—Shizuka's voice, Shefali's soul.

"What do you mean?" Shefali says. "Shizuka. Whatever it is that's troubling you—you have my sword to slay it."

Shizuka pinches her nose. Shame, again—she smells of shame. "I owe you a story," she says. "The letter you wrote me was so beautiful, and I . . . I should tell you, really, everything that's happened. There's . . . if you knew all of it, you might not . . . I owe you a letter."

When did the bold O-Shizuka start stammering like this?

"But I can't even do that," Shizuka says. "I can't even write to you. Because of the . . . Because of the water. I can't look at it. Just a bowl of it, Shefali. Just a bowl. Looking at it makes me remember, and—"

Shizuka sucks in a breath, shivers, trembles. As if she is trying to cry but the tears will not come.

Shefali holds her wife tighter. "When you are ready," she says, "I will carry your weight."

"I couldn't ask you to do that," Shizuka says. "You carry so much already. My suffering is a grain of rice, and yours is a boulder."

Shefali kisses her on the forehead.

"You didn't ask," she says. "And suffering is not a contest. Losing a limb, losing a horse, losing a friend—the pain's different, but the crying's the same."

O-SHIZUKA

ONE

There are people who have never heard Barsalai Shefali speak. There are people who do not know the joy of a violet-gold sky, people who have never bitten into a ripe mango and felt its juice run down their chin, people who have never heard Tanaka Kyosuke's *Petals Landing on a Maiden's Hair.* Some things in life are so pure, so pleasurable, that once you've experienced them, all imitators fade away.

So it is with Shefali. Each word from her lips is precious poetry, each sentence a hidden hymn for Shizuka's ears alone.

"WE WERE GIRLS when we spoke our vows," says Shefali. "We have seen things, you and I. Done things. Some of them awful. Some of them are best left to fade into the clouds of memory. But, Shizuka, every day we were apart, I longed for you. Every day of those eight years, I dreamed of our life together. But dreams are the same as clouds, aren't they?"

She kisses Shizuka's nose.

"You say we are gods. I know you are right, and one day far from now, I will tell you how. You say heroes do not grow old. But for the next few months—let us not be heroes, then. Let us be normal women, in a normal marriage, content to be together. Let us live in the clouds. When the time to go north comes, we shall be glad we tasted the sky."

Is this how her mother felt, listening to her father? Is this how Minami Shiori felt, is this how Tumenbayar felt? How could any of the Hundred Heroes claim to know the love blooming in her heart?

"Shefali," Shizuka whispers. "Come here."

Words fail to capture it, how she craves this closeness, how she needs this reassurance, how Shefali's touch reminds her that she is real and they are real and they are here, together, in this moment.

The two of them take this night and stretch it over their heads, and make a tent, and when the morning comes, they will be safe.

The sky outside is already beginning to change color: violet-gold, to announce the dawn. Shizuka kisses the crook of Shefali's neck.

So HEAVY IS her duty that she feels it even now, nuzzled against her wife as the first rays of morning beg for her attention. Who melted down the Phoenix Crown, who poured that molten gold into Shizuka's veins?

She wishes to carve it all out. She wishes to see it driven out of her, this Imperial stain.

All Shizuka wants is to relax into her wife's arms—but her mind won't let her.

And nor will her servants. Just as Shefali begins to ask her what brought on this attack, they hear the shuffling of their arrival. Shizuka glances toward the massive clock on one wall. Baozhai presented it to her two years ago as a birthday gift; the note attached mentioned that a busy woman like the Empress might have trouble keeping track of the time. It was a good-natured joke, of course, since Shizuka had been late to the past three monthly advisory meetings in a row—but no one can doubt the extravagance of such a thing. In all the Empire, there are precious few of its like. But Queen Lai Baozhai was no longer an Imperial subject, and so she had paid no mind to such constrictions.

The large hand points to the Grandfather beating a sword into shape atop an anvil. Shizuka tries not to wonder about him as a man, or even a god, tries to think of him only as a symbol. Second Bell, then—though the small hand tells her it is nearly Third.

Time enough to tell a story before the real world comes for her.

"Shefali," Shizuka says. Shefali's eyes flick over to her: the green and the steel. It has been so long since she last saw the steel that she forgets, at times, the character written upon it. *Peony*. A flower for bravery, a flower for daring; the flower of kings.

"Hm?"

Shizuka traces her thumb just beneath the steel eye. When Minami Shiori forged the rays of the sun into three swords—had she expected they'd end up in a place like this? Shizuka can think of no place more fitting; her wife's gaze is more precious to her than all the light of the world.

"If . . . We have some time, if you'd like to hear it. The story," Shizuka says.

"If you are willing to tell it," Shefali says.

Will that light still shine on her once the story is done? It will do Shizuka no good to wonder.

She can only hope, and begin.

And In Your Wake

Inconsolable.

If I had to choose a word, I think, that would be it. Mind you, I do not think it comes close to describing what I felt.

My uncle exiled you on the seventeenth of Nanatsu. That date, like the ninth, is carved into the walls of my heart. On the seventeenth of Nanatsu, the doors of the Bronze Palace slammed shut between us. My uncle commandeered the Xianese guard to escort you to the border; he did not want to sully the hands of his men with touching you.

If my uncle had commanded his stolen guards to hold me down that day, if he cut into me like a deer, if he cracked apart my ribs and bit into my heart in front of me—I would have been in less pain. If ever a poet captures that sort of agony on paper, I hope they are wise enough to burn it.

You know what it was like, my love. I hate to dwell on this particular pain when there is so much you do not already know. Suffice it to say that in the face of my world collapsing around me, I resolved to live on in the ruins.

I stopped brushing my hair, so that it would retain some of your touch. You left behind a pair of pants I wore for seven days straight, although I not once left my rooms in the Bronze Palace. I hardly even left the bed—in the mornings, I would wake expecting to see your face, and when I didn't, my weeping began. I fell asleep each night holding on to one of your unfinished bows. Anything to feel closer to you, Shefali, anything to convince myself that you would be gone only a month.

Within the four walls of my room, I wept until my eyes went crane-feather red. I bit my lips until they bled; I sobbed until my throat split like bamboo beneath a mallet.

Yet I was not alone in my suffering, no matter how much I wished to be. Baozhai and your brother were not on speaking terms given what he'd done, but they'd come to an agreement regarding me. Every Bell they were awake, one or the other would come to ask if I wanted company. I did not. Especially not the company of a man who'd sold me out to my uncle.

That sort of sadness is a strange thing, isn't it? So heavy and so immense that it crawls out from your mind and lies down at your side. Like a lover, it caresses your throat, your heart, your stomach. Everywhere it touches is alight with agony. You want to run, but if you do—well, who would hold you then?

No one.

Not you.

And so I lay there in my bed and I clutched my pillow to my chest just to get the scent of you.

When I woke on the twentieth, Baozhai sat next to me with a tray.

Had she been there all night? Xianese chairs weren't comfortable; her back had to have been aching.

I swallowed and called out her name.

Baozhai snapped to attention.

"Lady," she said. "Eight pardons for intruding. You have not eaten."

Though she spoke half in a haze, her manners were impeccable. I wondered if she had sprung fully formed from her mother's womb.

My head throbbed and my lips were dry. But I did not want to eat. Eating meant . . . the last time I'd eaten was with you. And if I ate now, I could no longer say that. Besides, what was the use in eating? To keep myself alive? What did it matter, when I did not have you to share my days?

Whatever sharp retort I had came out in a garbled whine.

Baozhai took that as an invitation. She set the tray on my lap and poured me a cup of now-cool tea.

"I understand you may not feel hungry," she said, "but I promise you that you are. If you have trouble holding your chopsticks, I shall be happy to help. But I am not leaving this room until you eat. You are not your wife, Lady, you need to eat."

Wife.

She said "your wife."

Hearing someone else say it brought me some relief. No, you were not here with me—but we were married.

You were so handsome, Shefali, reciting your vows. Have I ever told you that? The candles flickering, your skin so warm and golden, my hands in yours. You were so happy. You smiled so much, your eyes wrinkled.

The memory of your face soothed me. The memory of your touch, your voice.

My wife.

Baozhai leaned over me. When she frowned, spidery lines ruined the confident strokes of her face. She took the bowl into her lap. With the chopsticks, she heaped a ball of rice onto a flat wooden spoon.

"Your uncle is Emperor; you will rule after him, and into eternity, if the Lady of Flowers is kind," she said. To hear her now, one would never assume she'd just woken up. "But this is the Bronze Palace. So long as I live, it is mine, and I rule it. Imperial blood or not—I will not let you starve. Not in my house." A beat. She touched her fingertips to the teapot and sighed. "Even if I did serve you cold tea. Eight pardons, once more."

I reached for the cup. My hands shook, which terrified me—I have never been a woman who trembles. I held fast to the cup of tea and allowed my focus to drift for a moment.

Have you ever noticed, Shefali, that I never drink anything cold? Even in the midst of the steppes, on the coldest of nights, steam rose from my cup. The reason for it is as simple as it is difficult to explain: there is some sort of fire in my veins. Just as you have never been bothered by the dark, I have never truly been bothered by the cold. It started when I was five or six, I think, after our first meeting. For weeks, I used to set everything boiling with a touch, and I found that I could stick my fingers in the liquid without getting burned.

Of course, I immediately used this unchecked power for evil. By the third time I evaporated my mother's prized Smiling Fox rice wine, I'd learned to control it out of necessity. O-Shizuru was not a kind woman when it came to destruction of her property.

You may be remembering all those times I asked to share a bedroll with you on the steppes—all the times I complained that I was near freezing and would surely die without your company. I'll tell you now that I was faking it. I wanted so badly to be close to you—but I couldn't think of a better way to ask. And so I said I was dying of chill, when in fact I was almost unbearably hot.

I am sorry you had to find out this way.

And so it took only a moment for a curl of smoke to rise from the teacup Baozhai had brought me.

Lai Baozhai has been all her life a diplomat. Hokkarans often speak of maintaining our faces—making certain we look neutral even in times of great duress. Baozhai excels at this, except she does not look neutral. "Vaguely amused" is a finer term for it, as if you have told her a joke that she has heard before but enjoys nonetheless.

When she saw the smoke, her mask slipped. Astonishment overcame her amusement. Her lips parted.

But do not forget what I have said—she has spent a whole lifetime at this. Her astonishment was as a cloud passing over the sun; when she gathered herself, she seemed all the brighter.

"Lady, was I not clear enough? This is *my* palace. Though the flowers turn to face you, and the light clings to you like a cloak, make no mistake: this realm is *mine*. Drinking tea does not count as eating, and you will eat."

Precious few people spoke to me in such a way. It was surprising, but it should not have been. If not for the reprehensible actions of my great-grandfather Yoshinaga, Baozhai would be Queen in her own right. Though my ancestors tried to deny her the crown, she'd forged one herself, from the love of her people and pride in her own nation, from the ink she'd spilled at the White Leaf Academy. There could be no doubt who was the more regal between the two of us. How foolish of me that I had not seen it until then.

I inclined my head as I would have to the lords of Shiratori or Fuyutsuki, if I'd cared about etiquette when it came to those two. "As you say, then."

She held the spoon in front of my face. I took a bite, then reached for it myself. To my horror, my hands shook too much to get a good grip. The spoon fell to the bed, scattering grains of rice everywhere.

Another coil of misery around my throat. I could not even feed myself. I, Jewel of the Empire.

"I'll get a new set of sheets," said Baozhai. "Keep eating."

She held up another portion, and another. It was clear from her bearing, she'd brook no arguments on my part. The more I ate, the more my stomach protested. And yet—I did feel better. I had to admit that. It was the smallest bit better, but it was something.

By the time we got halfway through the bowl, I was too full to continue. Baozhai kept trying to feed me anyway. Only when I mustered up the strength to speak did she stop.

"If I have one more bite," I said, "I will be running for my chamber pot."

Baozhai narrowed her eyes. "Are you certain?"

"I am always certain," I said. But you know already that I am not. The trick to decisiveness is to make your choice before the fear starts setting in. Luckily for me, I am always afraid, and so I have very little time to make my choices. Once I've voiced them, once I've committed—there can be no room for doubt.

If I falter, you see, if I allow myself to fall—it is not just me that crumbles. In many ways, I do not exist. Only Princess Yui did, only Empress Yui does. From the day two pine needles fell on my unsuspecting brow, I have been the hope of a nation. Peacock Princess, Daughter of Crows, Four-Petal Princess, I have been all these and more.

But I can only be Minami Shizuka with you.

"My husband wishes to speak with you," said Baozhai. The words came from her as if yanked out by a string.

"Why should I listen to him?" I asked, for there must have been good reason. Baozhai was as frustrated with him as I was.

"Because he has two good Qorin horses his mother gave to him, and he wants to meet your wife before she leaves," said Baozhai. "The captain in charge of escorting Barsalyya is an older man with a bad hip. No doubt he will call for stops along the way. Kenshiro is convinced this will allow him to catch up to them. He means to set out as soon as he has spoken to you."

The beats of my heart rumbled through my body, as if I lay on the skin of a massive drum. Could he really catch up to you, though so much time had passed? What had taken him so long to say so? Kenshiro may have been Qorin, too, but he did not have your way with horses. Surely he'd ride them both to death at best. Surely he would not be able to reach you. And yet . . .

I would be able to send you one final letter.

I would cut through all eight of the Fallen Gods, one by one, for the privilege of speaking to you one more time. I would have used their blood for ink and their bones for brushes, Shefali.

To my blasphemous heart, speaking to your brother was hardly a price at all.

"Send him in," I said.

"Are you certain? If you would rather prepare a letter and give it to me, I'd pass it on for you."

"If he means for this to be his apology, then I want to see his face when he delivers it," I said. "I want to hear it from his mouth."

After a moment of consideration, Baozhai nodded. "Then I shall fetch him."

I watched her, in her day-old gown, walk to the door and leave. For a brief span I sat alone in the room. So much of it seemed preposterous now. The sheets I'd flung and the furniture I'd knocked over, the spilled ink and the faint smell of my own filth. Up above the door, the altar I kept for my parents; in three days I had not changed the rice. What would they think, if they saw me in such a state?

The memory of my mother in her final days came to me. She'd cried out for my father until her last moments.

Perhaps she would have understood.

But she would have insisted I do some cleaning, at the very least. My mother was always particular about her surroundings. Living in the Jade Palace, there are only so many things one can change without drawing the Emperor's ire—but my mother changed everything she could. The mats she replaced with those her family had made. All the art—portraits of my ancestors and all the gods alike—she replaced with portraits of Minami Shiori. A few of them were nature paintings for my father's sake. An antique set of robes belonging to Empress Yumiko embroidered with painstakingly small leaves was sent back to the Imperial archivist in favor of displaying a saddle Burqila Alshara had given her.

"You've got to keep control of your space, you hear me?" she'd said to me. "Even if you can't control anything else. I've slept in a stable more than once, but you can be sure I chose to do it."

Well. I had no saddle to display, and there were no paintings of my forefathers here staring me down. And this was, as Baozhai had reminded me, not my palace. Still—if I asked nicely, perhaps Baozhai could be convinced to let me do a little decorating. So few of the things in this room were mine. The teapot, my robes, a screen with Minami Shiori and the fox woman painted upon it. As I looked around me, a beam of light fell upon my mother's remaining two swords.

An idea came to me. Baozhai spoke of writing a letter to you, but what would I say? If these were the last words you and I shared, though I dreaded that thought—what would I say?

Letters are only paper. They may tear or fall apart or burn or eighty other things. Words can live forever, if we give them voice. Like leaves on a breeze, they float from one mouth to the next. And though

you are not the type to share them aloud, Shefali, you do hoard them
as a frog-god hoards his brains. Words are your lifeblood, poetry your
breath.

If only I had my father's talents.

And so, if words failed me, then I must make a grand gesture.

A gift. But what to give you? All my favorite things, you've given
me. The flower you plucked from Gurkhan Khalsar, which I keep between the pages of my father's poetry. A wooden phoenix sitting on
the Dragon Throne—you carved that for me when we were teen-
agers. The quiver you lent me once and I failed to return. My robes,
my combs, my brushes—none of it mattered to you. None of it spoke
of us.

But those swords spoke of me, and if I tried—perhaps I could make
them speak of you.

Just as the idea—the foolish idea—solidified in my mind, Baozhai
returned with Kenshiro in tow. As a criminal awaiting his sentence
so did Kenshiro stand, with his head bowed and his eyes focused on
the ground. The first thing I noticed about him was that he was in a
deel and riding pants. I don't think you approved of that deel. Xianese
silk in Spring's Promise Green, embroidered with winged horses
and cherry petals. Cherry petals, Shefali.

The second thing I noticed? You will think it foolish, but it
had been days since I actually looked at him, you must understand. Kenshiro looks more like your father than you do, with the
exception of his broad cheeks. He always looks like he is smiling,
even when he isn't. You, on the other hand, always look as if someone
has told you something you disapprove of but cannot find a polite
response to. His eyes are a duskier shade, and his hair closer to brown
than blond.

But he looked like you.

The resemblance struck me like a blow to the back of the head.

Pain exploded behind my eyes. What if the only way I saw your face from now on was in your brother's? My lip started to tremble; I covered my face with my hand.

Thankfully, he spared me the pain of having to look on him for very long. The moment he crossed the threshold, he sank first to his knees and then touched his forehead to the ground.

"If you cast me from your sight until the stars fell from the sky, that would be more than I deserve," he said. "A thousand apologies are not enough."

I am no Qorin, and yet the mention of stars falling from the sky prickled me all the same. Your family often spoke of the stars, of the heroes they represented. Surely Kenshiro could not wish for them to be forgotten? But, then again, perhaps his love of poetry was getting the better of his good sense. Baozhai—who kneeled next to him as if we were at court and not simply in my room—wore a face of perfect serenity, in spite her earlier frustrations.

I'd asked to hear his regrets in person, but at that moment I wished I hadn't. How was it that he made things worse with an apology? But there was no time to dwell on this if his plan had any hope of working.

"Are you certain you can catch up to Shefali?" I asked him. I did not want to suffer through his pantomime any more. "You are here because you are family to me, however repugnant your recent actions. If you fail, know that I will not hesitate to cast you from my mind."

I did not want to have to shun your brother. But if he failed in this regard, if he gave me false hope of speaking to you one last time—I could not imagine what wrath would overtake me.

He hesitated before answering, which told me he knew how impossible it seemed. "Yes," he said. "If I should fail, then I will return in white with my death poem already composed."

Baozhai flinched. I did not blame her. There had not been a ritual suicide in decades; Kenshiro was being maudlin now.

"Let me be the judge of your punishment, should you fail," I said tersely. "And do not assume you will fail to begin with. A duel is won before the first stroke."

In return he granted me only silence. I could almost hear him reaching for something to say, within his mind, and so I did him the mercy of continuing.

"With that said, my dueling days are behind me," I said. I gestured to my scarred face, though only Baozhai could see. "I shall write her a letter, yes. But I shall have something else, too."

I took the short sword. It never felt right in my hand, anyway. Like a serpent aching to pounce. "Take this to your blacksmith. Have her forge an eye from it. Send that along with the letter."

"A steel eye?" said Baozhai. "I have . . . I have never heard of such a thing. And from your mother's sword, Lady?"

"I've no use for it," I said. "Lest I lose my other ear."

"You didn't lose the ear completely," said Baozhai, who meant well.

"I lost the ear," I said. When Baozhai had washed the wound, I felt what little remained: a nub two fingers wide. My hand went to it anyway. To have that dog wound me in such way, to have him scar me, made me sick. I'd wear this mark for the rest of my life. What would people think of me when they saw it?

Baozhai pressed her lips together. She must fix things, you see. That is the core of her being, the same way the core of mine is arrogance and anxiety, the same way yours is stubbornness and caring.

"I will take the sword to the blacksmith myself," she said. I gave it to her—my mother's short sword—and I went back to bed.

Kenshiro hadn't left. What was he waiting for? Did he expect me to thank him for his service? When all of this was his fault—how could I do such a thing?

No, he must have been waiting for the letter.

I began setting up my calligrapher's tools: smooth paper, an inkstone more expensive than some jewelry, my brush, a bowl of water. After grinding my ink and laying the paper out before me, I began the work.

It was then that your brother looked up at me. Often, in happier times, he would watch me write. His own calligraphy is . . . lacking. Like many other scholars, he employs the White Leaf style, noted for being easy to read. Unfortunately, it is about as appealing as a plum crushed in the mud. I think he hoped to learn how to improve upon it by watching me.

I wished that he would not watch, but it would divert my attention if I told him so.

"Your father bought me my first good brush," he said, as if he did not know how much concentration proper writing required.

My father's generosity did not surprise me. Few who knew him spoke ill of him.

"With Yuichi for a father, he said, I would doubtless be writing out Oshiro's penal codes as practice within a year. I was eight. He was right."

I wanted to reply—but it would've interfered with my breathing. Scholars go on and on about the proper way to hold a brush, or the proper amount of tension to have in your wrist. I tell you the secret is in your breathing. The secret is being decisive and holding your breath.

But I did allow myself a small smile in spite of my anger. My father gave me this set, too.

"He was a good man, Shizuka-lun," said Kenshiro.

I almost didn't hear him. I kept thinking of what I was writing—

how you'd react when you read it. Thinking of the characters. Qorin letters are simple, yes, but don't you find they all look the same? With so many simple strokes and nothing to differentiate them, I worry about spelling—particularly when I was using Qorin letters for Hokkaran. You and I had worked out a system, but it wasn't a perfect one.

In truth, though I've learned a little of the language in your absence, I worry about my spelling even to this day.

But at that moment, spelling did not matter. Even my calligraphy did not matter. As long as you could read it.

And yet . . . what if?

I could ask Kenshiro to read it over—to my shame, your family are the only people I know who can read Qorin—but to do so would have invited him in. There was no need for him to know what I'd told you. No need for him to be involved beyond as a messenger.

Only when I finished—when I signed my name at the bottom—did I look back at Kenshiro.

"You haven't earned the right to call me lun again," I said. "And speaking of my father won't improve my opinion of you; delivering this letter might."

He slunk away, defeated, leaving me to my memories of you. I tried to imagine what you would look like with a steel eye. Desperate to have some image of your face, I tried to paint you with my brushes: your wide face, your kind eyes, your mouth meant for mine. None of it seemed right. What a fool I was, to try to capture you in paper—and yet the idea of forgetting what you looked like terrified me. I shut my eyes and tried to imagine you on your gray: your broad shoulders slumped in resignation, your white hair frizzy in the humidity.

But imagining you meant remembering how it felt to be wrapped in your arms. It meant becoming keenly aware that you wouldn't be holding me anytime soon. Who would guard me against the lightning itself, who would keep me safe? Who was I, without you?

It seemed I would have to discover this now.

THREE DAYS, KENSHIRO said it would take. And so three days we waited. Three days spent Baozhai and I in the hollow of a drum, waiting for the beat. Tatsuoka Village—the Village of Three Kings, as the poets called it—would be his best bet for catching up to you. Xian-Lai and Hokkaro both maintained roads to it. In the years before the Wall of Stone was built, there was even a beaten path used by your people. Merchants from the East often entered at Tatsuoka rather than through the gate near Oshiro precisely *because* Tatsuoka was so easily accessible. The Dragon Guard sent weekly patrols down Three Kings Road even then.

Kenshiro was never in any real danger. No bandits were brazen enough to take on a patrol's worth of Dragon Guard—not the Sons of First Winter, not the Lion's Fangs, not the Rain of Daggers. Roving blackbloods were more an issue in Shiratori or Shiseiki or Fuyut-suki. Demons were a threat, yes, but so was a comet falling from the sky and crushing him; they, too, tended to keep north. So long as he did not come across any irate minor gods, there should be nothing to harm him.

But that is reason talking, Shefali, and you know well how much louder speaks worry.

Baozhai never spoke of it aloud. Why would she? It was in her nature to tame storms, not to be swallowed by them. Every day she continued to visit me, continued to read me poetry, continued to inundate me with court gossip so that I would not think of how much I missed you. And every day, the bags beneath her eyes grew darker.

Two mornings after his departure, Baozhai brought up a breakfast to my room—thick rice porridge with fish, and fried sticks of dough for dipping; pork floss and pine-pattern eggs on the side. She laid this bounty out on the broad eight-sided table and apologized for it. "We have to make our rice last as long as we can," she said, and I wondered about the bowl she'd served me yesterday.

Now, as then, she stared at me until I finished my porridge.

But she not once reached for her own bowl.

And I knew well what hid behind her eyes then, for I'd felt it since the moment you left. Gnawing worry. Would her husband return? What a silly thing to worry about, yet there it was: the far-off look, the idle wringing of her hands.

"You should eat," I said to her. "You've my uncle to deal with; do you mean to face him on an empty stomach?"

This roused her attention. She started, as if from a dream, and met my eyes before remembering it was forbidden to do so. "Forgive me," she said. She picked up her bowl and took a sip from it then—but only one sip. "If it comforts you to know, Lady, your uncle will be departing the Bronze Palace this evening."

Leaving without a word to me? I had no wish to speak with the man, you understand, but I *did* wish he would treat me with more respect. I was his only heir, and with his presence, this now technically counted as court. For appearance's sake alone, we should perform the farewell ceremony. To skip it only fostered notions of my illegitimacy.

But that was what he wanted, wasn't it? To paint me as a petulant child to the other lords? And thus he might rule well into his decrepit old age without abdicating—for who would want a brat like me for Empress?

So I drank my tea. "Don't think this gets you out of finishing your porridge," I said instead.

Two Bells later—at Sixth, which was a terrible time to depart on a journey—I heard the drums and horns of the Imperial procession. From my window I watched them leave: the Dragon Guard marching in formation, their pole arms held aloft like blades of grass, my uncle's palanquin and those of his wives following soon behind. The sky above was washerwoman gray—and in less than an hour, it began to rain.

As the first drops began to fall, Baozhai again returned to my rooms. This time she brought with her a letter, which she presented to me without much preamble. We both knew from whom it had come.

Just the sight of it filled me with rage.

If the Son of Heaven writes you a letter, then everything about that letter should be perfect. Only the finest paper can be used; only the darkest, smoothest ink. When you hold the letter to your nose, it should smell of peonies, or if the news is bad, violets. The cord tied around it must be a particular color, depending on how you feel about the recipient. Basic things, Shefali, that any monarch learns within five years of existence.

But my uncle fails on almost all accounts.

This letter was written on paper two grades more coarse than standard Imperial. If I held it to my face, I could see black and green flecks: the stems of whatever unlucky flower was used to make it. Because the paper was little more than pulp, the ink feathered around the edges. Which is not to say that this was good ink. My uncle could not properly grind ink if he had a stone the size of the sun. When he is given terrible charcoal, he is, effectively, dragging little rocks across the page.

And his hand! Who hurt him as a child, that he has such handwriting? The start of each stroke must be confident and precise. My uncle's is always wavy or jittery. The end of each stroke should be elegant—there my uncle overcompensates for his starts. He always finishes his characters with bold flourishes that make them illegible.

If I am being honest, I would rather read your handwriting. If you write to me in Hokkaran, I know it is the result of great effort, as you struggle so to remember the characters. How long did it take you to write my name upon the gift you sent me? For it was your handwriting, and not your cousin's. You wanted it to reach me, and you knew I would recognize your work the second I saw it. Had you hired some scribe I might have tossed it aside.

Your writing the two characters of my first name took more effort than my uncle has put into anything in his whole life. That is true beauty, that is true dedication.

The letter I held in my hands, tied with a gray cord (gray had no meaning; what was he thinking?), was a slap in the face.

Dearest Niece,

    Since you are so taken with the local wildlife, we have decided to let you stay in Xian-Lai. We are certain you will find Oshiro's library to be enlightening. A girl as well read as yourself may yet discover hidden truths there. All sorts of laws lie dormant, waiting for some young upstart to rouse them.

    There is one law you will not find in the young scholar's collection. We declare, both in this letter and in proclamations to be posted in every village, that anyone who speaks the name of your little heathen pet will be subject to four-by-four lashes, delivered at the start of Twice-Second Bell, in the nearest common area.

    We hope you find the architecture pleasurable, and your

room comfortable, for you are not to leave the palace unless
you are returning to Fujino. And you may not return to Fujino
until you renounce this sham of a marriage.

Eightfold blessings.

He did not bother signing it.

It is a wonder I did not burn the thing the moment I finished reading it. Baozhai would not have let me do it—but trying would've felt nice. Instead, I crumpled it and threw it as hard as I could. It bounced off one of Baozhai's vases and fell to the ground.

"Lady," she said. "I am very sorry for the circumstances, but know the Bronze Palace will always be home to you. If there is anything I may do to make your time here more comfortable, say the word, and it will be done."

Bring back my wife, I thought.

"Do you have any wine?" I asked.

I saw Baozhai's disapproval. She was twenty-three and I was seventeen, but we were both married. I was no less adult than she was. If I wanted wine, then I was entitled to it.

It was a long moment, her studying me, but I did not care. At length she sighed. "You know wine is not the solution."

"I did not ask for a solution," I said. "I am asking for a little comfort, and I'm told wine is just the thing in these situations."

"And who told you that?" she asked. She took a sudden interest in fixing the vase I'd thrown the letter at.

"My mother," I said, and it wasn't that much of a lie. She'd never spoken the words out loud but I remembered wandering through our rooms late at night and seeing her, leaning against my father, cup in hand.

Baozhai knew better than to needle me about bad habits. Once she was done rearranging the flowers, she came back to me.

"Then I shall send for a bottle," she said, "but you will not drink it alone."

"BAOZHAI," I BEGAN, but she was saved from my misplaced temper by the servants' arrival. The brief reprieve granted by their bringing in the wine allowed me to reconsider, to swallow the ugly response building in my throat. Where had it come from? Best to let it drown in the wine. After a quick toast, I downed the cup all at once. It burned its way down my throat—but I've always been fond of burning.

And so one cup became another and another and another.

Soon my head was spinning and I couldn't speak properly, but I could not stop myself from drinking. As the world spun away from me, so, too, did my worries. Everything seemed so much happier, so much funnier, and when I was reminded of you, I told stories about you instead of wallowing. The time you drank two whole skins of kumaq through a funnel because Dorbentei said you had a westerner's delicate stomach. How, when you laugh, your eyes crinkle. All the bawdy jokes you used to tell me just to see me turn red. I remembered some of the jokes, even—and to my surprise, Baozhai didn't get any redder at all.

Well, not from the jokes, anyway. By her second cup, the skin of her neck and chest was ruddy. Perhaps because of this she began drinking water instead. Nevertheless, as I rambled on and on, she listened to everything I had to say, and when I was too drunk to stand, she said we should get some rest.

At first I thought she was going to help me to my bed and leave for her own rooms. Part of that was true. In spite of her own drunkenness, she remembered etiquette well enough; without permission to touch me directly, she instead gave me a walking stick to lean on. Once she'd drawn the sheets over me, I expected her to leave.

But she lay on the floor instead.

And these were not Hokkaran floors, covered with mats. They were cold stone, colder in the winter, and dreadfully uncomfortable. If she slept there, she'd wake with a backache for sure.

I rolled to the edge of my bed and extended a hand. "Come here," I said.

She looked at me as if I were speaking Qorin. I was drunk, so that was possible—"come here" is among the few phrases I know. I repeated myself, this time forcing myself to focus on speaking my native tongue.

"Come here," I said. "It's awful down there."

"It's not awful," Baozhai protested. "I have these floors cleaned every day."

I sighed. "You don't even have a pillow," I said. "Come here. It's warm."

I remember her brown eyes went wide, and that flush on her neck went pale. Baozhai's lips parted. I caught sight of her rosy tongue, just behind the two slices of red.

"Lady," she says. "Are you certain? You are drunk; what if you're displeased in the morning, when you find me lying next to you?"

Maybe she was the one speaking Qorin, then, for I couldn't fathom how I'd be displeased by finding her in my bed.

"I'm not going to be angry that my best friend is sleeping comfortably in bed. I might be angry if I see you slept a whole night on the floor for my sake."

I held up the sheets and waved for her to come in.

So she did.

I thought nothing of it at the time—I slept the same way with Daishi whenever she came to stay with me. The all-seeing eyes of eti-quette could not penetrate blankets, you understand.

But then Baozhai spoke in little more than a whisper.

"I miss him."

Like the first drop of rain heralds the monsoon, so did this whim-per herald her tears. Before I could think of anything to say, she was sobbing against my back.

"I know I shouldn't," she said. "He was awful, wasn't he? Because of him, all of this went wrong. I hate what he's done. I hate that he didn't think to *speak to me* about any of it. Am I not his wife? Shouldn't we help one another?"

The plush blankets of this Xianese bed became the soiled rags of my mother's deathbed; Baozhai's open mouth went thick with blood; her crying became my mother's plaintive "Itsuki, Itsuki . . ."

"Screaming at him doesn't ease the pain. I thought sending him away might, but now I just keep worrying. What if something hap-pens to him? What if the last thing I said to him was . . ."

What had my mother said to my father before the darkness swal-lowed him?

"Lady?"

Before the demons ate him alive?

"Lady? Are you all right?"

It wasn't until she touched my shoulder that I remembered where I was. As forcefully as I could, I shunted the memory away, but it stuck in my throat and brought tears to my eyes.

"It's . . . ," I creaked. "He'll be all right. He's on the Three Kings Road."

I don't think she believed me.

But Kenshiro arrived all the same three days later, having run one horse to death and the other very near it. Baozhai and I were having dinner when we got the news. All at once, she was on her feet and rushing to meet him, without even a word of farewell to me. I followed her, though I could not fathom why. There he was, covered in dirt and grime, about to head into their rooms when Baozhai threw her arms around him.

How happy she was to see him! She leaped off the ground to better embrace him, and he, so much the taller, held her up in his arms so that her feet dangled above the ground.

I watched them and I thought of you, and I returned to my room and wept.

BARSALAI SHEFALI

TWO

"Your Imperial Majesty."

Three words—three arrows through the screen keeping the real world away. Shizuka flinches as if struck, and Shefali wants nothing more than to reach out for her. In the end, she can't help herself. As the servants announce that Lady Fuyutsuki has arrived for afternoon tea, Shefali squeezes her wife tight.

"I don't want to deal with her," Shizuka mumbles.

Wear the Phoenix Crown only if you do not mind getting burnt, Shefali thinks, but the thought feels off—as if she is repeating something she heard someone else say. Yes, Shizuka should be focusing on her work—but she really has not gotten much sleep. To fault her for this would be cruel.

"You don't want me to deal with her either," Shefali whispers to her. Shizuka lets out a small laugh. She begins to stand, and Shefali stands with her, scooping her mask up off the desk. The two of them don't discuss this. There's no need to.

Together, they said.

And so when Shizuka calls for the servants to open the door, she does so hand in hand with her wife.

Shefali caught Lady Fuyutsuki's scent earlier. Dried flower petals, starting to turn; a hint of salt; powder and makeup. Nothing in the woman's appearance contradicts it. The dried petals are so like her skin, the salt evident in her unkind eyes, the powder and the makeup doing their best to fill in the crevices of her age.

When she sees Shizuka standing before her in her sleeping robes, the stubs of her eyebrows strain to meet. When she realizes who it is that is standing next to the Empress, the corners of her mouth turn downward.

For a court flower like Lady Fuyutsuki, these small gestures are pained screams.

It is a good thing the mask is hiding Shefali's smile. There are few things in life she enjoys more than upsetting Hokkaran courtiers.

"Izumi-shal," Shizuka says. Shal, really? The woman has got to be at least seventy. Isn't it time to switch to the Mother, or the Sister's honorifics? "A pleasure as always to see you. Have you had your rice?"

Lady Fuyutsuki's eyes flick over to Shefali. It is illegal to make eye contact with Shizuka, but no such laws protect the Empress Consort.

"I have," she says. "Has your—?"

"My wife's condition means she no longer has to eat," says Shizuka smoothly. "And if she did, I'm certain she'd avoid rice as long as possible. She's never liked the stuff."

"Never," echoes Shefali.

Lady Fuyutsuki stiffens. It is not quite hatred that Shefali smells on her. It so rarely is, when it comes to people like this. Pity, confusion, discomfort—but rarely hatred. "Fascinating."

Shizuka is about to say something cross. Shefali can smell it—the spice in the air is tickling her nose. Part of her wants to let her—she does delight in Shizuka's sharp tongue—but she cannot let the Phoenix Empress behave in such a childish way.

"I'm intruding," Shefali says. "Going to the gardens."

"Shefali—" begins Shizuka, but Shefali shakes her head. Her wife will be fine from here. It is only tea.

"Dinner," Shefali says. She brushes her lips against Shizuka's hand—an Axion gesture she grew fond of during her travels—to remind her that she is not alone. "Whistle if you need me."

"Whistle?" says Shizuka, but by then, Shefali has already taken her first steps away. She does not bother to bow to Lady Fuyutsuki, and why should she? She is Barsalai Shefali, the Tiger-Striped Princess, and she will not bow to anyone beneath her.

She waves to her wife. Just before she turns down the hall, she lifts her mask up and grins.

"You'll do great," she calls in Qorin.

"I'm going to throw you," Shizuka calls back, her Qorin as jagged as the face of Gurkhan Khalsar.

But she is trying.

And that is reason enough to be proud of her.

SHEFALI HAS TRIED to understand all her life what her wife loves so much about flowers. Now, nearing the end of her twenty-six years, she sits in the gardens and searches for the answer.

She asks the gardenias, and the camellias, and the peonies. They turn their colorful faces away.

She asks the daisies, and the sagiso, and the white magnolia, but they do not hear her.

She asks the dandelions, and the roses, and the chrysanthemums, but they don't want to talk to her.

For hours, she sits, taking in the scents of the gardens and watching the sun sink lower. For hours, she watches the gardeners care for Shizuka's creation. And it is Shizuka's creation—her touch is on every petal in this garden. So few of them bloom in their natural colors—the Imperial Garden is awash in blues and greens and dazzling violets.

And gold.

There is gold.

Shefali visits the golden flower at the center of the garden—the fabled daffodil. There she spends most of her time. O-Shizuru's things jut out of the ground at odd angles: the corner of a medicine drawer here, a golden pipe bowl there; an upside-down statue of the Mother, only her feet and the blade of her sickle visible above the ground. Shefali cannot say she knew the woman well, but standing here among her most valued possessions feels as if she did.

The flower—the daffodil—sways like a dancer in the afternoon breeze. The sky above, fast purpling, lends the gold of its petals a sublime sort of bruising. How soft it looks, though its petals are gilt! Part of her longs to drag her fingers along its stem, but . . .

No, no.

This flower was never hers.

Instead, Shefali sinks to her knees before it, in the garden O-Shizuru planted.

"Thank you," she says. The words come without her having to think on them.

The wind whips up. A gust, strong enough to bend the tallest oak tree in the garden, nearly unseats Shefali. She plants her hand on the cool grass to keep from toppling over.

When the wind settles, she notices two things.

First: a feather, black and iridescent, sits before the gleaming daffodil. Two pine needles are caught between the spines.

Second: the wind carries the scent of the sea.

Shefali knows a sign when she sees one. With a second, quieter thank-you to the wind that carried her mother-in-law's kind gesture, she picks up the feather and tucks it safely within her deel. Her heart is racing: she must tell Shizuka what has happened, must show her the message O-Shizuru left for them.

As the sun sets, Shefali practically races back toward the palace. The wind does not let up, carrying that floral scent to her long after she has left the gardens.

And yet something catches her attention, even over the feather burning in her chest pocket. A new scent calls to her. It tickles the back of her brain like a half-forgotten lyric. Familiar, so familiar, and yet not at all. Paper, ink, horses, jasmine—

A mop of light brown hair wrapped in Xianese green, throwing its arms around her knee. Shefali starts. A child? Part Qorin, too, from the looks of her skin and hair. Why is she hugging Shefali? Isn't she afraid?

She doesn't smell afraid. That familiar scent's coming off her.

Shefali kneels, takes off her mask. The girl continues to press her chubby cheeks against Shefali's knee. Her whole face is screwed up, her thick brows like clumsy brushstrokes.

"Where are your parents, little one?" asks Shefali. "I must scare you."

The girl giggles. "But you're my auntie," she says.

Shefali swallows. Her aunt? Is that why she—? That's it! She smells like Kenshiro and Baozhai!

Kenshiro has a daughter?

Thoughts race. Her brother has a daughter. Her brother! Gods, is this her? How can she be sure this is real, and not imagined, how can she be sure—?

Shefali is smiling, ear to ear. Happiness robs her of fear, of suspicion. Her throat closes up when she tries to speak. Yes—look at that nose, so like Shefali's own; look at those fingers, thin as Baozhai's; look at her downy hair. Shefali cannot keep her hands steady.

The girl scrunches her nose and giggles. "Are you okay? Am I scary?"

"No," says Shefali at once. "No, you're the cutest girl I've ever seen."

The girl narrows her eyes. "But what about Aunt Zuzu?"

Aunt Zuzu. Name of the Grandmother, Shefali did not know happiness could ache this much.

She taps the girl on the nose.

"Aunt Zuzu," she says, "is a cute woman. You are a cute girl. What is your name?"

"Lai Baoyi," she says. Not Oshiro Baoyi. Curious. But, then, Baozhai did outrank her husband. "And you're Auntie Shefa."

Shefali laughs at this, covering her mouth to hide her teeth from the child. Shefa. Only her mother called her that.

"I am," she says. "Where is your father, little one?"

Baoyi points with her tiny hands. There, down the hall, is Kenshiro. He's peeking out from around a corner, the hems of his robes barely visible. Shefali scoops up Baoyi and approaches him. She's held children before, of course—her cousins, her second cousins, the cousins of her clanmates. But she's never felt quite so . . .

Quite so at peace.

Does Otgar know? That is her second thought. It's an old truth that if one Qorin knows a thing, they all do—gossip travels fast as horses among Shefali's people. There aren't many Qorin here, but there . . . well, there is Kenshiro. He must have told their mother, and if their mother knew, then Otgar was likely to know soon.

The two of them parted ways outside the Wall of Stone—just as they'd planned to during their travels. Back then—surrounded on all sides by Ikhthians in opulent masks, the gentle ebb and swell of strings in the background—Otgar had said returning to Hokkaro was more chore than reward.

"I don't understand you, Needlenose, truly I don't," she'd said. It was her fourth cup of wine. The sharp, bitter smell coated Shefali's tongue. "Why return to the northerners, ah? Why not return to the clan? Your wife isn't the only woman who has missed you; your mother has, too. Why plant yourself among the pine trees?"

The two of them—mostly Otgar—had turned a fair profit in Sur-Shar already. If they brought the money back to the clan, they'd live well for the rest of their days.

But that meant a life exiled from her wife.

And was that a life worth living?

The answer, to Shefali, had always been obvious: She and Shizuka must be together, as earth and sky, as flesh and soul. And so she had smiled at her cousin beneath her fox mask.

"I am a pine needle," she'd said, "and so is Shizuka."

Otgar guffawed at that, slapping her knee so hard, she knocked a mug off the table in the process.

But what will Otgar say when she lays eyes on this child? For she is perfect, and brown, and so healthy that Shefali must fight back the tears biting at her eyes.

Three generations ago, the Emperor of Hokkaro sent forth General Nozawa to conquer Xian-Lai. Two generations ago, the next Emperor of Hokkaro decided to experiment on the Qorin people. Decades later, the Empress's Qorin-Hokkaran wife greets her Xianese-Qorin niece in the halls of the palace.

"Ken," Shefali calls, "you finally made something beautiful."

Her brother steps out from his hiding spot. Shefali's startled by how different he looks. A patchy whitish beard ages him—or maybe eight years have done that all on their own. His cheeks have lost the last of their baby fat. There are faint lines across his forehead and fainter ones near the corners of his mouth.

But his smile hasn't changed at all.

"I take offense to that," he says, "my poetry is delightful."

Shefali smirks. "Not so delightful as her," she says. Otgar really will love her—Shefali's certain of it. Has Kenshiro already taught his daughter to wrestle?

Pride. Joy. Something beneath the other two that Shefali cannot place. Pity, perhaps.

"It's good to see you, Little Sister," he said. "Have you changed your hair? You look so different."

How like him to make that joke. At least he isn't disgusted by her. To say that it is good your own brother does not find you disgusting— what a low bar she has for him. Yet it is one he's earned, given what happened in the Bronze Palace.

A liar.

Her brother is a liar, and even if Shizuka did forgive him—Shefali has spent eight years wondering what their lives would be like if her brother hadn't invited the Emperor to the palace.

"How come you're gray?" asks Baoyi. Shefali's shaken from her thoughts.

Kenshiro's eyes go wide. He moves to cut her off, but Shefali raises a hand. It's fine. A reasonable question for a child to ask, really, as much as it pains her to admit.

"I spent so much time away from your Auntie Zuzu," says Shefali, "that I turned colors."

Baoyi nods along as if that makes perfect sense. "And why are your teeth pointy?"

"To better eat the fat from a sheep's cheek," Shefali says. That much is true, or would be true, if she could taste.

"And how come your ears are pointy, too?"

Shefali laughs. What a quick mind she has. What else should she have expected from the daughter of two White Leaf scholars? "To hear you better," she says.

Baoyi starts tugging at her own ears. Shefali hands her over to Kenshiro.

"How come I don't have pointy ears?" she asks her father.

"You'll grow them in time," he says, "but only if you're as quiet as your aunt."

Shefali watches them. When was the last time she saw Kenshiro so happy? So at home? For with his daughter in his arms, he is almost a different man, at ease and all joy. Being near him feels intrusive—as if she's a horse grazing outside a full stable.

"I missed you," she manages. And she means it, truly she does. She has missed *this* part of her brother more than she can say.

Kenshiro pinches her cheek, the way he used to when they were younger. "We missed you, too," he says. "Your wife especially. Not a day went by without her pining for you, you know."

Not something Shefali wishes to dwell upon. She is aware how many days they spent apart. Worse, she is aware how many days . . .

Ah, but at least she will spend them surrounded by family.

She swallows.

"Where is she?" Shefali asks. "And where is your wife? Has she come, too?"

Grandmother Sky shaped Kenshiro's face for sly looks. He kisses his daughter on the forehead. "Oh, the lady's in her chambers, I think," he says. "Alas, my wife is not with me. Baozhai has much to attend to as of late in the Bronze Palace. A shame, really;

she wanted so badly to come see the lady. But I admit, that isn't why I'm here."

"It isn't?" Shefali says. She has been back in the palace for only three days—there is no way Kenshiro could have arrived in antici- pation of her. If he hasn't come to visit Shizuka, and he isn't here in an official capacity . . .

"I came because I wanted to peruse the libraries here for more in- formation on your condition," he admits. "That you've returned to us is surely a Sky-given sign. I'd like to speak to you, when you are ready. In your absence, I've been doing a lot of research—"

Shefali narrows her eyes. Unbidden, the words spring back to her: *Your brother will lie to you.* Why does he wish to speak of such a thing? They were doing such a good job of being civil to one another.

"When I'm ready," she says. Her voice is as firm as her resolve. Every day, her body falls apart more and more; she doesn't wish to speak of it. Not to him who betrayed her.

For he is both the elder brother who helped her make her first bow and the elder brother who told the Emperor where they'd been hid- ing. Which wears the skin of the other? Which is the lamb, and which the wolf? She cannot help but think he brought Baoyi to the palace on purpose. He knew. He knew that the moment Shefali saw her, she'd stop in her tracks, that she'd be in a good enough mood to speak with him. . . .

A tremor takes Shefali's right hand. Her disgust is getting the better of her; if she is not careful, it will start to shift, and she cannot let Baoyi see her for a monstrosity.

"Until tomorrow," Shefali says. She can smell her brother's guilt and shame, she can smell her niece's disappointment; she will bear the weight of both. Deep in her heart, she wants to embrace Baoyi before she leaves, to smell the top of her head and her cheeks, but—her fingers are starting to spasm. In place of a proper Qorin good-bye, she bows like a northerner. Before they can return the gesture, she's turned away down the hall. She clutches her twitching hand.

BAOYI.

Baoyi. She chooses to focus on Baoyi, on how perfect and how happy she is, on the woman she is going to grow up to become. If they have no others, then Baoyi will inherit all of Xian-Lai, all of Oshiro. Perhaps it is best if she has a sibling. Oshiro and Xian-Lai are nowhere near one another, that's for certain; ruling the both of them would drive a priest to drink.

Except the younger sibling would inherit the greater province, and Baoyi would be left with Oshiro.

On second thought—let Baoyi rule it all.

What if she and Shizuka have a child? It is not unheard of—not really. Sanvaartains create fatherless children often enough that there is a term for it—urjilinbaal. The ritual is recent, yes, and not without its flaws, but it might be worth attempting.

The image of Shizuka holding a child almost stops Shefali in her tracks. They'll have to name the child after Shizuka's parents, one way or the other. That is all right. She'll have Shefali's dark skin and Shizuka's dark hair, and she'll ride like lightning at night, and speak perfect Hokkaran with no accent, and she'll be able to read and write it without issue, and she'll know Qorin, too, and . . .

And Shefali will never . . .

What a foolish thing to dream of. She doesn't even know if a child is something Shizuka wants. They will have to talk, the two of them, and soon—but the thought is a set of stones tied around Shefali's neck.

Shefali can smell her now. She takes a deep breath. Peonies, chrysanthemums . . .

She slides open the door to their rooms.

Shizuka isn't home yet. Only the *things* are there to greet her. Shefali lets out a sigh. It can't be helped, can it? The court calls, and it is better that Shizuka is at last heeding it. She must be doing something important.

Her hands hurt too much to whittle. She holds the feather instead, and wonders what she will tell Shizuka when the time comes.

O-SHIZUKA

TWO

Barsalai Shefali may wear a mask around most of the world—but a mask has never been enough to hide her from Minami Shizuka. Shefali's wide face has always been as easy to read as O-Itsuki's scrolls.

Now, for instance. A Bell and a half after leaving her alone with Fuyutsuki Izumi, Shefali sits on their bed, looking as if she's swallowed poison. In her hands is a black feather—a strangely beautiful one—but it is her expression that troubles Shizuka. She's worn that look once before: when Burqila Alshara exiled her.

Burqila is thousands of li away, wherever she is; Shizuka hasn't heard from her in half a year. Her aaj has plenty more pressing things to attend to than her daughter-in-law's emotional whining. For once, Shizuka is grateful for the distance: it means that whatever troubles Shefali now, it is not so bad as exile.

"Beloved?" she calls, for Shefali has not stirred. "Is everything all right?"

Shefali does not answer.

Four hours spent in absolute boredom and misery are instantly forgotten. Shefali needs her now. Shizuka sits down next to her and laces their fingers together.

An errant bit of moonlight lands on the feather. Instead of shining silver, it only grows more violet.

"How beautiful," says Shizuka. "I never see you stare at the phoenix feather like this."

Shefali meets her glance. Good. She is not so far gone as to imagine she is alone. "The phoenix feather reminds me of the Womb."

In the days since her return, Shefali has not spoken of her journey at all. Shizuka has not pressed her. The details will come when her wife is ready. For now, the two of them are together, and that is all that matters.

"Your mother gave me this," says Shefali. "Earlier today."

A crushing sensation in Shizuka's chest. "What?"

"I went to see the daffodil," she says. "A sea breeze left this for me. See the needles?"

The daffodil? Shizuka has gone to see it more than once, but she's never . . . there have been no feathers for her. Joy at such an obvious blessing wars with the jealousy of being passed over for it.

Why Shefali? she thinks—but she can almost hear her mother's reply.

To teach you humility. And one of you has got to have her head on right.

She reaches for the feather, and Shefali lets her take it. Aside from the phoenix feather—which now decorates Shizuka's crown—it is the most otherworldly thing Shizuka has seen. For a long while, she studies the way the light plays upon it.

And yet no matter which way she turns it, the pine needles never extricate themselves.

"She approves," says Shefali. "I was excited to show you."

She approves. But would she? Her mother wanted a peaceful life for her, a normal life—and marrying a Qorin woman was anything but normal.

And her mother would have stopped speaking with her four years ago, at any rate.

But Shizuka stares at the feather all the same. She does not quite allow herself to dream of her mother's approval—she knew the woman too well for that—but she allows herself to dream of her father's.

It is the thought of O-Itsuki that lightens her mood, that eases the tension from her. She lays her head on her wife's shoulder.

"The sort of gift only you could ever give me," says Shizuka. "But why were you so upset when I came in? You certainly didn't seem excited."

Shefali grunts—but she leans her head against Shizuka's. "I saw my brother."

"Ah," says Shizuka. Her wife normally reserves such vitriol for Shizuka's uncle alone. "Yes, I should have warned you—I ask him to bring Baoyi for visits whenever he can. She's—well, you've met her. A delightful little bundle of rambunctiousness. Nothing like her parents."

Shefali shakes her head. Arranged as they are, she ends up nuzzling against Shizuka. Silence, then, while Shefali considers what she will say. Shizuka has gotten used to waiting to hear her wife's thoughts.

"You've forgiven him."

It sounds like an accusation. Shizuka bites her lip. The memories—they are coming back to her now. The river, the bodies. "I have . . . a different view of family, these days," she says.

"He betrayed you."

"He's trying," Shizuka answers with a sigh. "That is all I can ask of him. Without his help, I would not have been able to send you that last letter, Shefali. I know the wound is still fresh for you, but I've made my peace with him."

Another long silence. Shizuka worries for a moment that she has misspoken—that they are about to have an argument so soon after their reunion—but Shefali soon proves her wrong.

"How?"

"How did I forgive him?"

Shefali nods. "It isn't like you."

Well. She promised to tell Shefali the story, didn't she?

"It wasn't like me when you left," Shizuka says. "And it wasn't like me for years afterwards. It is a long path to forgiveness, my love, but it starts with a letter I received in Xian-Lai."

Blossoms Out of Season

I like to think of myself as the most important woman in the Empire. On most days, it's true.

But the most important woman—the most important *person*—in Xian-Lai is Lai Baozhai. So it has been since her father named her the heir to his kingdom; so it has been for near twenty years.

It won't surprise you, then, to hear that she did not always have time to keep me company.

Xian-Lai, though a province of the Empire, was once a kingdom in and of itself. It had lost no land during its annexation, and thus it employed seasonal courts just as Fujino did. Autumn Court was the largest of them, and it was due to start within the month. Baozhai had to be ready.

And I . . . I had to be . . .

Something. Someone. I was a warhorse free of my stable, Shefali, with no idea where to go or what to do. Some days I spent at the library, some in the gardens. Once, I visited the markets, but the number of guards I was forced to take along made it a terrible inconvenience for everyone around me.

In the mornings I would rise, light my prayers, and practice my sword forms. Everything after that was a mystery I unraveled anew each day.

Change was inevitable. Queens were not immune to it, nor were kings. Even the gardens were shifting into their autumn dress.

Why should I be immune to the changes? Because I am a god?

No—I think the reason you and I were born and have lived as mortals is that so we *can* change. So that we can learn, in the proper way.

Change came to the Bronze Palace one evening in Baozhai's pampered hands. A letter, accompanied by a small box, held past and future alike.

I didn't need to hold it to my nose to smell it—its floral perfume near brought tears to my eyes. The cord holding it together was Nishikomi Foam Green, a strange choice. Green meant "family." I had no family remaining in Nishikomi after the deaths of my grandparents. The paper, too, was curious: it was finer than that which my uncle had sent, and indeed almost fine enough to be Imperial Grade, with one exception. A cherry blossom was pressed into the back.

No one used cherry blossoms in paper.

"Who sent this?" I asked, for there were kinks in the cord already—someone had read it before it got to me. Baozhai or one of her servants, no doubt. Few people knew I was here; something like this was naturally suspicious.

"Would that I knew," said Baozhai. She was rearranging the flowers in my vase. I'd budged one of the flowers ever so slightly; fixing it was driving her half-mad. "I leave the matter to your judgment. If the sender is who she claims, then it is curious indeed she has never come forth before now. If she is not, then sending this at all is an affront, one that I would not tolerate if I were in your position."

Just who was Lai Baozhai when I was not with her? It occurred to me that I'd rarely seen her interact with her subjects; I'd been whiling away the hours with you. Baozhai the woman was well known to me, but Baozhai the sovereign was a mystery.

"Had it not been handed to me by one of my navy captains, I would have thrown it out without a care," she continued. Xian-Lai had a navy? I supposed it made sense; Peizhi Lake emptied into the Father's Ocean. "Yet the woman who gave it to me belongs to an old family, one that has served mine since before the Taking of Dao Doan. She swears that it and the bundle accompanying it are genuine."

The Taking of Dao Doan, and not the Adoption of Dao Doan. What a story lay in that choice of words. The two of us had never discussed my Empire's history of annexation, but I knew now where she stood on the matter.

We were in agreement, then. And I could not allow her to think otherwise. Just as I knew the person and not the sovereign, so, too, did she. I'd never told Baozhai how sickened I was by the actions of my forebears—but it was something Queen Lai needed to know.

"May her family serve you still once the threads are severed," I said. At this she stopped mid-motion. When she turned to face me, there was astonishment in her eyes—but a quiet joy, too.

"Indeed," said Lai Baozhai. "May the Lady of Flowers grant that day to her children."

I will be honest with you, Shefali—I had no idea who the Lady of Flowers was at the time. I thought perhaps she was referring to me instead—a play on the name she'd given me. If I had known what I was about to say was blasphemous—well. I would have said it anyway. I have been blaspheming since the day I was born.

"Oh, don't say 'my children.' Hearing that makes me want to take a bath."

Her lips curled; her brows came together. She turned back to her flowers. "Of course," she said. "My apologies, Lady. We'll speak more of this in the gardens."

In the gardens, where we were alone, and the servants kept greater distance than they did in the palace. What better place to discuss the pruning of an Empire?

I turned my attention away from intrigue and to the letter. As Baozhai had said, there was a small bundle of silk next to it—cheap silk torn from a singing girl's robes. Let the letter speak for it, then.

To Her Imperial Highness Minami Shizuka, Imperial Niece, Peacock Princess, and all of that, make sure you get all the ones I forgot.

I'd like to start this off by saying that if the handwriting is terrible it isn't my fault. I'm paying one of the other girls to write this for me. Everyone says she's got the best hand. It looks pretty enough to me—but I'm a painter, not a scholar.

With that out of the way, let's get straight to the point of the thing. My name is Sakura. I work at the Shrine of Jade Secrets in Nishikomi, where my mother left me when I was a baby. Before you get any ideas I should tell you that it isn't a shrine at all.

The madam—we call her a High Priestess, for the theme—took me in and raised me as her own and made me swear an eightfold oath never to tell anyone who my parents were. Well, it's a good thing the gods are probably dead, because I'm breaking that oath now.

My father was Minami Keichi, which means I'm your cousin.

Don't throw the letter away! Keep reading. I'm no idiot; I wouldn't send this if I didn't have proof. Ask Captain

Cheekbones for it—she should have a little bundle with her. Open it up and you'll see a seal, probably one that's familiar to you. My mother stole it from my father and tied it to my cradle when she abandoned me. If that's not enough then there are some letters, too, although I don't suggest you read those, since my father died when he was pretty young and you know how young men are when they miss a woman. He signed all of them too. From what I can tell he didn't know I existed either, so there, you've got something in common with your good uncles. Our good uncles, I guess.

I know it isn't much, but it's what I have.

I'm writing this to you because I've always thought of you as my cousin even if you're just learning about me now. Madam Yanagi—I think of her as my mother—always said I shouldn't bother contacting you because you'd never believe me, and with what happened to your mother there aren't many people left to verify things. She said you'd have me executed for mocking you.

But I listened to all the news I could anyway. We get a lot of it. Today the Xianese navy people showed up and told us what the Toad did to you down in Xian-Lai. Losing your wife like that, getting your face all cut up—that's rough business, all of it, and you shouldn't have to suffer through it alone if you don't want. You need as much family as you can find in times like these.

And I'm family, I guess.

So, I'll come visit, if you'll have me. I might not have much in the way of education, but you learn a lot about talking to people in a place like this, and if you need a friendly ear you won't find a better one in the whole Empire. You don't have to pay me or anything; you don't have to give me anything at all.

If when I show up we look nothing alike or you think I'm a
liar, that's all right, strike me down. But I'm being honest
with you here, and I hope you get that sense even though
someone else is writing.

Humbly,
Minami Sakura

Long moments I held this letter—long moments studying the calligraphy, the flower on the back. The silent words on this page were like thunder drums between my ears; I could not gather myself enough to think. When I did, all my thoughts came rattling to me at once. A cousin? A *singing girl*? Never had my mother mentioned such a possibility—but speaking of her fallen brothers pained her, and so I had not learned much of them.

"I TOLD YOU it was far-fetched," said Baozhai.

And it was, but there is a sort of truth that is so bald, you might mistake it for a lie. I wished she'd been able to write it herself. Calligraphy reveals all liars, Shefali, at least so long as I am the woman reading it. You spoke of hearing the voice of your horse as swaying grass. Ink sings to me.

Another reason I so hate reading my uncle's letters.

Reading this one, I could be certain of a few things. A woman had written it, an older one with a calm hand that'd gone a little wobbly. Her laugh was as easy as her strokes were light. And she believed every word.

But what was that worth? Perhaps this Sakura—if she existed at all—had hoodwinked the whole pleasure house.

I reached for the silk. Sure enough, there was another bundle of papers—smaller letters tied together with Plum-Flesh Red cord. Sitting atop the letters was a small cylinder of black-lacquered wood—an old-fashioned sort of seal, but a seal nonetheless.

Except this was not simply my uncle Keichi's seal, which would have borne his name along with our family's. That was something he would have kept with him every day. In all likelihood, *that* now lies beneath the loam beyond the Wall.

This was something else entirely.

It was not wood, as I had first thought. Smooth horn met my fingertips instead—and I had not known anyone to use horn for their seal in a hundred years or more. What a strange thing it was! To hold it was to hold a living flame: the longer I held it, the hotter it became, the more the black faded in favor of a brilliant gold. Only my own affinity for flame kept it from burning the skin right off my hands. In all my life, only three things have reacted to me in such a way, and one of them now sits in the socket of your left eye.

The Daybreak Blade and its two mates.

Minami Shiori forged them from sunbeams. In the hands of a true heir to the Minami line, they remember their former lives. In the hands of anyone else, they are only metal and rayskin, only swords.

Just as this seal had been only horn before I touched it.

I didn't need to see the name upon it to know whose seal this was—and yet I held it up all the same. Like picking at a wound better left to heal on its own.

"The temerity of some people. How it boils my blood, Lady, to know there are those looking to take advantage of you already. Forgive me for giving you the letter at all; I should have known it for a charlatan's work—"

"Baozhai," I said, for she had lost herself in arranging the flowers. "I don't think she's lying."

"What do you mean?" she said. At last she looked up from her work. To this day, I remember the wide-eyed distress, the yelp that left her. In a flurry of steps, she was standing over me. "What is *that*? Is it burning you? Lady, are you—are you all right?"

"I'm fine," I said. "But there's no doubting it. This is the seal of Minami Shiori. This Sakura woman—she's either genuine or very committed to her lie. I'll send for her in the morning."

As water pouring in and out of a noisemaker were my words in Baozhai's ears. Her eyes remained fixed on the burning seal in my hand. I dropped it and held up my open palm.

"See?" I said. "It's fine."

"There's *smoke* coming off that thing," she said. She reached for it only to draw back at the last instant. "It's hot as a coal, Lady. What were you doing holding it like that?"

Truth be told, Shefali, I am only saying what I think Baozhai must have said. I could not hear her. Or—I could, but I was not listening. Minami Shiori's seal was burning like the summer sun in my hands.

It was a beacon. A signal fire.

And if I ran toward it, I'd find something precious at its base. Something that even I, with all my Imperial wealth, could not buy.

Family.

"HAS SHE ALREADY ARRIVED?" I asked. Sakura—my new-found cousin—had written that she'd take the first ship she could find; I'd sent along a cash seal to make the process easier for her.

"She has," said Baozhai. "You're truly certain you want to meet with her?"

"I'm always certain," I said. "You seem doubtful."

Baozhai pressed her lips together. "Well. She will be waiting for us in the drawing room, with the others."

"So you've planned a celebration, then," I said. "I cannot say I'm surprised."

Her expression softened. "Lady, who would I be if I did not pamper my guests?"

The others. More than simply Baozhai, Kenshiro, Sakura, and myself, then. How many had she invited?

Social interaction is little more than a bladeless duel—and let none doubt that mine is the finest sword in the Empire. My eight robes were my armor; my face-paint my war mask. Whoever lay in wait, be they god or man—they were no match for Minami Shizuka.

When we came to the drawing room, Baozhai stopped us outside.

"I wasn't certain if you'd want Kenshiro to come," she said. "And so I've asked him to wait for your word. Shall I send for him or not?"

In the days since his return, Kenshiro had kept a respectable distance. Aside from one brief meeting to confirm he'd caught up with you, I had not spoken to him much in person. Messengers provided me with two books he'd chosen to give me—histories of Hokkaran–Xianese relations from both sides. The Hokkaran edition written by Daishi Hibiki was of course no accident. I'd no idea that Akiko's father was such a scholar—but I heard his voice in his words all the same, and saw his stern face in his careful strokes.

Yet was I ready to face Kenshiro? Did I want to include him in a celebration? Well—if I cast him out, would that make me feel any better? It would not change what he had done. But nothing could change that now, nothing except his own future shame at his mistakes. Baozhai had found her peace with the man.

And though I'd discovered a new cousin, the fact remained that I had precious little family left.

Could I trust him? No, and perhaps I might never truly trust him again.

But I might be able to abide him, at least. Since he'd done me the favor of reaching you.

"Send for him," I said. Baozhai clapped her fan against the palm of her hand; the serving girl outside the drawing room bowed and took off.

"Ready?" she asked.

"Are you?"

"Very funny," she said. And then she slid open the door. A light melody welcomed me in—one of Handa's more famous pieces. Two biwa players, accompanied by a woman on zither, started up in one corner. In the center of the room was an eight-sided table piled high with sweets—sweetcakes, candied orange slices, a bowl of coconut lychee pudding as big as my head. Baozhai hung one of my father's poems on each of the three walls; beneath each of them was a matching flower arrangement.

All of this would have been perfect enough on its own—but when I saw whom Baozhai had invited, my spirits soared. Sitting at the table, stuffing a sweetcake into her mouth when she thought I wouldn't notice, was my cousin Daishi Akiko.

I hadn't seen Daishi in years, not since she started attending military academy in Fuyutsuki. She isn't really my cousin. Not my first cousin, or my second, or anything like that. My great-great-grandfather Emperor Yoriyuki had one son and three daughters. The eldest of those three daughters was named Yuriko. Yuriko married a man named Daishi Akira, and that is Akiko's lineage. "Fourth cousin" is the technical term.

And yet there is enough jade in her blood that she always attended my parties when I was a child. She and Uemura were the only consistent guests. Since Uemura is four years older and Daishi only two, I naturally gravitated toward her. We used to plot all sorts of mischief. She was the one, for example, who taught me how to tie a sheep's bladder so that anyone who sat would sound as if they were breaking wind. Once, we managed to get it onto my uncle's throne. I wasn't allowed out of my room for an entire month after that incident, but the look on his face was worth it—and Daishi visited me, anyway.

(My mother tried to discipline me over this but kept breaking down laughing whenever she tried. Eventually she settled for making me swear never to use the sheep's bladder again, and I agreed, on the condition that I could still call my uncle the Toad when it was just the two of us.)

As time wore on, Uemura won his position as Champion, and Daishi went off for training. No one attended my parties but my parents. They did all they could to make up for it, telling wild stories and dressing up in masks.

But then they passed, and I ran away.

Daishi was nineteen in those days, scrambling to her feet as I entered. The wily smirk on her face suited her well; grinning always looked strange on her. Her brows were thick, her eyes more brown than amber. She kept her hair in the common style, straight and loosely bound beneath the shoulders. She did not stand the way other soldiers do—stock straight, shoulders back. She slouched, her hands never too far from her waist. If it were not for her Imperial Guard armor, one might mistake her for a cutpurse.

I always liked that about her.

When I saw her, I smiled from ear to ear. My scars pinched at my skin.

"Cousin," she said, "is it true what they say about you these days? Have you forgotten how to laugh?"

"I know how to laugh, Daishi," I said. "All I have to do is look at your outfit."

A jacket of Imperial Gold trimmed with Deep Scarlet Pink, her wide pants also Deep Scarlet Pink. Honestly. Baozhai had allowed her into the room in that getup?

"That's tough talk from one peacock to another."

This voice was unfamiliar—but the accent! As if I were listening to my grandparents prattle on to my mother about bamboo mats again.

Seated on the other side of the table was a woman with a slice of orange in one hand and a cup of rice wine in the other. Nothing about her was proper. Like a child, she wore her robes loose and overly long—they hung slack behind her neck and pooled up at her feet. I hadn't worn my sleeves that long since I was eight. In contrast with her childish dress, she wore her hair bound up like a married woman. Cherry blossoms fell from the enamel pin near her ear to just past her brow.

Now that I had her in front of me, there could be no doubt we were related. Beyond our mouths, we didn't share many features, but a painter doesn't need to use the same colors for you to recognize his work. Our broad strokes were the same. The way she sat, for instance, so straight and so proper that it became aggressive; the way we held our heads. Even her tone mirrored mine.

"Sakura-lun, yes?" I said. "I'll get you your Imperial Golds, and then you can join the peacocking."

She scoffed and took a sip of her wine. "That'd save me effort, I guess," she said. "Imperial Gold is always in season."

How nonchalant! As if she'd deserved to wear the Gold her whole life!

"She's got to be from your side," said Daishi. "I've been here with her for an hour, and all she's done is make fun of me."

"Well, you see her," said Sakura. "How could I not?"

So afraid I'd been to enter! Yet now the laughs left me easily. Baozhai, however, looked like a soldier awaiting a warhorn. Her eyes kept darting from one of my cousins to the other, waiting to see which of them would land the first mortal blow.

But she didn't know them as I did.

Duelists spar so that they might recognize their opponent's styles. This was no different. These barbs weren't sharp enough to draw blood, but they were sharp enough to cut the tension. We could have ignored Sakura's goading, all of us—but that would have told her we wouldn't indulge *her*, either. Court propriety would get us nowhere with a woman raised so far from Fujino.

"We must always seize the opportunities presented to us," I said by way of agreement with Sakura.

"Especially when they cause such pain to the eyes," she answered. Daishi guffawed. "It is good to meet you, Cousin. I was worried you'd be like Her Highness over here, lantern-delicate and glare-heavy. But you're not."

Baozhai's brow twitched ever so slightly. If she did not live and breathe hospitality, she might have said something. I could almost hear it forming behind her lips already. But she glanced to me and swallowed it down and set about making us tea.

"My wife keeps me humble," I said.

"Is it true she's taller than Lai-lao's husband?" Daishi asked. "That man, he's taller than our horses. I can't imagine a woman taller than that! Do you carry a stool around when you want to kiss her?"

Daishi wasn't bothered that I'd married a woman. A weight came off my shoulders before I realized it had ever been there at all. "He's a little taller, I think," I said. "Two or three fingers and no more."

I did not answer her about the stool. I was lost in the memory of you kissing me from the ground while I was mounted. I'd hardly had to lean over to you at all.

"He's Qorin, isn't he? And your wife, too," said Sakura. I braced myself for something ignorant. "Can't say I've ever met one."

"Ah, they're people like any other," said Daishi. "Sore about the plague, and I don't blame them for it. But they're trying to get by, same as everyone. One of the women in my unit's part Qorin. Every Qurukk, she chops off a goat's head and fills the carcass up with these hot stones. I've fought people to get a second bowl of that stew."

Now I was really smiling. Your uncle Ganzorig made the best stew in creation. This was a well-known fact beyond the realm of dispute. But it pleased me nonetheless that Daishi didn't look down her nose at your people.

For a while, our conversations drifted in these small circles—Daishi asking how I'd been and how many fights I'd gotten into, Sakura saying she'd been in more and maybe meaning it. Baozhai tried her damnedest to bring up polite subjects, like her prized gardenias, only for Sakura to comment that she'd painted gardenias on her colleagues' robes only a few days ago. She had a bit more success with Daishi, who kept up to date with the latest novels despite being holed up in the barracks of the Kyuuzen Mountains. The perks of Imperial blood, I suppose.

But it wasn't all perks. She was serving under an old Doanese man who—rightfully—hated the monarchy. Daishi being who she was, she was always stuck cleaning out the stables or the privy. The most action she'd seen, she said, was when the cooks served spicy fish.

I pitied her. If I had not been born to my station, I imagine I would've lived a life like that—hard labor and grunt work. Only the accident of my birth saved me. Oh, Daishi grinned as she spoke, and her ridiculous stories had us clinging to each other for support, but I pitied her all the same. This was not what she wanted when she left home.

And yet . . .

There was something honest in all that work. Something admirable. When Daishi went to teahouses, they did not need to be cleared of other patrons. People *touched* her without hesitation, people looked her right in the eyes without a bit of fear. She could walk among them without eight of the Phoenix Guard keeping up a perimeter. What was that like, being among the commoners, hearing their concerns? Surely they knew about the Troubles better than anyone in the palace. We got only the most severe reports.

My uncle did not want me to leave the Bronze Palace. What if I did—but not as O-Shizuka-shon?

Kenshiro's arrival stirred me from my thoughts. He bowed low to me and congratulated me on getting a year older—a practice I've never understood, but a wish I accepted. I caught Sakura eyeing him up and down. Her eyes, like mine, settled on the jade green box in his hands. When he set it down, he was so ginger that I wondered if it held a bird.

Baozhai rose to stand at his side.

"If I may," Kenshiro said. "Baozhai and I got you a present."

I resisted the urge to say it was Baozhai who'd gotten it for me, whatever it was, and that there was no need for presents when they'd somehow gotten Daishi across the Empire in time for this little get-together—but in truth, I've never met a present I did not want to keep. Even the useless ones my old suitors gave me.

"That is kind of you," I said. "You've already given me so much. I'm afraid I cannot accept."

"We insist," said Baozhai. Whatever was in the box made her eyes sparkle.

I had to laugh. Her enthusiasm was infectious.

"I cannot," I said, "for I am living beneath your roof and eating your food, which is present enough."

I did not think this. I did not in any way think this. And yet.

Baozhai leaned forward. "It is my honor to feed you and my honor to house you, and if you do not accept this gift, then I shall take it as a personal affront. I insist."

Sakura laughed. "So we're really doing this?" she said. "Where I come from, you accept a gift right out."

"Shizuka-lun doesn't want to do this any more than you want to sit through it," said Daishi.

"Nonsense, Aki-lun, I am being *perfectly* sincere."

"Of course you are," said Daishi. She stuffed another cake into her mouth. "Of course."

"And it really *would* be remiss of me to accept such a gift. If I were to enter your service for a decade, I would leave it still owing you a debt."

Baozhai stifled a laugh. How glad I was that she was the one doing this ritual with me, and not your brother.

"Now you're the one speaking nonsense! Well: if you do not accept this gift, then our goldsmith will be so ashamed, she'll throw herself from the balcony. I insist."

The third refusal now overruled, I was at last free to open the box.

When I opened it . . . I had not seen something so beautiful since the last time I saw your face. To say simply that it was a small golden phoenix would do it a great disservice. I might as well say that you are sometimes handsome in the right light. Every line on every feather was rendered in perfect detail. Tiny rubies added flashes of fire to its body, its eyes. Its plumes were covered with topaz and emeralds. The whole thing was so finely crafted, Shefali, that I worried it'd light my hand on fire.

I covered my mouth. Baozhai and Kenshiro were Lord and Lady of Xian-Lai, yes, but even my father would've balked at the cost of such a gift.

"You like it, then?" Baozhai said.

"Where did you find such a thing?" I asked, for I could not imagine human hands had crafted it.

Then Baozhai smiled in the way a cat does when it has caught a mouse. "As I said, our goldsmith made it. It was traditional for Xianese women to wear such adornments, until . . . well. It is an old custom. Wait until you see how it's worn."

I noticed a cuff on the back of the phoenix, hidden in the swoop of its feathers. Baozhai picked it up.

"May I?" she asked.

Touching the Heir is the sort of thing you brag about for decades. Baozhai was my sister-in-law, yes, but . . . No, I could not worry about it. Baozhai was my sister-in-law. My best friend.

"Yes," I said, "of course."

She moved for my right ear. A pang of fear shot through me; for a moment, I wanted to flinch away from her.

"Tell me if I'm hurting you," she said, but her touch was gentle and light. With little effort, she slipped the phoenix's cuff over the stub of my ear. It was heavy, but it did not hurt.

Kenshiro beamed. "It looks lovely," he said. Daishi was smiling, too. Sakura, true to her upbringing, let out a whistle.

But Baozhai glowed. Seeing her there with her hands clasped together in joy, I felt as if I could venture outside again. As if I could deal with courtiers and critics and those who would gape at my injury.

"Thank you," I said, "truly. I have not received anything so lovely in a long while."

For the rest of the evening, I found my fingers flying up to that phoenix. As Kenshiro rambled about Hokkaran customs, as Daishi told us how she got that scar on her chin, as Baozhai reminded us that the Jubilee was coming up and nagged us about our outfits, as Sakura told us more about her upbringing, I touched it. After a while, my own body heated it, and I swore it was alive.

I thought of what Baozhai had said—that it was an old custom, from before my people invaded. I thought of Daishi carting manure from the stables to farms that needed it. I thought of the kingdoms we'd crushed and the people who looked on the Imperial seal with hatred.

And these things came together in my mind, one by one, like notes in a song.

Later that evening, when Baozhai and Kenshiro retired to their rooms, the musicians left behind their instruments. The only song left was our own wine-warmed conversation.

Sakura wasn't content with that. She picked up one of the abandoned biwa with a grin.

"I'll play you something *festive*," she said. "Something to wake us all up. We'll call it the first part of my welcome gift."

At first I thought she must be joking—but soon I saw that she was serious. The melody she played was a raring one, full of coy little hooks to tug the imagination. Daishi started singing along. The lyrics were far less coy than the melody itself. Honestly, I'd rather not have all the details of a shepherd bedding a lord's wife, but Daishi and Sakura seemed to enjoy it well enough.

Perhaps this was my upbringing at play again. Would I be so prudish if I'd been raised like you, or like Daishi?

When the song came to an end, Sakura mock-bowed and Daishi sincerely applauded. I sat there, red as could be. Sakura grinned.

"Haven't heard that one before?"

"No," I said. "Is it a common song?"

"It is," said Sakura. "Especially lately."

Ah. A lord who could not please his wife, the wife turning to a commoner for pleasure. Of course that sort of thing was popular at the moment.

"Maybe I'll hear it more in the future," I said. "I had this idea earlier."

"Was it your idea or the wine's?" asked Daishi. We'd finished the bottle a while ago.

"Mine," I said. Even wine could not be so bullheaded as I am.

"Well, let's hear it," said Sakura. "While I get part two of my gift ready."

She rose and walked to one of the corners, where a large scroll lay in wait.

"On the third of the Jubilee, when everyone's off celebrating, I'm leaving," I said. Daishi near spat out her drink, but I continued. If I stopped now, I'd never get to my reason for all this. "Xianese rulers used to work for two months at the Grand Temple. Why shouldn't I?"

"Shizuka-lun," said Daishi. "Do you . . . do you speak any Xianese?"

"No, but that's all the more reason to learn! The best place to learn a language is among its people, isn't it?"

I said that knowing full well I'd learned only a few words of Qorin in four years.

"Do you know anything about that place? Your safety's important—"

"I know," I said. *My body is not my own.* "I've yet to lose a duel, save one against a cheating dog."

"But it won't be duels," Daishi said. She was leaning forward now. "There are people out there who hate you, and they won't be walking up to challenge you. They'll wait until you're headed to the privy in the middle of the night. Creep up behind you, cut your throat, that's it. You have to be *careful.*"

"You think monks are gonna cut her throat?" Sakura said. She sucked her teeth. "If we've gotta worry about monks, we've gotta worry about everyone."

"Sakura-lun's right," I said. "I doubt anyone will be plotting murder at a temple. That you're considering such a thing—Aki-lun, that's why I've got to go. Everyone here hates me, and they've every right to, but I refuse to be equated with my uncle. I'll prove to them I'm better."

Daishi sank back into her slouch. She narrowed her eyes at me, pursed her lips. I thought for a moment she might continue the argument—but she swallowed her arguments with the last sip of wine.

"If you're set on this, I won't stop you," she said, getting to her feet. "I know better than to get in your way. Just—remember what I told you, all right? Be careful out there."

"Going to bed already?" I asked. "All this worry and an early bed to match it. You really are getting old."

"I'm being serious," she said. "Some hard work would be good for you, you're right, but you've got to be certain of things before you do them."

"I'm certain," I said. Why was she so against this? It wasn't as if I were planning to run off into the jungle.

"Then may the Eight smile on Heaven's Niece," said Daishi. When she said it, it sounded sincere—but I will not lie to you, I could go my entire life without hearing those words again. "I'll see you for breakfast."

As soon as she left, Sakura helped herself to Daishi's abandoned sweets. "I can help you, if you want," she said.

I thought I'd misheard her. "What?"

"With the whole 'running away' thing. If you haven't heard 'A Roll with My Lord,' you haven't been out enough. Right now I think if you put on anything less than silk, your skin might fall off."

"I wear fur sometimes," I said, which was true enough when I was out on the steppes.

Sakura's grin was wolfish. "Really? Queen Lai'd go up like a Jubilee firework if she heard that, I bet."

Would she? True, I could not imagine Baozhai touching fur. She'd married a Qorin, though. Surely it had happened.

AND ALL THIS was assuming I didn't want to tell Baozhai before I left.

But I didn't.

Somehow I had not realized it until that moment. If I told Baozhai where I was going, she'd only try to stop me. I, with the weight of my history and my future, was an iron shackle about her wrists—but she did not see it that way. Almost a year spent in my company, and she'd already gotten used to the weight.

Well. It was time I set her free. She had better things to do than console a lonely princess.

Sakura began to unroll the scroll she'd brought. "I said in my letter I wanted to help you. Let me help. Once you're out of town, I'll tell her where you went, and that'll be that—you'll have your peace and your shit-shoveling."

We'd met only this day, and yet Sakura was willing to trick the Queen of Xian-Lai for my benefit. That sort of fool thinking clearly ran in our blood. "Thank you, Sakura," I said. "I didn't know what to expect, from your letter, but . . . it is nice to have you here."

"Sure hope you think so after you see this," she said. "Had to wait until the others left, but it's my finest work, if I do say so myself."

She unfurled the scroll then.

There are all sorts of stories about the warrior monks in the Kyuuzen Mountains. You've heard some, I'm certain. It is said that by entering a deep, meditative trance, they can extinguish a raging fire with only their own will.

I have never met a Kyuuzen monk, but I know something of focus. It took all of mine not to spit my rice wine onto the painting.

Rendered in bright ink before me was a single room within a pleasure house. Five singing girls sat within, two in the corners playing their biwa, two surrounding their client, and one pouring tea for all of them. How much time had Sakura spent on their clothes? Each stitch of their embroidery was painstakingly rendered, so that to look too closely at any one of them transfixed the eye. Perhaps the richly decorated clothes were meant to distract from the subject.

Sitting between the two plumpest singing girls was a mercenary— that much was clear from the detailed tattoos spiraling down her outstretched arm. That she was a vagabond and ne'er-do-well was also obvious—she held in one hand a long pipe of Sister's Blessing. Before her was a cup full of rice wine, on her face was a familiar blush of red. In no way was this a hero.

Yet I knew the cup that sat before the woman, the cup my father had given her on her birthday. I knew those robes of Imperial Gold and Reeds-in-the-Stream Green. I knew that fine ivory pipe, which she'd bought from a Surian merchant for a week's wages back in her Nishikomi days. I knew the flowers blooming in ink on her skin: pink-hearted swamp mallows unbecoming of anyone but the Swamp-Water Queen.

My mother, deep in her cups, sat between the two singing girls, preserved in history as she was not in life.

And she was so *happy*, Shefali! How rarely I'd seen her like this! All the weight of her position and her past lay somewhere outside— sitting near the threshold with her shoes, perhaps. The ruddy joy on her face was honest in every way, honest in ways I'd never seen when

I spoke to her. This was a part of her past she long sought to conceal from me.

To see my mother like this, so beautifully rendered, so happy and carefree—this was a fine gift indeed. From anyone else, it would've been a grave insult—but from family?

My scar hurt again. I'd done more smiling on this day than I had in the whole month.

I kept that painting. Even after I left, I kept it. You see? It is that one, right over there. When you first saw it, did you know that it was my mother?

This story is sort of like that painting, isn't it?

And we've yet to reach the worst of it.

You MIGHT WONDER what it was about the temple that possessed me so strongly. The answer, I'm afraid, is as simple as it is unsatisfying: I wanted to work hard, and it was the hardest work I'd heard of, absent enlisting in the army.

And you know better than any other the fervor that overtakes me when I set my mind to something.

SAKURA AND I drank together every night for a month. Toward the end—when the details of our plan were falling into place—Sakura unburdened her own purpose.

"Before you go, could I ask you a favor?"

At that point, she could have asked me for anything and I would have obliged her. "You want me to give your guardsman a promotion?"

"Of course not, then I'd never see him," she said. "I *do* want you to put in a good word for me, but it's with your brother-in-law. The Qorin."

"I have only one brother-in-law," I said. It bothered me that she'd add "the Qorin" on, as if it were the sum total of Kenshiro's personality. "What do you want me to talk to him for? Can't you say whatever it is yourself?"

I wanted to tease her more for being so shy—but drunk as I was, the look on her face convinced me otherwise. She'd drawn back into herself. When she next spoke, she avoided looking me in the eye.

"I can't read," she said.

"O-oh," I said. Right. How careless of me to have forgotten. "Yes, yes, of course. Are you sure you want him? Baozhai can read Hokkaran, too—"

"I want it to be him," she said, a little firm. When she saw my confusion, she continued: "I want to be able to read old things."

Well. I couldn't say I understood the urge, but it was a simple request, and I did want her well educated. Kenshiro, for all his faults, was an excellent teacher. The very next day, I caught him in the hallway nearest the library and told him of Sakura's request. He was as perplexed as I was, but happy to have someone who might listen to him. It just so happened he'd gotten a few new scrolls on the history of Nishikomi, old ones that needed translating, and translating was the easiest way to learn any language.

I was a little surprised how well they struck it off—and more surprised still at how it warmed my heart. I hadn't expected to feel such . . . joy when it came to Kenshiro. But with him and Baozhai and Sakura, the four of us all sitting at dinner . . . it was the closest I'd come to a family dinner in ages.

I had a place I belonged.

And I was going to cast it all away.

I want to say that I knew what I was doing. That I understood the magnitude of this sacrifice I was going to make. I didn't, but perhaps the sleeping part of my mind did—I found whatever excuse I could to follow Baozhai to court.

I told myself that it was because I wanted to practice my poor language skills. I did not speak a word of Xianese, you see, and that gave me something in common with my uncle. Learning the language would help me understand the people, surely. Understanding the people would distance me from him.

Yet Xianese is not a simple language to learn. I'm afraid I made quite the fool of myself. On my third day at court, I offered one of the other courtiers a fruitcake. The man went stark white. Baozhai slid into the conversation and smoothed things over. It was not until much later, over a cup of wine, that she told me the truth: I'd offered *myself* to him instead in the most vulgar terms possible.

Needless to say, I wanted nothing more than to disappear from court forever after that.

And soon, my chance arrived. It was the fifth night of Jubilee, and my cousin was waiting outside my door.

"ARE YOU READY?" she said.

I had to be, of course, if this was going to work—but trepidation filled me all the same. The last time I cut my hair was when I said my final good-byes to my parents. To do so now felt wrong, as if by cutting my hair for such frivolous reasons, I would rob my parents of their proper due. What would they think of all this? My mother would've been furious, in spite of having spent much of her youth as a brothel tough.

But my father—he would have found this poetic.

He would have said that it was all right, for I *was* in mourning. Mourning for the girl I had been.

"I am," I said, and I waited for the cut.

MY HEAD FELT lighter now that I'd cut my hair, and my face felt warm beneath my Jubilee mask. I left the palace, slipped into the crowd, and became one of thousands.

The crowd was no bigger than it might've been in Fujino, but in Fujino, no one touches me. Here I was no one of note. Here I was an ancestor, perhaps, or a smith's daughter, or a papermaker. For the first time, people bumped into me!

Oh, I was furious about it the first time it happened. The woman in a bear mask was late to some appointment or another—she almost didn't stop. But then she did, and she looked me right in the eye without any fear of retaliation.

"Sorry about that," she said. "Hope you're not one of mine."

And that was that.

Imagine! Someone spoke to me and bumped into me, and looked me right in the eye. I smiled. Of course I did. Who wouldn't? I felt almost as free as I feel when I'm with you.

I started bumping into people on purpose. Complimenting their costumes. Taking whatever food I could from the passing street vendors.

There was . . .

There was one vendor. Thinking on this hurts my head, but there was one vendor. She wore a . . .

What was it? Why is it so hard to remember? A bird, I think. A crane. I do not think it was a crane, but we shall say it was a crane.

She was tall—almost as tall as you—with spindly limbs. I didn't notice her blackened teeth until I'd scooped up a bottle of rice wine off her tray.

But it wasn't rice wine when I tipped it to my lips. It tasted like a mouthful of . . . bitter and earthy and metallic.

I spat it out and she smiled at me with those blackened teeth, those pointed teeth.

"Four-Petal," she said. "A taste of your future, free of charge."

"What are you on about?" I said. "You're letting other people drink this?"

She laughed. The crowd swallowed her up, and she was gone.

Yet I heard her in the back of my head: *No others. Only you.*

My hand went to my sword. I couldn't draw it without announcing my identity. Would I need to draw it? Not for long. One stroke. Where had she gone?

I tried to shove my way through. When that didn't work, I barked at the people in front of me to get out of the way. But in that mask, I was only a small girl, only someone's lost daughter, and they paid me no heed except to call lewd things in my direction.

Not that I cared. I might be small, but when I have a goal in mind, I am unstoppable.

To that end, I rammed the butt of my sword into someone's ankle just to make headway. As he crumpled behind me, I half ran after her. I could see her at the end of the crowd. As the sunlight played upon her mask, I saw flickering characters above her head, writ in gold.

Her name was Hachiko.

She was a demon, or else a demon in human skin.

I kept walking. She turned down an alleyway and I followed—

—but I bumped straight into a large man who shoved me to the ground.

He spoke to me in a voice like burning paper, then spat at my feet.

Xianese, of course, but I did not need to understand what he was say-ing to understand his intent. One of the others at his side was the man I'd knocked over.

I didn't have time for this.

I kicked off my shoes, darted forward, and hit him in the same spot. Then I took off running. Hachiko had turned not far ahead; if that man's friends stopped to help him, then I'd have time to catch up. Mud sprang up between my toes.

As I skidded, tripped, nearly fell, I turned the corner. On either side of me were two large stone watchtowers. Up ahead, a gate in the shape of a yawning lion's mouth, leading into a cavernous tunnel. Baozhai had taken me here before. The tunnel was built centuries ago. Lovers used to stand on either side of it blindfolded. If you walked through the tunnel and bumped into your lover, the two of you were meant to stay together.

This was the one place the crowd thinned out. Besides myself, I saw no one else, not even in the guard tower.

Not even Hachiko.

But I could feel in my bones that she was near, and so I ran through the gate, too.

Now—I told you I saw no others ahead of me.

How was it, then, that a woman in a bronze fox war mask was leaning against the tunnel walls?

"Four-Petal," she said, "you're not going to catch her today."

"I won't if you keep trying to speak to me," I said. I walked right by her and tried not to dwell on the impossibility of the situation.

"Listen to an old woman!" she shouted. "You will catch her eight years from now, and not a day sooner. What you want to do is turn right once you leave the tunnel."

She was running after me. I did not bother looking back, but I heard her.

"Did she go right, old woman?"

She groaned.

"That blood does keep," she said. "No, she did not go right. But I am telling you that is what you must do. Turn right."

The exit was coming up. The outside world seemed overly bright, now that I'd spent five minutes walking through the darkness.

Should I keep going straight? Should I turn left?

Or should I listen to this strange woman, and turn right?

"You should know I approve of your wife," said the old woman. "Your mother does, too. She says she knew it was going to happen the moment you pulled that stunt with the flowers. She used to find you curled up in her bed, and when she'd try to pull the two of you apart, you'd cling to her. You said you were keeping her warm."

I stopped.

"How do you know that?" I asked.

"I know many things," she said, "and you can ask me when all of this is over. Turn right."

When I turned, she was gone.

That is the way of things, I suppose. But my choice was clear.

I stepped out into the light and turned right.

And there stood a priest dressed in Mother's White, calling in broken Hokkaran for volunteers to take back to the Grand Temple at Xian-Ru.

I fell in line with them. A man next to me lit up a pipe full of Blessing. Two women argued that he needed to share, because it was a holiday, and so he started passing it around with a pained look.

The other woman passed me the pipe.

Tonight was the night to meet with your ancestors, wasn't it?

I took a long drag. *Are you watching me, Mother?*

In the stories, when you hear from your ancestors, time stops. Everything's dreadfully somber.

But for me, at that moment, it was much more direct. As the smoke filled my lungs, I nearly hacked them back up.

I took it as a sign that my mother did not want me smoking on the way to the temple.

BARSALAI SHEFALI

THREE

Eventually, sleep comes for Minami Shizuka.

It does not happen quickly, or all at once—it is a slow thing, lurking behind her for hours. Shefali sees it in the hollows of her wife's eyes, hears its rattle in her shaking voice. When sleep slips its coil around Shizuka's neck, Shefali does nothing to stop it.

But it does not keep its hold through the night. In fits and starts sleeps Shizuka, twisting this way and that. There is no screaming tonight, but there is a war with an unseen foe.

Whenever Shizuka wakes, Shefali is there to soothe her. She cannot remember the last time she slept. She safeguards instead the small slip of eternity she has married.

SHIZUKA'S BEGINNING TO open up to her; to press the issue would be to drive her further away. The story she has told so far cannot be the whole of it; there must be more to explain the state she's in.

So why is she starting so far back?

Perhaps it is like breaking a horse. At first, you tie two small stones to it. The next day, two more, and so on, until at last it will not mind the weight of a saddle. Shefali had tied the stones to her gray herself.

Perhaps this part of the story is a small stone.

She does not voice these thoughts as her wife rises up out of bed. She only watches. Shefali left Shizuka's robes folded together near the bed last night; she does not look at them as she makes her way to her desk. The silvered mirror tries and fails to capture the faint glow about her—but Shizuka isn't concerned with that this morning. Instead she draws her fingers along the dark circles beneath her eyes; instead she holds up a shock of her hair and sighs.

"Can't confront the real world like this," she says.

"The makeup—" Shefali begins, but Shizuka's sad smile cuts her off.

"Yes, yes," she says. "The makeup. My handmaidens will be here soon to change me into a perfect little doll. But they will still see me in this state, Shefali."

Such disdain. So she does not *want* to wrap herself in so many layers? Why do it, then? This smacks of politics; it is too early in the morning for politics.

(She thinks this, as if time matters to her anymore beyond "today is one more day with my family.")

Shizuka turns away from the mirror. "Why don't we stay in today?" she says.

"We stayed in the first night," says Shefali.

Shizuka's smile is anything but sad then, as her cheeks go a little red. "I—well, I didn't *mean* it in that way, but . . ."

"Aren't you too tired for that?" Shefali teases her.

"It's been eight years, Shefali," Shizuka says. "If you wanted me in the middle of court, I'd let you have me."

The idea—Shefali cannot help but laugh. How the Hokkaran courtiers would flush! Would they turn away, would they make their excuses to leave? For so many of them looked on Shefali with disdain in the old days; just her presence in court would be enough to make them shift uncomfortably. But to so openly display their affections . . .

"It'd make court interesting for once," says Shizuka. On her desk is a brush. Shefali recognizes it—it is one of the few things in this room that has not changed. A tiger prowling through the reeds, rendered in vibrant enamel. O-Itsuki-lor gave Shizuka that brush shortly after her ninth birthday. "What a fool I was to think it was awful when we were children. At least no one will look at you strangely for snapping at someone if you're a child, or for being half bored to death. Every day it is the same set of complaints and praise; every day I must sit there on my dais and listen to them prattle . . ."

She drags the brush through her hair, so long now that she must pool some of it in her lap as she goes. "I would *love* to shock them a little."

Shefali should have expected no different. Court is not a pleasant place to be, it is true, no matter whose court it is. In Hokkaro, the rules of etiquette bind her in place; in Sur-Shar, she was bound by Debelo's contract to do whatever he wished; in Ikhtar, her bindings were far more literal. All of this is unpleasant, all of this chafes at her, and all of it is necessary.

Shizuka wrote that she would devote herself to ruling.

How can that be the case when she speaks of it with such disdain?

"Shizuka," says Shefali. Her tone is sharp; Shizuka starts mid-brushstroke as if struck. "Shizuka, you're Empress now."

"So I am," says Shizuka. "But does that mean they are entitled to so much of my life? I want to run, Shefali. More than anything. To look on them every day and know how they hate me, to hide my disdain . . . I am suffocating beneath the weight of this tradition. I hate it. With all my being, I hate this."

The brush and her hands both lie atop her pooled hair now. An unseen weight slumps her shoulders. Unseen—but familiar. Shefali has seen that slump before. It tears at her—but she cannot let it stop her. A wife must not let her wife wallow away.

No matter how difficult that might be.

"Court is terrible," Shefali says, "but you must go."

She wants Shizuka to look at her. She wants that, desperately, for if Shizuka looked at her, then they might truly be having a conversation. Instead she stares out the window.

"*Shizuka,*" Shefali says again. Her joints are stiff, and she aches just thinking about moving—but she won't be able to convince her from the bed. Slowly she forces herself to the edge. She bites her lips to keep from screaming, she leans over to shove her leg down where it should be—but she stands. "You promised you'd rule well."

And still Shizuka does not look on her.

This pain is a shackle. She cannot see the chains, but they are there. The cuffs bite at her ankles and the tender skin of her knee, and if she moves—if she moves, the skin will tear; if she moves, she wonders if she will be able to stand afterwards at all. To take a step is to accept that risk. It would not be the first time she's fallen on her face in the early morning—something about the sunlight turns her joints to iron.

Shefali sucks in a breath. With all the strength she can muster, she *forces* her leg up, her foot forward. When her foot lands again on the ground, it is as if she's stepped on a knee-high spike. She staggers, sways; for a moment she thinks she will fall—but she rights herself in time. Pain throbs up from her knees to her head; she kneads her thigh with one hand, and it does not help, it does not help.

"Shizuka," she says. "You *promised*." The stress of her condition has turned her voice into a ragged saw blade.

Shizuka closes her eyes. She lays her hand along the bridge of her nose—along the scar—and breathes. The peonies in her scent have given way to something else, something more insidious that Shefali cannot place. "I did," she says. "I just . . . I wanted to stay here with you and pretend a little while longer. Is that so terrible? Will you be-grudge me this?"

And no—she cannot. The world can wait a Bell or two.

Even if Shizuka's recalcitrance does bother her.

Another step. Another. It gets easier, the more Shefali does it. She wraps her arm around Shizuka, and Shizuka leans against her as if taking shelter from a storm.

"Rest," Shefali says. "At least a little. I'll wake you when the hand-maidens come."

How many silences have they shared together? Shefali knows them all by now: the soft hush of brush on paper, the gentle rumble of her snore, the whisper of silk on silk.

She knows this silence, too. It is an old one. The first time she heard it, she'd thought it a dream she had after the tiger nearly killed her.

"*I'm sorry*," Shizuka said then.

And she says it now, too.

"Promise me we'll have tonight?" she whispers.

Shefali nods. "We always have the nights," she says. "No matter where the day takes you."

When Shizuka brings their lips together, Shefali tastes salt.

"Will you carry me to bed?" Shizuka says.

Will you tear yourself apart for me?

"Of course," Shefali says.

She promised to carry her wife's weight, after all, regardless of how much it would pain her.

SHIZUKA IS RIGHT—they do come for her at Third Bell. Precisely at Third, as it happens, the whole line of them appearing outside the door like a column of tulips that sprang up overnight. Each one wears draped scarlet and yellow; each one wears her hair long and unbound. Their perfume is so thickly applied that Shefali can hardly catch their scent. It gives her a headache.

But she rises when they come, and she hobbles her way toward them. Ten minutes, it takes her to cross the room—and that with each step the absolute focus of her attention.

She could have shouted at them from the bed, but that would have woken Shizuka. And she did deserve to rest.

So Shefali makes her journey across the deserts and the mountains of the room, and so she slides open the paper door the way she'd rolled aside the boulder that guarded the Womb.

It is only when she opens the door that she realizes she's forgotten to get her mask.

The first girl outside the door is young enough that she has heard of Shefali only as Barsalai, only as Steel-Eye—and then only recently. Hers is a life of relative ease. The Empress is demanding, yes, but beautiful in all the ways that matter, and if the mood struck her, she'd gift her handmaidens a new set of robes. To serve her is to live in absolute luxury, as far as possible from the horrors beyond the Wall.

She is not prepared to face Barsalai Shefali.

But it is admirable how well she keeps her face. Only her eyes give her away, shrinking small; only the barest twitch of her lip.

"Empress Wo—" she begins, but Shefali cuts her off before she can finish the unearned title.

"Give her another hour," she says.

The girl bows again. Somehow the cups of tea on her tray do not rattle when she does this. Shefali wonders where one learns skills like that. "Of course, your Imperial—"

"Barsalai," she says. "Thank you."

She closes the door, having already exhausted her energy for dealing with strangers.

And because she is in pain, she sits there and waits for them to return. In her mind, she plots the letter she will write to her mother when she is feeling better: *Come to Fujino, and I will make you another deel,* she will write, though she has no idea where she'll find another tiger. *We need to speak about Shizuka,* she leaves unwritten.

But she does need to speak about her.

It is said by the Surians that there is a merchant for every need. For meat, the butcher; for shoes, the cobbler; for medicines, the alchemist. *Do not visit the butcher for medicine.*

The first time she heard the saying, she'd thought it morbid in a way that reminded her of the Qorin. The second time, she understood.

As she understands now.

For gossip, go to the madam.

She cannot say she is *sad* at the idea, or that it displeases her. Most of the last week has been spent in the Imperial Garden—Ren's establishment only a stone's throw away from its namesake—and most of that week has been pleasant. She cannot say she had any worries except that of her condition—Ren provided her constant entertainment when she wanted it, and silence when she didn't. Music, or stories, or simply a fragrant blend of tea to smell—she had a talent for knowing what Shefali wanted without being told.

It had been good to see her.

It would be good to see her again.

If only it were under better circumstances. Perhaps the storm clouds on the horizon have darkened Shefali's view. Perhaps things are not so bad as they seem. Perhaps Ren will sing the praises of Empress Yui.

But perhaps a tortoise can outrun a colt.

Either way, she must know.

When the girls return for Shizuka, Shefali tells them she will be the one to wake her wife. The hours have chipped away at the unseen cuffs; she is a little less stiff.

When she stands, when she turns to face Shizuka . . .

There are many types of beauty. The smile of a woman you favor. Plum petals on snowbanks. A painting, slaved over for years and years and years. Each is, in its own way, a joy. Each one warms the soul.

But there is another kind of beauty—the sort that hits you right in the chest, the sort that robs the breath from your lungs, the sort that forces you to kneel and admit that you are small and insignificant, that nothing can surpass this eternal moment. That is the beauty of mountains. That is the beauty of lightning crackling across a starry sky. That is the beauty of the dawn playing across hundreds of li of silver grass.

It is the beauty of Minami Shizuka, curled up in her bed, with her thumb slipped between her lips. With every breath, her chest rises and falls; with every breath, she is a wave lapping at a white shore.

When Shefali scoops her up into her arms, when Shefali pulls her in close—

Yes, that is something like divinity.

She lets it fill her lungs. This, too, is Shizuka, for all that her waking self is worry-wracked.

To wake her is a tragedy in itself. Shefali does it as gently as she can, kissing the stub of her ear, kissing her cheek and chin. When at last Shizuka's eyes flutter open, she forgets why she is so worried about her.

"Shizuka," she says. "It's time."

"No," Shizuka mumbles. "Send them away."

"I've already done that once," Shefali says.

"Do it again," Shizuka says, but it is the playful whine of a child. She is already looking around the room, already awake. A kiss on the cheek and she has hopped out of Shefali's arms, landing like a cat on the mats.

She kisses Shefali on the cheek again—though now she must stand on the very tips of her toes to do it.

"Don't duel anyone," Shefali tells her.

"Hardly a duel if they don't even finish the draw," Shizuka says. There is more color to her now that she has slept—and now that she's gone a few hours without drinking. Shefali wonders if she should have said *Don't drink* instead, but the deed is already done. "I will love you always, even if the rest of me is a mess. You know that, don't you?"

Her hand is on Shefali's cheek. Shefali covers it with her own. Their eyes meet, and she remembers what Shizuka said once—*I know you as I know my own reflection.*

And of all the things she has doubted, she has never doubted that Shizuka loves her.

She kisses Shizuka's hand. "I love you, too," she says. "If you need me—"

"I'll yell," says Shizuka. She touches her thumb to Shefali's lips, and Shefali watches her go.

It will be hours yet before she feels well enough to leave this room.

SHEFALI'S HEAD IS still pounding. The corners of her vision are dyed a deep burgundy, like the wine Otgar drank so much of back in Ikhtar. The streets now are empty save for bedraggled Imperial servants awaiting their next shifts. Barsalai sees them through the open doors of teahouses as she passes. There are more teahouses now, aren't there? And packed, each of them. A familiar shamisen melody caresses her as she makes her way through the vine-narrow streets.

Look inside, it says.

But it is a difficult thing even to *glance* inside. Here, for instance, there are two dozen Imperial couriers seated around a massive circular table. Their cheeks and chests are already ruddy. One of them has his cup raised.

"To the one-eyed mongrel," he says. "The Sister herself couldn't improve the Empress's moods, but a Qorin can. That's the world we live in!"

He is met by a chorus of laughs.

Eight years, she journeyed. She has wrestled with lightning-maned lions—for this. There is no helping some people.

Her pain spikes, like a piton driven at her temples. Barsalai Shefali teeters, doubles over, and finally squats down in the middle of the street. She cannot be standing, not when it hurts this much, not when her body may change again at a moment's notice. Her tongue sticks to the roof of her mouth. Nausea twists at a stomach that has been empty for a decade. Trembling, growing frantic, she begins to count her fingers. Ten. Good. Two arms, too, connected to her solid torso, and two bowlegs beneath.

Barsalai, she whispers to herself.

You are Barsalai Shefali, and you must hold on as long as you can.

She runs her hands over her hair, over her thick first braid and the thinner ones Otgar gave her. With each link, she repeats to herself: *You are Barsalai Shefali, and you must hold on.* Like a prayer it leaves her. Each repetition is an arrow against the corruption in her blood, against the influence pulling at her leash. Her voice hitches.

This does not always work. It did not work earlier, when her temper got the better of her and she forgot to assert herself over the dark. Why should it work now?

Because she is in control, she tells herself. Because she is the daughter of Burqila Alshara, the Wall-Breaker, and no ink in her blood will be her master.

One gasping, gulping breath. Stars bursting behind her eyes. Another breath. Her stomach twists again, and she hikes up her fox mask. The pressure is mounting—she is going to retch, and she knows it, but what fluid will leave her is a mystery.

She forces herself to stand and stagger behind the teahouse. A man playing the flute has joined the woman playing the shamisen. Each note drives the stake deeper into Barsalai's temple. How easy it would be to break through those thin walls, to crunch them between—

Her jaw cracks and grows into a toothy maw. Barsalai whimpers.

You deserve to rule them. You're better than they are. You've always been better.

No. This isn't who she is.

Just as she wills her jaw back into shape, the retching comes upon her. For what seems like hours she stays there, on her knees, vomiting up something viscous and black and awful. When it is over, she is slick with sweat, heavy with shame. The puddle in front of her is large enough for children to float paper boats across it. It stinks of rot—how long will it be before someone comes back here to piss and sees it there?

No—she isn't willing to risk it harming others. But what is she going to do about it? Burying it surely won't help; the corruption would seep into the ground then, and some foul tree would sprout in four days' time. Burning it was also out of the question. Was she meant to scoop it up like gathered herbs in her deel and . . . carry it somewhere else?

She sighs, leans back, tugs on the mask that makes her feel more human. The perfumed rags she's stuffed into the fox's muzzle have lost their scent. Grumbling, she reaches into the pocket of her deel for another.

It is then that her fingertips brush on a skin full of kumaq.

Didn't Tumenbayar work miracles with kumaq? Yes—she kept the demons at bay with only a smattering of mare's milk. That was why all the sanvaartains used it. Kumaq was as sacred to the Qorin as rice wine to the Hokkarans. Hope is like water on her now parched lips.

Shizuka said they were gods, when they were younger. She'd been wrong about a great many things in her life—but never about their divinity. This, Shefali knew. And if kumaq was good enough for Tumenbayar, it would be good enough for Barsalai Shefali.

She pulls the skin from her deel and sucks in a breath. It felt like sucking in a breath was a thing you should do before you blessed things. How was it done? No one discussed that in the stories; it was a given that there was kumaq, and that it was blessed, and the how of it all was left to the listener. Why hadn't she asked the other gods when she met them on her travels? Seemed like a pertinent thing now.

What a fool you are, said the foul voice—the old one, and not the new. *It shouldn't be surprising that an illiterate cuckold like you can't piece this together, and yet . . .*

Anger simmers within her—but she has been down that road enough times to know it is a tiger trap. She is Barsalai Shefali, and—

That's it, isn't it?

She pours kumaq into her right hand—the hand with the pale scar across it, the hand that swore she and Shizuka would always be together. It goes cool against her skin. Smelling it is like entering a ger; smelling it is coming home. The memories wash over her and she lets them: her aunts arguing over which of their daughters best deserved that strapping boy from the Arsalandai clan, her uncle Ganzorig's stew filling up the ger with spicy aroma, her cousins about to come to blows over a game of anklebones.

Shizuka, trying to shoot a bow and missing even the largest of targets.

"Oh, what will it matter?" she said after missing an entire oxcart. "You'll be there to hunt for us, anyway."

Another breath. Despite her deel, despite her mask, despite how well covered she is—she can feel the starlight shining down on her, the moonlight painting her soul the silver of the steppes. She leans over, breaths out.

A cloud of silver engulfs the kumaq in her hand.

When she at last opens her eyes, the small pool of milk is glowing silver.

Barsalai Shefali stands. She looks down on the puddle of black she has left here, in an alley behind a teahouse, and speaks.

"I am of the sky and the steppes. So long as the steppes are flat, so long as the sky is full of stars, you will answer to me."

When the kumaq pours from her hand, it is a shimmering veil of water, it is a promise, and when it lands within the slick black fluid, it is more beautiful than an inkwash painting.

It feels right.

And, watching it, *Shefali* feels right. As if the fire raging within has at last died down, and flowers sprout from the wreckage.

There is no such thing as being too careful when it comes to the blackblood. She kicks dirt onto it, then pours a little more kumaq onto the resulting mound. Only then does she turn.

The way to the gardens is a familiar one. She walks the path, composing more letters with every step.

BARSALAI SHEFALI

FOUR

One of Ren's servants scurries over with a decanter of rice wine. She gets as far as setting down one of the cups before Shefali waves her away.

There is a saying in Hokkaro: No knife cuts deeper than your favorite. In Qorin, the saying is, the dog you raised has the most painful bite—but the meaning is the same. Thinking of Shizuka staggering home angry and drunk, the thought of her ignoring her duties, hurts her worse than any knife.

SHE TAKES A deep breath. Ren's done her best to conceal the omnipresent scent of sex, burning incense and oils in each room. The resulting miasma makes Shefali's headache worse. She squeezes the web of her hand, between forefinger and thumb. Kenshiro told her when they were young that it would help with headaches.

It doesn't.

She tries not to hold it against him now.

Ren sets aside the cup of rice wine. Shefali smells her concern as she leans forward, her hand coming perilously close to Shefali's.

"My darling Barsalai," she says. "You came to me once to soothe your worries. I hoped that, when you returned to Fujino, you'd leave them all behind—but I see now they're following you. Please—my home is your home; you can relax here. Let me carry your burdens."

Where to begin? The knot in Shefali's chest tightens. She wonders if speaking out loud will loosen it or wind it tighter. Is this a betrayal?

"You are safe here," says Ren. "I have promised you that, and I promise it still."

Ask her.

Shefali closes her eyes. It does little to drown out the presence of Ren, whose scent wraps around her like a thick fur stole, but it helps. "What has my wife been doing?"

Ren tuts. She withdraws her hand, and Shefali hears the chink of the teacup on the table again. "Ah," she says. "You've come for a little knowledge, that's all?"

A little knowledge. Yes, that is the truth of it. Why does it seem so looming, then?

"She seems . . . ," Shefali begins, but she is not sure what the next word will be. Different? But the core of her is the same.

"Troubled," finishes Ren. Shefali nods. "Lighting herself on fire for a lark, from what I've heard. Have you seen the statue?"

"Hm?"

"In the throne room," Ren continues. "A statue of the former Emperor Yorihito, although you can hardly tell anymore. She sliced it in two one night, drunk as a vagrant."

Shefali thinks back—did she see such a statue? She's hardly been paying attention; she is too distracted by Shizuka and the courtiers. But splitting statues in two, *lighting herself on fire* . . .

"One woman goes to war, and another returns, as the saying goes," Ren says. "She hasn't been the same since Ink-on-Water."

"Ink-on-Water?" Shefali says. "War?"

Ren raises a brow. The playful spark in her eyes dulls; she traces her fingertip along the rim of her cup.

"Did she volunteer?" Shefali asks, for that is the only way she can imagine this happening. Perhaps Shizuka wanted to prove her godhood; perhaps she wanted to do what her uncle never could.

"No," says Ren. "The Toad got it in his head that another assault on the Wall, after all these years, was just the thing to topple the Traitor. But instead of sixteen warriors, he sent thousands. He conscripted your wife and most of Xian-Lai's youth, to go lend aid to our Northern Provinces. Off they went, singing their war songs, dying in droves. . . ."

Her eyes go distant. She is remembering something sacred. If Shefali takes a deep enough breath of her scent, she might be able to peek. It's a tempting thought, but one she banishes. Memories are precious things.

"Have I told you much of my home?"

Shefali shakes her head.

Ren pours another cup of rice wine.

"Emperor Yorihito gave my father twice-two li of land, just past the river. Considering how fertile Shiseiki is, that was a generous blessing. We used this godly bounty to grow daikon."

Has she ever had a daikon? Shefali scratches her chin.

"It was hard work, but it was ours. My father would put his hands on his hips and look out over his land. 'This is what men were meant to do,' he'd say. 'Feed the land, and she will feed you.'"

Ren tosses back the second cup of rice wine. "When the first bandits came, long before you and I met, they razed the fields, of course. After they left, I stood where my father once did. Where he saw opportunity, I saw dirt. This place had never really been my home, I told myself. When my brother and I left for the camps— where Tsetseg and the other sanvaartains found us, and offered me the help I needed—I spared not a thought for the farm or my father's crops, believed it had nothing to do with me."

Bitterness stains the back of Shefali's tongue. Wherever Ren is going with this story, it is not one she likes to tell.

"Twice-two years ago, Emperor Yoshimoto proved me false," Ren says, spitting the man's name. "Yoshimoto sent your wife north, to the Wall of Flowers, along with his sniveling army. And they upset the river god, and the river god took her vengeance, and . . . after I left, the Qorin taught me that home is a white felt ger, of course. But I had more than that once. And then the wave—"

Ren takes a deep breath.

"Shiseiki is gone."

"Gone?" says Shefali. "The whole province?" What wave could do such damage? With knots in her stomach, she remembers the river in Shiseiki, remembers how wide it was. An entire day it took to cross it. Yes—it would take a god to demand such vengeance, the might to do such a thing.

As a child, Shefali had wondered if she and Shizuka really were gods, or could be one day; and her wanderings east of the steppes had proved the possibility more than once. Shefali had met other gods over the last eight years. Minor ones, for the most part, tied to a specific place and unable to leave it. At some points they'd helped her.

And at others—Shefali now knows that even to her refined senses, the blood of gods is far sweeter than that of a mortal.

"We can't know how many people died," says Ren, "but it was in the thousands. Drowned, all of them. Have you ever seen someone drown, Barsalai? That is the worst way anyone can die."

Shefali, at a loss for words, touches her friend's shoulder.

The sweet melody of an old Hokkaran love song wraps around them. Two precincts' worth of guards sit in the pavilion one floor down, with two dozen girls to entertain them. Their laughter, boisterous and sanguine, clatters against Shefali's heart. Only layers of wood separate joy from sorrow.

Ren screws her eyes shut. She almost rubs her palms in her eyes, but, as if thinking of her makeup, she sighs instead.

"You've asked me what has happened to your wife. I admit—I don't know all the details, but you may not like what I do know. You can mend a tear, Shefali, but the stitches remain. Are you sure of this?"

"I am," she says, even if she isn't.

"The first thing you should know, then, is that *most* people are pleased with her," says Ren. "The commoners *idolize* the Phoenix Empress, and the lower-ranking military do, too—even among the merchants and the nobles, most agree she's better than her uncle. Which isn't saying much. But I am saying it to you, anyway."

Shefali appreciates the gesture.

"The commoners like that she's feeding them, after years of lean living. The merchants, of course, hate that she's doing it by raising taxes on them. The nobles hate the tax issue, as well, but they're more in a froth over—" She gestures. "—other things."

"Like?"

"I will say this for your wife: There isn't a dull moment with her," says Ren. "She's liberated Xian-Lai. Dao Doan and Hanjeon, too, though those weren't so immediate. Ten years left for Dao Doan, twenty for Hanjeon—after that, they are free."

Shefali's mouth hangs open. Why did she ever doubt Shizuka? Of course she is going to sever the ties, of course she is going to undo her ancestors' great evil! No matter what clothes she wore, no matter the way she painted her face, she is still Shizuka, still casually doing the impossible.

"With the South no longer paying their tribute, she's had to raise taxes even more on Fuyutsuki and Shiratori," says Ren. "Unpopular, to be sure, and unwise given their positions. When I heard, I had half a mind to move to Nishikomi for stability's sake, but she continued to impress."

"Oh?" says Shefali. The knot in her chest—it is unwinding, unwinding, settling warm now in her stomach.

"The makeup," Ren says, lifting her cup. "The hair, the clothes. All of it. Lords Shiratori and Fuyutsuki are both nearing seventy. Their bones are tradition, nostalgia their blood. Dressing like her own great-grandmother's tricked them into thinking she's on their side." She smirks. "It's the sort of thing *I* would have done."

There is even a reason for the clothing! No wonder it wore on Shizuka so to go to court—she is trussing herself up like this to appeal to men she doesn't like.

"She's told them that Hokkaro doesn't *need* Xian-Lai. Xian-Lai wasn't part of the empire when they were young, after all, and weren't things just fine then?" Ren shakes her head with a laugh. "I cannot *believe* she'd think of that. And I cannot believe she made them believe her. But—what a wonder. It is good, Shefali, to see such a thing finally in our past."

"Thank you," says Shefali. "I was worried about her."

"You should worry," says Ren. She leans forward now. "That's the good, Barsalai. The bad is that she spent *perhaps* three days of her first few reigning years sober."

Not . . . not surprising. But Shefali counts then, realizing that Shizuka returned from war nearly four years since, and so her reign is more soaked in wine than blood, surely. Shefali thinks back again to Shizuka's drunken staggering.

Shefali shifts. So—there is good, and there is bad, but above all—there is hope. Except—she has no idea where to go from here. Four months of peace with her wife, Shefali wanted, and now it seems she will have to speak to Shizuka about her drinking instead—a task as far from rest as Dao Doan is from Ikhtar.

"If you are looking for my advice, which is, sadly, the only reason you're here . . . Barsalai, you are aware that she's . . . spent time with other women?"

"How do you know that?"

Ren has the courtesy not to smile, but her eyes glint. "My darling, what sort of crime lord would I be if I did not have eyes in the palace? Come, now."

Well. That does make sense.

"A WOMAN IS like a horse . . . ," Shefali says.

"She can roam wherever she pleases," Ren finishes in Qorin. "I was worried you'd be upset over it."

"Why?" says Shefali. Oh, it hurt to imagine while she was traveling—but she is here now, and they are together now, and that is all that matters to her.

"Your love for her is so *singular*," says Ren.

"I only want her to be happy," says Shefali. Her jaw's tingling. Why is her jaw tingling? "I was away. Others . . . weren't. She needed company; she found it."

Ren *hmm*s to herself. It is a long moment before she speaks again. Instead, she runs her finger along the rim of her teacup over and over.

"You're right," says Ren. "She does need company."

And then—pain. Horrible pain, shooting through the right side of her jaw. Ren is still speaking, but Shefali can no longer hear her, no longer focus. Where is this coming from? The poison in her blood, the stain on her soul. Why now? She's been doing *so well*. . . .

"Barsalai?"

She turns away, screws her eyes shut. Taking another axe to the face would be more pleasant. Not this creeping, as if spiders are burrowing into her flesh.

Shefali is starting to shift.

And already—the very tip of her chin is coming apart like the corner of a sack. She tries to breathe, knit herself back together, and for a moment, it seems to work.

When she turns back, she finds Ren wide eyed.

"Sorry," Shefali mumbles. The word comes out garbled, but her mouth isn't holding together, her mouth isn't *holding,* and soon the rest of her won't, either. . . .

"Shefali," says Ren. "I—I'm going to help."

She's up in a wash of silk that Shefali cannot follow, up and walking to a collection of vials and contraptions on a small table near the door. Shefali cannot watch her; she cannot afford to lose her focus. She must imagine herself. Barsalai Shefali, she is Barsalai Shefali, that is the name she's earned twice over, and this is her body, this is her mouth. . . .

She is Barsalai Shefali. These are her legs. They've carried her onto her horse, they've carried her across the world, they are—

They are giving out on her.

As paper lanterns crushed beneath heavy stone, her legs: she crumples to the ground, hitting her head against the carpet. Higher and higher the stitches climb—it is not just her mouth now but her nose as well, and soon it will be her eyes. Her fingertips tingle. She wants to scream, she wants to plead for this not to happen, but it will anyway; she is spiraling, spiraling, as her fingertips bloom, too.

"Barsalai, listen to me," says Ren.

Get away, she wants to say to her.

But how is she to speak with a mouth like this? Her tongue is anteater long, spilling out of her and wriggling through the air with a mind of its own. No. She could not answer Ren even if she wanted to.

"Swallow. I need you to swallow."

Swallow?

A taste like a smith's day-old quenching water. Someone is holding her head back, she thinks, so that the liquid can pour down her throat.

Swallow.

There is enough of Barsalai left to follow instruction.

SKIN KNITTING TOWARD skin, teeth sinking back into flesh. Warmth, as the potion spreads through her. *I am Barsalai Shefali,* she thinks, *that is my name twice-earned.*

This body of hers is wet clay, and she *will* shape it, she *will* . . .

Slowly she forms herself again, until she is lying facedown, in pain but whole on Ren's floor.

And Ren has sunk down to her knees next to her.

Like two warriors lying in the squalor of the melee—the two of them curled up next to each other.

Who will speak first?

What is there to say?

"Sorry," Shefali mumbles. She can think of nothing else. "You shouldn't have seen that. . . ."

She props herself up on her elbows. Now she can see Ren truly: her hair has worn free of its bindings, strands of black sticking out like straws of hay.

"Ren, are you all right?"

For long moments Ren does not answer, only stares at her, wide eyed and mouth agape.

"Please," Shefali says. *No, no, none of this was meant to happen.*

But this is your lot in life, Steel-Eye, says the old demon to her. *A plague on those you know.*

"Ren," Shefali says again. Her voice is cracking. "Ren, please say something."

"Shefali," Ren whispers. "How long have you been dying?"

BARSALAI SHEFALI

FIVE

All journeys meet their ends. All flowers, no matter how beautiful, wilt and fall away. The beauty of the clouds settled atop Gurkhan Khalsar lasts for only a Bell—the wind soon scatters them. Only the memory remains.

Two years ago, Shefali would've shrugged off such Hokkaran ruminations on transience. Now?

Now she comforts herself by thinking of clouds and flowers and the sound of falling rain.

She feels the changes whenever the sun rises: the lead in her bones, the throbbing ache. Her vision blurs at the edges. During the day, she's navigating more by scent than she is by sight.

Three days she'd spent with Shizuka, and her wife had never noticed it. Shefali wasn't certain whether she should be proud of how well she concealed her symptoms or disappointed in her wife's ignorance.

Sitting before Ren, she decides that disappointment is more appropriate.

Four months.

The words leave Shefali's lips as whispers; they meet Ren's ears as claps of thunder.

Tears well up in her brown eyes, though she is trying not to shed them. Color drains from her painted face. "Four months," Ren repeats, her voice cracking.

Shefali can hardly bear to look on her. She sinks back down to the floor. "I'm sorry," she says, for it is the only thing she can think of. "Someone reliable told me I had only twenty-six years in this world. The moment I heard, I hurried back as quickly as I could, but Sur-Shar is far, and . . ."

The double first is half a year away now—but it creeps closer every day. Shefali has never had a particular fondness for her birthday.

"Someone reliable?" Ren repeats. The venom in her tone! "Who? Who told you this?"

Shefali averts her remaining eye. "The Mother."

Ren has given up on holding in her tears. Shefali feels them soaking through her deel. She lays her head on Ren's lap; she has not the energy to sit up properly. "I'm sorry," she says, over and over until the words no longer even seem like words.

"Promise me you'll visit," says Ren. "Once this is all over with— promise me."

"I will," Shefali says.

"You've got to give me your word," says Ren. The weeping has put a shrill note into her voice. "I can't . . . This can't be the last time I see you, Shefali. You're . . ."

Shefali cannot summon an apology strong enough. It isn't fair, truly it isn't—and there is nothing she can do to change it. Even if she were to cut herself open and tear out everything that her disease has corrupted, she'd be tearing out her own organs. That she'd lived this long is a miracle in and of itself.

But Ren does not see it that way, and Shizuka won't, either. Shizuka with her dreams of growing old together, her dreams of a happy married life that they will never share.

"Promise me you'll send for me when it's time," says Ren. "I don't . . . I don't want to wake up one morning and hear you've gone without saying good-bye."

"I will," says Shefali.

She lies there swaying with the madam for five minutes, for ten, for fifteen. Slowly, the crying ebbs away into silent little gasps—and then into nothing at all.

"WHEN I MEET the Mother," says Ren, her voice now full of purpose, "I'm going to have a word with her about this. Did I upset her in some past life, that I should meet you only when there's death on the horizon?"

Shefali stifles a chuckle. She imagines Ren standing before the towering being that was O-Akane, fanning herself, demanding more time. Like a mouse petitioning a tiger for a head start.

"You'll have to ask," Shefali says.

"I will. Don't mistake me, it'll be years yet before I go to meet her, but I'll remember this," she says. She touches Shefali's cheek once more before moving to her collection of vials. "And I won't let her have you without a fight."

Ren picks up a vial already half full of a deep red liquid. Shefali has seen such color only once before: a glass of wine Debelo once enjoyed, brought to him all the way from the pale lands. She spent ten minutes marveling at it then, and now is no exception—she finds herself sitting up just to get a better look at it.

Ren takes Shefali's hand.

"Darling," says Ren in a tone so soft and sweet that it can mean nothing good, "I'm going to need your blood for this to work."

Shefali draws her hand back and holds it close to her chest, as if it is a serpent that might strike out at Ren. She shakes her head. "My blood is evil," she says. She has seen what happens when it mingles with the living—she has seen it over and over when Debelo ordered her into the fray. "You've already—"

"If you're worried about contamination, you've nothing to fear," says Ren. She holds up her hands. "No wounds to be seen, yes? No risk of my catching it."

Shizuka said the same thing when they first lay together after the infection. Straddling Shefali, her hand hovering above that vital spot, she'd traced Shefali's jaw.

I know there is a risk, she'd said. *But it's one I'm willing to take, if you're willing to allow it.*

Shefali squeezes her eyes shut. She doesn't want to remember Shizuka that way, not now. Not when there is a stain of black on Ren's cheek, too.

"What if I tell you what it is I'm working on?" says Ren. "Would that help?"

The answer to Shefali's condition does not lie in some vial on a singing girl's table—even if that singing girl trained with sanvaartains. If it did, then Alshara would've found out about it years ago. Calling for the sanvaartains was the first thing Alshara had done when Shefali returned. Whatever hope she'd had for a cure was crushed when, after four days, they announced there was little they could do to help her.

"She was never ours to heal," they'd said. "And now she's *his*. Keep her around, and the horses will start to rot, you mark my words, Burqila."

Shefali's chest aches. She'd spent every evening with the clan as far from the horses as she could out of fear. If one came to harm because of her, she didn't know what she would do.

And now Ren is saying she can help.

She feels small.

Ren touches Shefali's cheek, light as dawn.

"Shefali," she says. "You're safe here. Always remember that. If you don't want me to continue, I won't—but I would like if you heard my reasoning."

Shefali, biting her lip, nods. Listening won't hurt. And Ren treats her a far sight better than the other sanvaartains. Better than the so-called surgeons of Shiseiki Province, too, whose knives and scissors haunt her more than the bloodied jaws of wolves. "No cutting into me," she says.

"I'd never dream of it," says Ren. She does not make the request seem outlandish, and for that, Shefali is grateful. "Now. Godly corruption is beyond even my capabilities, but I've shaped at least a hundred bodies in the past year alone. I'm good at it. Better than most sanvaartains, I'm not too humble to say; Tsetseg wanted to keep me around for a reason."

Tsetseg is a common enough name, but there is only one sanvaartain bearing it. One of Alshara's cousins, if Shefali remembers right, born to Grandmother Nadyya's eldest sister. Shefali met her once or twice; she always had an extra sweet ready for Shefali's gray mare and a story to tell around the fire. Of all the Qorin Shefali knows, Tsetseg is the softest.

She is the one who taught Ren?

Shefali tries to picture them next to one another, but it's like trying to fire a Hokkaran bow on horseback. Nothing about Ren fits on the steppes.

But then, Shizuka always looked strange, too, lying around the ger in her fine silk robes.

"There are times when the ritual doesn't *quite* take. You've got to focus on what you'd like to look like, ideally, and your body shapes itself to match. But maintaining focus while your bones are cracking themselves open is a difficult thing. If your focus slips for long enough . . . ," Ren continues. She breaks eye contact, presses her lips together. Whatever is coming next pains her. "That's never easy. The patient's body will start growing in places it shouldn't, or hollowing out . . . the first time it happened to someone I was helping, I didn't move quickly enough."

Shefali squeezes Ren's hand. The madam squeezes back. "I was heartbroken. Tsetseg told me it was a possibility, yes, but I always thought it was some failing on the sanvaartain's part. And I didn't have any failings." She sighs. "So, I swore that I would never allow that to happen again. Years of work later, and I think I've got a handle on it. The problem is that the magic's will overwhelms the patient, and so I made a potion that counters it. Concentrated self, if you will."

Concentrated self? Sanvaartains keep their secrets close as their deels, but this sounds strange even by their standards. Yet the symptoms Ren mentioned match up so neatly with Shefali's own experiences. How is it that none of the others have mentioned this to her? Her face goes hot. All these years, the sanvaartains knew about people losing their shape, and yet they did not help Shefali when she'd asked?

"I will need a bit of your blood," continues Ren. "What I made you earlier, when you were struggling . . . that was a dose I'd prepared in case a customer turned up in need. Normally it takes me only a few days to prepare—but you'll need multiples, I think, and your blood isn't the kind I typically work with. So let's call it a gift, yes?"

A gift.

Four months.

There is a plum tree above her, just beginning to blossom. Shizuka stands at her side, pouting because she had not gotten her way. She-fali is trying not to stare at her. A passing breeze sends her hair sway-ing; petals fall where they will.

As ice melts when held near a flame, so does Shizuka's pout melt into a grin. Her eyes crinkle at the edges. Shefali's cheeks go hot—and hotter, still, when Shizuka reaches for her face.

"Careful," she says. "Someone will mistake those cheeks of yours for a sweet."

Shizuka brushes the petal from Shefali's cheek with a small laugh—a furtive little bird of a sound.

"Shefali."

It takes her a moment to realize that it's Ren speaking.

"Let me help you. Please. Let me try, at least," she says.

Four months. At least she'll see the plum trees in bloom one more time. If Ren's right about this, then maybe she'll be able to walk be-neath them, too, and see the petals spiraling like snowflakes onto the ground. How sweet the air would be. . . .

"All right," she says. "A gift."

BARSALAI SHEFALI

SIX

It is Seventh Bell by the time Shefali finishes her trip back to the palace. This though she rode most of the way. Contrary to popular
opinion, she was not born in a saddle; her horse's steps sent shocks
rumbling through her. On her good days, these rumbles make her
feel alive. Today—today she rode only because she did not trust her
legs to keep their form the whole way back.

You have to tell her about this, says Shefali's gray, and she is probably right. How much longer can she keep up this lie? How much
longer can she pretend there was nothing wrong? As the moon climbs
higher in the sky, some of her strength returns to her, but that is only
a three-bell solution. When the sun rises again, she will be suffering
again.

It hurts. Sky, how it hurts. But this has been her life since she returned from the Womb.

She cannot let Shizuka know.

Shefali stables her gray herself: feeds her a sweet before she leaves and makes her promise not to cause any trouble. Her gray cannot make such a weighty oath as that. Shefali tries to get her to promise she'll at least *try* to make the hostler's life easy, and there they can both agree.

The twisting halls of the palace taunt her as they did the night before, as they have every night she has spent within them.

She will hardly notice when you die, says the demon in her mind. One of the older ones, and not the man who has turned up recently.

Shefali has had enough of it for today. To address the thought at all is to indulge it—she turns her attention instead to her wife, who must surely be waiting for her in their rooms. Already Shefali can smell her.

Peonies, chrysanthemums, steel.

Not a drop of wine.

She's started drinking again to forget how ugly you've become, Steel-Eye. You should see the way she looks at you when you aren't paying attention. As if something has died in her mouth.

No. Pay it no attention.

Step after step she follows the scent. A melody soon joins it. One of the handmaidens must be practicing her zither. Shefali hums along; it helps to fill in the silence. She knows this tune—what are the words? They're waiting for her to remember them like dogs waiting to be let out of the ger.

Closer she comes, the two Phoenix Guards now plainly visible to her, the melody louder than ever. With a smile, she realizes that it is Shizuka playing.

She stops at the edge of the hallway to listen.

If she comes any closer, Shizuka will see her shadow. She's always hated playing for audiences—guards not withstanding—and Shefali has always loved listening to her. How many years has it been? More than eight. The last time she heard Shizuka play was before . . .

It was a long time ago.

Barsalai Shefali closes her eyes and leans against the wall. The melody becomes the only thing in the world for her—everything else has gone dark. From this darkness, Shizuka paints a new image, one rendered by the bright strings of her zither. She stands on the hills just south of Fujino. It is spring, or perhaps early autumn; late Sixth Bell, or early Seventh. Rice paddies go violet as the sun starts to sink beneath the horizon; in the distance, she can see the sloped ceiling of the Jade Palace, see the verdant green of the hunting grounds around it.

Her bones ache, her feet especially; she cannot remember how long she has been walking. The heavy pack on her shoulders has bent her spine like a bowyer; the wound at her rib has not yet healed.

The palace is home.

But it was home before she left for the war, and now she cannot imagine wandering its halls again.

View from Rolling Hills. This is the melody Handa wrote for *View from Rolling Hills.*

The Qorin always say songwriters live forever. You shave off a bit of your soul every time you write a song, after all. If it is good enough, the wind itself will learn the words—and then there is no killing you.

She stays there, unmoving, until at last Shizuka plucks the final notes. Only then does Shefali dare to enter. Quickly, too: if she waits too long, another song will start.

A second scent makes itself known to her before she opens the door: one quite like her own and nothing like her at all. When Shefali slides open the door, she is not surprised to see Baoyi sitting in front of Shizuka—but she is happy about it. Her niece is wearing a child-sized deel and trousers, with a mock Qorin hunting cap atop her sandy hair. The perfect little picture of a hunter! Better still when she sees Shefali—she claps her hands together and gets to her feet, running over to hug her knees.

"Ah, you *were* right," says Shizuka. Seated behind her zither, her face painted and her hair carefully arranged in streams of black, she almost looks like a proper courtier. "Your aunt Shefali *did* want to hear my playing."

Baoyi giggles as Shefali picks her up. "Told you," she says. "I'm always right, Auntie Zuzu."

Is this Kenshiro's daughter or Shizuka's? Shefali finds herself grinning as she lets Baoyi ride on her shoulders. "Missed me?"

She cannot see Baoyi nod, but she can hear the soft little sound she makes as she does it, the bright *mhmm*. "You can't keep running off like this. Not unless you're going to get a feather for me, too."

"Perhaps if you're well behaved," says Shizuka, "we might be able to find you one for your birthday."

Well, Shefali knows where to find the Phoenix if she wanted to— but there is no time to make the trip twice.

As a wrestler enjoying a friendly match finds blood coating his side and realizes he's torn open an old wound—Shefali's heart sinks. When was Baoyi born? Shefali might not even live to see her next birthday.

"Do you promise, Auntie Shefa?"

What is she to say? Shizuka's eyes are on her, and she looks so *relieved,* so at peace. As if she has journeyed eight long years to watch Shefali play with her niece like this.

"I'll do my best," Shefali says. She cannot bring herself to lie.

Baoyi harrumphs. She wanted something a little more solid—but this is already promising her the clouds for her palanquin.

"Now I'm sure Aunt Shefali is tired," says Shizuka, "isn't she?"

"She doesn't sleep," says Baoyi.

"I still get tired," Shefali says. There are days where it is the exhaustion that shackles her and not the pain—days where her bones go heavy as lead and it is all she can do to lie in bed.

Baoyi leans over Shefali's head, so that they are eye to steel eye. "Are you tired now?" she asks.

She isn't. "Long day," she says.

Baoyi pouts—but she doesn't argue when Shefali picks her up and sets her back down on the ground.

"Hideki-zun, come in for a moment," says Shizuka. One of the guards opens the door, takes a single step inside, and then touches his forehead to the mats. Shizuka hardly waits for him to finish before continuing. "Escort Lai Baoyi to her father. I trust she will be safe with you?"

"Yes," says Hideki. "I'll guard her with my life."

"I'd hope so," says Shizuka. "I will see you tomorrow, Baoyi. Try not to vex your tutors."

"No promises," says Baoyi. Grinning, she bows to them both and says good night.

Hideki gets to his feet, only to bow to Baoyi at the waist and ask her to lead the way. How preposterous—she walks down the hall windmilling her arms and he keeps pace eight steps behind her out of deference.

Shefali closes the door behind them. Shizuka's begun to put away her zither, though she's done nothing to hide the small smile on her face.

"Too much like me," she says. "That girl . . . She is *far* too much like me."

"That's for the best," says Shefali. She sits behind her wife, wraps her arms around her waist. "You'll be a good aunt."

Shizuka leans against Shefali's chin. She takes Shefali's hand in her own and traces the lines of her palm, her face scrunching as if she is trying to decipher a badly transcribed poem.

"We'll have to set good examples for her," she says. "Kenshiro hasn't taken her hunting, you know."

Of course he hasn't. "She can ride?"

"Oh, yes, your mother gave her a horse for her fifth birthday. A blue roan! Beautiful creature, although she's not very bright. The hostler keeps complaining about her licking the poles in her stall. . . ."

Shefali chuckles to herself. She'd met a few horses like that in her day—and she had seen a blue roan when she stabled her gray. She should've known it was a gift from Burqila. Where else would you find a coat so gleaming except among the Qorin? And if she was a filly still, it explained why she was no larger than the other horses. It'd be a year yet before she grew to her full size.

"She named her Wudi," Shizuka says. She shakes her head. "What a cocky child. I never named *my* horse anything so presumptuous."

Barsalai Shefali has known her wife since they were three. She does not know what her red's name is, nor has she ever asked. You don't call another person's horse by name unless you're married. Which—well. They were, now. But Shefali hadn't mustered up the courage to ask.

Shizuka knows she's eliding the question. She touches a finger to Shefali's chin. "Matsuda," she says.

"A good name," Shefali says. She'd expected something about him being red—Red Hawk or Scarlet Rabbit or Carmine Fury. Pine Needle was sedate in comparison. Thoughtful, even.

"I thought you'd like to know," says Shizuka. "You told me Alsha's name. When I was reading your letter, I realized I'd never told you Matsuda's."

Shefali kisses the top of her head.

"I . . . I was unfair to you, in those days," says Shizuka. "Asking you to follow me wherever I went. Demanding it. I'm sorry. Truly, I am."

"You never had to ask," says Shefali. "I would follow you into the sun."

"But it's my fault that you're . . ."

Shefali squeezes her. "You couldn't have known," she says.

The old demon in her mind is far less polite—but she again pays it no mind. She is here with her wife, and the rest of the world has fallen away; she is here with her wife, who is clearheaded; she will not let the moment be ruined.

"But I should have," said Shizuka. "I never thought things through. It took . . . I didn't *start* until you'd already left. Until the war. You deserve better than that, Shefali. I've hurt you over and over again, haven't I? Even these past few days—I've been ignoring my duties and drinking more when I promised you I wouldn't. I promised you I'd become a better woman, and I . . . I haven't."

How strange. Can she not see that by admitting her mistakes she's proving herself wrong? Shefali cannot imagine the Shizuka of her youth speaking in such a measured manner about her shortcomings. It's . . . strange, yes, but it soothes a little of the hurt Shefali felt yesterday.

She's trying, isn't she?

"You freed Xian-Lai," says Shefali. "And you did not drink today."

"You heard about Xian-Lai?" says Shizuka. Shefali draws in a breath; she lets it out when Shizuka quickly continues. "Of course you have. News like that will travel. What else have you heard?"

"Hanjeon and Dao Doan," Shefali says. "Taxes on Shiratori and Fuyutsuki. Your uncle sending you to war. The wave. Shiseiki."

Shizuka flinches at the last; Shefali instantly regrets mentioning it. It feels as if the two of them are locked in a dark room together. On the floor someone has scattered shards of broken pottery. Shizuka knows where all the shards were—but Shefali is still figuring it out.

"I'm sorry," Shefali says.

"No, no, it's—it's only a name," Shizuka says. "I . . . I'm going to have to tell you about it eventually. You need to know."

"Take all the time you need," says Shefali. "Did you want to keep talking about it?"

Shizuka nods against her. "You deserve to know," she says. "And maybe it will help sort out . . . everything."

"Then I will listen," Shefali says. "But sleep comes first."

There—Shizuka's soft laugh. "Is that so?" she says. "I'm the Empress. My word is law."

"If you don't go to bed at a reasonable time," says Shefali, "I'm going to tell everyone about your thumb-sucking."

"No one will believe you," Shizuka says in a very serious voice.

Shefali touches the tip of her nose. "Is that a risk you're willing to take?"

And in the end, it isn't.

But she does insist that Shefali carry her to bed, and lie with her—though she knows only one of them will be getting any sleep.

"You make an excellent pillow," is her argument.

Shefali would not dream of arguing.

O-SHIZUKA

THREE

Water fills her lungs.

Her eyes shoot open. Dark blue, all around her. Up above, there are lighter patches, where the sunlight fights against the waves—but the light does not reach her. In the cold darkness of the filthy water, there are shapes surrounding her.

Get away.

That is her thought, that is her only thought, that is all she wants. It dissolves into panic. She flails, and flails, and flails, but only sinks deeper. Fetid water rushes in when she opens her mouth to scream. The salty-sour taste turns her stomach. Just as she covers her mouth—as if that will help her hold in the vomit—it happens.

Something grabs hold of her ankle.

No.

No, no, no, she's not going any farther down, if she goes farther down, then she'll see them, she's not going to see them, she's not—

She reaches for her sword, but she's not wearing it, she's not wearing anything, her skin crawls—

Screws her eyes shut, covers them with her hands, tries to hold in the scream building at the base of her throat, tries to tell herself that this can't be real, it's been years, it's been years—

It's a hand on her ankle.

It pulls.

Hand on her head, forcing her down. She grabs at it, tries to tear it off, but the arm isn't attached to anything, it's a severed arm and it's pushing pushing pushing—

"Look at what you did," says the river.

But it isn't her fault! She didn't make the decision, she didn't send them north, she tried to save everyone she could and—

No. No, this *is* her fault. Go north, she'd told herself—go north and slay a god. What was she thinking? She went alone when she knew in her bones that she needed Shefali at her side. She hadn't fought back when her uncle summoned her.

It is Shizuka who made the bargain; it is Shizuka who held the sword.

Fingers prying at her eyes, severed fingers crawling on her face and pulling her eyes open and laughter, cruel laughter—

Houses submerged beneath her. Dolls, dark green with algae, float past her, never to be used again. A bucket tied to a well. Statues of local heroes, remembered forever by the terrors of the depths. Shrines where only squids will pray, scarecrows becoming barnacle idols.

Bodies.

There are so many that at first she thinks they must be large fish, but she knows better, knows in her soul what this place is. A woman bloated as a puffer fish, wearing a tattered set of robes that must have cost her a year's wages. A stocky horse with its legs bending in directions they shouldn't bend, a man with fish swimming out of his rictus.

Severed arms. Severed legs, still wearing standard-issue Imperial Army boots.

The heads are the worst.

The heads turn to face her as they float by, the heads with their open mouths and their unblinking eyes and their swollen tongues and their skin going black and and—

Hands around her throat.

She wakes up screaming. The early-morning Hokkaran air can't seem to fill her the way the water did. She gasps, clutching her chest, trying to gulp in as much of it as she can. The ground moves beneath her as if they've gone to sea, as if the ocean is clawing at the hull of her ship, hungry and undeniable. There's someone in front of her, someone trying to hold her down, and all she can think of is the hand on her ankle, pulling, pulling—

"Shizuka! Shizuka, you're safe!"

That voice.

Shefali?

No, Shefali's been gone for eight years, eight long years, and when she returns, she won't be happy to see this wreck of a woman where her wife used to be, won't be happy to know what she's done or what she's seen or how useless—

"Shizuka, I'm here, I've got you. You're safe."

That is her, isn't it? She can't let, Shefali can't see her like this, can't see her being such a burden.

Shizuka covers her mouth. Bites down on her hand. It hurts, but it keeps her rooted enough in the current moment that she can recognize her wife.

She's real.

Shizuka's mind is still reeling, still spinning. She grabs Shefali's pointed ears like handles, holds on to them, reminds herself that her wife is home.

"Breathe," says Shefali. "Remember? You have to breathe."

And there is the faint memory of the two of them sitting in that awful tent, of raindrops against canvas, of a poem she made up so that Shefali could remember the count.

Yes.

She remembers.

Breathe.

She is the master of her own body. She is jade and iron and light. She can breathe.

Shefali holds her. She whispers things to her, things that only the pair of them know, things only the pair of them have seen. She takes Shizuka's right hand and their palms meet, and she says the most important word of all.

"Together."

What feels like a whole Bell later, Shizuka can feel the severed fingers crawling up her spine only faintly.

"How long was I asleep?" she asks. She rubs her throat to try to smooth out her cracking voice.

"A Bell," says Shefali. "It's the start of Second."

Shizuka allows herself a sad smile. "A whole Bell," she says. "I'm almost proud of myself."

"You sound like me," says Shefali.

"I've been getting about the same amount of sleep," she says. She takes Shefali's hand and lays it over her heart. It'll be an hour or so yet before it stops racing. "And I won't be getting any more tonight."

She wants to curl up on Shefali's shoulder the way they used to in that terrible tent—but that does not feel right.

She settles for kissing Shefali's cheek before standing up. To her surprise—and joy—Shefali is hesitant to let her go. It's another few kisses before she does, before Shizuka can make it to her calligraphy bench.

One by one she arranges her supplies: her inkstone, washed one week ago, before Shefali's return; the inkstick itself, given to her by

Oshiro Yuichi as a gift; her fine paper, buried beneath the missives she has not the energy to indulge; the brush she took from her father's desk, after he left her; the bowl . . .

The memory returns to her. The last time she tried to write, her eyes fell on the bowl, on the bits of charcoal floating like bodies, and she . . . she had been unable to continue, so she hid it within the desk.

Useless, useless Empress.

But she is confronting her fears already. From the depths of her heart, she summons enough courage to open the drawer, to pull the bowl out and lay it atop the desk.

"Shefali," she says, turning her back to the bench. She bites her lip. Her wife is over in an instant.

"Yes? Is something wrong?"

"The bowl," stammers Shizuka. "Clean the bowl. There's too much—I need you to clean it."

Shefali pauses for a moment. Then, when she realizes what Shizuka means, she picks up the bowl and dumps some of it out the window. "Do you want it all gone?"

"Leave as little as you can. A quarter of the bowl," she says.

Shefali sets it down once the task is done. Shizuka forces herself to turn. There's less now. She can deal with this much. Baozhai bought her this bowl. She tries to focus on that.

Breathe.

Shizuka begins writing.

Shefali stands behind her, watching. Only when Shizuka has finished does Shefali speak.

"A letter?" she asks.

"No," says Shizuka. "Writing down that nightmare."

It is not pleasant work. She tries not to think on it—tries to let the words come out as they will. The best state of mind is no mind at all, as her tutors used to say. Without care for punctuation, without care for grammar, she writes. The familiar trance of calligraphy over-comes her.

Then, when she is done, she pinches the paper between her thumb and forefinger. The trance is vital—she can feel the threads begin-ning to tug at her—and she must not let it go to waste.

Burn, she whispers to the paper.

And it heeds her, as it always does—the fires of Shizuka's heart soon consume the page. Still holding it—heedless of the fire, which shall not burn her—she walks to the window, where she holds the paper outside and watches it burn. Wind scoops up the ashes and sends them swirling toward the sky.

Let the dead gods deal with her nightmares.

Once the paper is gone, Shizuka breathes a sigh of relief. Shefali comes to stand next to her. She takes Shizuka's hand and waits.

That is the thing about Shefali—she will wait a hundred years if she has to, but she will wait right there next to you. Sure as the moon.

Shizuka has been certain of three things in her life. One: that the Phoenix Throne would be hers when she came of age. Two: that she is a god, in some form or another. Three: that Shefali is as integral to her life as all the bodies of heaven.

It is good, she thinks, to feel her wife's rough hand again.

"Does it help?" asks Shefali.

She nods.

The Qorin wraps an arm around Shizuka's waist. She leans against Shefali. For a woman who so despises being compared to trees, She-fali quite resembles an oak—tall and sturdy and brown.

"Writing your letter helped me," says Shefali. "Getting thoughts down."

"Getting them out of my head," Shizuka echoes. "I am not so fine a writer as you, my love, but I am happy to say it helps."

Silence. Her wife must, as always, consider what it is she wants to say next. Shefali never says anything she does not mean. This has lent a sacred air to whatever she *does* say; Shizuka often finds herself turning over something her wife has said months after the fact.

"Family helps, too," Shefali says. A statement and not a question.

"Yes," Shizuka says. She traces the lines of Shefali's palm. "All of you do."

"All of us," Shefali says. "There weren't many, before."

"Most of my family is yours, to be fair," Shizuka says. Though it has been some time since Burqila last visited. The Kharsa-That-Was-Not can travel to Fujino only twice a decade without her people planning a mutiny.

"But not all," Shefali says. The sound she makes is a little amused, a little perplexed. "You haven't mentioned this . . . Sakura much."

"She stays in Xian-Lai most of the time," Shizuka answers.

It wasn't always that way. When Shizuka returned from the war, Sakura had made her way to Fujino immediately. It was she who saw the new monarch cut her grandfather's statue in two; it was she who saw the Phoenix light herself on fire. In the end, it was Sakura who got O-Shizuka the help she needed.

But they have not gotten to that part of the story yet. It is another sword hanging above their heads, waiting to fall.

Will Shefali stay, once she hears the worst of it?

"I gave her the Minami lands," says Shizuka. "Since the rest of us are all dead. Technically, she's only the steward until I retire, but . . ."

"You'll retire," says Shefali.

More accurate than she thinks. Shizuka nuzzles against her. She really should be cleaning, or working, or doing anything but lying here.

But it's so hard to leave.

"Xian-Lai interests her more than our ancestral homeland," Shizuka continues. "Learning to read the language opened a door for her, I think; she'll read whatever she can get her hands on these days. The Minami clan didn't keep a library—and Xian-Lai's is centuries old. An easy choice for her. She does most of the administration from the Bronze Palace."

The concept of owning land has always perplexed Shefali, and Shizuka can read that on her face now.

"I miss her when she's there," Shizuka says, to fill the silence. "Sakura reminds me of you in some ways."

"You can tell me more of her," Shefali says.

Shizuka wants to laugh. "Oh, I will. But her part in the story is over for now—after I left the palace, I didn't see her for . . . four years? Five?"

It is so hard to remember anything after Shizuka returned to Fujino.

"You do not have to tell me your story, if it pains you," says Shefali again.

It will pain her. But it is important that Shefali knows, isn't it? Important that she understands how it all came to be this way.

"Neither of us will be getting any rest," she says. "Now is as good a time as any."

How Quickly They Fade!

Y ou are not the Toad's niece."

The woman in front of me had more wrinkles than skin. When she was young, she must've had cheeks as round and full as yours. Now it looked as if someone stuck two empty waterskins to either side of her face. Her hair had a curl to it, the same curl I know I'm going to get if I make it to that age. There was more ash to its color than snow—but her eyes were dark as coal, and burned as hot.

"I am," I said.

She looked me up and down in that infuriating old-woman way. Then she sucked her teeth. "Nice disguise," she said. "Come here." She grabbed my bad ear with no hesitation, no fear, and a grip of solid iron. I yelped.

"Pah," she said. "Can't take pain, can you? Spoiled northerner."

"I came here to humble myself before my ancestors. Would you like me to name them? Prince Yohei, O-Itsuki-lor, is my father;

O-Shizuru-mor, Queen of Crows, is my mother; Emperor Yorihito and O-Kimiko-lor my father's parents—"

The old woman twisted the stub of my ear. I yelped again. As much as I wanted to berate her for her conduct, it would do me no favors.

"Stop rattling off names," she said. "Hokkaran names. So long. Get to the point, I say, or don't bother."

"Are you satisfied with your inspection of my ear?" I hissed. "Do you want to tear the rest of it off?"

Humility happens all at once, it seems, or it does not happen at all.

"One last thing," said the woman, smirking. "That sword has to go."

I stood. With one comment, she'd kindled all the fuel I'd been trying to keep away from my ever-present fire.

"No," I said. "I'll clean your stables, I'll sow your fields, I will scrub the whole temple down with the smallest brush you have—but you cannot take this sword from me. My mother gave it to me, as her mother gave it to her. It's been with our line even when we had to live in that awful swamp—"

The old woman clapped once. It caught my attention long enough that I stopped my ranting.

"Girl, think of why you came. Everyone gives something up when they come here, even spoiled brats who think they are Queens. Prove your devotion or leave."

I held it tighter. The rayskin of the handle was, at once, smooth and rough against my palm. Sunlight made the gold glow. Gaudy filigree, impractical decorations, and yet—not a single scratch on it. Despite all the throats it has bitten, the Daybreak Blade remains pure white to this day. If I dropped it in the snow, I'd have trouble finding it again.

"Can't I shave my head instead?" I asked. The few Xianese monks I'd seen kept their hair closely cropped, whether male or female.

"If you have to ask that," she said, "then you already know what is more precious to you."

I trembled.

You, of course, have heard the story of my conception—my desperate mother, on advice of a wily priest, buried the dagger that matches the Daybreak Blade in the Imperial Gardens. She had tried everything, and it was her last hope.

The next day, a golden sprout emerged from the dirt, and I was conceived shortly thereafter. And then—well, my path has always been promised.

I took the blade from my belt and handed it to Lady Zhuyi.

"Keep it safe," I said. "The palace will raid this place if you don't."

She scoffed. "Let them try."

When she took it, I swear I felt a tugging on my soul.

It continued throughout the day.

Cleaning the stables distracted me for most of it. Hard not to focus on such a task when the smell alone brought tears to my eyes. That reek got caught at the back of my throat and wrapped itself with my tongue. And that was before I had to shovel. You cannot clean stables without handling manure.

I am thankful that your mother made me care for horses during my time with you—otherwise, I would've vomited. She said it built character to wash your own mount.

I think she was right.

The others I was with—a woman with a brawler's brand on her cheek, a man with one hand, and a man without a nose—didn't complain at all. As much as I hated the way the mess felt as it squished beneath my feet, as much as I hated the weight of it, as much as I hated getting on my knees—the others didn't complain.

So I wouldn't, either. I hiked up my monk's robes, tied my sleeves up, and got to work.

By the end of Sixth Bell, I was lurching forward with one hand on the small of my back. Exhaustion overcame me. Cold stone, my bones; my burning soul nothing but smoke and cinders.

After filling our bellies with a thick broth and sticky rice, I was led into the sleeping quarters. Volunteers are all put in a set of barracks. Each wood block pillow came with a thin sackcloth blanket and a bamboo mat. One would think that the Grand Temple would have enough blankets and pillows to keep their volunteers warm.

One would be wrong.

You see, it was sixty years ago that my grandfather sent forth General Nozawa to conquer Xian-Lai. Ancestor worship far outstripped worship of the Family back then. But as generation passes to generation, my people stripped away Xianese culture like plucking the plumes off a feather. No one wants to worship gods that abandoned them. No one wants to face the shrines of those who died in vain.

And if no one goes to temple, then no one donates.

If no one donates, then the Imperial Heir must share a blanket with a girl whose name she doesn't know. It was . . .

I hated the feeling of someone next to me. I hated how warm she was, I hated how, in her sleep, she kept lacing her feet between mine. I hated how she snored and I hated the sound of her grinding teeth and I hated it, I hated that she wasn't you.

It struck me then, as I lay there in the cold hours of the night, that I was alone again.

Really alone.

Strange how that can happen when you are surrounded by people snoring or fornicating or muttering to themselves about how much they, too, hate to be here in this place.

Loneliness and I are good friends. Like you and silence, I suppose. It is like . . .

It is as if there is a bowl sitting on the back of your neck. Every few seconds, a grain of rice drops into it. At first you are used to the weight. You continue about your day. It's comforting, almost, to bear that weight. Like the hand of someone you love. As time wears on and it starts to wobble, you begin to worry. You become more conscious of everything you do because you don't want to spill it.

But in your worrying, you forget your form, and you stumble, and suddenly there is rice everywhere and everyone can see it. It will take half an hour, at least, to clean it all up.

It felt like that.

I woke before Third Bell. Silence and darkness ruled the world. I thought of going back to bed, but then it occurred to me that I might be able to pick my own chore for the day if I got started early enough. Grooming the horses, cooking breakfast, caring for the shrines, folding clothes, washing clothes, greeting visitors—anything but cleaning the stables.

Despite the hour, I heard others padding their way through the halls. Breakfast for two hundred must be started in the middle of the night.

As I made my way down the many flights of stairs, I tied up my sleeves and hair. I tried to make up my mind about what I'd tackle. Seeing as I had no idea where the kitchens were, or the wash-room, I settled on the shrines. I found a bucket, filled it, shoved six washcloths into my belt, and picked up a brush.

I was ready for battle.

I LEARNED MORE at the temple than I had in eighteen years of private tutors and expensive ritual lessons.

There is magic in the world, we know this. Your sanvaartains are masters of their own bodies, sculpting flesh to better suit themselves. Healers can give years of their own lives to cure disease or speed mending. You can draw back that bow with the same hands you use to pluck fallen hairs out from my eyelashes.

Magic.

There is magic, too, in routines.

A season passed, and I noticed only when Lady Zhuyi gathered the others. I knew enough Xianese by then to catch bits and pieces of what she was saying—our time was up, we were free to go.

Some broke off as soon as the words left her lips. With little more than a hushed good-bye, they made their way toward the clerks to claim their things. One by one, I watched them go.

I thought of returning to Xian-Lai. I thought of going to Baozhai's parties, I thought of her homemade cakes, I thought of the garden where I practiced with brush and sword alike.

But returning to Xian-Lai would not bring you home any sooner, and the time passed so fast when I was boring myself half to death. How impressed you'd be when you held my hands again, when you felt how rough they'd become.

Would you be proud of me? Your mother tried so hard to instill hard work in me. Of course, I'd been too stubborn to learn for years, but now—now it felt good.

And so I watched them go, one by one.

Kenshiro's letters started not long after that first season. Your brother's penmanship is almost as bad as yours. He and every other scholar in the Empire use the same blocky, inelegant hand. You can't tell any of them apart. Your penmanship should be a reflection of yourself; that is half the point of writing to people. How am I to know if someone is decisive, or anxious, or pragmatic, or . . . there are books dedicated to this. There are ways for a writer to flirt with the reader simply by changing their handwriting.

I'M BORING YOU. Suffice it to say that I hated your brother's hand-writing but loved what he wrote. He'd include a brief lesson on

Xianese history in every letter, as well as the proper way to write two or three words. He is the sort of person who writes the same way he speaks.

Baozhai wrote, too. She wasn't pleased with me for running off the way I had, but she could not quite fault my reasoning. No one in the Imperial line ever worked a season at the temple. So—though I'd worried her, she wished me all the best.

And told me all sorts of things about the Xianese courts. Her letters became my favorite source of entertainment in those months.

And so my days went.

Awake before Third Bell. Clean the shrines. Eat, and read the latest letters. Go to town and beg. Eat, and write responses. Sleep.

The next round of volunteers came. We ate together, and we slept in the same room, but I told them nothing of who I was. I learned quickly that I had a name in Xianese—but it took me months to discover what it meant.

Princess Dog-Ear, they were calling me.

I didn't mind it. At least they didn't think of my scarring as grotesque.

And yet something about me was . . . separate. No matter how much I tried to mingle with them, only certain acolytes bothered to acknowledge me at all. I'd become one of the fabled shrine ghosts: whispered of and named, but never addressed. Only the old man who cared for the shrines ever spoke to me directly.

So it went for four seasons of my stay, until the day I saw the woman in the fox mask again.

THE WOMAN WORE that fox mask in the same way you wear your eye now, my love. I didn't notice at first, but when she inclined her head toward me, I saw the striations where flesh met bronze. The pits of the mask's eyes shone with a fiery light, like two flaming arrowheads aimed right for me. She wore Hokkaran clothing so old, I'd seen it only in Kenshiro's scroll collection, and at her hip hung an empty white scabbard. The way she stood reminded me of the tiger we fought as children—I could not shake the feeling that something had wronged her, and I was the nearest target for vengeance.

I did what anyone would do when confronted with a frightening stranger in a room full of shrines to the dead.

I held my broom as a sword and leveled it right at her.

"You dare haunt this place in my presence?" I snapped. "I am O-Shizuka. I am the arrow of dawn, I am the lance of dusk! Speak your message and leave, or I will slice you from creation myself!"

Oh, it was a grandiose thing to say. I've no idea where it came from. Whenever I open my mouth in the face of danger, whenever I say things that would make the most melodramatic playwright cringe—it pours out of me. You wrote once that it was like being an instrument played by some other person. I think it's rather like being a brush, dipped in ink, trembling above the paper. I know words will spring from me, and I know they will be beautiful—but I never know what they will say.

The ghost's shoulders shook as she laughed. "Your blood is true," it said. "I mean you no harm, Four-Petal, and I shall trespass no longer than I must."

My knuckles went white around the broom. The ghost's voice was the touch of a stranger on my neck. Could brooms hurt spirits? If I was the one wielding them. Did I want to test my theory?

No.

No, I did not. But she did not need to know that.

Those burning-arrow eyes fixed me in place. Impressive—but mine are Imperial Amber, and they are not without spark.

"Speak," I said. "Or did you come to try to frighten me? I do not know fear."

The ghost reached for her empty scabbard. Her hand opened, closed, grasped only air. This upset her: two plumes of smoke rose from the eyeholes in her mask.

"Lying does not suit you," she said. "You know fear well already. You are afraid of my tidings."

"I am not," I countered, taking a step forward. I held the broom tighter. Was she like you? Could she smell my emotions? Then I must banish all traces of fear. I must cut it out of me, screaming, and crush it beneath my bare foot.

Yet fear is a slippery creature, much more easily taunted than tamed.

The ghost flickered. Startled, I blinked. In that split second, she closed the distance between us. The broom went right through her chest and stuck out on the other side. Her armor brushed against the backs of my knuckles. A chill ran through me and my vision went white. It is only now that I know for sure what I saw. At the time, it was like looking at a white ink painting against white silk.

Before me was the vague shape of a woman floating downstream, faceup, surrounded by floating corpses.

And then, another blink, and I was staring down the ghost again. The scarred rim of its mask made my stomach turn. Deep in the core of my being, I wanted to step away—but I was Minami Shizuka, and I would do no such thing.

"Dramatic of you," I said. "A vaguely worded warning would have sufficed."

A long pause. The smoke coming from the ghost's mask made my eyes burn. Tears rolled down my cheeks, to my irritation. I was supposed to look imposing.

"The Toad sends you north soon," she said. "Remember: you are a swamp lily. You will float, so long as you do not allow yourself to sink."

Someone screamed behind me. The old man. When I turned to look at him, he'd fallen backwards onto his hands, horrified and shocked.

"Master Li," I said, "there is no reason to worry; I've everything under control."

He pointed toward the spirit. I followed his gaze back to her, too. She hadn't moved at all. With one hand, she cupped my face. White flooded my vision again. This time, I saw the stacked roofs of a temple; I saw a man sitting in a stately Hokkaran-style room, alone save for a single bowl of water before him.

I blinked.

The woman was gone. How like an ominous spirit.

Li lay there, terrified. I offered him a hand. He took it, then launched into a prayer. I left him to his comforts. If the ghost was right—and they always are, in the stories—then my uncle's messengers were on the way.

I'd need my sword.

Given the hour, there weren't many others wandering the temple. I made my way down one floor, and another, and another, my feet tracing the familiar path. No one stopped me along the way. I was a ghost myself, after all.

But the farther down I got, the more I heard footsteps—the more I heard voices. I caught a few errant words of Xianese, something about soldiers and fighting.

And then I heard the Hokkaran.

"Attention, heathens! You harbor in your midst the fugitive Imperial Niece, Princess Yui! You will find her and produce her, or we shall help ourselves to your grain stores. It appears you haven't been paying proper taxes to the Dragon Throne, if you've this much saved. What a shame it would be if your people went hungry!"

This, I thought, is why everyone hates my people. Second Bell, and they're threatening a temple. A temple! The enemy does not dwell in houses of religion; the enemy dwells beyond the Wall of Flowers, massing an army greater than any of us can fathom.

As I neared the entrance of the temple, where the Hokkarans gathered, I approached the altar Lady Zhuyi set out for the Daybreak Blade. The guard posted next to it nodded to me. I couldn't get it in my hands fast enough. With its rayskin handle against my palm, I felt whole.

Mostly. I did not have you. But I was whole enough.

"Who dares call for me at such an hour?" I said, emerging through the doorway. "Have you no respect for a woman's rest?"

I expected eight messengers—a small unit capable of defending themselves if faced with bandits or rebels. Sending eight of anything implies wholeness and good fortune.

My uncle sent eight, all right. He sent eight-by-eight. A whole military unit, albeit the smallest one. A force large enough to overrun most villages, just to find me.

No—not just to find me. To make a point to the Grand Temple.

The captain wore violet with a stylized mountain emblazoned on his chest. Fuyutsuki-kun the younger. What was his name? Daigo? I hadn't actually met him, only heard stories. He spent most of his time training in his own province. He was tall and broad, with a rare full beard. He struck me as the sort of man who wears his body hair as a badge of honor.

"Captain Fuyutsuki Daigo," he announced, "cares only for executing the will of heaven. Who are you to question the Son of Stone?"

Ah, he did not recognize me. I could have a bit of fun with him.

"Fuyutsuki-zun," I said, "you do not pay attention to court gossip, do you?"

I stood in front of him and all his men. From the looks of it, they were all cavalry, and all from his province. I saw no wear on their armor, no chinks, no dings. No use. In contrast, I wore sackcloth monk's robes dyed a hideous orange. Streaks of ash painted my cheeks. I had no brush for my hair, and so I wore it in a loose ponytail, tied off between my shoulder blades. The only crown I wore in the temple was a crown of frizz.

"I have no need for the chattering of women," he said. "You have yet to answer my question, whelp. Who are you? From whom did you steal that fine blade?"

Never mind that I spoke court Hokkaran—he took me for some Xianese thief. "I stole it from my mother," I said, "who stole it from her mother, who stole it from her mother, and so on and so forth until Minami Shiori stole a ray of light to use as her weapon. Would you like to have a closer look, Fuyutsuki-zun?"

By now, a few of his soldiers caught on, but none were brave enough to stop him. What a shame. I promised you that I'd stop dueling, I was trying to be humble—but Shefali, sometimes the opportunity to humble someone just falls right into your lap.

Fuyutsuki leveled the tip of his glaive at me. "You dare?" he roared. His brows were like two storm clouds on his face. "You dare threaten a noble? Twice I have asked you who you are, twice you've ignored me. Answer now, or face the question of steel!"

The question of steel. It hurts my mouth repeating that. Who taught him how to boast?

"Ask your steel question," I said. "If you are so noble."

And here he made his grand mistake. Shefali, you have never held a glaive in your life, but you know they are not thrusting weapons. This is elementary. You use them in wide, sweeping cuts. The blade is made for such motions; the tip is not pointed enough to easily break flesh. If you want a spear for thrusting, you use a spear. Any farmer can tell you this.

Now, I expected Fuyutsuki to know enough that he'd try to chop at me. I underestimated his stupidity. He went for the thrust. That meant I had less time to react, and I had to abandon my plan of splitting his glaive down the middle. No matter.

Here we have it: he thrusts his glaive.

I draw my mother's sword.

One, two, three perfect cuts.

Back into the scabbard.

One, two, three pieces of the glaive fall to the ground.

"And so you have your answer," I said to him. "I am O-Shizuka."

MY UNCLE HAD sent me another one of his scrawls.

> *Errant Child—*
>
> *Since you are so enamored with the inferior people that you would rather be their servant than our Heir, we have decided to intervene.*
>
> *You are henceforth enlisted in the Imperial Army. We have been so kind as to grant you leadership over the Conquered People. We are sure you will flourish in the post. You will follow Fuyutsuki to Xian-Lai. You will claim your army. You will march north, with the others, and you will reclaim the land Beyond the Wall of Flowers.*
>
> *This should prove a simple task for one as exceptional as you.*

He did not bother to sign it.

There is no one who fills me with fury the way my uncle does. An army—a Xianese army? Did he mean for me to be assassinated? Why

put a Hokkaran in charge of a Xianese army? They would not listen
to me. They'd actively disobey. How was I going to sleep, knowing
I was in charge of thousands of people who wanted my family line
extinguished?

And marching beyond the Wall! Didn't he know? Hadn't he seen
what the Fourth's armies could do to us? It did not matter how many
men we sent when a demon could tear them apart as easily as an
arrow through a paper screen.

To say nothing of going without you. When I imagined us going
north, Shefali, I imagined just that: us. To go without you . . . I knew
in my bones that nothing good would come of going on my own.

I could refuse his edict. I could tell him that the word of a king—
even an Emperor—was nothing before a god. This prophecy I'd so
often turned to—that you and I would go north and slay the Traitor—
was of my own creation; I could decide how it was fulfilled.

I didn't have to heed its call if I did not want to.

I could have stayed at the temple. I would have cut down Fuyutsuki and all his men if I wanted to—would it be easy? No. But I could
have done it, and I could have waited for you before going on this
fool's journey.

But more men would come. I was sure of it—my uncle's petty
temper would tolerate no less. I could fight for an eternity, or so I
thought at the time, but the Xianese . . . they would surely suffer for
my arrogance. And would it not be better to be with my people when
my uncle sent us all to our deaths? I could save some of them, maybe.
I could keep them safe. Whatever scars they bore, I'd bear with them;
whatever they saw, I'd see with them.

I should have run away. Oh, Shefali, I should've run.

But I was eighteen, and I was so confident that my presence would
mean something on the battlefield. That war is only a longer duel.
That I could make a difference.

"I shall fetch my things," I said, "and go with you from this place. If you so much as breathe a word to any of the people here, it will not be your glaive I slice in two."

THE JOURNEY ALONG the Three Kings Road was a long one, and not entirely worth recounting. Safe to say, Fuyutsuki's men found my shabby robes hilarious, though no one said anything about it to my face. Two days in, we stopped near a bathhouse. The others didn't dream of suggesting I enter—but they did make a point of stopping there and emptying the place out. I washed my hair and body, and came closer to my old self.

BARSALAI SHEFALI

SEVEN

Every morning, silver changes to gold. This is a natural thing, an expected thing, and yet it is not without its own magic. As Grandmother Sky closes one eye and opens the other, the pain in Shefali's joints returns. Whittling will be out of the question until the night falls again. At the moment, even standing seems a distant dream; the dull ache in her knees tells her they will not cooperate with any of her plans. She wonders, not for the first time, if she should simply shift into a wolf again. Stiff legs matter a little less when you've got four of them.

But Shizuka does not know about her wife's shifting, and it is Shizuka who needs stillness now. Her own voice has at last gone quiet; a silence that is a war drum for anyone who knows her.

And so Shefali holds Shuizuka, and does not shift. She wraps her arms around her wife, and for a stretch eternal and ephemeral, they speak instead of nothing. Fashion. The changing cooks in the kitchens. Shizuka's favorite papermaker being unable to fulfill her order this year. Shizuka speaks and Shefali listens, and eventually—blessedly—Shizuka returns to sleep.

Later—later, they will speak of something much more important.

Barsalai Shefali loves her wife, has loved her since they were children.

If Shizuka had her to pluck the stars from the sky, if she had asked her to sing songs long forgotten, if she had asked her to dance upon the moon—all this Shefali would have done happily. Nothing in the Empire or beyond it was too great a gift, so far as Shefali was concerned.

And so, when Shizuka asks if they might travel together with Kenshiro to Xian-Lai for the winter, Shefali can hardly refuse her—no matter how confusing it is to hear. Has all this talk of Xian-Lai stirred up nostalgia within her wife's breast? That must be it. She longs to return to the palace, to the place they found comfort before their world was so upended. Shizuka longs for a place free of her uncle's influence.

Shefali can read all this on her wife's face as easily as she can read bold Qorin characters.

Shefali makes her arguments.

"What about your duties?" she says.

The smile on Shizuka's face is as heady as the morning itself. Outside, the dawning sun strains to match the brilliant amber of her eyes. "We shall wait a week before we leave," she says. "Plenty of time to hear the last supplicants of the season. The rest of it, I can simply send in by courier."

"Is that safe?" Shefali asks, for it seems unwise to trust documents of statecraft to messengers.

"I use only Qorin messengers now," says Shizuka, "so perhaps you should be asking your mother that question."

Well. It is good to see her time on the steppes had imbued her with a little bit of sense. Qorin messengers are quick and above all loyal to Burqila, and Burqila had sworn to look after Minami Shizuru's daughter.

"What about the other lords?" Shefali asks. She trusts them about as far as a child can throw them.

"They can write to me, if they've need of me," says Shizuka. "What's the matter, my love?"

What a war this conjures in Shefali's heart! For she cannot deny Shizuka, not really, and yet any day spent traveling is a day she cannot spend with the Qorin. Shefali told Otgar that she would meet with the clan again here—and now she is going to have to change her plans, for her wife's sake.

If they leave Fujino, there won't be time to return. The trip to the palace alone will take the better part of a month and a half. Less, if they sail down the Jade River, but there will be no sailing with Shizuka in such a state. If Shefali chooses to go south, she'll be choosing to die there.

And part of her wants to die instead on the steppes.

Oh, it is an impossible dream. The Mother had been clear: She will die on the first of Qurukai, after taking up arms against the Traitor. Returning to the steppes and going north, over the remnants of the Wall—there is time only for one of them.

Now there will be time to go north only if they sail from Xian-Lai, and . . . well.

Yet how to say all of this? *I'm dying, and I need to make certain I have time to meet my destiny when the time comes.*

When Shizuka's fires were burning again, when she'd gone three days without making a drunken fool of herself—how can Shefali say such a thing to her?

"What is it, then?" Shizuka says. She lays her head in Shefali's lap, her hair like a fan out around her. "Whatever the matter, you *can* tell me. It hasn't been so long as that."

But it has.

"I wanted to meet with my family," Shefali says. "Dorbentei was going to speak to Aaj about it."

Shefali sent a letter to her mother yesterday, to help convince Burqila that time was of the essence. Shorter than the one she'd written Shizuka by a far margin, but by no means short. There were so many details. So many things to say, in case the messenger took too long, and then the letter reached Alshara too late.

You were right to exile me when you did. I was a monster, she'd written, each stroke a cut.

And then:

If nothing else—here is the story of what I did beyond the sands. Dorbentei was with me for most of it, if you've any doubts. Share the story. Please, share it. Tell it to everyone who will hear it. I know now I will never be Kharsa, but, please, let me still be a hero to them.

I've failed you, Shefali confessed, *but I would like to see you one last time. I am with Barsatoq in Fujino—and if you come, I promise I will share my kumaq with you.*

Writing it had been . . .

Writing it had been agonizing. There is no other word for it. Shizuka's letter was a comfort to her, a way to be near to her even when they were apart—a gift to remind her wife of how they had fallen in love.

This was different.

This was her legend. Shefali knew it would be. At least she was lucky in that she'd be writing it herself.

Still. She hoped to share that kumaq with her mother. She hoped to dance around the fire and to force herself to drink her uncle's stew, even when she could not taste it.

Hopes are clouds, of course, but she loves to look at them.

"My love," says Shizuka. She cups Shefali's face with her hands.

In their time apart, her palms have gotten rougher—but Shefali loves them all the same. "If you want to see them, of course we can see them. Why not invite them to winter with us in Xian-Lai?"

"I've already sent—"

"We can send another," says Shizuka. "If we do it today, the messengers will find her before she's too far on the path to Fujino. I'm certain your mother would love to see Baoyi again. They'd be there in time for the Jubilee."

The Jubilee that starts five days before her birthday. What state will she be in? Will she be able to stand? Will she even have legs by then, or will she melt like lard on a hot pan?

"Please?" says Shizuka, pouting, and then pinches what is left of Shefali's cheek. Isn't she afraid of her wife? Of her sharp teeth? "I've already got your outfit planned out. You can be a wolf, and I'll be a phoenix, and everyone will marvel at the two of us."

And in the end—what is Shefali to say but yes?

So they wait their week in Fujino. The Autumn Court is the longest of the seasonal gatherings, and the most well attended. Shizuka announces she'll be departing afterwards to force any issues to the forefront. Shefali goes to court with her twice out of her own curiosity. She does not recognize many of the new Hokkaran lords, and they do not recognize the woman in the laughing fox mask who stands at the base of the Imperial dais.

It really is a dais now, with a bamboo screen to keep the lords from seeing Shizuka directly. In the old days, courtiers were not trusted to keep their eyes to themselves. That is fine, by Shefali's standards. A screen would've kept Kagemori from seeing her.

She's ready to tear off another head if it comes down to it. That is part of the reason she came—to see if all Shizuka's courtiers are who they claim to be, and that they treat her well within the bounds of reason. It is fine to dislike her, fine to argue with her, even, but if

Shefali catches the faintest whiff of the Traitor or that awful lust—
she won't hesitate to hunt the perpetrator down once night falls.

Part of her looks forward to it. She has always been a hunter at
heart. The prey has only gotten bigger.

Instead she encounters only mundane evil.

Lord Fuyutsuki the Elder, having shaved his head in the traditional
way, argues that it is not his responsibility to feed the whole of the
Empire. Shizuka answers him from behind the screen, her tone as
demure as it is firm: "Fuyutsuki-tun, your duty is to the Empress,
and Our duty is to feed the Empire. You would do well to remember
this in the future."

Winter approaches. On the steppes, the elderly and the guardians
of the very young now brace themselves for the worst. Cold kills more
than age—cold and the hunger it brings with it.

And this man is arguing that it is not his *duty* to keep others alive?

Easy to see why Shizuka is so eager to be rid of this place and her
court.

Yet Lord Shiratori, for all he radiates hatred, brings forth a salient
point.

"Your Imperial Majesty," he says, "who will guard the North while
you more pleasantly winter in the South? The Traitor's forces amass
still behind the Wall; the sky there is black as pitch no matter the time
of day and, too, strewn with columns of fire. To say nothing of the
raiding parties still coming down through the mountains."

Shizuka's scent shifts. Regret, anger—when she speaks, Shefali
expects her to snap. Instead her words are measured and heavy, each
syllable like the crash of a thunder drum.

"We have blackened the Traitor's eye already; he shall not break
through the New Wall. However—your concern is a reasonable one.
We will send a quarter of the Dragon Guard to reinforce your northern borders."

The New Wall? Shefali truly has been away from the Empire for a long time. Through all her travels, she never heard tell of a new wall. Is this the third one, then? Why is it that Hokkarans try to solve all their problems with walls?

Lord Shiratori barely keeps his disappointment from reaching his face.

Shefali ponders anew. What was he expecting? The entire Dragon Guard? If Shizuka is leaving the palace, she cannot spare an entire army—not with the wolves circling like this. Yet if he has another argument to make, he does not voice it, and the subjects quickly return to the mundane. Merchant Prince Debelo had insisted that as his honored guest, Shefali would attend all his council meetings, but only as a protection; all their business had been conducted in Surian. Burqila had more impatiently insisted that, even as a young child, her daughter attend all her mother's meetings, too, and insisted that she paid attention, but the problems that vexed the Empire were never brought up there.

Much of the discussions at the Empire's heart centered not on budgets and infrastructure, but on minor laws concerning who could fish where.

Shefali understands little of it—but she is not there to understand. Shizuka is. If it were up to Shefali, they'd all have to learn to barter and everyone could fish wherever they wanted. Laws about where you can fish! This is why the Hokkarans have such trouble: They think they own the land.

She imagines that she is a horse, not for the first time, and that she is racing Shizuka along the perimeter of the hunting grounds. It is winter, and the air is thick with the scent of pine. They wear no crowns save the blazes upon their brows; they can outrun death if they choose, the two of them.

It is a good dream. She thinks of sharing it with Shizuka, but then, she already has.

Shefali peeks at her whenever she thinks she can get away with it. She edges the screen open just a little with the tip of her foot and peeks behind. There: Shizuka sitting on several cushions, the perfect picture of a northern princess.

"Worth the eyebrows?" she mouths to Shizuka.

The Empress of Hokkaro sticks her tongue out in return.

Shefali laughs. She can get away with it. They *are* married, after all.

ON THE SEVENTH DAY—their last day in court—Shizuka makes a final announcement.

"We thank you, as always, for your continued devotion to the Empire," she begins. "Those of you with pressing concerns will see Us once more at the Winter Court, graciously hosted by the Thorned-Blossom Queen.

"As Our last proclamation of this court, We formally bestow upon Barsalai Shefali Alsharyya the title of Empress Consort," says Shizuka.

Should she laugh or groan? Groan, more likely. The eyes of the court are already boring into her. Is someone going to challenge her? She wishes someone would. That would be less awkward than simply standing here.

"You may recall that We bestowed the title upon her when We first took the throne," Shizuka continues. "As Our first act, no less. At the time, there were whispers that We were unwell. We wish to assure you all—We have been surer of nothing in Our life than this. We have loved Barsalai Shefali since the day We laid eyes on her, and that should be reason enough for all of you."

Well.

Now they can see a Qorin blush.

"We will not brook any dissent or discussion on the matter. Those of you with comments or concerns should address them to the gods, who may descend from on high to try to stop Us if they like."

Shefali worried, at times, that in her letter, she overplayed Shizuka's cockiness. Nostalgia is a liar, after all. If anything, she'd muted it. Isn't the point of the hair and the makeup to project an affection for old Hokkaran tradition? Such arrogance clashes with it.

Shefali wants her no other way.

Later that night, Shizuka calls her Empress Wolf and pulls her by the collar into bed.

Shefali cannot say she minds.

But long after—hearing another voice while Shizuka lightly snores—Shefali does mind.

How many others have held her like this? the voice says to her. The oldest of them all. Shefali does not need to see the creature to know the form it takes. She's seen it enough already, seen its decrepit parody of the woman she loves.

Does it think this line of questioning will bother her? Shizuka is a woman grown; Shefali had been away. What she did in her own time was just that—her own.

Shefali holds her tighter.

How long will she settle for you, when she's had others?

The demon is nearing, she feels it now: cold breath on her neck, clammy skin pressed against her bare back. Insects wriggle down her legs. Shefali retches in her mouth. She wants to shift, but Shizuka is such a light sleeper—the slightest movement will wake her. This is the first night she hasn't woken up screaming since Shefali's arrival.

Nothing is going to interrupt that.

So Shefali lies there instead, doing her best to shield Shizuka from the demon with her body. When it wraps its arms around Shefali, the thing's skin sloughs off onto her; when it hooks its leg around her, its open sores scrape against her hips.

She has to keep Shizuka away from it.

All you are to her, all you have ever been, is a mouth and a rough set of hands.

So it coos into her ear. Its tongue flicks her earlobe.

Anger wells up in her breast. Her fingers twitch in Shizuka's hair, and she wonders, wonders: How quickly can she kill the demon? For that is the easiest way to be rid of them when they manifest like this. She learned that traveling through the desert. All it will take is a snapped neck, and she'll be free of it for a few hours.

She's found better than you. You know that, don't you?

Its hand settles on Shefali's throat as a lover's. What is that awful sound, that awful sensation? It is rocking back and forth, as if . . .

Right here on this bed. A mouth shaped for poetry, fingers like flower stems, skin smooth as milk—what does she need you for?

No. No, she isn't going to indulge this any further.

"Sorry," she whispers to Shizuka. "Please keep sleeping."

If you had only heard her, Steel-Eye!

Joints pop, bones crack, skin melts into skin. She's stopped being squeamish about this long ago—so long as she is the one shifting herself.

The things she said!

Faster, the demon. It reaches through Shefali's breast, and Shefali is ready for it. The demon gurgles, but does not let go.

Stubborn one.

Shefali's shoulder starts to ache. As the spears of a hunting party entering a boar: the demon's hand, trying to break through her skin.

When at last it stops struggling inside her, Shefali forces her body back into its usual shape. The moonlight makes it easy. Easy, too, to grip the thing passing through her body and fling it into the corner of the room. As easy as throwing rotted fruit; but the scent of ghosts and demons lingers long.

One night in the desert, Shefali was visited by four such fiends, and each one had remained staring at her after its death for two hours. Staring at her with those eyes full of maggots. In those days, she'd been so desperate for company that she spoke to the corpses.

Now—Shefali has someone precious nearby instead.

So she closes her eyes again and buries her nose in her wife's hair. Part of a person's soul is in their scent. Shefali intends to share as much of Shizuka's with her as she could.

BARSALAI SHEFALI

EIGHT

They say that if you ride far enough east—past Sur-Shar, past Ikhtar, past all of it—you will come to the place where Grandmother Sky rests. You must be kind when you approach her. Take a skin of kumaq with you, and the finest gray wolf pelt you can find; take a bag of anklebones and dice; take the bow you have shaped with your own two hands and the arrows you have fletched to shoot from it. These are the gifts you will give her. Lay them before you—the anklebones and the dice both set with their best sides facing up— and call to her.

"Grandmother Sky!" you will say to her. "I have ridden through the hills and the forests of Hokkaro, through the swaying Silver Steppes; I have traveled through the sand and over mountains to come here. You have taught us to saddle lightning and brought us forth from wolves—all this I know. And yet I would ask you another favor."

If the fur is soft and the bones favorable, if the bow shoots straight and the arrows do not wander, and—most important—if the kumaq is good, she will answer you.

"What is it you wish? For I have given you much, my child—some you do not even know. Tell me, what is it you wish?"

And that is when you ask her for the horse that will outrun your troubles.

It is easier to ask her for it than to ask Grandfather Earth. He never leaves his mountain unless his wife comes to him, you see, and so it is simpler to ask the Sky.

She might grant it to you, if you deserve it.

Shefali wonders if she does. As they ride south, she makes a list of her deeds. At eight, she slew a tiger; at ten, a demon; at sixteen, a demon. She has survived the blackblood (mostly), she has resisted the charms of a fox woman, she has wrestled a woman with stone arms, and she has returned from the Mother's Womb in one piece.

Surely all of that will entitle her to the horse. Or—preferably—will grant that speed to her gray. She isn't fond of the idea of switching mares.

But she can use the speed, especially now. Part of her hopes that the change of scenery will help soothe her soul. The Qorin say it is staying in one place that makes your mind grow roots, and she was in Fujino for a little over a week and a half. That is longer than the Qorin stay in any one place. Traveling, she tells herself, will help.

In some ways, it does. The farther south they go, the cleaner the air starts to smell. Hardly noticeable at first, but by the third day of the journey, Shefali swears she can taste it. As if she's been drinking from a well and suddenly stumbles upon a lake. It feels *nice* to breathe, in a way she cannot quite place. And the scenery—that is good, too. They are traveling southwest between the Jade and the Sound of

Stone Rivers, so that they have to ford them only once. It is not a path often taken, thanks to the hills, but it is a beautiful one, and when the sun strikes the rice paddies at dusk, they gleam dozens of different colors.

Shefali loves to look on them—but Shizuka retreats to her palanquin when they pass the paddies, and so Shefali most often follows. A nice view is a small price to pay for her wife's comfort.

The medicine, perhaps, helps most. Ren had been near to pretty tears when she handed it to Shefali.

"You promise me you'll return?" she'd begged.

Shefali could not.

But she *had* given Ren a parting gift. An expensive one, at that. During the week Shefali went tiger hunting, deep in the night while Shizuka was yet absent. Fortunately, the Imperial Hunting Grounds remained well stocked. Slinking through the forest after the tiger aroused powerful nostalgia within Barsalai. For once, she used the bow. To do it otherwise would've felt wrong.

So she killed it, and skinned it, and sewed together a jacket that was, frankly, an affront to fashion of all kinds. Yet it was a thing she'd made with her own two hands—and no other woman in Hokkaro could claim to own a tiger pelt coat. (No one would even imagine wearing one, another sign that Grandmother Sky never intended for those people to live through a proper winter.)

It was a good thing that Ren is only *mostly* Hokkaran.

And in exchange, Ren's gift: a box engraved with Tumenbayar before her clan banners. Inside it is hope: two hundred vials no larger than Shefali's forefinger, each filled with inky black liquid. The box itself smells of cedar—Shefali loves to open it and get a whiff, even as she ponders the medicine itself.

"It is about time the sanvaartain helped you," says Shizuka. "After all you've suffered for them!"

"It wasn't a sanvaartain that sent them," says Shefali. Better to get the truth out in the open. "I saw Ren again before we left."

Shizuka looks down at the box and crosses her arms. Before they left, she stopped shaving her brows—there was a little stubble, and so it is plain to see her brows coming together.

"Ah," she said. "Her doing."

Frustration builds within Shefali; she is about to say something to defend her friend—but Shizuka's petty temper breaks first.

"I . . . Sorry," she says. "It's a wonderful gift. Really, it is."

Who is this woman, and what has she done with Minami Shizuka? "You mean that?"

Shizuka nods. She drags her fingertips along the vials.

"I swore to you we'd find some way to cure you," Shizuka says. "I meant it. If this treatment works, then it is a step in the right direction."

A step toward oblivion, or away from it? Shefali cannot be sure. Not that she can say such a thing to Shizuka. Instead she picks up one of the vials—their glossy color so like the beetles that had tried to eat her amongst the Rassat—and pops it open.

The stench turns her stomach inside out. What is *in* this concoction? It smells of piss and blood; it singes her nostrils with every breath.

"My love?" says Shizuka. "Is something the matter?"

"The smell," Shefali says.

Shizuka sits beside her. She leans over and—closing her eyes, holding her hair out of the way—takes a breath of the potion. Shefali watches her for any sign of a reaction. There isn't one. That would be troubling, except that watching Shizuka is always a source of comfort.

"It smells like tea," Shizuka says. "That's all."

"To you," Shefali says.

"Hmm. Do you think that bodes well?" Shizuka says. "If it smells awful to you, perhaps it's reacting with your condition in some way."

Perhaps. And the chorus of screams in Shefali's mind—the chorus she mostly ignores—certainly doesn't like whatever it is.

Well. There is only one way to know for certain. Shefali pinches her nose.

"Let's find out," she said.

So rancid is the smell that tasting ash is a relief. She is half-expecting the same cacophony of fumes to take up residence on her tongue.

"Do you feel any different?" Shizuka says. She leans in closer as if she might see the signs written on Shefali's skin.

Shefali smirks. "Give it time," she says.

Before long, she feels it: the cold in her stomach radiating outward. Cautiously she opens and closes her fingers, flexes them one by one. The pain is lurking—but whatever is in this medicine has cowed it.

"What about now?" says Shizuka. "Are you . . . I only worry, my love, now that you're drinking strange concoctions made from who knows what—"

"Ren knows what," Shefali said. She kisses Shizuka's cheek. "It's working."

"It is?"

Shefali nods. She squats down and then stands back up. This, too, is easier than expected, as if it were the dead of night and not Third Bell. It takes her longer than it would have a few years ago, yes, and her back creaks as she reaches her full height—but that she can do it at all is encouraging.

As a child of the South taken up into the mountains to see snow for the first time—this is Shizuka's expression. She races to Shefali's side, her feet slapping against the floor with no care for decorum. Is she hopping up and down?

"It *is* working!" she says.

But just how well? There is one test left for Shefali to conduct. A scholarly one, of course.

She scoops Shizuka up into her arms and kisses her nose. "You're excited," she says.

Does it hurt? Yes. As if someone affixed a hook to each of her shoulders, and to each hook a length of iron chain. The chain they'd tied onto a horse's saddle—and the horses are starting to pull.

This is not something she can do for long, but she has no need to. The bed *is* right there.

TAKING MEDICINE JUST before sunrise quickly becomes a habit. Riding in the day is *almost* pleasant again. Riding, of course, is always pleasant at night. On the sixth day of their journey, Barsalai teaches the guards that she really *can* pick a coin up off the ground while mounted. Shizuka watches that demonstration awfully closely.

She doesn't watch the next one, and for that Shefali is grateful.

In the middle of the night—after the others have gone to bed—Shefali stands rubbing her gray down. Better to do it in the night. No one can stare at her this way, and more important, no one can stare at her horse. Her gray loves the attention, yes, but Shefali doesn't.

There she stands, rubbing and humming an old Qorin song, when she catches sight of Kenshiro. To her surprise, he's changed into his deep green deel, trousers, and boots. Does he mean to impress her?

"Little Sister," he calls. He has the nerve to smile at her. Shefali has half a mind to throw her brush at him. "I hear you were doing tricks for the men earlier."

Shefali keeps rubbing at her gray. *At least give him a chance*, Alsha says.

Ridiculous. "It's his fault I got exiled, that Shizuka has been alone these eight years." The words are only uttered with a breath of quiet sound—the tongue of swaying grass.

Kenshiro's belabored voice is much louder than that whisper of wind. "You did one coin, didn't you?" he said. "I wanted to show you. I've been practicing my trick riding. I can do *three* now."

Choppy Qorin. Well. Riding can be practiced in solitude, but language is best practiced with a partner. Whom would he speak to—Baozhai? Shefali can't imagine what she sounds like in Qorin. And it isn't as if their mother ever spoke to Kenshiro. She has as little to do with him as possible. Shefali used to think that was harsh—but she now understands with perfect clarity.

He's mounting, says Alsha.

"Let him," Shefali mumbles. "Three coins. Hrmph."

His stallion isn't pleased about this, says the gray. *He was trying to sleep.*

Why? Why is her brother like this?

He's going to fall, says Alsha.

Shefali wants to ignore him. Truly, she does. If they were on the steppes, she might, for there'd be plenty of people around to tend to him, and proper, lush grass to cushion his fall. There is none of that here. If he falls—if he would disgrace himself and all his Qorin blood by *falling from his horse*—he might be truly injured.

And as much as she wants to punch him, she doesn't want to see him get hurt.

Barsalai Shefali groans as she turns toward him. Kenshiro already is hanging half out of his saddle, the three coins laid out in front of him. He'll be able to get low enough to scoop them up—but his foot isn't in the stirrup properly. The moment he tries to pull himself back up, it'll twist, and so will his ankle. If he is lucky, he'll fall off. If he isn't, he'll end up getting dragged.

Shefali shouts, "Ankle!"

Maybe she shouldn't have said anything at all. Now that he knows there is a problem, he panics; Shefali should've expected he'd have that reaction. Instead of putting more weight on the saddlehorn so he can reorient his foot, he starts windmilling, teetering, teetering—

Her brother crashes against the ground. His forearm takes the brunt of it and bends backwards, cracking like split bamboo.

Shit.

"Stop!" she shouts to Kenshiro's red dun, whom she's never actually spoken to. Thankfully, he listens. Her feet beat against the earth as she runs to her brother's side. He's curled in on himself, his brown skin going ruddy as he lets out a hiss of pain.

"Idiot," Shefali says. "Don't move."

He continues rolling back and forth like an injured child. Which he is, only that he is taller than most Hokkarans, and also a man of thirty years. Looking at the break, she can't blame him *too* much for being in such pain: a clean snap in two a third of the way up from his hand is bound to hurt. The skin broke; a little of the bone peeks out.

More important, he's bleeding.

Shefali's mouth waters; her stomach rumbles. Already she can taste—

No, she tells herself.

How do you fix a broken bone? Shefali always just set it back in place and slept it off, but her brother doesn't have the advantage of her unusual healing. But for anything else, she needs materials—

"Sp-splint." Kenshiro winces.

Shefali wants to hit him. "I know," she says. "Do *you* see any wood lying around?"

"Tr-trees?" he says.

Trees.

Well. He isn't wrong. And he is very lucky he has Shefali for a sister.

"Lie back," she says. "Don't move."

A beech tree is the nearest, its lowest branch high enough that she has to climb it. Shefali hates climbing trees almost as much as she hates traveling by ship, but everyone must make sacrifices for family. Even if her brother should have known what he was getting into. Three coins. Three coins! What was Ken thinking?

She grabs the branch and pulls. The wood creaks and groans and finally snaps like an overlarge twig in her hands. Shefali tucks it under her arm as if it weighs nothing at all, and gives thanks to the Sky that her brother at least has the sense to hurt himself at night when she can function. She makes her way back over to him and sets down the branch with a heavy thud.

"Nothing smaller?" Kenshiro asks. "That's . . ."

"Working on it," Shefali says. She grabs the branch again and breaks it over her knee—a branch thicker than a man's arm, snapped like tinder. Kenshiro gawks at her. She tries not to let it bother her.

"How's my horse?"

"Doing better than you are," Shefali says. She shapes her hand a little—only enough to give herself proper claws—and splits the branch down the middle. Tearing apart the wood sends awful shocks through her bones. She hates the feeling. She hates everything about this except for Kenshiro.

She can't hate him, though she desperately wants to. Months are all that remain to her—why mire herself in hatred any longer than she has to? He is her brother now, and he will be her brother when she dies.

"That's good," Kenshiro says. From the look on his face, from the sweat on his brow, he's trying not to scream. Shefali considers shoving a smaller piece of wood between his teeth so that he can gurgle freely, at least, without waking anyone. It is a good thing the guards patrol only the outer perimeter of the camp and not the inside of it, or they'd be laughing at him.

Finally she has two pieces of wood at the proper length. What else does she need? Something to tie them together. There's rope in her saddlebags—she gets some and sits back down.

He's going pale. The smell of her brother—sweet, sweet fear. Oh, shame is there lending the whole thing a terrible stench, but it is the fear that comes to her first. She kneels in front of him with the two pieces of wood, and her hands tremble.

The bleeding. The blood. A puddle of it around his wrist. Blood caked onto his brown skin, blood turning his green deel an awful dark shade; blood beneath his fingernails like half-moon promises.

Barsalai Shefali is hungry. Hungrier than she's been in seven years.

Her mouth starts to twitch.

No.

She swallows. There is work to be done. She has to hold on at least a little longer. Why is this even happening? The one thing she learned among the Rassat was how to keep control of these urges. Why are they coming back to her now?

"Let me help," Kenshiro says. She is too consumed with her hunger to argue. He sits up, and she helps him, looking away from the wound as much as she can. With his free hand, he sets down one of the blocks and holds it close to her wrist.

Her now clumsy fingers fumble through a simple knot to keep everything in place.

"Tighter," Kenshiro says. "I can't be able to move it."

Tighter. When she can see her fingers starting to change shape, starting to go more slender and hooked—he wants this knot tighter.

You do it, she wants to say, but she swallows it down and tries again—

She pulls the splint tighter, and her brother yelps. The smell of him in pain!

Isn't he pathetic? say the voices. No—the voice. There's only one tonight, and it isn't one she's familiar with. An older man, from the sound of him, with an almost incomprehensible Hokkaran accent. *If only he'd listened to you, Steel-Eye. If only you could make him listen.*

Disgust comes over her, disgust and hunger. The twitching is getting worse.

"That'll do for now," Kenshiro says. "Ugh . . . Baozhai is never going to let me hear the end of this. . . ."

But Shefali is not listening to her brother. Where is her fox mask? Bad enough already that Ren has seen Shefali having an episode; she cannot let Kenshiro see this, too. She can't trust him to keep his mouth shut—to say nothing of his delicate Hokkaran-comforted constitution.

There—it hangs on a cord around her neck as always. Her hands close on cold bronze. With the mask in place, she does not have to worry about hiding how long her teeth have gotten, how her mouth and nose come together as a snout.

All she has to do is get away.

Except that her brother is *determined* not to let that happen. He throws an arm around her—his left arm, the unbloodied one—and draws her close against her will.

"You'll have to forgive me for that stunt," he says. "I was trying to show you I'd changed—"

Close, she is so close to his arm, her teeth are sharp, and all it will take is a second to snap it off—

This can be your kingdom.

"Shefali?"

It already is, if only you would seize it.

Are those her talons closing around the splint she made?

No, Sky, no. These aren't Shefali's thoughts at all. Something—someone—is coating her soul in filth. It's taken her this long to feel it, but there's no mistaking the sensation now. Filth. It clings to her like bogwater, like the smell of death.

And she cannot let it rule her. Whatever this presence is, the scent of blood summoned it. She needs to drown out the scent if she's going to regain control.

"Kumaq," she rasps. "In my deel."

She can't look away from the wound—the blood so like smashed fruit in the dark—but she hears him reaching into his own deel, hears the slosh of a filled skin of kumaq. He keeps one with him? What, so they can share it together when she can't even—

Now is not the time to be angry with him.

He opens the skin.

"On the . . . On the wound," Shefali says.

"That's—you can't be serious," he says.

All Shefali's efforts are focused on *not* changing into a horse-sized wolf hungry for human flesh.

"Do it," Shefali snarls. The low rumble of her voice surprises even her. Certainly it inspires speed in Kenshiro—whatever doubts he has about sanitation, he pushes aside.

Kumaq soon mingles with his blood, white swallowing up the red.

But this masking of scent is temporary, and her brother will lose his arm from the fermented drink if the wound is left like this for long.

In Fujino, Shefali had projected herself, seemingly, onto that spilled kumaq. Her will had worked over it, as Ren had proposed. Can Shefali do the same here again? In Fujino, she'd only been keeping the black waste from spreading into the ground. Now she has to contain danger and grant Kenshiro some of her own healing.

In times of great stress, a Kharsa must be a banner to her people. So Shefali, if she ever has been her mother's daughter, must strike decisively.

Grandmother Sky will sort out the rest.

For the moment, Shefali's body is all her own. She places her hands along Kenshiro's broken arm, the half-clotted liquid warm against her palm.

"What are you doing?" Kenshiro says. "We have to clean this out—"

"Do you remember our hunting song?" Shefali says. Before, thoughts of the steppes granted her the clarity she needed for this sort of thing.

"I—Yes. I do," he said. "Do you need me to sing it now?"

She nods, closing her eyes and allowing herself to focus only on the melody. Kenshiro's singing voice hasn't improved since they were children. In some ways, that helps. Easier to imagine the two of them as children on the steppes, before all the changes. Yes: the two of them, sitting outside their mother's ger at sunset, working on their bows. Kenshiro is the one who taught Shefali how to bend hers into shape, Kenshiro is the one who taught her to wrap it in birch lest the moisture get to it.

He is a terrible hunter. Always has been. Once, when Shefali was young enough that he carried her around on his back, a half-crazed marmot bit him. On the arm, too, wasn't it? Yes, it had been on the arm. The sanvaartains—they poured a little kumaq on the wound, too, didn't they?

Shefali wasn't strong enough to look at it herself then.

But she is now.

The Ninth Winter cold prickles at her lungs in her imagination. Her fingertips tingle, and her lips, too, but she knows this is of her own making. With every breath, it grows colder within her—and with every breath, she feels her power growing.

"Flesh and bone, needle and thread," Shefali says.

The cold pours out from her hands into Kenshiro's skin. For eight breaths, she allows this; for eight breaths, she forces the cold into him, until she is herself empty and spent.

Until she is certain that awful presence overtaking her soul is cleansed.

She opens her eyes.

A thin coat of snow covers Kenshiro's arm, as if he fell asleep outside the ger during a blizzard. The man himself stares, mouth agape, but . . . is he smiling?

"It doesn't hurt," he says. "Shefali, you— It doesn't hurt!"

Part of her wants to brush away the snow, but another part of her—the part that never misses a shot, the part that always knows which way is north—knows it needs to remain until it melts.

"I knew it!" he says, now fully grinning. "You *are* a god!"

She is too tired for this. Instead she lies backwards on the ground. Her deel sticks to her skin—she is covered in sweat. Breathing is harder than she expects it to be, and the pain is worse than it normally is at this time of night.

But she's done it. She's healed a wound.

"Shizuka's been telling you for years," Shefali says.

"Well—yes," Kenshiro says. He unties the splint and lets the blocks fall away. "But I *am* a scholar. After all she's done in her rise to Empress, I was certain of her, but I . . . I've never seen you do anything like this."

"I tore off a man's head," says Shefali. She is a little dizzy. More than anything, she wants to crawl into bed with her wife, but she is too tired to do that at the moment.

"That was your condition back then," says Kenshiro. "It changed you into that . . . Thing."

"The wolf," Shefali says, for she is fond of giving her forms names. It makes them easier to remember.

"The . . . The wolf, all right, if you'd like to call it that," he says. He is flexing his hands, squeezing the space where the wound once was. "What I mean is—I can be sure you're a god, too, now. And that means my theory is right."

That he'd doubted her does not disappoint Shefali, for she is already so disappointed in her brother, but it does surprise her a little.

Some of her strength is returning. She can stand now, she thinks. She does not want to talk to him about his theories. "Tomorrow," she says. "We're done for the night."

She's already indulged him enough tonight. He hasn't even thanked her for healing him. Why had she expected him to?

"Wait," he says. He stands and walks after her, hopping over the branch Shefali's left. "Sister, wait."

"Get yourself to the stables!" Shefali shouts to the horses. She does not stop walking.

"Shefali, please," Kenshiro says.

He tries to take her hand. He tries to keep her from leaving.

Why? Why is he like this? She pulls her hand away from him. "What?" she says, turning the word into a hammer against his bones. After all she did for him tonight, after the miracle she worked for him—this is how he speaks to her? As a *theory?*

"You need to listen to me," he says.

Barsalyya Shefali would've listened—but it is Barsalai who stands in front of Kenshiro now. So he is a king, what does it matter?

She is a god.

And he is not the first king she has ignored.

"I *need* nothing from you," she says, and closes the door behind her.

In the morning, Shizuka asks for them to travel together apart from the entourage. Shefali is happy to indulge her, and so they ride onward.

BARSALAI SHEFALI

NINE

They arrive in Xian-Lai on the first of Nanatsu with a cool autumn breeze at their back. It feels as if autumn comes earlier every year, but perhaps that is because she's been traveling so long. Sur-Shar hardly has autumn at all; the trees in Ikhtar are always more orange than green. Not every place gets the same attention from Grandmother Sky.

Xian-Lai, however . . . Xian-Lai must be one of her favorites. How else to explain this sight? For the green she remembers so vividly from their youth has grown somehow *more* vibrant in her absence. As if she's spent all her life staring at a faded deel, and someone's suddenly presented her with a new one. There is green *everywhere*, granted by the canopies of the towering trees around them, whose roots crawl along stone like hands in search of purchase.

But it is not the only color—and that is what separates it from faded Fujino. The very first things they see are the vendors at the bazaar—

each in a high-collared jacket in deep, jeweled colors. A fruit merchant has crates full of produce in all shapes and sizes, from smooth violet grapes to huge, spiky golden durian. Next to him is a dressmaker of some renown. Gone are the flat, pale colors favored in Fujino—here everything has a gleam to it, a shine; gone are the painted robes, in favor of intricately embroidered jackets and flowing dresses in soft gradients. Even the pants the men wear are a bright, unstained off-white.

And color, of course, is not the only vibrant thing about Xian-Lai. Music meets them as well, beautiful zither and mournful flute, the hum of the crowd like the quiet rumble of distant drums. There are as many people here as there are shades of red and yellow and blue; in the markets they are packed shoulder to shoulder. All *sorts* of people, too, and not the relative homogeneity of Hokkaro. Shefali always hated that about the Empire. In Fujino, if you see a Qorin, it is only ever two or three at a time; if you see a Surian, only one; if you see an Ikthian, it is the same.

Here in Xian-Lai, there are Surians selling fragrant coffee and chocolate and more Surians among the crowd. Here in Xian-Lai, there are Ikthians in their masks and tight dark shirts admiring woodcuts near and far; here in Xian-Lai, she even sees flame-haired Axions playing their six-stringed shamisens.

Shefali watches it all and wonders: When was the last time she saw a city like this? For it is unmistakably a *city*. Up on the hill, the red roof of the Bronze Palace gleams like a promise to its people. To the west—behind them—there are masts and sails of many nations upon the lake. There is hardly room for the caravan to move at all, and no one seems to care about their Imperial banners.

Why should they? These are no longer Imperial citizens.

And look how happy they are for it!

This city is a wild mare, and Fujino an old gelding.

"A lovely sight, isn't it?" Shizuka says. She remains in her palanquin, does not want to risk seeing the lake.

Shefali nods. Eight of the Phoenix Guard are trying to clear a path at the moment, and the nearest magistrate—a squat Xianese woman with gray in her hair—is not making it easy for them. Kenshiro can make it easier for them with a word, but Kenshiro is sitting on his red dun, trying not to look at her. So it has been since he broke his arm. Only Shefali knows he broke it; only a jagged patch of white on his skin gives away that he's been hurt.

After all she has done for him, he looks at her like a kicked dog.

Shizuka has not noticed, of course. Shefali loves her wife—but her wife does not notice much.

Baoyi is atop her blue filly. She waves at Shefali, and Shefali waves back.

"Wait until you see the palace," Shizuka says.

What she means, as Shefali is soon to discover, is *Wait until you see the Queen*.

The palace approach is splendid, yes, as it was when they were younger. The banners have changed from the Imperial Dragon to a sign Shefali does not recognize, a violet flower on a field of green. There are more soldiers now—at least twice as many; thousands, maybe—and all of them are outfitted from head to toe in bronze scale. They look like dragons, Shefali thinks, like real dragons, and not the sort that Shizuka employs. Each soldier carries a thick curved blade at their hip, a bow and quiver on their back, and a long spear in their hands. As the Imperial convoy approaches, this unit of ten thousand moves as one: they plant their spears in front of them and salute.

But they do not kneel.

They can see straight down the walkway and up the steps to the raised platform where Baozhai awaits them. The platform is new, isn't it? Shefali does not remember it before, but it towers so high that only the roof of the palace is visible behind her. The woman she thinks is Baozhai stands in the center, an imperious smudge of purple, flanked on both sides by dozens of handmaidens in identical dresses.

By now, all their servants have dismounted. Shefali is relieved when Kenshiro and Baoyi remain mounted; that means she does not have to dismount either. She *does* do so long enough to help Shizuka out of her palanquin, for she is the only one present who can touch her without fear of the gods striking her down or whatever nonsense the Hokkarans fill their head with.

"My lady wife," she says, offering her a hand.

"You're insufferable," says Shizuka. She smiles as she takes Shefali's hand, as Shefali lifts her up and sets her down sidesaddle on her red gelding. Matsuda. That's the horse's name.

"You love me," says Shefali with a kiss. So what if there are people watching? She's earned the right to kiss her wife in public.

She mounts back up. Her gray says that she is going soft, and she is right, so Shefali does not argue the point.

Kenshiro rides ahead of them with Baoyi and her blue on his right. Of course. He is the King here, and she is the Crown Princess. As they wait for their cue to follow, Shizuka takes Shefali's hand.

"Thank you," she says, "for coming here."

"Wherever you lead, I'll follow," Shefali says to her. *Until I no longer can.*

"I know," Shizuka says. "You say that often, and I know you mean it, but I don't *thank* you for it often enough."

Perhaps she really did learn something at the temple. Shefali cannot remember Shizuka thanking her much when they were younger. She means it now: she's looking Shefali in the eyes, her mouth a mirror of the scar across her face.

Shefali, a little mystified, can only stare at her.

The others are eight lengths ahead of them. It's time to go now, but Shizuka waits before advancing. For a long moment, she studies Shefali. Then, a little ashamed of herself, she turns toward the palace.

"I hope one day I can be worthy of such devotion," she says, and with that sets off.

When did her wife become such a puzzle?

Shefali follows after her. It is an easy thing to catch up; her gray is just as concerned as she is. Her wife wears her Empress's mask—her shoulders held back and head held high. Authority emanates from her like heat from a fire.

Shefali wants to tell her that she is already worthy, that she has always been worthy, that it is foolish to argue about the worthiness of love at all. Love is something you grant someone regardless of—in spite of—their flaws. Love is a promise you make, a thing you grow *together*, and you cannot do that if one of you is ruminating over worthiness.

But it is the Empress atop that red now, and not her wife, who will hear her.

So she follows.

And as they come at last to the raised platform, Shefali finally sees her: the Thorned-Blossom Queen. Shefali's first thought is that she's chosen an awfully imposing name for herself, when not all that much about her has changed. There is Baozhai in a high-collared green jacket over a gown that goes from white to violet. Her collar is higher, her jacket more intricately embroidered. There are rings on each of her fingers now, great emeralds and amethysts; there is green by her eyes and a circle of violet painted on her lips.

But she is the same Baozhai.

So Shefali thinks at first, until an idle thought occurs to her and the rest of it falls into place.

Nothing about her clothing is Hokkaran—not the silk, not the patterns, not the dyes.

Nothing about her hair is Hokkaran either. She wears it neither unbound nor styled into the half circle favored by Hokkaran women. Instead it is piled atop her head, jutting a little outward.

Oh, she is smiling when she sees them—but she does not bow to Shizuka, or even incline her head. Her handmaidens bow, yes, but she remains standing, her hands delicately held at her chest as she looks the Empress of Hokkaro in the eyes.

"Empress," she says. "We are happy as ever to see you. And it is of course a pleasure to make your wife's acquaintance."

What? They know each other well. Shefali frowns before the meaning becomes plain to her: Shefali may have met her sister-in-law, Lai Baozhai, but she has never met this Queen. What's the protocol in a situation like this? Shefali decides she doesn't care—crown or no, Baozhai is still her sister-in-law. A simple nod will do.

"Thorned-Blossom Queen," Shizuka says. "It is a pleasure to be in your company. We thank you for hosting Us through the winter." She does not bow, either, but there is a deference in her voice that confuses Shefali. She sounds as if she *might.*

"You have asked and We have given, it is no more complicated than that," says Baozhai. "Generosity is a pillar of our monarchy."

Baozhai is speaking in Hokkaran only for Shefali's benefit. She's certain of that, somehow. The lightness of her voice is only a courtesy; she speaks as Debelo speaks. They are on *her* land.

A smile comes to Shizuka then, a small one, a crack in her mask. "To Us, everything is complicated," she says. "Something you well know. Shall We refuse this gift three times, as well?"

Shefali expects Baozhai to smile. She does not. Her scent glows a little brighter, though. "If you do that, Empress, We will leave you to prepare your *own* welcoming feast."

"Oh, perish the thought," says Shizuka. "Cooking is not among Our many talents."

"I could make bodog," offers Shefali. They won't have bodog at this feast, she's certain, and truth be told, it isn't really a feast without one. Even if she can't taste it.

Baozhai's eyes flick over to her. Is that disapproval, or amusement? It's hard to tell by looking. She sniffs a little, trying to get a better feel for Baozhai's scent. Lavender, still, with no trace of peppery anger.

"What's bodog?" says Baoyi. She has leaped from Kenshiro's arms to stand at her mother's side. Shefali can see the resemblance between them, even as Baozhai does her best to keep her mask on.

Kenshiro winces. So does Shefali, for an entirely different reason. "I'll make you some," says Shefali to her niece. She doesn't look at her brother at all. A beat later, she realizes she's on Baozhai's land, and the Xianese, like the Hokkarans, think they own land. "If I can hunt here."

"We'd be honored to have you," says Baozhai. "News reaches Us from all over the world about your hunting, Empress Wolf. So long as you respect the laws of the palace, and confine yourself to the designated hunting grounds, you are free to do whatever you wish."

The way she says that makes Shefali wonder—has she heard about the incident in Ikhtar?

"However, it might have to wait until tomorrow. It is nearly the Hour of the Hearth. Dinner awaits us inside, and We are certain you are all hungry from your travels."

The Hour of the Hearth? It is an hour or so before Seventh, is that what she means? Hour of the Son? What did the Fallen Son have to do with the hearth? Must be the Xianese name for it. Shefali's head is already starting to hurt. They had different gods, didn't they? Bad enough she has to remember thirty-two honorifics when she only ever uses three. Now she is going to have to remember two different sets of names for the time of day, when the position of the sun should be enough.

This city is grand—but she misses the steppes.

"We *are* hungry," says Shizuka. "And We do hope you've made cakes again."

"We are the Thorned-Blossom Queen," says Baozhai. "We do not make cakes."

But she tells a different tale when they are inside, for by then she is Lai Baozhai again.

KENSHIRO KEEPS TRYING to *speak* to her. As if he's earned the right, with the one moment of connection.

It starts at dinner, or at least begins again in earnest. Because he has Baoyi with him, because he has Baozhai with him, because they are all together enjoying one another's company—he thinks he can try to bridge the divide between them.

"But you must know all about Surian pudding!" says Kenshiro to her after Baoyi mentions there's none on the table. As if she will conjure pudding from within her deel and pour some out for her niece. She would, if she could, but that's beside the question.

He knows she cannot taste anything. He knows she wouldn't have tried any.

She does not answer him then.

"Tell us about Ikhtar," he says to her, bouncing Baoyi on his lap. "Baoyi wants to hear about it."

"Do they really wear masks everywhere?" Baoyi asks.

The thought occurs to her that perhaps Kenshiro does not actually love his daughter; perhaps he only uses her in cases like this, where someone does not want to speak to him. She feels sick for thinking it. "Yes," she says. "Fine ones."

"Tell us more," says Kenshiro. "You can't simply leave it at yes!"

Shefali stares at him. He's smiling at her with his mouth while his eyes beg. Her niece is smiling, too, but hers is genuine.

She wants to tell the story. She does. But it's not one that Baoyi should hear until she's older. The Queen of Ikhtar was not a kind one.

"Later," she says. The word is beginning to grate on her.

"But I don't want the story later," says Baoyi. "I want it now."

Beneath the table, Shizuka takes her hand. "Your aunt Shefali's just getting settled back in," she says. "She's been through a lot to get back to us."

"And it is impolite to pry," says Baozhai.

This seems to soothe Baoyi a little, or at least it tells her that she won't be getting the story. She heaps more rice onto her plate. Shefali notices there are no vegetables on it, not a single one, and wonders how long it will be before Baozhai notices. Five minutes is the answer—the Thorned-Blossom Queen picks up her daughter's plate and adds a healthy serving of peanuts and spinach. Baoyi huffs—but she knows better than to argue when her mother says, "You must eat properly."

A shame the girl isn't growing up in a ger. Then she could have all the meat she wanted. Shefali really will have to make her bodog, but she'll have to do it without Kenshiro realizing.

"Are you all right?" Shizuka whispers to her. "My love, you seem a little . . . tense."

She glances again at her brother. Her jaw hurts. *Later,* she almost says. As Baozhai and Kenshiro share a conversation about the curtains in their bedchamber—they are new, Baozhai is proud of them, and Kenshiro is politely refusing to say he hates them—Shefali leans in closer to Shizuka. Being so near to her makes her head swim. How is it that her eyes are such a warm shade? Who allowed it? It isn't fair.

She forgets what she meant to say, looking at her wife, and so she only leans her head on Shizuka's shoulder.

Shizuka traces shapes in Shefali's palm—an echo of the way they'd spent part of their morning. "Has the medicine been working?"

Shefali nods. The presence is bothering her more than the pain. A very real part of her wants to jump into Peizhi Lake for cleansing.

"Good," says Shizuka. She smiles at her—and this is a real smile, rare to see on her these days—and squeezes her hand. "I was worried you'd be suffering the whole time you were here."

"As long as I'm suffering with you," Shefali says.

"You say that, but I think you miss that fox woman," Shizuka teases.

The memory makes Shefali wince. "She tried to eat me."

"I can hardly fault her," she says.

Shefali can. Jiyun tore her throat out in the middle of a crowded market. Shefali couldn't speak for a week afterwards. To this day, she bears a scar at the base of her neck. Either Shizuka hasn't noticed, or she has and decided not to ask.

There are many new scars her wife has yet to ask about.

But that is the way of their relationship now—old scars and buried stories.

"She called me Rotten Peach," Shefali says.

"Oh, well, that's a different story," says Shizuka. "She didn't know you at *all*."

Shefali laughs. She forgot how comfortable it is to speak with Shizuka—how little she has to try.

In stark contrast to the man across from her.

Four months left; she shouldn't spend them ignoring him, but . . . her brother makes it so tempting.

A cascading zither melody rouses Shefali from her thoughts. The musicians have stopped playing their usual piece in favor of something else. She glances toward the door, for she can smell someone new coming.

And yet—that scent isn't entirely new. Beneath the powder and the old books, beneath the ink and perfume, beneath the soft spice of confidence—the spray of salt water Shefali always associates with O-Shizuru.

Minami Sakura arrives, smiling, twenty minutes late to dinner with the Queen of Xian-Lai and the Empress of Hokkaro. Only a Minami could do such a thing with such reckless swagger—the woman knows that everyone is looking at her and *revels* in it. It is like watching a flower bloom in real time, to see her drink in all the attention. The grin on her face, the sparkle in her eye—no, she does not look like Shizuka.

But she does look like O-Shizuru, without the armor. She hasn't even bothered to wear traditional Hokkaran clothes, either. Instead she's combined the high collars and vibrant textiles of the Xianese with the wide sleeves and painted landscapes of the Hokkarans. The short jacket she wears over the ensemble, crusted with pearls as it is at the collar, would look ridiculous on anyone else.

Minami Sakura doesn't think she looks ridiculous—and so she doesn't.

Shefali finds herself smiling, too. This lateness, this blatant disregard for authority, this ostentatious dress—it's all very Qorin.

"Had trouble picking out your dress?" Baozhai asks her. She has spared Sakura only a passing glance. Her posture now is closer to the Queen than to the woman.

"Oh, you know how it is," answers Sakura, "can't make up your mind which robe to wear, so you wear them all together. Like with food."

She has the nerve to smile at Baozhai after saying this, after gesturing to the feast in front of them.

Really, it's funny—she sounds just like Shizuka and speaks just like Otgar. Shefali hasn't known what to make of her from the story. She half expected her to betray Shizuka later on, she showed up so suddenly—but it is good to meet her in person.

"Is this your wife, Cousin?" she says to Shizuka. "She's bigger than I expected. You weren't joking."

"This is my Shefali, yes," says Shizuka. "And no, I wasn't. I believe you owe me a new robe."

"Oh, come on, Cousin," says Sakura. "That was a *friendly wager*. I'm a very in-demand woman, you know, especially this time of year." She finishes piling food on her plate and points to Shefali with her chopsticks. Shefali can almost *hear* Baozhai's spirit break. "Can you believe her? She's trying to get me to work for free with the Jubilee coming up. You see where I'm coming from, right?"

Shizuka keeps smirking at her, as if she expects no different from her cousin. Maybe she doesn't. "I can wait," she says. "It can be after the Jubilee, in Qurukai, when everyone's locked themselves up inside their own manse."

"After Qurukai!" says Sakura. Now she's making wild circles with her chopstick hand. Baoyi is laughing; her mother is trying very hard to pretend Sakura is not at the table. "When everyone's going to be getting ready for the long night festival here? No. No, no. Got to pay me."

"No discount for your own cousin?" says Shizuka. "You said, 'If your wife is that tall, I'll paint you whatever you like.' You never said anything about price."

"All right, fine," says Sakura. She scoops a bit of rice into her mouth, chews, and swallows before continuing. "It'll be ready by the Jubilee."

"But you just said——" begins Shizuka.

"Speaking of the Jubilee," cuts in Baozhai, her voice once more that of the Thorned-Blossom Queen. "I have here some of the cakes I was planning on serving. I'd thank you all for your opinions on the various flavors, if you could please turn your attention to them."

As she speaks, servants pick up the remaining plates and place down the cakes. There are eight different flavors to choose from and six of each cake—forty-eight of them painstakingly arranged in a flower on the table. Baoyi sits up on her knees in her seat; Baozhai quietly squeezes her shoulder and whispers a remonstration.

"Suit yourself," says Sakura. She is the first to reach for a cake—one of the peach-filled ones—and speaks before she is finished chewing. "Hey, Barsalai-lao——"

"Barsalai."

"Barsalai," says Sakura. She nods, grateful for the correction. "Your brother talk to you yet? About what we're working on?"

We're?

Shefali tilts her head. Wait. Sakura is sitting right next to him, isn't she? And Kenshiro mentioned something about an apprentice that night. Sakura is working with him? *She hardly seems the type.*

Ugh. Where did that thought come from? The Minami women are clearly strong willed, and Sakura had wanted to learn to read old texts, hadn't she? That is all that matters—that she is doing what she wants to, and that she isn't hurting anyone doing it. So far as Shefali is concerned, that is all that matters.

Unfortunately, Hokkarans—especially nobles—have a habit of hurting others.

But Sakura—she seems all right, so far. Likable, even.

"No," she says.

"Well," says Sakura. "We're on the verge of something real important, we're pretty sure."

Kenshiro has learned better than to say anything, but he nods as she speaks. She can feel him searching her for any hint of interest.

My brother thinks of me as a theory, she wants to say. *How do you think of me?*

Baozhai's disappointed sigh is an axe; the conversation bamboo. "We do not discuss *work* at the dinner table," she says. "It is a place where we can be among *family*."

"Right, right," says Sakura. She sets down the peach cake, half-eaten, and proceeds to the plum.

Shizuka went for the plum straight off. She's on her third cake. There's a smear of fruit at the corner of her lip; Shefali thinks it is the luckiest piece of fruit in the world.

She spares no more thought for her brother, or for her cousin, or for anyone but her wife.

Later that night, the two of them settle into their rooms—the same rooms they were given a lifetime ago. Now, as then, Shefali lifts Shizuka up onto her shoulders so that she can properly place her parents' shrine. When she sets her back down on the ground, Shizuka takes three steps backward and falls onto the bed.

Shefali is quick to follow her. Any excuse to hold Shizuka is a good one. If it were up to her, she'd hold her all the days of her life.

As there are only two and a half months left, she plans to hold Shizuka for as many of them as she can.

Shizuka throws her arms around Shefali's shoulders and curls up against her. "It feels like home, doesn't it?" she says.

The room around them has not changed much in ten years. Shefali is fairly certain that box in the corner contains one of the bows she'd been working on before she . . . Before she had to leave.

"I know what you are going to say, my love," says Shizuka. "Home is a white felt ger, home is wherever I am."

She isn't wrong.

"Home is right here," Shefali says. She kisses Shizuka on the nose, and when she laughs, Shefali thinks that no matter how many times she hears that sound, it will never be enough.

"In my nose, of all places?" she says.

"I like your nose."

"Enough to *live in it*?"

"To live where I can see it," Shefali says. Her face is starting to hurt from smiling—but look at Shizuka going red and redder.

"I forgot how much of a flatterer you are," says Shizuka.

"Was the letter not enough?" says Shefali. "Next time, I'll send a longer one."

Shizuka laughs again. Yes—it is for this that they traveled. For this girl laughing in her arms, smiling, her crown a distant memory.

Shefali does not ask Shizuka to continue her story that night. She hasn't the heart to. They spend the night together, making this place their home. Only when Shefali is sure that her wife is safely asleep does she leave her, and even then it is a difficult thing to do. What if another nightmare comes over her? No, she cannot wander far.

She passes the time instead writing to her family. The letter she sent before they left Fujino was short, only a page to say she was leaving, and no real updates on her condition.

We've arrived safely in the South, she writes. *The horses will be happier here.*

There's something freeing about writing in Qorin. A directness that she cannot nurture when speaking in Hokkaran, a bluntness that is in its own way as refreshing as clear water. She loses the better part of an hour and a half discussing the journey, although she is not quite certain of why. Perhaps since she has already sent them one overly long record, she feels the need to send another.

She writes to them of the pain, she writes to them of the presence, she writes to them of nearly losing her shape—but will she tell her mother of Kenshiro and the horse? For losing her shape is one thing. Only *she* can lose her shape, since only she can really change it at will to begin with.

But falling off your horse . . . When a man falls from his horse, it is Grandfather Earth telling him his time is near. So goes the saying. If she tells her mother about it, Kenshiro will surely never live it down. Her mother has never liked him; that much is clear. She named him Halaagmod for a reason. And he wears that name like a badge of honor because it is the only name he will ever get from her.

Shefali sighs.

She thinks of her brother lying, near tears, clutching his arm.

She thinks of him calling her his theory moments later.

She thinks of him across from her at the table, trying to ingratiate himself when he has not earned the right.

She leaves out the horse. He broke his arm in a simple fall, which no one will question. Kenshiro has never been a physical sort of man.

But thinking of that night brings more questions to mind. Why is it that blood set her off, when it has not done so in years? What is this feeling coating her? For even her time with Shizuka does not wash it from her. She can feel it still on the walls of her lungs, can feel it hiding in her throat—this *wrongness*.

That man speaking to her: Who is he?

She can think of only one woman who might be able to answer.

And so Barsalai Shefali writes to Madam Ren.

> *Your medicine's working.*
>
> *In the mornings, I can now leave bed as spry as a man of eighty. You will laugh, I think, but listen when I tell you that this is a marked improvement. Now that we are settled in Xian-Lai and I have been taking it for weeks, the pain is more memory than fact.*

I have only one complaint.

Two weeks ago, I smelled blood. I have told you a little of how that used to affect me. You remember, I hope, the haunted look on my face when I crawled to you in Shiseiki. It was the blood that drove me to attack then.

And had it not been for a skin of kumaq I carried with me, I think it would have driven me to attack again. I have not felt such a hunger in years, Ren. Years. If you tied me to a chair and set before me an endless feast, I would feel only a fraction of what I felt then. It was as if my stomach had changed to a hungry pit.

And as the hunger grew, another sensation followed.
A wrongness.

Biting into a crisp apple only to feel the maggot burst in your mouth. Finding your prized hunting dog covered in ticks. Opening a pot you forgot to clean two weeks ago only to confront the creature now living inside it.

This is the wrongness I'm speaking of.

I write to you because I don't know whom else to ask—what is happening to me?

BARSALAI SHEFALI

TEN

The evenings are always kind, but she expects to feel awful in the morning. As Grandmother Sky opens her golden eye, Shefali braces herself for the familiar ache in her joints, for the throbbing in the back of her head, for the stiffness.

Yet on this morning, the sun is shining down on her now through the windows—there are so many windows here, the Xianese are not afraid of the sun—and she feels no different than she did in the evening.

Luck, it must be. She does have days like this on occasion—days that make it easy to forget the severity of her condition, days that make her think that she can *really* take up whittling again. It will pass. She must remember that it will pass. As petals are pink one day and brown the next—it will pass. Hokkarans love flowers not because they are beautiful, but because they are transient.

Now, so is she.

Will Shizuka love her more for it, when she finds out?

In the back of her mind, she knows she must tell her eventually.

"We can't simply leave before the flowers bloom," says Shizuka later that morning over tea. "Baozhai's got a new variety of camellia in—we can't just leave before they're ready for a proper viewing."

You can see them with her, if you like, after I'm gone, Shefali wants to say. But that would be a little rude, wouldn't it? The sudden heat of jealousy she feels tells her so. That, too, feels like the thought of another person. What is there to be jealous of? Shizuka has never done well alone, by her own admission. She will need company, once Shefali is gone, and she and Baozhai have always been excellent friends.

There is nothing to be jealous of.

And yet that heat is there all the same. More unkind words come to mind: *I journeyed for eight years, and you drag me here to stay with her? How selfish are you?*

A hunter rides out one morning with his three sons. While pursuing a stag, he kicks his gelding into a gallop and rides into the northern forests, assuming his boys will follow. Only when the stag wears a necklace of arrow points does the father turn away from it. By then, the two older boys have arrived: their father has given them excellent horses, and they are skilled riders besides. The forest poses no danger to them.

But the youngest is not among them.

The father goes cold with worry. The northern forests have been hungry since Tumenbayar left them thousands of years ago; he journeyed within them only because winter is near and the stag will feed an entire ger. Fear sinks its teeth into his neck. He tells his two sons to skin the stag and take it back to camp while he searches for their brother.

Hours, it takes, but eventually he comes across the boy. His youngest son sits atop a branch in the forest, staring down at him.

The father freezes in place.

That is the deel his aunt made for him. She bought the rich blue dye for it from a Surian merchant caravan, and traded her five best wolfskins for it.

That is the hat he made for the boy with his own hands, with wool sheared from their own flock.

That is the bow his brothers made with him, those are his brows, those are the beads in his hair his mother gave him two months before the Sky took her.

And yet he looks that thing in the eyes and knows it is not his son.

So it is with Shefali, with these thoughts that slink into her mind like wolves in the night.

"WHAT DO YOU think?" says Shizuka. Her voice is enough to snap Shefali from her maudlin thoughts, this lightest touch a post to tie her soul to. "Let's stay. At least until the flowers bloom."

"If you'd like." It is all Shefali can trust herself to say.

Shizuka's brows come together, her mouth something like a pout. "Are you *certain* you're all right?"

"Are you worried?" Shefali says. She tries to keep her voice light when she says it, tries to smile and keep the truth of things far from her own mind.

"Of course I'm worried," says Shizuka. She pushes her tea aside to take Shefali's hand in both of her own. "Of course I worry over you. My love, I swore that I would help you slay this beast within yourself, to stay by your side no matter what came between us. You know how it pained me when you left—how can you ask me if I worry?"

What is she to say that can possibly make this better? And there are the unwelcome thoughts again: *What a thing to hear from you! The woman who put this poison in my blood, the woman I lost an eye for— what do you have to worry about?*

She closes her eyes. This isn't the time. That isn't her voice. Those aren't the words. Sky, what *are* the words? It is one thing to write them—one thing to sit at your desk and whittle your thoughts into the right shape, one thing to debate the merits of "austere" against "stark," but to speak of something so important? With so little preparation?

Her throat closes up; her tongue sticks to the roof of her mouth. To even think the phrase "I am dying" is to tear open her own stomach.

"Shefali, please." Is Shizuka truly struggling, too? Impossible. Shizuka has always been a light in the darkness; she has always been an unerring arrow. Except . . . Shefali remembers Ren's story. Staggering home drunk in the middle of the night, lighting herself on fire . . . "If there is anything, anything at all that's troubling you— my heart beats alongside yours. Whatever is threatening you, whatever is wearing on you—only tell me, and together we will face it. But you must *tell* me."

I am dying, Shefali thinks, *and there is nothing either of us can do to stop it.*

"I . . ." Shizuka has learned, over the course of their years together, the value of patience. Shefali loves her for it even as she continues to flounder.

I am dying, she thinks, *so you had better take your heart back.*

"There is . . ."

You've never been anything more than a spoiled child. You'll be useless when I'm gone. The old man's voice is sharp, pushing the words through Shefali's heart.

"It isn't so simple. . . ."

"Take your time," says Shizuka. She runs her thumb along the curve of Shefali's cheek. "The Empire can wait."

Can it? Barsalai thinks of Fujino and Xian-Lai again. As a village and a palace, these two cities, though they should be alike in nature. How much of that is Shizuka's doing? The thought is a bitter one, but bitterness sometimes brings clarity.

"Shizuka," Shefali says. "My burdens don't matter. Yours do."

"How can you say that?" says Shizuka. Her voice cracks; she sounds on the edge of tears. Shefali wants more than anything to reach out for her wife's face—but she does not know what she will do if Shizuka pushes her away.

"You've an Empire to—"

"I don't *care*!" The Empress—no, Shizuka—snaps. She is on her feet now. "I never asked for any of this, don't you understand? If you told me today that you wanted to run off into the wilderness with only the clothes on our backs—Shefali, I would do it. Without hesitation, I would do it. How I've *dreamed* of a day like that! The two of us running off somewhere, anywhere. A place I don't have to wear this crown, a place that we can be ourselves . . . that's all I've ever wanted. To be with you. And now you tell me that your burdens do not matter?"

When her wife speaks, Shefali hears condemnations. Words elude her. Only emotion remains, a fist closing around her heart. If an unseen assassin drove a pike through her, it could not heighten her agony. Her wife, looking on her in such a way—her wife, letting these fires burn the tears from her body.

Three words. All she must say are three words. But Shizuka speaks first.

"Shefali, I would strike the head from the Mother's body to keep you here with me."

Selfish.

Shefali closes her eyes again. She tries to find her own voice.

"If you say that your burdens don't matter, Shefali, then what's left for me? You're all I have. You're all I've ever had. If I don't have you—"

Selfish, selfish, selfish . . .

"—If I can't even help you, then what use am I?"

The word, over and over, shouted in the strange cadence: *selfish*.

And though the thought is not hers, Shefali cannot say the old man is wrong. Eight years, they were apart. Shizuka swore in that letter that she'd turn her attention to her people. She swore she was going to improve lives. Didn't she go to the temple to learn humility? And yet here she is, speaking in such childish terms. *You are all I have.*

No. She cannot tell Shizuka that she is dying when she is not . . . when she still thinks of the world only in terms of herself and Shefali.

Shefali would call down the moon if her wife asked her for it—but she does not have an empire to rule. When she returns to the Sky, her niece Otgar can still lead the Qorin. Only Shizuka depends on her, in all the world.

But the entire Empire—or at least seven provinces full of people— depend on Shizuka.

How long is she going to ignore them?

Selfish.

"Shizuka," says Shefali. The other voice is welling up at the bottom of her throat, a deep burn she must ignore if she is to focus. "I love you. I have loved you all my life, and I will love you . . . I will love you afterwards."

She opens her eyes. Her wife is looking back at her, her eyes the size of Surian coins. Shefali has kept a Surian karo with her throughout her travels—when the light hits them in just the right way, they shine amber. They are only a bare reminder of beauty.

"You have the whole world," Shefali says. As if the syllables are strung on a cord in the pit of her stomach, and she must draw them out one by one. "Thousands of people. Millions, maybe, need you. My life isn't worth more than theirs."

Like glass shattering—Shizuka's broken countenance. Shefali can hardly look at her, and yet she knows what she is saying is right. It *must* be said.

"When you understand that," Shefali says, "I will tell you what troubles me."

She cannot bear to stay in the room any longer, cannot bear to stay and watch as Shizuka falls apart. Shefali gets to her feet—how easy, when nothing else is—and reaches for her bow case.

"Shefali—"

"I'm going hunting," Shefali says. "Baoyi wanted bodog."

"Shefali, wait—"

Sky, her voice. Shefali can turn away from her all she wants, but it is impossible to run from her voice. If she leaves—if she walks out of the room they shared once and now share again—she will be breaking something in Shizuka's heart forever.

But it is only the Hokkarans who would put broken pots together with gold to fill the cracks.

She leaves the room.

As she closes the door, she hears the shards fall.

BARSALAI SHEFALI

ELEVEN

It is the simplest thing in the world to find a goat. Every farmer has one. Merchant families, too. Goats are hardier than sheep, after all, and you can use them for all the same things. Shefali is certain that she has known more goats in her life than she has people, although she's never bothered to talk to them. She used to like eating them. It'd be strange to talk to them.

Strange, too, given what she must do to the goat once she finds it.

She told Shizuka that she was going hunting, but in truth, that would be a fool's errand. There aren't enough mountains to find wild goats here; any livestock she finds will likely belong to some farmer or another, and it is wrong to poach. She wants to hunt—badly, in fact—but she has promised her niece a meal.

So Barsalai Shefali takes to the markets. Five years ago, being among so many people would've terrified her, but as busy as Xian-Lai is, it's no Salom. Here she is packed in so tight that she cannot move her arms. In Salom, she could not move at all unless the person next to her did.

She allows herself to take in the sounds, the smells of the place. So much food. She has not hungered since that night with Kenshiro, but the succulent street fare here is almost enough to make her stomach rumble. Focusing on the scent of herbs and slow-roasting meat allows her to ignore the more private things she might catch a whiff of. People's souls were in their scents, after all.

And the sounds. There are at least five languages here that Shefali can pick out. Maybe more. She understands a little of the Surian and less of southern Xianese. A Hokkaran merchant is selling off wood blocks featuring the Xianese royal family, but it is the Qorin merchant who interests her.

The Qorin merchant who is selling goats.

Shefali does not know the man. She doesn't even know the markings on his deel, which she takes to mean that he must be a northerner—she never spent much time among them. Still, there's something comforting about seeing him, and seeing him now in particular. As if Grandmother Sky knew that she could use a friendly face.

"Is that Barsalai?" he calls as she approaches. Yes—he is from the North, there's no mistaking the accent. "Burqila's girl, Barsalai? What're you doing all the way down here, Cousin?"

Every Qorin is her cousin. She's learned this from childhood. The man is old enough that she ought to call him Uncle, but since he's framed their relationship already, she will not alter it. He gestures for her to come close so he can sniff her cheeks. She does, but she does not remove the mask. "Making bodog."

The man laughs. It is a loud, crackling laugh; he slaps his knee and wipes away at a fake tear. She hasn't heard someone laugh like that in months. Beneath the mask, she finds herself smiling. "What's so surprising?" she asks.

"Oh, it's just—whew!" he says. "Haven't had bodog in *months*."

"You sell goats."

"Can't eat your own stock, Barsalai," he says. "I thought Burqila's daughter would be smart enough to know that!"

Ah. How nice it is to have someone nag her. It makes her miss Otgar, who by now would be neck deep in haggling. "I'll make extra, even so," Shefali says. "How much?"

"For the rice—"

"Don't call them that."

"For the . . . westerners," he says, a little upset at the change, "I usually charge two ryo."

"That's robbery," Shefali says. She's back to smiling at him now. Who in creation would pay two ryo for a single goat?

"It's not robbery if they pay it," he says. "Anyway, charge the locals one ryo, that's nice and fair. But for the daughter of Burqila Alshara! Why, what sort of man would I be if I charged you anything less than full price?"

Qorin humor. "Five ryo, then," she says, and starts rummaging in her deel. In truth, she does not have any ryo on her at all, only karo and Ikhthian foils. She has no idea if the man will even take them— but he must think she's willing to pay.

"Two ryo, and a skin of kumaq."

"Five mon and a hunting dog," Shefali answers, ready to blow a whistle to call a dog she does not have.

"No, no," says the man. "One good hide, a skin of kumaq, and one roll of felt."

Shefali thinks to herself. She's got only one skin of kumaq, and she isn't inclined to part with it, but Kenshiro might have more.

That would require talking to him.

Well. She's going to be talking to Baoyi today at the very least. Maybe his need to prove he isn't an awful person will drive him to give her his skin, if she asks for it.

"The felt and the hide now," Shefali says. "Give me a day for the skin."

"A hard bargain," says the merchant. "If it were anyone else, I'd refuse it, but there are only so many ash-gray Qorin in fox masks in this city. Take your pick."

He gestures at the goats. He has ten gathered around, in shades from black to dun, both male and female. Shefali walks up to the fattest one.

Hmm. For some reason, the pain isn't troubling her today. She might be able to just up and carry the thing away. Certainly it would be easier than leading it on a leash. Goats can be stubborn.

There's only one way to know. She squats down. With one hand on the goat's horns and the other on its hind leg, she lifts. She expects her back to creak and groan; she expects to feel the hooks again.

They never come.

Even when she stands back up, her knees give her no trouble at all.

Seems she will be carrying the goat, after all.

The merchant whistles. "I'd expect no less from you, with your reputation," he says. "Wouldn't want to wrestle you."

"My cousin's the wrestler," Shefali says. "I'll be back with the hide and the felt."

"See that you are, or I'll have to train them to ram you next time you visit," says the man.

The goat isn't happy that it's being carried. It struggles most of the way, which is fine by Shefali. Her mother always told her that the liveliest goats made the best meals. Burqila Alshara is rarely wrong—particularly when it comes to food.

Shefali makes her way back to the palace grounds. As she approaches the stables, she sets the goat down and ties it to a post while she rummages through her saddlebags. She's fond of her wolf pelts, a little too fond to let them go, and so she picks out her finest five foxes instead. Anyone would deem that a fair trade. The felt is easy enough to find. She slings the felt over her shoulder and prepares to walk back to the market when the hostler stops her.

"You can't kill that here," he says, pointing to the goat.

Shefali furrows her brow. "Why?"

"Nothing dies in the Bronze Palace," he says. "Queen's orders. King's orders before that. If you want to kill it, take it off the grounds."

And she thought the Hokkarans were strange. Well. She's already upset one Queen today; there's no need to upset another. "Right," Shefali says, and the hostler bows to her.

Back at the market, the merchant sits on a folding Qorin chair. There's a horsehead fiddle near him, and Shefali is surprised to see it—more surprised that he hasn't started playing it to try to drum up more interest. Hokkarans always love it when the Qorin conform to their ideals of "Qorinness." Is it the same for the Xianese?

"Barsalai!" he says to her. "Good, good, I'm glad to see you again."

He insists on sniffing both her cheeks again. It's unnecessary, but Shefali allows it, because it's the sort of unnecessary that makes her feel at home. That said—she doesn't take off the mask. He'll run if he sees what she looks like beneath it.

She hands him the felt and the pelts. The pelts he likes—"Fox fur this far south? I'll make a killing!"—but the felt is a little too thin. He grumbles that he should've specified beforehand that it was to be *fine* felt and not her grandmother's rejected scraps.

Barsalai's grandmother has been dead since she was three.

Yet she cannot begrudge him for it. Before she knows precisely how it has happened or why, she's spent the better part of an hour talking with him. Simple conversation: nothing complicated or deep. She used to hate small talk like this. Now she drinks it in. The more she talks to him, the less she has to think about Shizuka.

Except—it is difficult to live adjacent to your wife's nation without her coming up.

It happens as she is saying her good-byes. She thanks him for his time and tells him that she hopes the stars will guide his path.

"Tell the stars to guide your wife," he says. "Sky knows she needs it."

The mention of her is a needle. "What do you mean?"

"Look around you," he says. "Xian-Lai's doing well, now that they don't have her breathing down their neck. Hanjeon, Dao Doan, they'll be fine. But she hasn't said a word about us."

She must have misheard him. "What?"

The merchant scrunches his face, scratches at his thinning hair. "You've heard, haven't you?"

"No," says Shefali. "I've been away. What do you mean?"

"Your wife, she, ah . . ." He trails off, staring at the curled toe of his boot. "No easy way to say this . . ."

"Spit it out," Shefali says. Clearly she can see herself picking the man up and shaking him for information—but that is not *her* thought.

"She hasn't called off that nonsense with your mother," he says. "Hasn't given her her title back, hasn't cut the cord to the Qorin. When I heard about what happened here, I got my hopes up, I did, but . . . I'm sorry to be the one to tell you, Barsalai, I am."

It isn't his fault. She knows it isn't. To snap at him for the news would be the wrong thing to do—and yet she is tempted. Liberating Xian-Lai must've nearly provoked a civil war. Liberating the Qorin— whom the Hokkarans are not fond of, to begin with—would be a simple thing in comparison. Awarding Burqila Alshara her title would take perhaps ten brushstrokes.

And to know that her wife has had that power for four years and has not acted upon it . . .

What bitter medicine.

BARSALAI SHEFALI

TWELVE

She was worried, earlier, that she'd feel guilty, killing the merchant's goat after carrying it all the way to the palace. When the time comes for her to snap its neck, she feels only relief—and a wave of self-loathing soon follows it.

Barsalai Shefali sits on her Qorin folding chair in front of a pit she's dug a few horselengths off the palace grounds. There's a tree over-head. Every so often, a breeze ruffles its branches and leaves fall on her shoulders. They aren't pine needles. She isn't certain what they are, but they have wide, flat leaves, thick and waxy. She shrugs them off and keeps staring at the pit.

The goat's inside, hot stones and herbs stuffing its carcass.

The smell makes her mouth water, and she tries to focus on it instead of her thoughts.

If I am going to have to spend time away from you, then I am going to spend that time bettering Hokkaro.

Except Shizuka hasn't. And so, really, what has she been doing for eight years? So she marched off to war—to what end? What happened, before the wave struck? She said nothing of it, nor of the fate of Shiseiki since. Did she neglect it the way she's neglected the Qorin?

You have always known her for a brat, says the familiar voice. Shefali wishes it had the decency to manifest itself. At least then she could kill the thing. This voice, however—this wasn't anything like the Not-Shizuka that Shefali used to see when she'd first been cursed. Whoever it was spoke with straightforward confidence, no tricks. In her mind, Shefali saw him as an old scholar—like Kenshiro, twenty years from now, with his easy charm and absolute conviction of righteousness.

That Kenshiro came to mind felt at once horribly wrong and horribly right.

"Shut up," Shefali says to the voice. It has been a long day; she is not in the mood to indulge this new intrusion.

Am I mistaken? Only say the word if I am. That girl has only ever thought of herself.

Shefali grits her teeth. "She tries."

Does she? answers the voice. *You look on this so-called Empire of hers, and you think that she is trying? That this is the best she can do? You are mistaken, Barsalai. The Eternal Empire is within her reach— but she will never have the courage to grasp it.*

Barsalai? The sound of her own name like cold water dumped down the back of her deel.

The demons *never* called her Barsalai before.

The sun has its path. It does not stray. The mountains stand guard for centuries, never shifting. The stars you so value—everything in this world knows its place. In that order we find our meanings. The Phoenix Empress, the Dragon Emperor—no matter the name they wear, they must be as unchanging as the stars, sun, and mountains.

She is not.

Who does this man think he is to speak of Shizuka in such a way? As if the ability to change is a curse. No—the Shizuka that Shefali left behind just this morning is not the Shizuka she left behind eight years ago, but is that so terrible? A ruler must live at a remove from their people, a ruler must always tower just a little above—but they must be human, above all. Always address your soldiers mounted— but always address them, always fight with them.

As furious as she is with her wife, Shefali is not about to let her be insulted by a disembodied voice.

"I don't know what you're after," she says. "I don't know who you are. If you're trying to turn me against her, it won't work."

Won't it? replies the old man's voice—she could call him the Scholar, perhaps. *You've always been the reasonable one.*

"I will drink kumaq from your skull before I let you near her," she says.

"Ugh, please don't. Ken-lun let me taste some of that stuff once. I'm happy to let the Qorin have it."

Shefali starts. Was that an imagined voice, too? No—it couldn't be. She can pick out the scent now: peony and old books, rice wine and ink. Not one she is familiar with, but one she has smelled before. Who was it—?

Ah.

Sakura.

Shefali sees her now, two horselengths away, a Hokkaran-style parasol in hand. There's no mistaking her; few bother to wear Hokkaran robes here, and fewer still pair them with a Xianese-style jacket. Shefali can't make heads or tails of the style, but it seems the sort of thing you'd wear if you want people to look at you. Certainly Sakura does. You wear red that bright only when you want to catch people's attention.

Still—it suits her. Brings out the natural red of her cheeks and mouth. She looks so much like Shizuka that Shefali finds it hard to believe they are only cousins. The same nose, without the line running across it.

Shefali shifts. How to handle this intrusion? The Scholar's gone—she can't feel him sitting next to her anymore—but Sakura heard her speaking with him, or perhaps with her own self. Shefali feels as if Sakura has caught her while stringing her bow.

Sakura, on the other side, doesn't seem particularly bothered that her cousin's wife is talking to thin air. She walks up to the pit where Shefali has buried the goat and kneels at the edge of it. Unlike Shizuka, who wears her sandals so high that she sometimes needs help walking, Sakura wears hers low to the ground.

"Don't mind me if I'm interrupting," Sakura says. "Thought I'd come out to check on you."

Shefali sniffs. "Why?" She's met the woman only once before.

"My cousin's in a mood," she says. "Sitting in the garden with steam coming out of her ears. Figured there had to have been a fight, and I know how she gets."

Shefali had thought she could make bodog in peace. She had thought that she might find some respite from thinking of Shizuka, of her mistakes, of how badly she wanted to comfort her in spite of them. Grandmother Sky has other plans for her, it seems.

"We don't have to talk about her," says Sakura, "if you don't want to. I know she's frustrating."

Shefali turns her attention to the pit, to the smoke rising from it like a column of clouds.

"Don't know what it's worth, but she does love you," says Sakura. "That's the last I'll say on it. Even when she was so far gone she didn't know her own name, she'd ask for you."

"I know," says Shefali. None of that is the issue.

Sakura sighs. "How are you holding up?"

What a strangely normal question. Shefali isn't sure of the answer. The pain's coming back a little now, and sitting in one spot like this is making her knees hurt. There's a new voice in her head, one that knows her true name.

"Yeah," says Sakura. "Suppose I shouldn't ask someone who's dying how they're doing."

She says it so casually, as if it is a thing she has always known, as if they have been friends for years.

Shefali is too exhausted to raise questions. Maybe it is obvious. Maybe Shizuka knows, too, although for some reason, Shefali doubts it. If Shizuka knows, then her talk of their future is crueler than Shefali imagined.

"I'm not going to tell her, if that's what you're thinking," says Sakura. "She doesn't know. Ken-lun, he knows. It's why he's so desperate to make amends with you. I keep telling him he's being an idiot, but he doesn't seem to listen. Read a couple books, think you know everything, that sort of deal."

"You're his assistant," Shefali says. There is a branch next to her. She picks it up and pokes at the edge of the pit a little. The wood soaks up the smoke—she likes the smell of it.

"Doesn't mean I have to agree with everything he does," says Sakura. "I think the best assistants don't. Sparring keeps soldiers sharp; it's the same thing for scholars."

"You sound Qorin," Shefali says.

"I'll take that as a compliment," says Sakura. She flashes Shefali a smile, toothier and wider than Shizuka's. For all her interest in fashion, Sakura doesn't paint her teeth black.

"Why are you here?" Shefali asks. It's the question she keeps asking herself. Checking in on her—they could have sent anyone for that. Baozhai, maybe, although Baozhai probably has her hands full ruling. They might've even put the Qorin merchant up to it. Baozhai seemed the type to have the royal family covertly followed, and she'd spent hours in his company already.

Why Sakura?

The woman herself scoffs. "You don't trust me at all, huh?"

Shefali meets her eyes. For some reason, she expects to see amber there, instead of brown. "You're new."

"From a certain point of view," says Sakura. "I've been living in the Bronze Palace for seven years. You're the new one, to me." She squints. "What's in that pit, anyway? Smells incredible."

"Goat," says Shefali.

"Never had goat like that," says Sakura. "But then, back home, it's mostly fish. Here it's mostly poultry. Everywhere's got their thing. This has got to be bodog, right?"

Shefali nods. She hopes Sakura will stop talking, but of course she doesn't.

"In the archives, there's an old journal, belonged to a Courtier Second Rank by the name of Xu Taishi," says Sakura. "One of those shy types, like you, but wrote so much. Lots of it beautiful. Refreshing, even, like clear water from a stream—"

Shefali grunts. Sakura's beginning to sound like Kenshiro now, with his fascination for dusty old tomes.

Shizuka's cousin just grins.

"Getting to it. Half the time you're reading about him, you just keep muttering, 'Damn it, Taishi. Come on.' See, he was in love with a Qorin girl for most of his life. She and her clan raided Tastuoka; he was called in to dispense the Crown's justice and so on. Took one look at her and decided he couldn't order her execution. The line in the journal is, 'I beheld a woman whose beauty was as undeniable as the very laws of nature. When the Lord of Stone shaped her, he must have had in mind a beacon for all humanity.'"

It is a little jarring to hear her shift into a proper court accent for the quotation. Sakura sounds better with the Nishikomi accent, Shefali thinks—freer.

"He's never the same after he meets her," says Minami Sakura, "so you end up rooting for them. You want him to write to her. It was easier back then, without the Wall of Stone in the way, without the tensions that led to its being built in the first place. I know it's hard to believe, but there was a time when we *didn't* see the Qorin as plague-bearing barbarians."

She pauses. "Not that I've ever thought of your people in that small way."

Shefali only nods. Her exhaustion means she hasn't the strength for that particular argument—and besides, it seems Sakura still has a point to get to.

"So, Taishi, he had this girl's name and the name of her clan and everything. Wouldn't have been difficult to track her down. Instead he spends pages on pages agonizing over it, and never gets anything done. . . . I'm bringing this up because most of our written sources about Qorin from that time come from his journal," she says. "He was obsessed with them. He thought that if he learned more about them, then maybe he could show the woman he'd met that he wasn't like the others."

"Sounds familiar," says Shefali, and Sakura laughs once.

"Suppose it does," she says. "Anyhow, he has a bodog recipe in the sixth volume. Your brother, though, looked at it and said it wasn't anything special. Said your uncle made the best bodog the steppes have ever seen."

"He's right," says Shefali. Uncle Ganzorig's cooking is the finest she's ever had. The memory alone can sustain her at times. Has he given Otgar the recipe by now? Uncle Ganzorig is getting old. No, he isn't Otgar's real father, but it feels like the sort of thing you could trust her with.

"Well," says Sakura. "Your uncle never made bodog for Tumen-bayar, and my boy Taishi did."

Tumenbayar? Shefali doesn't know what to think. Tumenbayar was the first Kharsa of the Qorin; she taught them to saddle horses and ride lightning. It was she who had first brought the clans together, and her death that split them apart. All of this happened so long ago that the stars had not yet learned to shine—any Qorin child knows this.

"Ahh, I see I've caught your interest now," says Sakura. "It's true. I can show you the journal if you like. He met Tumenbayar. He wasn't the only one, either—there are a couple of reports of her tearing up the border villages in her youth. Did you know, Oshiro Palace isn't the first one? There was another a little farther out, smaller of course given the time, but still important. Tumenbayar set the place on fire. Burned for ten days straight."

Arbangaladai. Ten-Fires-Burning. Shefali knows the spot well—a pile of charred old stones that the steppes struggle to reclaim. These days it serves as a waypoint for the Qorin messengers, who often camp there before making their final journey into the Empire.

But the stories surrounding Arbangaladai are clear—Tumenbayar razed it to the ground because a pack of demons had taken up resi-dence there. She rode eight times around it and cast kumaq in her wake, but still they did not leave, and so she raised her sword and gave the order. . . .

How does Sakura know of Arbangaladai? Did Kenshiro tell her?

"Let me ask you something, Barsalai," says Sakura. There's a sly look on her face as she speaks, a curve to that smile that Shefali has seen elsewhere. On Shizuka, it has always seemed a scythe—but on Sakura, it reminds her of a drinking bowl offered by a friend. Her eyes glimmer in the same way.

"How did your Tumenbayar die?"

Shefali racks her mind for the answer. How many stories has she heard of the woman? Hundreds, at least. Some of them stories about her with Tumenbayar swapped in, though those are so recent, she hesitates to count them. Tumenbayar was born at the base of Gurkhan Khalsar before the stars learned their course through the sky. She grew to a young woman in the mountain's shadow, for the Qorin had not yet learned to travel. On grass and marmots she feasted; from the glittering Rokhon she drank. Even in Ikhthar, the Sky was watching over her.

Sakura, next to her, wraps her arms around her now-crossed legs. Shefali cannot remember the last time she saw a Hokkaran woman sit in such a way.

"You can't remember, can you?" she says. "That's all right. It drove me up the wall, too, when I was trying to find the answer. But Taishi—he saw it happen. In the morning, Tumenbayar had bodog with him. In the evening, he caught her and her husband staring up at the moon. They were arguing about something in Qorin, something he couldn't understand—so he kept his distance. In the end, Tumenbayar hopped onto her horse and rode off, right into the sky. Poor Taishi thought he was going mad, but the next day—the next day, her husband addressed the clan and said she would not be returning. So he hadn't imagined it.

"We never hear tell of her on the steppes, at least, after that day. All the other stories are apocryphal—I mean, written long after she died. And some of them are repeats, stories we've seen before word for word, just with her and the Qorin swapped in. Whoever Tumenbayar was and whatever she did—we don't know what happened to her after that day. She never died."

Sakura is right: Tumenbayar never died. The Qorin know everything about her life but that. She remembers now: asking the sanvaartains for the story only to be told that it was not one for her to hear. That it was not important how she went home to the sky—just that she had chosen it.

Is it because she never died at all?

Is it because she, like Shefali, had since birth heard a song in her blood that could not be ignored?

Shefali's stomach sinks. The world goes out from beneath her. Of course—it is so obvious. She's seen it happening already—the stories about Tumenbayar fading into stories about Steel-Eye Shefali, one god slowly replacing another.

It all seems so obvious now.

Tumenbayar became Grandmother Sky.

But if Tumenbayar is Grandmother Sky, that means that she *is* dead.

Akane was clear on that front: the Traitor had tracked down the other gods one by one. Akane herself survived only because she was already dead. Why did Shefali ever hope Grandmother Sky could escape?

The laughing fox mask hides Shefali's gray, inhuman face from those not ready to see it—but it will hide her anguish now, too.

The Sky is dead. Has been dead for . . . how long? Since the day Shefali first took breath? Is that what did it? The Hokkarans believe your soul keeps finding a new body, over and over, until at last you fulfill whatever purpose the gods have in mind for you; the Qorin believe that if you are courageous, the gods turn you into a star.

But what purpose can the gods have in mind for you if you are already one of them?

And who would turn her into a star?

"YOU AREN'T THE first person to become a god," says Sakura. "You aren't the second or the third, either. Traces of this sort of thing are hard to come by, but we're pretty sure you're part of the fourth set. Just——" She sucks in a breath. "——it's got its downsides. Like . . . people forgetting who you really were, and what you became. . . ."

Shefali doesn't want to hear this. *Being forgotten?* No. They shall clip her gray's mane when she dies, and they shall make a banner with the hair, and they shall plant it atop Gurkhan Khalsar where her soul can travel through the steppes forever.

Where the winds can sing her name forever.

That's what . . . That's what is supposed to happen.

They sing Tumenbayar's name still——but how much of what happened to her is real? How much is true? She'd told Shizuka that all of it was.

But what if it isn't? What if none of it is, what if these are all half-distorted memories cobbled together from the lives of others?

SHEFALI HANGS HER head back. Overhead, the clouds float across the sky, lazy as petals on a stream.

For the first time, she finds no comfort in them.

"Part of you dies, when it happens," says Sakura. "The human part. The people you know, they sort of . . . well, two generations gone, and there's no one left to talk about what your favorite color was. Three generations, and you're gone, for the most part. People start calling you by some title or another instead of your name. Meanwhile your name gets swapped into all the stories. It's happened with all of them."

"You're sure?" says Shefali. She knows already that Sakura is, but she wants to hear it from her mouth.

"I am. It's what Ken-lun and I have been working on," she says. "Never thought I'd be helping a scholar read thousand-year-old scrolls, but life has a way of surprising you."

"And you came out here to tell me this?"

"I came out here to check on you, as I said," says Sakura. "And because I want to remember you, too. Haven't known you that long, but you're the world, as far as my cousin's concerned, and I thought it'd be nice if we got to know each other a bit."

"This is what you call getting to know me?" says Shefali. She wonders what Sakura qualifies as an argument. Bringing someone's world crashing down around them, setting dark clouds on an already black horizon—is this not an argument?

"You're an honest woman," says Sakura. "You appreciate honesty, so that's what I've given you. My mother always taught me that's how you get to know people—you mirror them."

Shefali wants to scoff. She wants to tell Sakura that she must be wrong, that all of this is wrong, that she refuses to be forgotten before her time. Her own mother will always remember her, and Otgar will, and Ren. Barsalai Shefali Alsharyya. She will be remembered.

But, Sky, she is so *tired* of all of this, of all the unwanted revelations! Four months of peace. That's all she's wanted. Every day, the prospect of getting on her horse and riding somewhere far from here grows more and more appealing.

"We could talk about something else, if you want," says Sakura. "Taishi's journal says a whole lot of things about Qorin. We could talk about that. My cousin says you like poetry, but you can't read any on your own—I can recite some, if you want. I know a couple hundred. I'd ask you about your favorite kemari team, but I don't think you've got one—"

Barsalai is going to be forgotten in three generations, and Sakura wants to talk about sports. Shefali laughs. It's all that she has left.

"My cousin, Dorbentei, you'd like her," Shefali says. She shifts her weight on her folding chair and looks once more at the steam rising up from the goat's remains. "She won four hundred ryo betting on a kemari match in Sur-Shar."

"They play all the way over there?" Sakura asks. She's actually sitting on the ground. Won't that stain her robes? She doesn't seem to care. Shizuka would've waited for Shefali to give up her chair.

But Shizuka isn't here.

"They didn't, when we got there," says Shefali. "I taught Dorbentei, and Dorbentei taught them. She had the idea to start a kemari competition because—"

"Anyone can play it!" says Sakura.

"Yes," says Shefali. "It isn't riding or wrestling."

The story bubbles out of her without her having to think too much on it. There is no shifting, no fox woman, no Kings or Queens, Emperors or Empresses.

It isn't a story about Steel-Eye, or Laughing Fox, or whatever it is they will call her in a few hundred years.

It is a story about Barsalai Shefali, her cousin Dorbentei, and the trouble they got into once.

She refuses to be forgotten. So she tells Sakura a story.

THEY ARE TOO far away to hear the call for Fifth Bell. At first Shefali thinks it is because they are not inside the palace proper, but she realizes as the story comes to an end that it is because they aren't in Hokkaro anymore. She misses the gongs and the courtiers and the criers in their costumes. She didn't think she would. The distant thunk of bamboo on rock—she misses that, too. The cicadas in the summer.

She will not hear them again, but she can make the most of the current moment. A few minutes' ride away, the market is breaking off for dinner. The melodies carry all the way up the path—so many of them dancing with one another, like fireflies in the night. Behind them, the setting sun paints Peizhi Lake gold. A passing breeze carries the scent of fresh water to her, the scent of sweat and well-oiled wood and people, and she looks back with a laugh on the days the sea terrified her.

It scares her—but there is precious little that can scare you when you know the day you will die.

There's comfort in this—in cooking, in sitting around a fire, sharing stories beneath the sky. Part of her feels as though she's at home again, which of course she isn't. This fire is a small one fed by fragrant Xianese wood from trees she cannot name; there's only one person to listen to her story; the Sky is empty and uncaring.

But it feels *almost* like home.

It's another hour after she takes the goat from the ground and slices it into chunks before the stew is ready. The pot she's kept it in is an old one. Her mother picked it up at some point during her childhood, and it's always been there in the background of her life. The white paint and blue diamonds have faded to near invisibility, but she sees them perfectly well.

Shefali remembers them.

She remembers, too, how her mother taught her to tie a single length of rope so that she could properly carry a pot. She could, if she wanted to, palm the thing and carry it by hand in spite of its heat. It would burn her—but it wouldn't be the first time Shefali's been burned and it likely wouldn't be the last. Sakura wouldn't appreciate it, though, and so she carries it the old-fashioned way to the Bronze Palace.

"You know, you aren't what I expected," says Sakura. She keeps the parasol on her shoulders in spite of the darkening sky. Perhaps she just likes to twirl it.

"Hm?"

"The way Shizu-lun talks about you, I thought you'd be like a big, fluffy dog," says Sakura. "Suspicious of people you don't know, a little scary, but really a puppy beneath it all."

Shefali isn't sure how she feels about being compared to a dog, but Sakura means well. She understands the point even if she dislikes the metaphor. "Am I not that?"

"No," says Sakura. "You're not. You're a lot more confident than I thought you'd be."

Hm. Shefali's never thought of herself that way. She's suddenly conscious of the difference in height between them, of the way Sakura looks up at her. Eight years ago, she would've been fumbling over her words, walking with a pretty girl like this. Now she's able to choose them carefully—which sometimes means choosing silence.

"I think she's a little confused," says Sakura. "My cousin, I mean. She was expecting the big dog, too, and now here you are—"

"A wolf," says Shefali.

"Don't be overdramatic, but sure, if that works for you," says Sakura. "And you were expecting her to be who she was before you left, weren't you?"

Let the gods challenge me if they wish; I cannot be bested by my equals. Standing half naked near the door of the ger, she'd said that. Shefali can't imagine her saying it now.

"I think, maybe—and stop me if I'm wrong, or you don't want to hear it—I think when you got separated, you took a bit of her and she took a bit of you. Parts that you needed to get through whatever you've been through. I can't speak for your trip through the desert, but, well—whenever she talked about you, about how solid you were, how you liked animals more than people—it felt like she was talking about herself. Especially after the war. I think she's spent more time in the gardens than in the throne room, if I'm being honest with you. And when she's sober—*she's* solid. Hard to shake, I mean. People say all sorts of things right to her face, and she's endured without a word."

They cross the gates. Leaves land on Shefali's head, but not Sakura's. Ah. So that is the wisdom in keeping the parasol.

"*I* keep telling her that she should be a bit more assertive with them," says Sakura. "But I think . . . Well. I used to think that part of her got swept away in the waves. And now I think maybe she gave it to you, somehow, when you needed it." She sighs. "That doesn't make any sense at all. If my mother or your brother heard me—"

"It makes sense," Shefali says. Like two panels of a deel torn apart still share thread—yes, it makes sense.

More time in the gardens than the throne room. Well. She could sign treaties and laws in the gardens if she wanted. And Shefali still doesn't know what she went through in the war.

The girl has always been a brat, the Scholar said earlier, his sly poison in Shefali's ear.

He is wrong. Shefali is certain of it, as she is certain of the mountains and the silver grass that birthed her. If Shizuka were truly selfish, she would have gone into exile at Shefali's side. If she were truly selfish, she would have stayed behind when her uncle conscripted her, instead of journeying north with an army that hated her simply to try to keep them safe. If Shizuka were truly selfish, she would have abandoned her people hundreds of times over by now.

But she hasn't.

"SORRY FOR BRINGING her up again," says Sakura. "I know you're stewing over it."

"It's fine," Shefali says. "Dinner's coming up."

Sakura nods. "And no way are either of you getting out of *that*."

"Baozhai would kill us," Shefali agrees.

"She wouldn't kill you, oh no," says Sakura. "She'd send you trays full of leftover food, and instead of letting a servant do it, she'd deliver it herself, just so she can look you in the eye when she hands it to you." She wrinkles her nose. "'I noticed your absence,' she'll say, 'and I can't help but wonder if you weren't feeling well.'"

"Speaking from experience?" Shefali says, smiling beneath the mask.

"Ugh," says Sakura.

She changes the subject back to kemari, to the local teams, and Shefali lets her.

With every step toward the dining room, Shefali prepares herself.

She's trying.

What a brat.

I think you gave her some part of yourself, when she needed it.

Three thoughts, three minds, warring for Shefali's attention. Which will win? For she can feel their armies trampling across the battleground of her heart, see their banners and hear their warhorns. Cavalry charges down the hill only to meet entrenched pikemen. Arrows rain down upon the pikemen. Cavalry cuts down the archers. So it goes, the battle in her breast, so it goes.

But when Shefali sees her wife . . .

A column of light cuts across the battlefield. Warhorns give way to bright flute and zither. A thousand archers stay their hands; a thousand pikemen lower their arms; a thousand cavalry dismount as one.

There—a goddess stands with a cup in hand, her hair worn wild and loose, the deep red of her robes like the charred remains of her temper.

Their eyes meet. Amber so dark, it's gone honey brown; shame that forces the goddess to look away. She sets down her cup. Her lips part as if she is about to say something—but at the last moment, her courage breaks.

"Shizuka," Shefali says.

Again, their eyes meet. Hope swallows shame. Is it conscious, the way she leans toward her, toward Shefali? Is it conscious, the way the light shifts around her? For the armies have at last come to a rest.

She's trying.

It's written there, in the grace of amber: she is trying.

"I was wrong to pry," Shizuka says. "I've been trying to think all day of what to say to you, and—"

Shefali lifts her mask. She sets her pot down on the table Baozhai spent so much time planning out. There is a space for it—of course there is. "My beating heart," she says, "we'll have time after dinner."

"Oh, wow, there's duck again," says Sakura as she takes her seat. "That's so surprising, Baozhai, that there's duck on this table."

"Would you prefer the quiet solace of your room and a plateful of contemplation?" says Baozhai without missing a beat. "That can always be arranged."

Shizuka laughs, and Shefali laughs because she is laughing, and Baoyi joins in, too. Only Sakura is grumbling.

O-SHIZUKA

FOUR

"Before you say anything, I'd like it if you listened," says Shizuka to her wife. It is the first thing she says when they enter their chambers and properly settle in for the night, as she unties the belt keeping on her outermost robe. The words have been stewing inside her all night; she has saved all her storied courage for this. "If that's all right. I have a lot to say, and I've had a lot of time to think about it. If you'd like to start—"

"Go on," Shefali says. She sits on the bed, Qorin style, and perches her head on her hand. That's an old look from Shefali, who used to look at Shizuka that way whenever one of their discussions about history came up. "Go on," she'd say back then, too. Shefali and the other Qorin always let Shizuka speak long enough to prove herself wrong.

Shefali's condition might've warped her features, but her expressions are as easy to read as ever. Part of her should be upset, Shizuka supposes, that her wife expects her to fail at this, too—

but it's to be expected. Shizuka has done an excellent job of that lately.

"You're willing to let me speak first?" says Shizuka. "I was worried that you'd say I've done too much already."

Shefali shakes her head. "You've had time. I want to hear it."

The amusement leaves Shefali's eyes—there is only expectation now, and concern.

"Right," says Shizuka. The last moment before—it is a branch thrown between the wheels of her conviction. She wavers before finding her path again. In her wobbling, O-Shizuka reaches for her old comb. Her hair isn't in need of it, but the motion soothes her. "I'm sorry. I should begin with that. I don't begin with that often enough."

I'm sorry.

Shizuka pauses again.

Those words were once so unfamiliar to her. Like a prayer coiled at the base of her stomach—she had to pull it, bead by bead, out of her mouth. Apologizing for sleeping through meetings, apologizing for missing Baoyi's birthday—these were simple things. Small beads.

But at the end was a stone the size of her closed palm, soaked in the blood of the army and the waters of the Kirin.

In comparison to that—perhaps this argument is a small bead, too.

"I'm sorry that I've disappointed you. I'm sorry that I haven't kept my word to you. I'm sorry that you came back to find me like . . . this . . . when you were expecting your brash girl instead."

Easier and easier, to say all of this—and yet as she speaks, that fire returns to Shizuka. She remembers her rage from earlier; she remembers her indignation. The girl she once had been is there, gathering heat, waiting for the right moment to explode. Shizuka sets down the comb. The gesture is deliberate, the soft clatter of enamel against the wood of her desk like the crack of burning wood.

The flames are coming.

"But to hear you say that I do not care for my people? My love, you have known my soul from the day you were born. That you would say such a thing to me, or even imply it . . . I may not be the girl you left behind, but nor am I the woman you seem to see. I have bled for this Empire, Shefali. I have given years of my life to people who demand decades. I have crawled on my hands and knees among the bodies of my army—and you say that I do not care about them? That I have abandoned them, in pursuit of your affection?"

Her throat is going raw, but she continues. She must. Fires are cleansing—so she will let them consume her. Then there shall be only the ashes, and the seeds of their reconciliation.

"My heart beats in your chest. Yours beats in mine. Since we were children, it has been this way. I will love you until the sun swallows the earth, but do not think that I shall idly stand by and allow you to speak of me in such a way. I admit, part of this is my fault—I have taken my time telling you the truth of what happened, and so you do not *know*. You do not *know* what I have sacrificed, you do not know how I have bled. To you, yes, it must seem as if I've grown lazy and belligerent. To you, Xian-Lai must seem a paradise and Fujino a desolate waste. Do you think that I cannot see that myself?

"Do you think I do not ask myself *every day* what I might do to improve Hokkaro's lot? With demons attacking northern Shiratori, with the fish in Nishikomi harbor dying, with our fields fallow and the sky growing darker every passing day—do you think I ignore all of this?

"Four years I've spent on the dais, Shefali, and in that time, I never heard a *word* from you. And you say I ignored the Empire in favor of you?"

She comes at last to something like a stop—but she is not done. No, that's clear enough from the look on her face, the bared blade of her regard. She pinches her nose, as if by so doing she will put out some of the fires she's stoked within herself. With a wave, she gestures toward her writing desk, toward the papers stacked atop it.

"These papers you see here—they are merely *one month's* work. Minor laws and edicts that need only my signature to come to life. Do you know why I have neglected them?"

Shefali eyes the stack. Shizuka wonders how much she can see— the stack is on her left, and so more in line with the steel eye than the green. Her letter mentioned that she could see vague shapes. It's difficult to miss the vague shape of the stack, tall as it is. Baoyi, at five, is only a little bit taller.

Shefali's expression flickers with disgust. It's over in an instant— but the damage is done, the arrow already in Shizuka's breast.

You've been too busy drinking, she imagines her wife saying.

"Because they are minor?" she says instead. "You came here for peace."

"I did come here for peace," Shizuka answers, "but no. That isn't the reason. I wish it were. Maybe I wouldn't feel so disgusted with myself."

Her voice comes out thick with the venom she's swallowed. She hopes Shefali will not mistake it for anger. She isn't angry at her— not anymore, at any rate. Now she only wants her wife to understand.

And to understand, she will need to see, to hear.

The large bead in her stomach rolls.

She isn't willing to summon it yet.

Shizuka reaches into her sleeves. What she's looking for is easier to find, now that she has stopped tying flowers to her wrists. The habit of an untested girl.

Instead of a flower, Shizuka now holds a seal. Gold leaf clings to the characters, like moss to a tree. She hopes that will distract from her own shaking hands.

"This is how I sign my name these days," says Shizuka. "Since I've gotten back, or almost. It's an improvement, if you'll believe that, to have a stamp at all. For the first year, I refused to sign things outright, because the sight of a bowl filled with . . . with wa . . ." She closes her eyes, scowls, forces herself to continue. "Because the sight of water, even a bowl's worth, was terrifying to me. I couldn't . . . Everyone knows me for my calligraphy, Shefali, and I could not even do that. So I had this stamp made. And every time I use it, I remember that failure.

"Every time I use it, I feel like the useless lump of flesh I was when I returned from the war. Every time, Shefali."

It hurts to speak of herself in such a way—but no more than it hurts to think of what she's done. Of the people who are dead because of her. Of the bodies like leaves floating downstream—she sees them whenever she closes her eyes; how can she forget?

Useless, useless, useless. All the powers of a god, and she saved none of them.

Shefali's concern is written plain on her face. More than anything, Shizuka wants to run from the rest of what she must say—to bury herself in her wife's arms and hide.

But she has started this conversation, and she means to finish it.

"I CAN'T ALWAYS muster up the courage to do it. I will admit that to you, my love. I cannot always summon the will to confront that part of myself, and so the papers stack up and stack up, and soon their height begins to taunt me—but when I am feeling strong enough, I do them all at once. I confront that part of myself, over and over, all at once."

She lets out a breath, sets the seal down on the table next to the comb.

"I've put off telling you the worst of it for too long. I see that now. Speaking of what happened before the war is easier, but the easy thing often isn't the right one. All I ask of you is that you listen to me, when I tell you the story, when I tell you what I have given for this throne. If you think me cruel and uncaring after that—well. In truth, I haven't prepared myself for the possibility, but if you think of me that way—"

"I could never," says Shefali.

The relief Shizuka feels at that moment—is there anyone alive who has known its equal? All day, this thought has eaten away at her: that her wife thinks she is indiffferent. Like the giant she slew in Onozuka Village, it has towered over her, casting her in shadow.

And in three words, Shefali has slain it. "Before you begin—one question."

"Of course," says Shizuka.

The anticipation is its own little death, but Shizuka would die as many times as Shefali asked her to.

"I spoke to a man in the markets," she says. "Vachirgai. He sold goats."

Shizuka smiles a little. How like Shefali. "A goat salesman."

"They're good goats," Shefali says. "He raises them well. But he told me, Shizuka—he said that you have not freed the Qorin. You haven't given my mother back her rightful title."

SHIZUKA'S FIRST INSTINCT is to argue that she has been excellent to the Qorin. That she has made it a priority of hers to punish those who discriminate against them; that she has poured thousands of ryo into caring for the Qorin left displaced throughout the Empire.

But what is there to argue about when Shizuka knows she is so clearly in the wrong, and Shefali so clearly in the right? Once she stifles that urge to fight, it's clear to see: all she has done is better the lives of the Qorin within the Imperial framework—a framework none of them like.

If she truly cared, she would have cut these cords long ago.

Shizuka walks to the stack of papers. She riffles through them for a few moments, her long-nailed hands flat against the pages, before plucking one out by the corners and laying it on the desk. She picks up an inkblock and the bowl—but she does not touch the bottle of water.

"Help?" Shefali offers. Shizuka cannot turn her down. She nods, and so Shefali picks up the bottle. She takes the bowl from Shizuka and pours out a little of the water into it.

The paper is fine and white, without traces of the pulp used to make it. The handwriting upon it isn't Shizuka's. Shizuka's handwriting dares the heavens to strike at her. This feels . . . gentler. Soft as flower petals, with its swoops like stems in the wind.

Shefali cannot read a word of it. "What is this?"

"The piece of paper that will do what you've asked," says Shizuka. She points to the characters running down the right. "'Declaration from the Phoenix Empress Concerning the Qorin people and their ruler.'"

"Why not sooner?" Shefali asks her. "Why not at court?"

It is a fair question, and one that Shizuka must give fair consideration to before she answers. "Because I am a failure" will not suffice.

"Freeing Xian-Lai caused enough havoc," Shizuka says. "Fuyut-suki and Shiratori take whatever excuse they can to say that I am weak, and too kind to the 'conquered people.' The lords of Hanjeon and Dao Doan are more concerned with their coming freedom than with cooperating with me on the matter of Qorin rights. Shiseiki is too weak to come to Fujino's aid, should Fuyutsuki and Shiratori decide they'd like to try for the throne. At first, I was waiting until they'd settled down long enough, but—you're right. I've waited too long, and I've failed my own family."

If Minami Shizuru had instead been on the Phoenix Throne, she'd have beheaded Fuyutsuki and Shiratori and been done with it. Still a viable option, so far as Shefali is concerned, but not one Shizuka will ever take. She has absorbed the westerner politics, without insight.

"If you sign this now, from Xian-Lai, who guards the palace?"

"Your father, and my Dragon Guard," says Shizuka.

"A paltry army, it's true. . . . My love, a favor?" Shizuka says. Her hands shake as she grinds the inkblock; she gives the resulting paste to Shefali to mix with the water. In the meantime, she picks up a brush. Clawlike, her fingers around the brush; gone is the easy grip she once employed.

Shizuka stares at her hand, stares at her fingers, licks her lips, and tries to calm down.

Shefali squeezes her shoulder. "Will they attack?"

"Probably not," Shizuka says. "Shiratori has his own problems, as I've said. That report, there—it seems the enemy is striking farther south than usual. They're coming down the Azure Mountain Pass, tearing up villages in their wake . . . I've sent him two legions, and if he's wise, he will make use of them. Fuyutsuki himself won't try anything without Shiratori goading him into it. The man has no initiative."

Having something to focus on instead of the water helps—

"You're certain of this?" says her wife. That she needs to ask at all . . .

"I'm always certain," says Shizuka with a sad smile. "Haven't I told you that lately?"

Shefali takes her hand. "Together, then," she says.

"Together," says Shizuka.

The signature that follows is not perfect. No one would dream of calling it such.

But it is theirs, together, and it is a start.

BARSALAI SHEFALI

THIRTEEN

There is no paperwork to attend to when you are a Kharsa. The astute might say it is because the Qorin adopted a formal writing system only thirty-odd years ago, when Burqila Alshara commissioned one—but this, though technically correct, is wrong in spirit. Kharsas do not have paperwork, because everyone shows up in your ger to tell you, in person, all the things you have done wrong.

Shefali sat through many such meetings as a child. Burqila made a point, when planning the clan's route through the steppes, to visit all the other clans at least once. This gave them the opportunity to air their grievances, which they were always happy to take.

"Gaarughaal and his clan camped at the banks of the Rokhon two months early, when *my* clan has use of the banks."

"Sarangarel sold me fifty horses, and every single one of them is infertile, Burqila, every single one."

So it went. Burqila had indulged them, her face a mask of vague displeasure, and when they were done speaking, she'd sign something. Otgar voiced it, or Kenshiro before her, and the matter was settled.

"Drive your horses a little harder and get there before him next time. You have the best horses on the steppes—why are you being so lazy?"

"I'll have her send you fifty new ones—so long as you *told her* you wanted them for breeding, and not racing."

Quick engagements, all of those; the gathering of the clans every year was where the real rambling happened. Even then—Shefali cannot remember anyone speaking for more than a few minutes at a time. Burqila never would have allowed one of her people to grandstand over another.

Shefali thinks—not for the first time—that the Hokkarans truly have it all wrong. She and Shizuka have been going through the pile of paperwork for what seems an eternity. Shefali cannot read them, but she hates them all the same, for Shizuka must sit and read and ponder whether or not they are worth indulging.

And she asks, of course, for Shefali's opinion—on the proper amount to tax millet farmers and dye merchants, on trade agreements with Axiot and distant Galdun, a nation even Shefali has not visited; on plans for new White Leaf Academies in Kakize and Horohama. Every letter—already long—becomes an entire conversation about things Shefali cannot find the will to care about. She may be half Hokkaran, but these are not her people.

It is all terribly boring.

Boring enough, in fact, that soon Shizuka is nodding away in her seat. Shefali knows what is coming—she scoops Shizuka up in her arms and sets her down in bed.

"But the paperwork—"

"Can wait," Shefali finishes. If she has to listen to one more report, she will scream. She pulls the sheets up to her wife's chin and kisses her. "I'll keep you safe."

"Promise?" Shizuka mumbles.

"Always," Shefali says.

Shizuka falls asleep with her hand in Shefali's. No matter how many times Shefali watches her fall asleep, it never ceases to amaze her—all the tension leaves her in an instant, and soon she is breathing steady, steady.

For hours, too, Shefali sits at her wife's side. Whittling, for the most part—her hands do not pain her anymore, and so she is able to get more detail onto her wolves than usual. When she finishes one for the pack, she sets it down and takes out the feather O-Shizuru gave to her. The blessing.

She looks from the feather to her sleeping wife.

Like two pine needles, she thinks.

Shizuka shifts, the blanket leaving her shoulder bare, and Shefali is quick to tuck her back in. More than anything, she hopes that Shizuka will at last be able to rest. How many days has it been since she slept through the night? Shefali cannot remember her doing it even once.

Please, she says to the feather. *She deserves to sleep.*

But the Queen of Crows has been dead for years now, and cannot hear her anymore. Shifting becomes thrashing, and thrashing becomes screaming. Barsalai rocks Shizuka in her arms, back and forth and back and forth, whispering over and over that she is safe. To see the Phoenix Empress gasping for air, to see her hiccuping and tearing at her hair, to see her nose dripping—this is far from dignified.

Shefali did not marry Shizuka for dignity.

And so she wipes her wife's nose, and so she gently holds her wife's hands so that she cannot hurt herself, and so she whispers: *Breathe.*

How long does it take Shizuka to stop sputtering, to return to her former self?

How long does it take a flower to bloom?

Shefali holds her, all the same. When at last Shizuka is ready to speak, she creaks two words: "I'm sorry."

"No," says Shefali. "You don't have to apologize."

"I'm . . . I'm like this every night," Shizuka says. The color is returning to her now, though there are still bruised rings beneath her eyes. "I'm wasting your time."

"You aren't," says Shefali. How can she say such a thing? "Shizuka, please. Don't speak of yourself that way. You are my white felt ger, you are my endless sky—you could never waste my time."

Dark as it is, Shizuka's eyes are like cinders.

For a long while, they say nothing—but the silence closes in like rushing water, and she must find some way to stave it off. "I told you I would give you the whole story," she says, staring at her hands. "I'm not yet finished. We haven't even gotten to—"

"We don't need to," Shefali says. "Not tonight."

"I promised—" Shizuka repeats. Shefali can see where this is going. Like a maple seed torn in half spiraling to the ground—she will keep repeating herself.

Shizuka's spoken from her seat, and for the most part, Shefali has listened from the bed, where she's continued whittling her wolves. She sets the wolves aside—there are six of them now—and stands. The pain of the journey is a distant memory; it isn't hard to stand at all, and it isn't hard to scoop up the Empress of Hokkaro into her arms.

"I will be here tomorrow," she says. "And the night after that, and the night after that."

She presses her lips to Shizuka's, expecting to feel her melt a little, to feel her soften.

But she doesn't.

She clings to Shefali's deel, and she lays her ruined ear against Shefali's heart—but she does not soften at all. Whatever her Imperial
eyes are seeing, it isn't Shefali.

Perhaps . . .

Perhaps it has been wrong to press her to this degree. Shizuka had
reason, after all, for most of the things she's done. Why did she ever
worry otherwise? What had possessed her to be so critical, to be so
pessimistic about the woman she knew so well? Her own feelings felt
like a story someone else was telling, and now here was the result.

Her wife, curled up in her arms, unable to speak, thanks to the con-
quest of memory.

"Don't worry," Shefali says. "You're safe."

It is the only thing she can think to say. The most important thing.
More important than how much she loves her, more important than
how much she cares. Love is a powerful force—but it is no Daybreak
Blade. You cannot slice through your memories.

She sits on the bed with Shizuka laid against her chest, with her
legs over Shefali's lap.

"You're here in Xian-Lai, where nothing can hurt you," Shefali says.
"The birds will be singing soon. Sunrise comes earlier here, hm?"

There—Shizuka nods against her. So she's listening. That's a
good sign. Shefali thinks of singing a little herself, but she decides
it's best not to subject Shizuka to such a sound when she's in a delicate state.

"In Sur-Shar, it's hard to tell," Shefali continues. Maybe it's best
to distract her. "Salom is three cities piled one atop the other. In the
lowest of them, you can hardly see the sky at all. The walkways of
the middle city block it."

"You must have hated that," whispers Shizuka.

"I did," says Shefali. "Without you, without the sky . . . I was far
from home."

"You're home now," Shizuka says. Shefali hardly hears her.

You will never be home again, says the Scholar. Him, she hears clearly, his words swallowing Shizuka's. His presence comes upon her after his voice. There—the taste of rot at the back of her tongue; that clammy film that seems to cover her skin, as if she's cloaked herself in a frog's remains.

Not now, she thinks.

"I thought it'd be easier to talk about with you here," Shizuka says. She drags her fingers down Shefali's chest as if trying to find purchase on a mountain. "I . . . I'm sorry, I suppose it will have to wait until tomorrow. You must think I'm useless."

If she listened to me, she wouldn't be in such distress. But you're wiser, aren't you, Barsalai? You know sense when you hear it.

Her soul is broken into two horses running in opposite directions: the one that wants to comfort Shizuka and the one that desperately needs to be comforted.

His presence, like the scum atop a fetid pond, is difficult to ignore.

"I don't," Shefali says. She cannot close her eyes, so she chooses instead to train them on Shizuka's face—on her eyes, on her scar, on her lips and her brows. The face that she's traveled so long to see again, the woman who needs her. "You're not useless."

"I can't even tell the story, when I swore I would. I didn't liberate the Qorin immediately. I've spent my days drinking and my nights in shambles, waiting for you, and—"

Let me speak to her.

What? What is he saying?

"—now that you're here, I can't even speak to you properly. What sort of ruler am I? Ah, Shefali, you deserve—"

You heard me, Barsalai. She's only going to keep spiraling. What she needs is discipline. I can give it to her.

Discipline? Does he think Shizuka is a child to be bent over his knee? Shefali's jaw aches.

"Shizuka," she says. It's surprising how much effort this takes her. Her throat hurts, as if she has been screaming all day. "Please. I love you, I want *you*."

"But how can you say such a thing?" says Shizuka. She's spiraling faster, but so is Shefali, the two of them careening toward their separate destinations.

Shefali has to hold on.

"Because I'm certain," Shefali says. She must say it through gritted teeth. Her fingers are twitching. It's happening again, she knows it's happening again, but it feels—

It feels as if there are strings tied to the end of her fingers, as if someone is forcing her head under the water. The rot floating atop it is flooding into her nose and her mouth; she cannot breathe, she cannot breathe—

His voice, her mouth, the words like open sores on her tongue.

"Certain that you are a selfish whelp. How can you expect your people to—"

Shefali bites down on her tongue. Her mouth fills with the taste of metal—that's preferable to the bile she'd been spilling. She clutches a hand over her mouth as her mind races: What is she to do? Like someone else's brush, like someone else's song—

"Shefali?" Shizuka says. Gone is the hesitation, gone the shyness from her voice. "My love, you're speaking a language I cannot understand—"

"Have you not even learned the proper tongue?" says the Scholar, but Shefali stifles most of it by biting into her finger. "I'm sorry," she mumbles. "I don't know what's—"

Another wave of vitriol. Her stomach twists; she bites into her finger again as black blood wells up at the joint.

Shizuka's sitting up now, her self-pity consumed by the flames of her love. "What can I do?" she says. "Say the word. You're stronger than whatever this is, Shefali, and you've got me with you."

What *can* she do? This isn't like her other attacks; she isn't losing control of her form. Her body is the only thing keeping itself together as this *presence* drags her under, as her mind goes foggy and blank. How long will she be able to keep fighting this?

Will. Someone . . . Someone told her this is about will. Who was it? The smell of orchids and sweat and perfume. Flowers, long ago.

It doesn't matter who said it, only whether or not it is true.

Barsalai Shefali. Her name is Barsalai Shefali, and she earned it twice over.

But what does that *mean*? It is so hard to remember the details. Everything is falling into some sort of mist—

And this woman speaking to him! Is that Shiori? What is she doing here; doesn't she have Yasaru to trail after like a lovesick fool? He'd cast her aside if she weren't . . . If she didn't look at him in such a . . .

"Shefali? Shefali, look at me."

She's taking his hand. Why is she taking his hand? And what has she done with her hair? Cut straight across the forehead instead falling loose where it may. It gives her the look of a court camellia. When has she ever been a courtier? Yasaru loves her because she is wild and untamed—

She's tracing a scar on his palm.

His palm? No, this isn't his hand, and this crescent-shaped scar isn't—

What is she talking about? Those aren't her thoughts. Barsalai Shefali, she is Barsalai. She needed to *remember*. But how?

"Shefali," says the golden-eyed woman, the quiet woman, the Empress of Loneliness. "Listen to me. Do you see this scar?"

A crescent of silver against her brown skin—the woman traces her fingertip across it again and again.

White birch trees. The early autumn, before their ninth birthdays. A childhood lark that ended with . . . a tiger? Yes.

The tiger.

Two pine needles falling on her shoulder in Ikhtar.

A ger they shared once; a field full of flowers Shizuka grew overnight.

She's remembering.

Do you think you can hold me off? he says to her. *Do you think your little trick will impede me? You cannot hide behind your ice forever, Barsalai. One day you'll have to leave this palace.*

She's not certain what trick he means. There isn't any trick to this; only memory, only their love cast around her like a rope. He can continue trying to weigh her down if he likes—she will only keep climbing back up to the surface.

Shizuka lays her palm against Shefali's. Their scars line up.

As if they'd closed their hands around lightning, as if they'd spoken the true names of all the heavens, as if Shefali had swallowed winter itself! The cold shoots into her veins, and for the first time in what feels an eternity, she feels . . . at peace.

When at last she lets out a breath, it comes out in a cloud of cool vapor. Everything, everything is cold: her fingertips against her wife's hand, her beating heart, the breath running down her throat into her lungs. Everything is sharp and clear—and the Scholar's presence is at last gone from her.

"Shefali?" says Shizuka. With her free hand, she is cupping Shefali's face.

"I'm here," she says.

"Oh, my dearest," says Shizuka. All at once, she's gathered Shefali up in her arms as best she can, their foreheads pressed together. "Oh, I thought . . ."

"I'm here," Shefali repeats. She wraps her arms around her fretting wife. Part of her wants to relax into this embrace—to melt into it, to turn all her attention to the way their bodies fit together—but she is not sure how long it will last. She takes a deep breath of Shizuka's cheek. Hopefully, holding on to more of her wife's soul will help her fight off any further attacks.

Yet when Shizuka kisses her, Shefali welcomes it. This, too, is divine; this, too, is her soul; this, too, is an oath.

SHIZUKA TRIES TO warm her. They lie beneath the covers, Shizuka in the crook of Shefali's body, burning like a campfire in Ninth Winter. If Shefali tries, she can catch the smell of burning grass in her wife's hair.

Shefali clings to it now. She clings to anything that will remind her of home, of herself—of the things the Scholar cannot claim.

Wolves aren't fond of fire, after all.

How long does it take before Shizuka breaks the silence?

How long does it take for a Qorin to craft a bow?

Her love's voice is calming, even when the subject isn't.

"I think you should know," Shizuka says. "I think that if I don't tell you, part of me will wonder what you would've thought. If you would've left."

"I won't," Shefali says. After what just happened—Shizuka thinks Shefali will leave her?

"You're saying that now," says Shizuka. She bites her lip; her brows come together. "You do not know what happened—"

"I know enough to say I will stay," says Shefali. She kisses Shizuka's scar—three kisses planted along the raised line. "If you want to tell, I will listen."

And perhaps, in taking in her wife's sorrows, she might forget her own.

Shizuka nods.

She squeezes Shefali's hand.

And she begins, again, her story.

If I Only Knew

In the days before we arrived, we spoke of what was to come. Daishi was traveling with the Fuyutsuki army—she had been the
woman in the monkey mask, doubling over when I struck down
Fuyutsuki-zul. I spent most of my time traveling Xian-Lai with
her—though we parted ways once we made it to Fujino.

To hear Daishi tell it, the North was in shambles. The hole your
mother and mine used to cross the Wall had grown and grown; there
were three of them now. One stood near the Kyuuzen Mountains, one
near the village of Shigeoka, and one between them—all three spew-
ing darkness out into the forest. What few villages remained over
the river had been consumed; what game remained had fallen to the
Traitor's influence. Stags sported gnarled crystal horns; bears grew
to the size of homes. Even rabbits, once so docile, now hungered for
flesh.

For years, the river had been our savior. There were only two
crossings to the Kirin—the dam, a few li northeast of Kimoya, and

the Broken Crown Bridge. Not even a Nishikomi fisherman would dare try to swim across it, for the Kirin is as deep as it is blue, and its goddess is known for her hunger. If I sat here and wrote the names of each sailor she'd claimed onto a grain of rice, the resulting grains would fill a Qorin wagon.

And so Lord Shiseiki saw this natural border and said to himself that he might as well make use of it.

One year ago, at First Bell, he'd sent forth his army to destroy the Broken Crown Bridge. This he'd done without consulting any Imperial Authorities, who would have stopped him. That bridge was built on the very spot King Duc of Dao Doan surrendered to General Karekaze of the North—it was the site of Hokkaro's first usurpation. Lord Shiseiki wisely decided the importance of such a monument was secondary to the well-being of his people and so down it went, plank by plank and stone by stone.

He did this knowing there were soldiers on the other side. That would be no trouble, he told himself, for this would be a temporary trouble, and there was still the dam besides. Far narrower than the bridge is the dam: only one man may comfortably walk across it at any given moment. He stationed eight units there at the base of it in case anything foul should try to scurry across. Every day, eight messengers ran back and forth across it, and so they maintained communications.

By all accounts, this system worked beautifully, until the very moment it did not.

You see, all the blackbloods and all the demons that sought to cross the Kirin from either side now attempted to swim from one bank to the other. That made them easy targets for the Hokkaran army, who shot them full of arrows and bolts without care for the river itself. And so their blood seeped into the water. Their bodies, heavy with shot, began to sink.

And the river began to change.

It was slow at first. Fish with two heads. Carp with human teeth. Anyone might mistake these things for signs of the times. We will endure, as my uncle would say.

But then a fisherman on the banks was scooped up by a massive, watery hand, and pulled into the depths. Two days after that, a water spout landed on the head of a Hokkaran captain. His men, fearing a demon's influence, sliced and chopped and yanked and prayed—but to no avail. A crack heralded the end for him. When his body fell to the ground, water spilled from his mouth onto the mats of his post.

You are no longer welcome, said the river to the soldiers.

And what are you to do when the river itself turns against you? Lord Shiseiki called for a five-li retreat on both sides.

For the past year, he has conducted nightly offerings to try to reclaim that land. For the past year, the river has killed whoever has approached it.

"His Imperial Majesty wants us to try to rebuild the bridge," said Daishi. "It's his thinking that the river will not dare to swallow a member of the Imperial Family bearing the appropriate gifts. Eight priests will go with us as well, for whatever that's worth."

The two of us were alone in her tent, and so she could say "for whatever that's worth."

"And why rebuild the bridge at all, if the river is keeping us safe?" I said. My own destiny—our destiny—lay beyond the Wall, but we did not need an army at our backs to fulfill it.

Daishi thumbed her nose. "The bodies," she said. "They stopped sinking. She spits them back up, now, and where they land . . ."

How fragile you'd looked after Leng's blood corrupted you, my love. Like ash formed into a woman. Three days I'd sat at your side and watched you grow paler and paler. What agony you were in! Your eyes rolled back into your head, your chest rising and falling with each labored breath!

I swallowed the dagger in my throat at the thought of anyone else suffering through such a thing.

"Your uncle, he thinks if you speak to the river and rebuild the Broken Crown, then we can cross with the whole army and head through the gaps. Take back Iwa and the other lost cities."

And how many would die in the process? I suppose it did not matter to him. As a young man, he'd sentenced sixteen of his finest to death. You can come to know sixteen people very well. You can eat with them and sleep with them, you can drink with them and joke with them. You can remember their birthdays and their names and all the secrets they give you at First Bell.

I say "you," but I mean "my uncle." For he did all those things, and still he sent them to their deaths.

What was a few thousand more?

In Daishi's tent, I tipped a cup of rice wine to my lips and conjured a daffodil.

"For old times' sake," I said.

She laughed, but it wasn't the laugh we'd shared as children.

When your Grandmother Sky at last carried me off to sleep, I dreamed of you.

Only—it was not *quite* you.

Silver, your hair, the silver of the swaying steppes. Black, your skin, as a moonless night spent in the arms of a lover. One green comet had fallen from the sky and landed in your eye; the other glinted metal. Your deel was only a shade lighter than your skin. Thousands of stars blinked in and out of existence upon it, so that it never remained the same from one moment to the next.

Yet these are only physical differences.

When she smiled at me, I knew it to be you. A you with silver teeth, granted, but a you all the same: her eyes still crinkled up at the corners, there was still that dimple in her cheek.

In this dream I ran to her, in this dream she held me close, and she smelled of leather and horses and earth, and when she pressed her lips to mine, I swear to you I knew eternity. My soul hummed its song.

We tumbled through the sea of stars, the two of us entangled, and when at last we stopped, she lay curled up against me.

How I missed you! How the sight of you moved me to tears! For I knew it was a dream even then, and I held tight to this apparition before me. I pressed my nose to her hair to try to remember the scent of her—the scent of you—to try to remember when our scents last mingled.

At last I summoned my courage: I opened my mouth to ask if you were returning to me.

Yet what left my mouth was neither word nor sound.

A ray of light shot forth instead.

You turned toward me as my heart began to race, as my joy turned to fear. You wrapped your arms around me as I screamed, as more light shot forth from me, beams and beams of it like stalks of bamboo in a forest. The fire in my veins burned my Imperial blood and I heard it, Shefali, I heard the hiss of it in my ears, but you stroked my hair.

"You are being born," you said to me, your voice like the winds of winter, and more than anything, I wanted to run.

But I could not. How could I, when you were holding me?

Hotter and hotter I burned until at last the light pierced my skin—spears through lanterns.

But it did not *hurt*, Shefali, that was the worst of it. As I saw my own skin peel away, a giddy joy came over me, as if I sat on the branches of my father's dogwood tree, as if I'd beaten you at a race, as if we were in a field with no one else to see what we might get up to. With every flake of me that fell away, that joy mounted.

Was this being born?

For as the flakes of my skin spiraled into the dark, so did my fear. These flames would not hurt me! A forest consumed by fire blooms twice as beautiful and so, too, would I bloom—so, too, would I rise—

My vision swam with white.

I awoke in my cousin's tent, covered in sweat, on a flower bed I'd raised in my sleep.

Daishi sat next to me, her armor only half on. Her eyes were wide as rice wine cups, her lips slightly parted. She was nearly touching me on the shoulder—but some vestige of honor held her back.

"I'm fine," I said, though my mind was abuzz. Were we really the only two in this tent? For I heard voices in the back of my head, like the whispers of courtiers.

"There's a flower bed in my tent, Shizu-lun," said Daishi. "You've been screaming for the past ten minutes."

Had I really? My throat felt raw, now that she mentioned it. "I do everything loudly, Aki-lun, even dream. You should know this."

She wrinkled her nose at this. "I'm used to you calling out to your wife," she said. "The screaming is new."

I rolled off the bed and began to dress myself, if only so that I had an excuse to look away from Daishi. Discussing my dreams of you felt an awful lot like discussing what we did in bed—and that was a line I could not bring myself to cross. Not even if the dreams involved what felt like falling into the sun.

Daishi sighed. "Suit yourself," she said. "You'll talk about it when you're ready. And you do need to talk about it. Pain shatters the bottles you put it in, Cousin; don't think our blood exempts us."

I did not answer her, and it was only partly because my bottle was in fine shape. The voices were growing louder—I could make out individuals now. Five of them? Yes, there were five—but what were they saying?

The question vexed me. I found no easy answer that night, nor any of the nights to follow. Not for years yet.

No—the only voices I was to hear for the next few months were those of my soldiers.

IN THE STORIES, the army is always at the ready. All the hero must do is ride out into the courtyard, torch in hand. All along the ramparts, the soldiers will see this signal and throw up their fans, and so the army is mustered within only an hour. Ten thousand strong they stand, in their shining armor wrought with gold and silk and ivory. When the hero hoists his sword overhead—and it is always a sword—his army cheers and bows to him.

Victory is theirs before they have even left the courtyard.

Never have I read a story where the hero had to marshal her own troops. Never have I read a story where the hero, flanked on either side by her brother and sister-in-law, must tell an old farmer that the army has more need of his son than he does.

But that is the story I am telling you.

This was not a thing that happened once, mind you. This was a thing that happened over and over, at nearly every house we visited.

Would that I had had Daishi with me at least. It was not to be—she had to rejoin the Fuyutsuki army after I met up with Lai Xianyu. Xianyu was Baozhai's First Sister, and she was about as similar to her as a boulder is to a flower. I'd been hoping for a friendly face. I had Xianyu.

Here is how it would work, at the larger farms: we would approach the farmer's modest home with our banners raised. We tried it once without raising our banners only to send the whole family running off into the fields, and so afterwards it was always banners raised, no matter the dread they seemed to strike in anyone who saw them. I would call out first, for I was required to as the army's general.

"The Imperial Niece, on authority from the Son of Heaven, seeks able men and women for her army!" I would say. And invariably there would be no answer. The farmhands would stop, yes, and they would bow as was required of them—but they would not answer.

Again, I would speak.

"I wish to be here no more than you all do, but this is an important matter. I ride north, to march beyond the Wall of Flowers like my mother before me. There I will strike down the Traitor and restore order to the land. Who will ride with me?"

And here there would be one or two who cast down their implements, who shared nervous glances or who grinned at the thought of all that glory waiting to be had. They would call out to their overseers and run toward us, and Xianyu's lieutenant would take their names for the roster.

But most would stay, still.

Xianyu spoke last. It is her way to speak last, speak loudly, and speak once. "Make no mistake! We are asking you politely, but we will be forceful if need be. All able-bodied men and women are to report to us."

Here the protesting would start. The shouting. It was always the men who most dug in their heels on the matter.

"Who will tend to the crops?" they'd ask.

"The Bronze Army," I said, "and your lord's men."

"Why not send the Bronze Army north, then, if you are having them till fields in our stead?"

"Would that I could," I said, "but my uncle has made his feelings on the matter clear. We are to marshal forces from the people themselves."

How I hated repeating that. Every time I spoke those words, I hated him more, until my hatred for him consumed my waking hours nearly as much as my longing for you.

"And you allow this?" was always the response.

"There is nothing to 'allow' about the Divine Order," Xianyu answered in my stead. "If you've a quarrel, take it up with the Bronze Army. They will be happy to entertain you."

Xianyu was as firm as her youngest sister was soft. At times I thought that if you dragged flint across her skin, it would send sparks flying through the air.

When we'd met, she nodded to me once.

"General," she'd said. "I don't respect you and I don't respect your people, but for my sister's sake, I'll leave that aside."

How much she'd left it aside remained to be seen. The whole journey, she'd said perhaps ten words to me. Still, I was grateful for her steel at moments like this.

Because there was *always* a moment where we had to speak to the farm's owner, and explain what we were doing.

I tried to handle this myself as much as I could. I'd dismount, even, which I know would earn your mother's ire. A leader must always meet her people mounted, she so often said to us, but I did not want these people to see me as their ruler. I wasn't.

And so I approached them on foot, these wizened men and women who had once known a time free from my people, and I told them I was taking their sons and daughters to war.

They wept. They threw themselves at my feet and begged me not to do this thing, to go to some other home and steal their sons and daughters instead. From each and every parent, I heard that their own child was the most loving in Xian-Lai, the hardest working, the most needed here at home.

One man hiked up his pants to show me where the stump of his severed leg met his wooden prosthetic.

"Do you see this?" he said, jabbing it with his finger. "This is what I've paid your kind already. You think I can farm like this?"

I wanted to tell him that I would pass his house over. He had only one daughter, you see, and his field was large enough that it must have taken the two of them all day to get anything done at all. If I took his daughter, his crops would fail. I knew this.

And yet if I could not muster ten thousand, my uncle would empty the prisons to fill my numbers. And I did not want the farmers of my army to deal with the murderers.

"I know this is an unthinkable hardship for you, but I must do this all the same," I said to him. "If it were my own will, I would leave you and yours, as I would leave all the sons and daughters of Xian-Lai in their homes. But this is not a matter of my own will."

And it was Xianyu who went out into the field and spoke to his daughter, Xianyu who showed her where her place in our infernal marching column would be.

Never in my life had I walked so far on foot, let alone marched. The boots Baozhai had gotten for me were fine indeed, but they were new and not yet broken in. One day spent on foot split open my feet in ways I'd never known—thick, beetle-sized blisters full of blood sprang up at my heels. Only my own stubbornness kept me walking at all. At the end of the day, when we at last stopped to rest, Xianyu showed me how to wrap my feet in calfskin to lessen the pain—but it helped only a little. I hobbled through the second day, swallowing down my tears as I went, determined to provide a good example.

By the third day, one of the wounds had begun to fester. Xianyu insisted we hold a hot iron to it—but I knew that would not help.

"General, I understand you spent your childhood filling your head with stories, but no mortal skin can withstand this sort of heat," she said.

And so I grabbed hold of the iron with my bare hand. I kept my eyes on hers as I did this. She at first tried to yank it away, but when she saw that it did me no harm, even stodgy Xianyu gawked.

"Is that proof enough?" I asked. "Or will you have me tell you a story about it?"

She swallowed. "Poultices it is."

And so it was. I wrapped my feet in stinking herbs and bound them tight, and hobbled my way through another day.

I could have ridden. I could have. But to do so would be to admit some kind of defeat. I could not be the pampered princess I'd been in my youth. I had to be a leader, and that meant I had to suffer the same as the others.

Only I had to do it first, and I had to be seen doing it.

This was my fate. To rise in the morning with dawn, to hear voices I could not understand, to travel from farm to farm on feet that threatened to buckle beneath me with each step. To walk up to a farmer who had spent his entire life toiling on his land and tell him that I was going to take away his children. That I was going to lead them thousands of li north, beyond the Wall of Flowers, because my uncle wanted me dead and saw fit to kill half of Xian-Lai Province in doing it.

To bear their screaming, their tears, their begging. To look upon them in the greatest moment of their despair and tell them that I could not help them.

You will not be surprised to hear that some fought back. Etiquette is divine, as they say, but the love between a parent and child would spit in the face of the gods themselves if that was what needed to be done.

I did not wear the phoenix mask Baozhai gave to me when I visited the families, and so I was slapped often. I could tolerate a slap. I know you will not believe me when I say this, but my mother did not coddle me as much as you might think. It is . . . I do not like speaking of it, as I am not sure what to make of it now in my adulthood, but safe to say, she spared me no mercies when it came time for punishment.

So I let these farmers hit me as hard as they liked.

I took to planting trees and blessing fields. Coaxing them from the earth, really, as I so often did in my youth. My thinking was this: If the Troubles really did spread south, then these crops would be ruined, but perhaps my influence might keep them safe. It was not something I could be certain of, but I was certain in the way that children are. It deserved a try. The worst that could happen was an unwanted plum tree.

At first I brought it up with the parents.

"Nothing I can offer you can replace your child, should the worst come to pass," I said, "but I would be happy to bless your crops."

"What good would that do me?" was often the answer.

I knelt whenever they asked this and pulled off my gloves. I let my hands touch the cool green grass. As they stared, I forced some of that fire within me into the earth, and I asked for it to show me a flower.

Always, it was a daffodil.

When they saw the daffodil, they often relented. And so while Xianyu spoke to our new recruit, I would walk the perimeter of the farm, calling for flowers as I went. At the easternmost point—there I would call for a plum tree.

I have loved plum trees since the day we stood beneath one together, since the day you put a plum blossom in my hair. I have never told you this, but I kept that blossom tucked in my robes for days after you gave it to me. The smell of them alone returns me to that day. They brought me peace, and I hoped these trees would bring peace to their new owners as well. That they have often stood for endurance did not occur to me for years—I chose them only because they reminded me of you.

Of course, everyone thought I put a great deal of thought into the gesture. Poets have made much of it. Plum blossoms! Surely I swore to these people that if only they endured, I would return their children unharmed. Surely I'd sworn an *oath* to that at every single house I'd visited. I cannot count how many poems I've heard on the subject, how many wood blocks I've seen of it. For some reason, they all render me in the mask.

Even the road itself is not free from this revisionism. If you walk the path my army took around Xian-Lai, you will be taking the Road of Broken Oaths.

What would you think of this, if you were with me? Would you have been at my side as I went from house to house? Or would we have run away from this, as we'd run away from all the rest of our problems? Surely there was someplace in the jungle we could hide. The two of us, alone. You'd spend your mornings hunting, and I would spend mine coaxing fruit from the earth. Together, we could live, the two of us.

As often as I imagined this, I knew it was a false comfort.

Hiding away in the jungle would have made us happy—but we would have had to go north eventually.

Baozhai wrote to me. Her letter was the perfect piece of sugar-silk frippery. The Second of the Lai sisters, Lai Yizhen, had returned from five years abroad shortly after I left. Baozhai often spoke of her the way you spoke of your mother, or the way I spoke of my ancestor Shiori, and so I was pleased for her when I read the news. Having visitors would be good for her spirits—and her long-departed sister was the finest sort of company.

FOR AN HOUR I lost myself in the reading of this letter, for an hour I let myself be taken back to the Bronze Palace and the life-ending dilemmas of which color to wear to court. How comforting it was, to live this sort of crisis through her!

And yet how distant. The troops I marched with now hated me, and they had every right to. It was I who had yanked them from their homes. Xianyu was the one who set up the units, and she'd at least done them the mercy of keeping villages together, but that was little comfort to most. Always, when I approached, the conversation would stop like a fire snuffed out; always their eyes bored into me.

Why are you here? They wanted to ask, but could not. And so they bobbed their bows and returned to sitting in silence.

At first, anyway.

After two weeks spent taking my meals with them and leading them in exercises, things began to change. The conversation did not immediately stop when I took my seat among them. Indeed, I'd learned some of their names. Fenglai from Xian-Qun, for instance, stood nearly as tall as a Qorin with the shoulders to match. Unlike the others, he was a blacksmith's son, and he carried with him his own weapon—a sledgehammer he'd forged when he first saw our troops approaching.

Fenglai took a liking to me when I drunkenly boasted that I could pluck a log from the fire without burning. In all the Qun units, he was the only one who bet on me, and so he won a tidy stack of bu for his trouble. The next time we stopped at a city, he bought eight bottles of plum wine and presented them to me as a gift.

We shared two of them, Qun unit and myself, all of us sitting around a fire. It was a few days after my twentieth birthday, and the firebugs were floating about us, dancing their final dance of the year. One of Fenglai's friends, a cobbler's daughter named Mei, was telling us about Yuzhang and the Lightning-Dog. In great strokes she painted it all: Yuzhang's mother falling ill, his visit to a famed healer deep within the heart of the jungle, who told him only the fur of the Lightning-Dog could cure her; his journey north through the hills and mountains of Hokkaro in search of the beast. Three other creatures he encountered along the way: a splendid firebird, the sight of which transfixed him to a single spot for five days and nights; a coiling river serpent that dragged him to the unseen cities of the depths; a dragon who plucked him into the air and asked him what he wished for.

"For the safety of my mother and my people," he said, and so the dragon left him before the cave of the Lightning-Dog.

"Yuzhang crouched low to the ground," said Mei. "So low that the hairs of his beard dragged against the stone. The slightest breath would be enough to draw the Lightning-Dog's attention—therefore, he held his breath for an hour as he watched the creature's movements."

"An hour?" said Fenglai. "You tell me he held his breath for an hour?"

"I also told you he rode a dragon, and you did not fault me then," said Mei.

I laughed and took another drink of my plum wine. It is strange, isn't it? The sort of things that take one out of a story. Dragons and phoenixes are perfectly acceptable, but no man can hold his breath for an hour.

Mei held up her hands and settled back into her storytelling stance. "An hour he lay in wait—"

Jenai, another of the Qun soldiers, guffawed again. "Ten minutes, maybe! But an hour—"

"Let her finish!" I said. "He learned how to hold his breath from the river serpent, now let us continue."

The frustration on Mei's face gave way to relief. When she inclined her head and raised her cup to me, it felt genuine. I smiled my wine-hazed smile back at her.

The rest of the story was as riveting as the beginning. Yuzhang

crept into the cave and rolled in a pit of mud. Then, struck with a sudden well of bravery, he charged the Lightning-Dog and wrestled it
to the ground. When he got his clump of hair, he did so by tearing it
from the beast's back with his bare hands.

Of course, the Lightning-Dog was not pleased with this turn of
events. In one mighty bite, it tore the hand from Yuzhang's arm and
swallowed it whole. Now that he knew he'd been bested, Yuzhang
fled the cave. Once more he called on the dragon. The wise creature
appeared to him, but so, too, did the phoenix. The phoenix offered
him one of her feathers in exchange for the fur—a feather that could
cure even death itself—but Yuzhang refused. He'd paid his price for
the fur.

Yet he was not done paying it. When the dragon left him in his
village, Yuzhang had only the strength to return to his mother and
give her the fur before the blood loss took him. The village planted
an oak tree in his honor, which to this day has only golden leaves.

You will forgive me for recounting that story. I quite enjoyed it,
although my telling is lacking compared to Mei's. Perhaps one day
you will hear it done properly—by the time Mei finished, there was
not a dry eye in the camp.

It was Fenglai who brought you up. He turned to me, once the
story was done, and he said: "General Dog-Ear, do you think your
wife could have wrestled the Lightning-Dog?"

My temple nickname had spread among the ranks without my realizing it. You may think it gauche, as I did when it was jeered at
me, but there was a fondness to the tone here that I did not mind.
General Dog-Ear was a name for *me*, and it was more name than
Princess Yui.

Besides—I would take any excuse to brag about you. So rarely did
they come to me in those days! It was illegal to so much as acknowledge my marriage. No one at the temple dared risk mentioning it—

but here, I was the highest authority, and I was certainly not going to order anyone lashed for mentioning you.

"She could have," I said, "and she could have done it one-handed, at that."

(I was deep in my cups then, but I stand by this statement.)

Jenai scoffed again. "No mortal woman could do such a thing," she said. "She cannot be as strong as you say."

"She is," I said. "Stronger, even. Barsalai Shefali can lift her Qorin mare over her head as easily as I lift this cup."

I lifted the cup over my head, but of course I was drunk and so it toppled over. Plum wine spilled all over my face and hair.

Silence took the camp.

Two years ago, I would have been mortified.

But now? Now it was the funniest thing that had happened to me in *months*. To spill plum wine on myself! I, so renowned for my grace, my fine duelist's reflexes!

I laughed until I could not breathe, and, after a beat, so did everyone else.

What Waited in the Forest—

I have spoken to you a little already of marching.
A little.

Now it all begins in earnest, for now all ten thousand and two of us traveled the Three Kings Road to Shiseiki.

Baozhai had, in fact, been modest about the Troubles in the North. South of Fujino, the land was arid but workable. We saw farms as we traveled. Livestock wandered the fields. Cows munched on green grass without a care in the world for the darkening northern skies. As we traveled the Three Kings Road from Sodol to Fujino, the villages we came across were happy to see us. More than once, a village elder insisted on housing us for the evening, so that we might not all have to sleep out beneath the stars. This in spite of us wearing the violet and green of Xian-Lai Province, you understand, although in Hanjeon, those sentiments are not so strong as within the Inner Empire.

These gestures warmed my heart, and I was happy to indulge them. After hours spent marching, even a bed of hay was welcome.

In the mornings, I would rise with the dawn and call all the food I could as payment, while Xianyu and her captains led the army through their morning drills.

This all changed the moment we crossed into Fujino.

If the Empire were a fruit, then the first two bites were succulent and sweet, which made the maggot-riddled third bite all the more horrifying. None of the villages here welcomed us. Indeed, when we marched through them, they occasionally threw things at us. Food was too precious to waste on foreigners, of course—the land here was more grit than soil—but there were other things to fling. Waste. Insults. Threats.

To hear this, to see it, astounded me. This was not the Fujino I knew, where cows and sheep meandered across the golden hills. This was not my father's Fujino, where he'd often gone without his Imperial trappings to be among the commoners.

When these people screamed at us, when they raised their hands against us, their eyes went flat and the muscles in their necks went thick as bamboo.

"If I catch any of you near our fields, I'll skin you myself!" shouted a reed-thin man with a cleaver in hand. So old was he that he leaned on his grandson for support. I doubted he could skin a chicken alone—yet here he was, threatening to skin a whole army.

"You call this an army? Pah! Xianese have no fighting spirit!" said a woman without a single visible scar anywhere on her person, who stood in a fishmonger's stall.

To suffer this abuse for hours on end would try even the most patient people. It was not surprising to me, then, that by our third village, some of our soldiers had begun to fight back. Some shouted their own retorts, those who spoke Hokkaran well enough to do so. This I did not mind so much as those who took matters into their own hands.

Kunomi was the turning point. There, as I led my column through the village, a putrid excuse of a woman working at the blacksmith saw fit to fling hot coals at us. Mind you, she flung these coals at the most well dressed member of the army, the woman *in a solid gold war mask*. Stupidity and hatred are inseparable siblings, as the saying goes.

Whatever she expected, it was not me. As the coals soared through the air toward me and mine, I called for a halt. Then, quick as I could, I broke off from the group. If I sliced through the coals, that would only create more of them—the solution was to block them entirely.

And the finest way to do that was with my own body. It wasn't as if it would hurt me.

And so I flung myself into the path of the coals. Like stones from a sling, they shot into me. My armor took the brunt of the impact, but not all of it—one hit me in the chest hard enough to rob the air from my lungs. I had thought nothing of this through, least of all the landing, and thus when I hit the ground, I landed flat on my back.

"You deserve worse for wearing that mask!" shouted the woman. Somehow she'd missed that my undercoats were trimmed with Imperial Gold. "Who do you think you are?"

No one helped me to my feet, although several soldiers gathered around me in a circle. That should have been her second hint as to my identity. My ancestor Yaton had drowned in the Jade River because no one dared to touch him.

"I should ask the same of you," I said. As I got to my feet, I waved my soldiers away. Only when I was looking directly at the woman did I take off my mask. "But it is polite to answer the questions of others first, is it not? My name is Shizuka. I am the daughter of O-Shizuru and O-Itsuki. In my blood flow the Fires of Heaven. And so I ask—what flows in your veins that you would strike at another person with such vitriol?"

The color drained from her face. Xianyu, who'd broken off from the column herself, was rounding up behind her. Her eyes flicked to me, asking permission to arrest her, but I shook my head.

The woman fell to her feet. Over and over, she begged eight thousand pardons of me.

"I did not know!" she said. "I did not know!"

Some dark part of me wanted to step on her, to grind her face into the earth for what she'd done—but I cast this thought away.

"And if you had known," I asked, "would you have flung the coals at my soldiers instead?"

Her hesitation told me all I needed to know.

"Commander Lai," I said, "arrest her. Captain Lu, see to it that the magistrates hear of her crimes and rejoin us at camp."

I watched them drag her away, and I heard her protest over and over that she was not a horrible person—it was only, why should Xianese soldiers be entitled to live off a land that was not their own?

We made camp well north of Kunomi that night. Xianyu found me as I was drinking.

"Your people are dogs," she said, and I allowed that to stand without further comment. The muscles of her jaw worked as she looked me over. There was a bruise on my throat where one of the coals had struck me. "You'll have to ride from here. At least then you'll be visible. Dogs know their own masters, and if they see you on your red gelding in Imperial livery, they'll know you."

I shook my head. "No," I said. "Not while the others are marching on foot. We've precious few horses, Lai-zul, and we need them for transporting our—"

"General, perhaps you misunderstood me," said Xianyu. "I was not making a suggestion."

There was that flash of steel. I could count on one hand the people who would've dared to speak to me in such a way. Your mother, your cousin, you. Baozhai, perhaps. Above all, I admired this about

Xianyu—for all her blunt force, she was invaluable as an adviser. Her allegiance lay with keeping her army safe in spite of me.

I've mentioned my determination to show the others that I would struggle alongside them. In that moment, when Xianyu told me it was time to ride mounted—well. She knew the army better than I did, and certainly she knew better how a general should conduct herself. Had my uncle not been indulging his vendetta by placing me at the *head* of the army, it would have been Xianyu leading us.

I could have argued with her—but what would that have achieved? A fissure between the two of us, when unity was required going forward. No, it was not worth it to argue, and she was likely right besides.

"Very well," I said. "If you think it best, Lai-zul."

A flicker of surprise crossed her features. "No haughty argument about your honor?"

"The most honorable thing in the world is to safeguard others," I said. It was something the priests at the temple told me when I at first remarked that cleaning chamber pots was beneath me. "Second to this is recognizing the wisdom of others. So, if you think it best if I ride, then ride I shall."

Xianyu is nothing like her sister. There is no softness to her, no *give*. Her features are as severe as the rest of her.

In that moment, she *almost* smiled. "Understood," she said. "I shall have your gelding readied. Your uncle made no proclamations on which banner we fly, did he?"

"No," I said. I poured myself a cup of wine and offered one to Xianyu.

Just like that, the near smile was gone.

"Drinking alone, General?"

"A small indulgence," I said—though in truth, the question rankled me. Considering the circumstances, an occasional drink would do me little harm. I wasn't draining a bottle every night—not when I drank on my own, at least. I just enjoyed the taste. Was that so wrong?

"See that it is," she said. I reminded myself again of her good intentions—but I was going to finish this cup regardless of her opinion. One cup of wine would not bring the Empire to its knees. And why was she commenting on it, when I'd just relented to her?

"Continuing," said Xianyu, "I advise that we fly the Imperial banner alongside that of Xian-Lai. Our uniforms are green and violet, still, but the banners may earn us a reprieve from all this harassment."

To this, too, I relented, though I had no idea if we had any Imperial banners. Xianyu left after the briefest possible pleasantries. I was alone, again, with only letters and wine.

The next morning, I mounted my gelding and rode alongside the head of the column, instead of leading it proper. Somewhere within the depths of our stores, five banners had been found—I wore one mounted on a pole at the back of my saddle. As we prepared to march through the town of Nodaira, I braced myself for more vitriol.

But it did not come. Not with the venom it had before, at least. We were still treated to the Empire's finest glares and huffs of disgust, but no one in Nodaira raised either voice or hand against us. The town headsman even consented to let us rest in his field for the evening.

Xianyu had been right, as she so often was.

That did not change my evening routine overmuch. I poured myself a drink, and I read Baozhai's latest letter. This time I began my answer—but this was the only change. I told myself that I would listen to Xianyu when it came to army matters—but when it came to my life, I would be my own master.

And so I wrote to Baozhai, the wine making my strokes almost recline against the page.

A woman flung coals at me yesterday, I wrote. *Can you believe she tried to burn a phoenix?*

I thought nothing much more of it at the time. I hadn't been injured, not really, and besides—it was ironic that she'd chosen me of all people to try to burn. Now that the woman was safely locked away somewhere she would never harass anyone else again, I thought the whole incident a little funny, even. And this was only one line among the many in that letter, most of which centered on how I could not believe Lord Qin was still trying to court Lord Ru's daughter. He'd commissioned another poem from Kenshiro!

I did not receive Baozhai's answer until we'd passed Arakawa, and by then I had worse things to worry about than coals.

It was the twentieth of Akkino, and we were marching through the bamboo forests east of Arakawa. You and I avoided them on our way north—that was a decision I made consciously. For centuries now, Hokkaran artists and poets have found these forests enticing beyond any other. It is the permanent impermanence of them, I think, for bamboo is ready to harvest within only five years. In five years time, you may cut down an entire forest and have another rise up in its place, and that is the very definition of Hokkaran beauty.

For me—I have always preferred towering pine. It is my opinion that if you stand for a thing, you should do so proudly, and you should do so as long as you are able. Bamboo may be essential to the Hokkaran way of life, and indeed, it is quite strong—but it is nowhere near as majestic as pine.

And—well. The way bamboo towers up out of the ground reminds me of spider legs, and if I am being honest, I have never been fond of spiders.

Nevertheless the road did go right through the forest—it would be the quickest way to Kimoya, and the safest, too, thanks to the patrols. If the eight thousand bamboo legs of some unseen arachnid made me uncomfortable, that was my own problem. At least I was mounted, and at least I knew what a Hokkaran winter was like. Many of my army had never weathered anything colder than our spring.

Yet the moment we stepped within the forest, I felt in my heart a pinprick sensation, as if ants were running across its surface. A cold drop of rain fell at the base of my neck—impossible given both my armor and the freezing weather. Snow lay over the good brown earth; where would rain have come from?

And that was to say nothing of the bamboo itself. Though you and I avoided the forest when we traveled, doubtless you've seen some growing on your own. The stalks should be a pale green, darker near the ridges—but all I saw here was ash gray. Would the bamboo cutters be able to harvest any of this at all? For it seemed that even the slightest touch would send it collapsing into a pile of dust.

Worse—the bamboo was flowering.

Shefali, the last time the bamboo forests of Arakawa bloomed, my grandfather was a young man. And they certainly did not have red flowers then.

I told myself that it was my worry getting the better of me, yet the skittering-ant feeling grew worse with every step. I turned, was certain I felt a pair of eyes on me.

It is only your imagination, I thought, until the very moment I saw the creature.

If you stare at a fire long enough, you begin to see it whenever you look away—yet the fire is not quite itself. Instead of haughty red, you see arcane blues and greens, always flickering at the edge of your vision. So it was with this thing. Whenever I looked at it, I could not find it—but when I kept my eyes trained on the horizon, I saw the shape of it lurking in the woods, slithering like a serpent between the stalks of bamboo. Try as I might, I could not see its name, nor any details on it save for its shape. Yet how long it was! For ten horselengths it slithered on.

All at once, I called for a halt. Xianyu, brows furrowed, came to my side. "What's the meaning of this?" she said. "We can't make camp here, and it's another Bell to Arakawa."

"I saw something," I said.

"General, we cannot stop because you think you may have seen something—"

Now it was I who cut her off. "Commander Lai, you will note I said, 'I saw something.' Not 'I think I saw something' or 'I may have seen something.'"

Behind me, the soldiers began to chatter. Perhaps I'd been too harsh in my response, but if this thing was what I imagined it might be, then there was no time to spend debating whether or not to fight it. I swung from my saddle, sword in hand. "I will return with its head," I said.

"Don't be a fool," said Xianyu. "Take Captain Lu with you at least. To go alone is—"

"Is the safest for the army," I said. I put on my mask as I hopped over the barricade and into the woods. "If I am not back in an hour, then you may send someone for me—but not a moment before."

Xianyu continued to call for me, but I paid her no heed. A demon lurked within these woods—and that meant this was a personal issue. I could hardly expect my army to go demon hunting. And to send all ten thousand tramping into the woods was foolhardy, too. How were they meant to see the signal fans? We'd trained for combat on an open field—not combat among hundreds of towering stalks.

Going alone was the right thing to do. I was convinced of it.

But as the trees closed in around me, a cruel wind whipped through. So strong was it that it tore the flowers right off their stems. All around me, the red fell soft as a maiden's hair onto the white ground. My breath left me in plumes of smoke; it was cold enough that the metal of my mask was more pain than comfort. The crunch of the snow beneath my feet, the distant hush of the army—these things were the only sound.

Sixteen steps I took into the forest. Sixteen steps in, and the cold now froze the tip of my nose to my mask. To breathe was to swallow needles into my lungs. What little moonlight reached my eyes served only to make the shadows seem darker.

Darkness does not frighten me, so long as I am with you. But in your absence, I supposed my mother's sword would do. I ignited it with the seventeenth step. When I held the blade above my head, the blackness improved only slightly—and there was no sign of the creature at the edges of my vision.

Yet the ant-skittering feeling remained.

If the demon does not come to you—well, you shout at it until it does. That was always my mother's strategy. It served her well for many years, until it didn't.

"I am Minami Shizuka, daughter of O-Shizuru and O-Itsuki. It's my blood you hunger for, isn't it?" I called. "Come and take it."

I held my breath while I waited for the answer. One heartbeat, two heartbeats, ten.

Only the cold answered me. Only the wind.

Sixteen more steps forward.

"Do you hear me?" I shouted. Already my throat was raw. "I know you are there! What is it your creator made you for, if not to attack me?"

Only the hush of snow, only the falling flowers.

Sixteen final steps.

"Show yourself!" I said, for by then my voice was cracking in the cold and I dared not risk any more bravado.

Again I held my breath.

It was the arrow that answered me. With you as a wife, I know well the whistle of an arrow. The moment I heard it, I knew I'd made the right decision. You and I often made sport of splitting arrows during our travels through the north. I should thank you for that, my love, as it trained me not to fear them even as they shot straight for my heart.

A flash of gold. The arrow, two thick lines of black against the red-and-white ground.

"Coward!" I said. My eyes searched the darkness for any trace of movement, but there was none, Shefali, there was none. The arrow had come without the creak of a bow. Who was firing on me? Where were they hidden? The creature I'd seen was a snake—I knew no serpent that could draw and fire.

My eyes fell on the arrow itself, and my heart fell into my stomach.

There was a reason I'd known the sound of that arrow so well: it was a *Qorin* arrow. That fletching came from the small brown birds that always tried to steal our food on the steppes. Incredulous, I knelt down next to it, held it in my hands: there was no mistaking it. I knew those feathers.

"A-Aaj?" I called, for your mother was now my mother, and I worried what this arrow might mean. Blackbloods marched to the north once the infection had taken them; everyone knew this. Many might wander this forest, lying in wait for a meal to pass them by.

But it was years since I'd heard from your clan, and I did not want to believe, I did not want to believe—

Like the fireflies of our youth blinking into view: the glowing green eyes of the enemy. The enemy that had once been human. The enemy that had once been . . .

I . . . you won't want to hear what they looked like. Only that the cover of darkness and the light of my sword were not enough to shield me from the horror of them. The way their bodies bent, the gleam of their teeth, the rattle of their breath in the cold silence of the bamboo forest.

How many were there?

I . . . forgive me, Shefali, please forgive me, but I do not remember.

"Aaj?" I called again. "Tell me you aren't here."

The not-quite-silence that answered me was a knife. As the fear trickled down over my body, I remembered: it would make no difference if I called out to her or not. Your mother never spoke. And if she were to become a blackblood, her mouth would likely stitch together for it, and . . .

Desperately I searched their faces. Desperately, I held on to my mother's sword, the only light in that accursed place. I saw no one familiar among them—but then, who was I to say if their condition had transformed them? The characters I normally used to determine someone's name were not appearing to me now, or at least not legibly—instead of bright gold, I saw only dull yellow smears in Qorin, half the letters illegibly decayed.

Whoever these people had once been, they had long left that life behind them.

My heart was a drum in the night.

I did not want to strike at them. In the low rasp of their breathing, I heard the rattle of their pain. I thought of you lying in that bed in the barracks and I wished, I wished that I could see your defiance among them.

But these . . .

They weren't human anymore, Shefali. Their bodies shifted away from the light of the sword as if it burned them. Indeed, I saw curls of smoke coming up off their filmy gray skin wherever the light hit them. The eyes that stared back at me were hundreds of shades of green, but all of them burned with unimaginable hunger. Gnashing teeth, popping jaws, tongues lolling out of their mouths onto the snow-covered ground—whatever relief I felt at not seeing your mother's deel faded away into horror and revulsion.

I heard a crunching sound to my right. When I turned, I saw one of the changed Qorin biting into the head of a stag. Bits of bone flew from his oversized mouth, and the brains of the deer tumbled like a maiden's unbound hair onto the snow.

He smiled at me, Shefali, and I knew then that the best thing I could grant would be a cruel mercy.

The first cut was mine—the stag and the blackblood's hand alike falling in a spray of black. The creature looked at its bleeding stump and laughed.

And then they descended upon me.

To describe to you the battle that followed—I could tell you the motions that I remember. I could tell you of the stress of it all, the parries, the hands closing around my sword and the screaming that pierced my ears. I could tell you how difficult it was to keep track of what was going on at all when it seemed all the world around me had transformed into a den of tooth and claw. I could tell you how it must have looked, had you been watching: the flashes of gold, the towering black stalks, the crowd closing in around me like wolves around a corpse.

I could tell you those things, if you are in the mood to hear them, but to do so would be to rob the Qorin who had been, the people I faced then. To glorify the time I spent killing them in the bamboo forest.

I took no pleasure in it, Shefali. Every cut felt . . . I kept imagining you. Any of them could have been you.

When at last I stood alone again in the woods, the snow around me was black and half-melted; when at last I stood alone, my lungs burned and my shoulders ached. My knees shook as I beheld the work before me: the bodies of the fallen, the souls that the winds would never scatter to the sky.

There were so *many* of them. How had they lived here so long without notice? How many had they killed? How had any of this happened, and who had permitted it, who had . . .

I beheld the work before me and I thought of the Traitorous God living beyond the Wall. Streaked with sweat and evil ink, my throat burning from the cold, I wanted to call out to him. I wanted to tell him that he would pay for what he had done to these people.

But that was when I heard the scream—an all-too-human scream behind me.

I whirled on my heel. As fast as I could, I beat my feet against the snow-covered ground. Breath came to me in ragged gasps, but I continued onward, onward, cutting down the stalks rather than running around them.

Until at last I cut down the final one, and I came upon the serpent.

Would the horrors of this forest never cease?

Tall as two men the snake was long, though it was not all uncoiled. Unnatural greens and blues floated like clouds over the black of its scales. Four eyes it had, each of a different color. As its cavernous mouth opened, I saw that its flesh was violet—except where the gore of my soldiers coated its maw. The telltale shimmer of souls lent the whole scene an awful whimsy.

By the time I came upon it, it was in the middle of swallowing someone, their feet kicking uselessly as their body slid farther down its gullet. The army itself was in shambles—dozens were running into the woods, screaming at the sight, for they'd never in their lives seen anything like it. The remainder were trying to form a circle around the thing, and it was this crowd that I had to push my way through if I was going to do anything useful.

"Make way!" I screamed, barreling toward them with my sword raised, but with all the commotion, they could not hear me. Into the crush I went. A cacophony filled my ears—screaming and shouting and hissing and the sickening crunch of bone. Scent soon followed: sweat and waste and blood. Up ahead, Captain Lu was calling for a formation that no one seemed to recognize, and certainly no one was heeding him; instead a hundred spears jabbed uselessly at the serpent.

I heard the soldier fall at last into the serpent's mouth. I heard it swallow him, and I heard it laugh soon after, the *oh-ho-ho* of a pampered court lady. A moment later, it stretched itself up and swung its tail down like a club—crushing three of my men beneath it.

"How *delightful*!" said the serpent. "Oh, I haven't had thisss much fun in centuriess!"

This was wrong. All of this was wrong. All the training that we'd done, all the hours spent swinging our weapons at one another, all the speeches Xianyu and I had given—did they count for nothing? But what else did I expect from the children of farmers and smiths and swineherds? You can train a man to kill another man—but how can you prepare him for a gigantic snake that might swallow him whole?

More of the soldiers broke off for the woods—but more screaming came to my ears. I tried to see but could not, not with the others pushing me this way and that, not with standing itself being such a tremendous effort in the crowd. The woods were *not* safe. I knew this in the pit of my soul, no demon ever appeared alone. There would be more blackbloods waiting—

They were all going to die if they did not *listen*—

"Do you hear me? Make way!" I screamed. A struggle it was to hold my sword aloft, but I managed it—and it was this that at last won my purchase through the melee. The soldiers on either side of me scattered far enough that I finally had a path. "Broken Circle, on me!"

A knot in my chest loosened when I saw that the others were at last paying me heed—those around me began to form a semicircle around the creature, with my position as the open side. Their spears came together like the spines of a sea creature.

But the serpent now had eyes only for me.

It brought its tail up to its mouth and laughed again.

"Four-Petal! Come to play at lassst? I thought you'd be frolicking in the foresssst *forever*!"

I wished I were mounted. The serpent held itself taller now than some buildings; standing before it made me feel hopelessly small.

Small—but no less angry, no less determined to crush this thing beneath my boot. I scanned its surface for any sign of the golden characters of its name—none yet appeared.

"Your quarrel is with me," I said, "so you shall attack *me alone*."

"Isss that what you'd like?" it said. "All right. I'll fight you, Four-Petal. But then my friendsss—they'll be fighting yours."

SUMMER IN XIAN-LAI means monsoons. Do you remember, Shefali? We'd be out riding when all of a sudden the sky would tear itself apart, and the rain would fall down on us like a thousand stones all at once. Together we'd link hands and run to the nearest tree—you'd pull your deel off and hold it above us to try to keep me dry.

How I loved the memory of running through that field with you.

But now—now when I hear the rainfall, all I think of are serpents. Bursting forth from the forest like maggots from a corpse, Shefali, so many of them that the ground beneath us changed to writhing black. Some were thicker than a person; some were so thin, I could not see them in the shadow and the dark. Some stayed on the ground, wrapping themselves around the feet of my men, taking them down and feasting—some fell from the trees and dug their fangs into whatever flesh they could find.

My stomach sank. Deep within me was a girl screaming in horror at the death around her, deep within me I wanted to run.

But the only way to stop all this was to kill the demon summoning it—of that I was sure. Within me burned the fires of my divine rage—and so I fed my fears to the flames and charged.

Yet I could not find my footing amidst all the serpents, and the demon was ready for me besides. Only three steps I'd taken before I slipped. It seized the opportunity—quick as a bull, quick as a colt it struck at me, its mouth yawning open to swallow me. Even I, with my reflexes, slashed it only barely before it closed its mouth around my floundering bottom half. The gash I opened across its nose spurted evil ink onto my chest, onto my beautiful mask. Had I not shut my eyes and tucked in my head, it might've gotten in my eyes.

I was chest deep now in the serpent. Only my free hand saved me: I'd managed to grab hold of the corner of the serpent's mouth, and it was to this I held on for dear life. The furious hand of the Father could not have squeezed me any tighter. Only a second in, I felt a pop in my hip that heralded a wave of crimson pain. How I wanted to look down, to see my legs! For I could feel them no matter the pain, and perhaps if I saw them—

But to look down would be to confront the horror of my situation, and I knew that for folly. The trouble was—I could think of no way out that did not involve my dropping the Daybreak Blade, and that was not an option.

When the serpent laughed now, I felt it around my body—a moment of merciful relaxation followed by constriction worse than any before. If I escaped this without a broken bone, it would be a miracle.

I shook off my own despair—I was going to escape. Coated in serpent saliva as I was, half-swallowed as I was, I was going to find my way out of this if only I could *think*—

The world around me blurred as the serpent's head shot up. Soon came the downswing, my stomach threatening to empty, and then the moment of impact. As a melon beneath a hammer, my hand against the ground. The agony brought tears to my stinging eyes. My *hand*, Shefali. The fingers bent backwards on themselves, already they were swelling like grapes. What was I going to do without my hand? How would I write to you?

Another laugh from the serpent. It rolled its head and my hand dropped, useless, into its mouth. If it wrapped its tongue around me and pulled me farther down, this would be the end of Minami Shizuka.

Swallowed by a serpent, surrounded by her felled army of farmhands, who were also shortly thereafter devoured by more serpents.

I will be honest with you: as I felt its tongue wrapping around me, I thought to myself that there was nothing I could do. That I must have been wrong, all those years ago, when I said that we were gods. How foolish I'd been! We'd never truly defeated a demon, you and I, not without proper sacrifices—and now here I was, trying to fight one effectively alone.

I felt it begin to tug me down.

Would they find my body? No. What would they burn for me, then? What had Minami Shizuka left to the world except hundreds of cash seals, except the letters of a foolish girl who thought she could be a god?

Xianyu was screaming orders. I heard her even then, in the maw of the serpent, telling the archers to fire. I even felt the arrows land on the thing's neck—but it would not free me.

Deeper I sank into that stifling gore, until it closed its mouth around me.

And it was then that I saw the light. The only light, as it were: my mother's sword clenched in my unruined hand. How perfect it looked, even then, free of the blood and saliva and dirt that coated the rest of me. How beautiful it was.

And how hot it burned! The air around it bent like the air above a smith's forge. Across my palm, I felt a great heat, and I realized then that it was the scar you'd given me as a child. Our eightfold oath.

The gods themselves trembled before eightfold oaths, did they not? No, I could not die here. I'd sworn to you that I wouldn't. Wherever you were, beyond the Golden Sands—you were living for me.

And so I had to live for you.

I swallowed. My other hand was in agony still, but for this to work, I would only need the one. One perfect thrust. This was no different from the duels I'd fought—one strike was all it would take.

As the possessed serpent tugged me past the wretched gates of its mouth, into its throat, I threw everything into one final strike. A lance of light in the darkness—a thrust into the beast's skull and out.

Easier to thrust into stone! The tip of the sword broke the skin but would not break the bone. The serpent's jerk of pain bought me only a second more time. It was a second I could not waste—I twisted my body as much as I could, putting all my weight into the sword.

A moment of horror—and then! The blade at last punctured the skull. Farther and farther in it went as the serpent thrashed—but within its mouth, the impact was nowhere near as severe as it had been outside of it. Only when the blade's hilt met bone did I at last stop thrusting—only when the thrashing stopped.

I lay there for what felt like an eternity within the mouth of the serpent, delirious with pain. With its mouth closed, there was little air to speak of. In spite of my horror, I forced myself to breathe slowly and lightly, as I had at times within the temple. The demon was felled—for now—and thus the smaller snakes outside would also have ceased their assault. Demons and their minions are as a puppet master and puppet—if you slay the master, the puppet soon falls limp.

But that presumed I had killed it. Which I had not. Not until I spoke the name—a name that I could not see from within its mouth. And even then, only a severed head would truly put an end to it.

Perhaps Xianyu and the others would pull me out. No—how could they? They had a battle on their hands; I was but one participant. Either way, it would do me no good to wait for them inside my enemy.

Roaring with pain, I pulled the Daybreak Blade from its awful reptilian sheath. With it still in hand, I crawled forward, forward, toward its fangs. With the elbow of my wounded arm, I propped the mouth open—

And Xianyu grabbed me by the wrist of my sword arm.

"I've got her!" she shouted. Someone else grabbed me then—never mind the etiquette—by the other arm. Thankfully, they saw the state of my hand and opted for my wrist instead. Slowly, between the two of them, they dragged me from the mouth of the serpent.

The world was intolerably bright then, even in the black of night, and I saw it all as if through a screen of rice paper. Shapes and colors more than details. The only reason I knew one of the figures before me was Xianyu was her voice—but even that sounded distant.

"Lady?" she was saying. She was shaking me, I think. Someone took off my mask and another wiped clean my eyes, but it did not help me see any better. "Lady, answer me if you can. Someone check her for wounds!"

I shoved her away. You know what it is like to be in such pain,

Shefali—words are far too much effort. Instead I forced myself to stand.

Before me, a massive smudge of black surrounded by green and violet shimmer. Before me, amidst them, the puddle of evil ink. Where was the gold? None of this mattered if I could not find the name for the demon that loomed over us.

One step, and then a stumble. Another step. How much pain was I willing to put myself through? Still no sign of the name.

Another step. I felt the rumble of breathing beneath me—it would not be long before the demon rose to terrorize us again. I could not fight it. Not twice, not with this body.

Yet if I took another step—my grip on consciousness was so thin already. My feet may have been on earth, but my mind was in the floating world already. Another step, and I might leave this world for that of gods and heroes.

If I didn't, my army was going to be killed.

One more step.

There, the gold icons clearly visible in spite of my sorry state. Like water on your lips in the desert.

I leveled my sword at it as well as I could.

"Hakuro," I said. "Your name is Hakuro. I, Minami Shizuka, bind you here." Then, with the last of my strength, I turned to whoever was next to me. "Cut its head off, won't you?"

The rest?

Black.

Would I Have Dared it?

There is no name for that battle.

This puzzles me to no small degree. Hokkarans love few things more than assigning ludicrous names to their fights—why not this one? There is a name for each skirmish we fought by the river-bed, a name for the skirmishes all the other armies engaged in on their way to the Broken Crown. Why should this one be any less notable?

You will think it is a small thing to be angry over. What does it matter if a battle has a name or not? A name will not raise the dead. It will not mend the bones of the fallen; it will not cleanse the blood of the corrupted. In every practical sense, a name is useless.

And yet we name most everything. Colors, the layers of a lady's robes, flowers, bridges, roads, forests.

If a thousand people die like dogs in the middle of a bamboo forest—are they less worthy of a name than a noblewoman's robes?

Beyond the flaps of the tent lay the aftermath.

How like a dream it felt, Shefali, how like a nightmare! Had I really been swallowed by that demon? What a ridiculous thing to think, and yet when I tried to prop myself up in bed, a jolt of pain confirmed my worst fears. A splint held each finger of my left hand in place— the slightest jostle was enough to bring tears to my eyes. Seeing it made my heart drop into my stomach, for though it was splinted, my fingers had swollen up like firecrackers. It looked as if a child had drawn a hand and stitched it to my body.

Yet it was mine, all the same.

And if my hand was truly hurt, then that meant . . .

My mouth dry, my tongue stuck to the roof of my mouth and my lips splitting open, I tried to force myself to stand—but I'd forgotten about my hip. I caught myself on a table. Was even walking beyond me? No, no—the Daybreak Blade lay within easy reach. I could use it as a crutch. Priceless though it was, the sword was a tool before it was anything else. I was certain my mother wouldn't mind if I used it this way.

So, with the Daybreak Blade as my crutch, I left the tent.

I might as well have left the sword inside. What I saw brought me to my knees. The *blood*, Shefali. I thought I knew what war was like, I thought I'd read all the stories and seen all the paintings.

But the sight of the blood-soaked snow, the sight of hundreds of soldiers laid out on stretchers, the sound of them all moaning and crying out for aid . . .

Even those who remained standing were not well. I saw one of our surgeons moving from sickbed to sickbed, her expression so blank as she examined her patients that it may as well have been a mask. None of us in the van had escaped with our armor intact—so many around me bore smears of black, so many had their boots soaked through. There went the one-legged man's daughter, carrying on her back a man who'd lost an arm. How old was she? No older than me. No older than me, and yet . . .

Wherever my eyes fell on the camp, there was more fault to find—
and all of it was mine.

I had not seen to it that they got proper training.

I had agreed to this farce to begin with, when I should have remained in Xian-Lai or else had the decency to have left to follow you
wherever you were going. Empress? A Peacock Princess? What nonsense! Before me suffered my people, and I thought I had any right
to the throne?

I could not simply collapse there in the snow. I had to see it, all of
it. This thing that I'd created, this blight on the earth, this sore I'd
torn open.

I pulled myself up, and I hobbled through the camp with the blade
for a crutch.

The wounded were one thing, but the bodies were another.

At the very edge of camp, twenty minutes away from the sick
camps, was the pyre. In all my years, I'd never seen one so tall. Whole
stalks of bamboo were arranged in a pyramid to feed it. Beneath it
were piled bodies, ten or twenty or thirty deep, the flames licking
their flesh clean. You could smell it from the other side of camp: burning hair and sizzling meat, rot and burning wood. A massive pile of
armor and weaponry towered nearby. Soldiers were sorting all of it
into smaller piles as their friends burned.

Fenglai was there, on the pyre. I saw his face. I remembered his
face.

And so I stood and I watched the flames take him. That was what
the Qorin would do, was it not? Watch over a corpse until an animal came for it. Fenglai would've hated that. He would've hated
this, burning in a communal pyre with so many others. He would
have wanted a proper Xianese burial. On a hill somewhere, where he
could watch the sun rise, and people could pour wine on his grave-
stone.

Watching over him was the only mercy I could give him.

All of this was my fault.

Lai Xianyu found me. She must have known, of course, where I was. I wore my undercoat and your old pants instead of proper clothing—in truth, I wore your pants whenever I could find an excuse to do so. Who else in the army wore a coat trimmed with gold and Qorin riding breeches? She must have known, the others must have told her.

Yet she allowed me this time to mourn. When she found me, she urged me back to my tent. Quietly, at first, and then more firmly when I simply stood there as if I did not hear her.

Fenglai's face was almost unrecognizable.

"General," Xianyu said again, and I thought to myself that she must be thinking of someone else. "You cannot stay here all evening. With your wounds, you need rest."

But there would be no rest, couldn't she see? How was I supposed to sleep, knowing what had happened? If I'd doubled back sooner, if I'd ordered us to march in formation—if I'd done anything at all but run at something I'd seen from the corner of my eyes, what would have changed?

Would I still be watching my friends' skin boil and pop?

"General," she repeated. "If you do not move of your own will, I shall be forced to carry you."

I heard Xianyu approaching, and I decided I did not want to cause her any more trouble than I already had. Without a word, I turned and hobbled back to my tent.

I do not remember falling asleep.

I remember the dreams. You and I were swimming in the Rokhon, far away from the rest of the clan. It was the middle of the night—the only time we could get away with a swim in a sacred river. You stood on the banks though I was already chest deep in the water.

"Come on!" I called. "The water feels no different, for being so holy."

But you raised your brow at me and you shook your head. "I'll watch," you said.

I splashed you. The water landed right on your cheeks. In my dream, I commended myself for my aim. "Who will stop us?" I said. "Shefali, in all the world, you are the only person who can stop me."

You pressed your lips together as if you were thinking of doing just that, but eventually you let out a resigned sigh. "I will keep you safe," you said. "But not swim."

"Keep me safe from what?" I said, and the part of me that knew this was a dream knew there was much from which I needed safe-keeping. But the me who spoke—the me who spoke feared nothing. "Let the gods strike us if they will, it is just a swim!"

But instead of answering, you pointed to a man who stood south of us. So far was he that I could not make out his face, only his anti-quated robes, only the cold blue of his eyes, like winter itself.

The eyes knew me. I woke from this dream covered in sweat, only the idea of water in my mind, only the salt spray of the sea on my lips. Only when I wiped my face clean was I able to return to bed— and then only after an hour.

Yet that sleep was not rest! The voices that woke me. That day— the second day after the nameless battle in the woods—was the first day I understood them.

Grant my sword arm strength, said one. *Or I will never win her hand.*

Must I really marry that man? said another. *Grant me wings to fly, or carry me on the wind, to somewhere far away from here.*

Hokkaran accents, both of them: the first a courtly young man from Fuyutsuki or Fujino, the girl with the clipped syllables of

Dao Doan. Where were they? Were they the same as the other voices I'd heard? For they sounded different from the others. Every day, the voices had sounded different. Who were they, and why did they ask these things of me, when all I wanted to do was sleep?

Yet I did not deserve even that.

I ignored them instead, and went to meet with Xianyu. Still I used the blade as a crutch, still I could not quite walk under my own power. This was the longest I'd ever been injured in my life, Shefali, and I wore it as a monk wears their sackcloth. This was what I'd earned.

AND SO, TOO, did I earn the tongue-lashing I received from my second-in-command. Did I not realize how foolish I'd been? She'd told me to take a unit with me, or at least another of the captains—why had I been so bullheaded? She'd told me that we needed to travel in formation, and I'd said we would be fine in columns—why? She told me these things and many more. For an hour, she asked and asked and asked, and I had no answers to give her.

"If we are to make it back to Xian-Lai," she said, "then we need a general. Not a hotheaded child. Not a princess. Do you understand me, Lady? You cannot continue to think only of yourself. These flights of fancy will take us all to an early grave—do you understand?"

I sat there and I weathered this without a word, for she was right. Every word from her mouth was a righteous lash against me.

At the end of this hour, I had only one question, which I voiced with as much confidence as I could manage.

"Lai-zur, you have spoken true. Whatever you ask of me, I will give it. Whatever orders you have—I will see them carried out, or I will do it with my own two hands. All I ask is this: Where are the survivors who have succumbed to corruption?"

After an hour of screaming herself hoarse, her hair had fallen out of its bindings. A shock of gray stood out like a feather. "And why do you wish to know this?"

"So that I might bring them peace," I said. Best to speak such wounding words quickly, lest they cut to the bone.

"And you can bear the sight of them?" she answered. "Their twisted bodies, their wounds, the horror of the dying?"

I met her eyes and I did not blink. These words were more painful than the last—they'd cut no matter how quickly I spoke.

"The first time I saw a man die of blackblood, I was eight. My mother killed him in front of me as a lesson. The second time, I was thirteen, and the one in need of mercy was my own mother. The third time, Lai-zul, it was my wife who lay in bed for three days, and I sat by her side ready to end her if that was necessary. I know well what I am offering."

She studied me. All the stress had worn new lines between her eyebrows, as if someone had pressed an arrowhead there. "Very well," she said. "There's sense in you somewhere, I see. Captain Lu will accompany you. See that you are armored, General."

Already Xianyu had taken command from me. A year ago, I would have bristled—but it felt now as if she'd taken an iron mantle from my weary shoulders.

Captain Lu accompanied me to my tent, and two of his aides helped dress me. Doing so one-handed would have taken a terribly long time. They wished to be sure, besides, that there was no room for the blood to seep into me. Delicately, delicately, they put on my gloves and tucked them into my sleeves. I wondered how long it would be before I could write with that hand.

But I only needed the one to do what had to be done that day.

Oh, my Shefali. I shall not dwell long on the state of those I ended. You know better than anyone what the blackblood can do to a person's body. For you, there was hope, but for these people? Suffice it to say, I spent hours traveling from one sickbed to the next, making my single cut across the throat. It was a mercy.

It was a mercy.

How often I tell myself this. The words ring hollow now, as if they'd come from a play everyone has quoted half to death. *It was a mercy.* As if that will wash the blood from my hands.

As if that will wash the memory of their faces, their last words, their names, their pleas.

As if . . .

I could wash myself in the Father's Sea, I could wash myself with the tears of the Mother—I will never be free of this stain.

Going north was my decision, and my army paid the price.

THE CLOSER WE come to Ink-on-Water, the more I question if I will be able to speak of it at all. Yet you have asked for the truth of what happened in your absence, and so you shall have it. If I have to carve open my skull and pour my memories into your ears—you shall have them.

If I am honest, the days between Arakawa and our arrival at the Broken Crown Bridge are a fog. Is that the fault of the drink, or of the fear, or simply my own refusal to mire myself in those days of horror? All three, I think. All three.

Here are the things I remember.

We remained in Arakawa for two more days past the death of the wounded. By then four days had passed since the battle—we could be sure that no one had been hiding symptoms of corruption. In the mornings, Xianyu gave me our marching orders.

Never again did we employ the columns. From that day forth, it was Arrow formation at all times, unless we came across more of the enemy. Arrow formation—it is as it sounds. Two companies march at the head, each at a slight diagonal, so that they form an arrow. Two more ride behind angled the opposite way. Three final companies march horizontally at the rear. If you've archers, you position them mostly at the rear. The commander rides in the center of the formation—safe on all sides from attack.

I wish I could say that this rankled me, riding in the center, but it did not. I'd lost that part of me in the serpent's mouth. Better for me to be surrounded. Better for us to travel like this, so that we might be able to handle any oncoming threats.

Maintaining formations was difficult at first. Though we'd marched the whole way north, it is quite a different thing to do so in formation. The slightest deviation will not only slow everyone behind you, as it would in a column, but it will throw off everyone at your left and right. A single errant soldier can turn an Arrow into a Hammer with enough time.

And so the captains made sure *no one* was errant. Captains rode on horses with each company. With their war fans, they signaled their troops to move this way or that and better serve the formation.

I do not remember any blackbloods finding us before we passed Horohama, but as I've said, my memory has long since faded. Perhaps there was an attack. If so, then certainly it was smaller than the serpent's—blackbloods without a demon to command them. But I do not think there was, Shefali; it does not feel right when I say those words.

So—in the mornings we had our breakfast, we ran our drills, and we marched. I conjured what plants I could to supplement our meals, but I was only one woman, and the farther north we went, the less likely farmers and villages were to share with us. By the time we passed Kimoya, we marched on a single meal of rice and thick broth soup, supplemented with slices of whatever fruit I'd summoned. To say it was grueling was to name a boulder a pebble—when we stopped hours later, my stomach hurt so badly that I had trouble walking. I was not the only one. We'd set up camp quickly just to get more chance of rest.

But there was no chance of rest for me. Xianyu waited in my tent each night with a stack of battle plans she'd written herself. Famous battles found new life under her hand—we'd pore over the diagrams and analyze the moves of all the armies involved. Why had Qi Shaowan fielded only ten thousand pikemen against Wo Jihao's vastly larger army? Because General Wo had more cavalry than he had sense, and General Qi had dug trenches the night before. Why did Chen Luoyi wait until Fifth Bell to launch his attack on Huang Shanbo? Because Fifth Bell was sunset, and General Chen positioned his army to the west of General Huang's.

Most were Xianese, but there were Hokkaran generals represented, too. General Kazekawa's failed siege of the Ruby Palace, for instance, and General Nozawa's later successful one.

Hours we spent discussing these maps, until I could tell you with certainty what was on Chen Luoyi's mind at any given moment of his life. Xianese revered generals the way Hokkarans revered duelists, the way Qorin revered great hunters and warlords. The stories of them were endless—and Xianyu seemed *almost* happy whenever she discussed them.

Baozhai's next letter reached me at Kimoya. It had been only two weeks since the last one, but reading it after Arakawa was akin to reading it from another world. I read it only after Xianyu had departed for the night—these letters were the last private thing I had. I could not risk any of the others thinking me weak, or girlish; they must see me only in solemn spirits or bright. Despair and longing had no place in a general's heart.

They threw coals at you? Lady, you must take greater care! To know that you are assailed in such a way—did you strike them down?

I'd forgotten about the coals, about Kunomi Village.

There was more, of course, long since faded. More of the courtroom gossip. Their plum trees were now in bloom. She'd drawn one on the corner of the page. I ran my fingers over it in the lanternlight and hoped I might see them again.

To see a plum blossom in the winter—is there anything more trite, my love? Is there a path more well trod by poets than this? And yet this simple thing, this obvious thing, reminded me that I was not alone in the winter. It reminded me of a time when what colors to wear mattered more to me than which formations were employed by whom at what battle. A time when I was with you, and with Baozhai; a time when the flowers fell so soft to the ground that to hear them was to hear Heaven itself.

I wept.

It was the first time I wept since Arakawa. That I remember. I remember, too, how hot my tears felt as they rolled down my cheeks. The salt of them. The way my eyes stung . . . What a simple thing it is to weep, what a splendid thing. Every drop that left me carried with it some of the darkness I'd swallowed.

To tell you the truth—I have no idea what I wrote to Baozhai that night. I do not even know if it was legible, for the tears ruined some of the characters as I went and I had no care to fix them. It was less about the words and more about the *feeling* of the thing. Less of a letter and more of a bloodletting. Hokkaran literature places such emphasis on brevity that I'm certain my father would have wept at the sight of that thing.

But my father would have wept to read it, too.

Yet when I was finished, I felt cleansed. As if I'd spent the day in a . . .

They say fire is cleansing.

Let us say that in writing that letter, I burned all my emotions away. All the stories I could not share with the army, all the things I could not tell Xianyu. The things I would have told you, had you been at my side. But if you had been at my side—would any of this have happened to begin with?

I think not. I think you would have known not to go into the forest.

I SENT THE letter off before we left Kimoya. We stayed there only two days, which may surprise you—Kimoya is a city proper, larger than storied Horohama, which is only just to the south of it. Where Horohama is known for its art and culture, Kimoya is known for its artisans. Surely an army would have found whatever reason they could to stay there as long as possible. We had broken weapons and armor, we had horses that needed shoes, we had need of arrows. By all rights, we should have tarried there a month.

But the Fujino army and the Fuyutsuki army had done so already. Each of them fielded twice our number. They'd eaten through Kimoya's already modest stores of grain and rice; they'd bought up all the iron in the city. For an army of foreign farmers, there was little of anything to be had. The only reason we were able to get the horses shod at all was my own insistence: they could refuse a Xianese captain, but they could not refuse the Imperial Niece.

But they did not have to give me everything they had. Nails, for the most part, which we had to melt ourselves into horseshoes or arrowheads. Though we requisitioned all the forges in the city—well, that was not saying much. There were only ten.

No one threw coals at me in Kimoya, but only because there were no coals to spare.

WE MARCHED IN Arrow formation from Kimoya to the Broken Crown Bridge. Through the forests and the mountains we marched, the trees around us twisting into grasping hands, the ground going from good soil to gristle and rock. In the mornings, the sky was ash gray regardless of the weather; in the afternoons, woolen; in the evenings, a thick smoke permeated the air, making it near impossible to see. You might expect that it smelled of burning hair or something likewise awful—it smelled of cedar, instead. Many of the soldiers did not mind the scent, only the way it nipped at your eyes.

The scent was by far the most pleasant thing about the journey. From Kimoya to the bridge is a distance of only three hundred li—three days' journey for us.

And yet every day of that journey, we were assaulted.

The grasping hands of the forest were well suited to concealing attackers, you see, and blackbloods throughout the Empire were bound to travel north toward the Wall. When they arrived at the Kirin and found the bridge to be ruined, they either tried to swim across (and were swallowed by the river), or retreated to the forest instead.

And so every step we took, we were at risk.

The first time they found us, I think, was during the morning of the first day. Third Bell, perhaps. Between my memory and the lying sky, there is no easy way of knowing. As we marched between two hills, Xianyu commanded our pikemen to overlay their weapons, so that we marched like a massive hedgehog down the valley.

Did I think this was a silly precaution at the time? Yes.

Did I listen to Xianyu regardless? Thankfully, yes.

Sure enough, two dozen blackbloods— dog-shaped more than man-shaped—vaulted from the hills and landed on the pikes. Now, this was not the end of them. Their ferocity is a storied thing. Even with spears piercing through their stomachs, they tried to claw their way farther down, tried to eat those upon whose weapons they landed.

Here I feared the army would break, as it had when the serpents attacked. Watching from atop my red, I longed to shout something encouraging, or to command them to stand strong. Something, anything. If I was half as good a shot as you were, I could have fired a bow, at least, but my talent has always lain with the blade. Xianyu commanded us to stay put, regardless.

My fear broke when Xianyu gave her next set of orders. All at once, the pikemen raised their catches, and the archers fired. Like birds, the whistle of those arrows as they soared. Most even landed where they were meant to, piercing through the blackbloods. Evil ink rained on the soldiers—but here, too, Xianyu had been prepared, as all of us now marched as fully covered as possible.

Another shouted order. The pikemen removed their weapons, letting the blackbloods tumble to the ground—the arrows driven farther in by the impact. Then, all at once, they brought their weapons down on the heads of the enemy.

Not long ago we'd have scattered in horror at the sight of these creatures—but now, thanks to Xianyu's leadership, we crushed them. With proper preparation and sufficient numbers, this became no more difficult than hunting a boar. To see the black smears on the arid ground—to know we'd succeeded where last we failed—my heart swelled with pride.

"You can say something now, if you like," she said to me as the last of them died. "You're better suited for speeches."

"Xianese or Hokkaran?" I asked her. I trusted her now to tell me if my accent would do more harm than good.

"Xianese," she said. "Let them know you're trying."

To this I nodded—and then I stood in the saddle. Xianyu looked as if she'd taken a bite of a lemon. I'd no idea why. She asked me to grandstand. What better way than this? Besides, I was perfectly safe. You were the one who taught me to stand in the saddle. I could not stand on one hand the way you could—but I knew a little of trick riding, too.

"Our nighttime fears tremble in the face of the dawn," I said. "Look on these creatures and remember it was your hand that slew them. When next you feel terror's grasp around your throat— remember this, and stand tall, for you ride with the Dawn."

I had no idea what I was going to say until the moment I started speaking—but this felt like the right thing to say. Certainly the army seemed to take heed of it. When next we were attacked—only a Bell later, by only eight—the pikemen did not falter.

Nor did I.

When we began to set up camp that night, I said to Xianyu that we should change the arrangements. Normally we slept in a square, with rotating guards at each of the corners and my own tent the farthest in. I argued for a broken circle instead.

"Explain yourself, General," she said. She said it with no malice, only expectation. I suspect she hoped her lessons were settling in at last.

"We're going to be attacked again," I said. "It's folly to assume otherwise. Broken Circle is better suited to dealing with expected threats. All the blackbloods we've seen today have acted irrationally; there can't be a demon nearby giving them instruction. Even better for Broken Circle—they will charge into the wedge, for they will see the fire there and assume our force is smaller than it really is. Then we simply collapse in on them. Is that what you wanted to hear, Lai-zur?"

She did not smile, because Lai Xianyu never did. But she nodded in a way that might have been a smile to anyone else. "Very well," she said. "I'll send out the orders."

And so it was done. In truth, Shefali, I thought of Broken Circle not because of the lessons I'd taken with Xianyu, but because of hunting trips with the Qorin. It was hardly a formation with only seven riders—but that was the shape your people often used all the same. And the blackbloods we'd seen to that point were little more than animals.

Horrible animals, to be certain, but animals all the same. Dogs and stags with once-human features; great birds with teeth in their hungry mouths. To see them—oh, it churned my stomach. To know that they had once been human!

This, more than their might, was what disturbed the men. I began to hope that whatever attacked us would look as inhuman as possible. Creatures with four mouths and two heads, walking on all six misshapen legs. I wished for fur. I wished for scales. I wished for anything but human skin stretched so thin you could see through it in places, anything but eyes that could have belonged to a cousin or a friend or a lover.

My prayers were not answered that night. The blackbloods that found us then were akin to spiders, with their human heads in the center and eight creeping limbs spiraling around them. They were not large—perhaps the size of a cat—but there were plenty of them. Fifty, at least, launching themselves into the air like grotesque fleas.

The sight of them was so upsetting that a few of the soldiers were overcome. We lost five in the night. I came for them in the morning and offered them my small mercy.

For the whole of our journey, it was like this—attacks every few hours from animalistic blackbloods. Had the other armies really marched through here? I wondered. For if they had, they hadn't done any work at all clearing out the enemy. Worse was the idea that they *had* been attacked—that they'd seen still more of the enemy than we had, and we were dealing only with the remainders.

Every single blackblood we killed had once been a person, after all. We'd seen hundreds by the third day at least.

How many had fallen to this plague?

I thought of your people—of the empty gers some set up in remembrance of those you had lost. The stories people your mother's age told, which always involved cousins and siblings who no longer rode on the steppes. The paranoia whenever someone so much as sneezed.

How many of these blackbloods had once been Qorin? More than had been Hokkaran.

I began to think of this, too, as a mercy. We could not leave their bodies out for the birds—but I could say a few words to myself whenever we threw them on the pyres. I could hope that there were horses wherever their souls were going.

We reached the remains of Broken Crown Bridge at the end of our third day of marching from Kimoya. It was a longer march than usual—we saw the fires of camps up ahead, like lanterns in the smoke, and decided it best to try to meet with the others before setting up camp. When we did . . .

It was as if I'd spent five years of my life toiling away on a painting of peach blossoms, only to present it in the summer, when everyone is presenting paintings on peach blossoms and theirs were all much nicer. Peach blossoms in the hair of a beautiful woman; peach blossoms painted on robes; peach blossoms on the corpse of a fallen warrior. All these things and more—each one finer than my simple painting of a branch.

So it was with the other armies. After the incident in Arakawa, we'd spent so much time working to improve ourselves, and we had suceeded, but the moment we arrived, it was clear the others would never respect us. Our armor was cobbled together from Bronze Army castoffs and whatever we could buy on the march north—while they wore gleaming steel. Where we had spears and rattan bows, they had glaives and fine yew. Even our uniforms—stained as they were from Arakawa—paled in comparison to theirs. Brilliant Fuyutsuki Violet, Shiratori Blue so deep and soft, it was a dream of the sea— what was our dull green and worn violet to all of that?

I rode at the head of the army as we approached the camp, donned my Imperial Gold to shine bright. A makeshift wall separated the great camp from the rest of the forest, the gate wide enough for twenty to march through abreast. Eight guards were posted, two every five shoulderbreadths, when four would have done. On either side of the gates rose lookout towers. It was the lookouts who first spotted us coming. I motioned for our flags to be held high. That morning I'd unfurled our last clean flag for the first time—I wanted it to be clear who was approaching, and I wanted it to be clear that I was proud of those with whom I marched.

Yet when the lookouts saw our banner, when we approached them, they had only just barely stifled their laughter. The sight of it stoked the fury in my heart.

And so I sharply addressed them. "You, who stand guard at the bridge—you who have eaten your fill at Kimoya, you who wear unblemished armor—what right do you have to laugh at me and mine?"

Nervous glances between two of them—but the other six bowed. The two who remained wore the dark blue and verdant green of Shiratori Province.

Long has Shiratori vexed my family's throne, Shefali. Since the raising of the Wall, in fact. In the old days, all the foreign ships would land at Iwa, and trade would flow downward from there. When the Traitor seized those lands for his own and the Wall went up— Nishikomi's port became the gateway to the Empire. If you sailed any farther south, you'd have the Father's Teeth to contend with, and if you sailed any farther north, well, many ships that tried to skirt the Traitor's Lands failed to reach their destinations.

Thus, Nishikomi's ports are the lifeblood of the northern Empire. Without their trade coming in from foreign lands—without our trade *leaving* for foreign lands—we'd be beggars. And so the lords of Shiratori have continually reminded us of this for *generations*. My uncle won a brief peace only by lowering their taxes: a boon to Shiratori and an intolerable cruelty for the rest of the Empire, who now had to try to make up the difference.

As soon as I ascended the throne, I was going to undo this. I'd not told anyone, of course, but I think Shiratori Ryuji knew all the same that his days of wealth were numbered.

So I should not have been surprised that his guards gave me such a difficult time. He'd likely told them how much better off the Empire would be if some mishap came upon me. What would the Empire do then? Well, Shiratori's son Ryusei was such a strapping young man, and so well educated, perhaps something could be arranged. . . .

"What right have you to wear a phoenix?" one of them shot back at me.

"More right than your lord does to wear a dragon," I said. The trick with people like this was not to indulge them. They want to enrage you, and oftentimes they do—but you must not let them have that power over you. I kept my tone firm and confident—but I was careful not to sound too angry. "I would invite him to meet me on the field if it truly causes him undue distress, but I know he is not here. Nor is his son."

I did not know this. I did not, in any way, know this. This was at best a guess and at worst a brazen mistake. Yet I spoke it all the same, for I knew Shiratori Ryuji, and I knew Shiratori Ryusei. Neither of them was a warrior.

The guard's pained swallow told me I was right.

"Think well where your allegiance lies. What worth is it to throw your life away for a man who will not even ride with you?" I continued.

The guard bowed. "Eight apologies. Proceed if you will, O-Shizuka-shon. Will you be in need of a crier?"

"No," I said, "but if you're in need of a better leader, you know where you may find us."

I did not want him to join us, you understand, but at times you must say things like this to remind people of their place. To question the Imperial Niece!

Granted—he was right. Wearing the phoenix was staking my claim on a throne that I had not yet inherited. And to wear it in spite of what happened at Arakawa—what sort of Empress was I then? What sort of god, either?

Yet he knew nothing of the struggles we'd undertaken just to reach the bridge, and thus he had no right to comment on them, however right he might have been.

That was what I told myself as we advanced through the gates.

"Well handled," Xianyu said as we crossed the gates. I thought I had misheard her.

"Truly?" I said. "You hate the princess, do you not?"

"Without her, we'd be camped outside, I imagine," she said. "I do not hate her tonight."

As much as I hated to think of it—she was right.

The lodgings we were given were not much better than they would have been outside, mind. The Shiseiki army had constructed barracks for their own army, and barracks for the others, but by the time we arrived, there was little room left. All eight thousand of us had to fit in the two remaining barracks. The dustiest barracks, the ones crawling with insects and rats. For beds we had little more than a single piece of cloth and a bundle of hay. The walls were so thin that a strong breeze sometimes made them wobble—these foundations were far from proper.

But it was what we had, and so we slept there. For that night, at least. In the morning, I was going to have a word with the others. Daishi was with the Fuyutsuki army—as much as I was excited for a friendly face, I knew she wouldn't be in charge there. Fuyutsuki-tun likely wouldn't, either—perhaps he was in a situation similar to my own, where someone handed him orders. Somewhere around here was Uemura Kaito, likely surrounded by women who wanted to bask in his presence. I wasn't looking forward to dealing with him—I had the feeling he'd take the news of my marriage as a personal affront, and I did not wish to have to explain to him how serious I'd been in the Bronze Palace all those years ago.

And so in the whole of the army, I knew perhaps five Hokkarans.

How strange that seemed. All these people knew me. At times they knew details of my life that even I had forgotten. Anyone five years older than me likely remembered where they were when the news of my birth reached them, even, and so they had known me from my very first moments.

But in this crowd of fifty thousand, I knew only five.

Is that the lot of an Empress, Shefali? Or have I erred somewhere along the way?

IN THE MORNING, I donned my armor. I had it in my head that I was going to find the generals of each of the other corps and . . . Duel them? Talk to them? I wasn't certain, to be honest, and how they treated me would be the deciding factor. Either way—my army needed better accommodations. We deserved barracks at least as nice as everyone else's.

So I went, armored, my mask and helmet under my arm. Through the winding streets of this makeshift city I wandered. Through seas of Shiratori Blue, through fields of Oshiro Tan, through the crushed-fruit red of Dao Doan, through the impossible violet of Fuyutsuki, I went. As I passed, those who noticed me bowed, and those who did not were made to bow. Was I a scythe cutting wheat, then, and not a woman?

But it was when I saw the Imperial banner that I knew I'd come to the right place. There, in the rough center of this camp, stood a barracks finer than any of the rest—one with a tiled roof instead of thatch. How they'd found the time and money to tile it, I had no idea. Perhaps it had been here before—its foundations looked solid enough, and it had the air of oldness some buildings come by with the years. A talented artisan had engraved the door with twin dragons. Outside were posted two of the Dragon Guard, who, when they saw my mask, looked as if they'd swallowed eggs.

I did not bother announcing myself. I did not stop to speak to them. Why should I? It was not as if they could stop me. Besides, if I allowed them the opportunity, they'd warn my childhood companion Uemura that I was coming, and I wanted to catch him unaware.

I made certain to take off my boots before entering. As angry as I was, I'm not a monster.

Uemura, my uncle's Champion, was indeed within the barracks. He and six others sat around a war table larger than any I'd seen before, decorated all over with flags and string. A serving boy had just set down a teapot and the appropriate number of cups; when he saw me, he leaped backwards and ran to another room. To his credit—

the others were afraid of me, too, and they were scarcely better at hiding it.

With one exception.

Daishi Akiko was with them, and she grinned from ear to ear.

"O-Shizuka-shon," she said, bowing from the shoulder. "How nice it is to see a familiar face."

"Nice to see you're in a joking mood," I said. "Family finds you in the most unfamiliar places."

Now it was I who was surprised. Daishi was leading the Fuyut-suki army? For there was no mistaking the chrysanthemum crest on her armor, the crest borne by the six others in the room. She hadn't been wearing it when I last saw her.

I returned her bow as I scanned the room. Uemura sat in the center, looking dreadfully uncomfortable in his armor. Gray had crept into his sideburns; new wrinkles winged his eyes. It had been a long two years for him.

Uemura bowed. He was smiling, too, but it was a polite smile at best. He gestured to an empty space before the table. "An honor, as always, to be in your presence, O-Shizuka-shon. Will you join us for tea?"

I did not want to stay for tea. In no way did I want to share a cup.

But if I refused a cup of tea, my father might materialize from the ether to express his disappointment in me. And so I sat, and I felt guilty for thinking of how nice it was that they had proper bamboo mats here.

"You have met Daishi-zul already," said Uemura. "It is my eternal pleasure to introduce to you Jeon Siyun, bravely representing her mother's province; Doan Taichi, middle son of Doan Jiro; Kasuri Jun, serving at the behest of Shiratori Ryuji; lastly, we have Shiseiki Haru, on whose land we now tread."

I did not need the introductions when the names materialized in gold near their bearers. All the same, I indulged him.

Jeon Siyun wore plate, a bow at her back and a quiver on the mats next to her. You may wonder how she was allowed to keep her weapons indoors. If you had seen her face, you would not be wondering: she had the sort of beauty that is near infuriating to witness in person. If you switched her plate for eight robes, she'd look every bit the proper court lady—but there was a hardness to her eyes that told me she preferred to be far from Fujino.

Doan Taichi resembled his father, as most of his brothers did. I'd never met him personally, but I'd met each of his six brothers. Why had Doan-tul sent such a young man? For he was younger than I was, and I knew the eldest Doan son, Masaharu, was more than capable on the field. I worried for him, though we'd not said a word to each other.

Kasuri Jun wore the clothes of a woman twice her age. Antique robes painted with antique patterns peeked out from beneath her lamellar armor. Shiratori's general was well appointed—her armor was studded with gems, and two large emeralds adorned her ears. From the twitch of her lips, she'd never met an Imperial before—Daishi excepted. My eyes are occasionally off-putting to some people. Or was she staring at my scar?

Shiseiki Haru was a curiosity to me, for I had never before heard of Shiseiki Takumi's having a daughter. There she sat before me, heedless of her impossibility. Of an age with Daishi and Uemura, she wore her bangs in the court style. That meant she'd had to cut her hair before departing. Curious, I glanced at her hands, and found them uncallused. Strange and stranger still.

After an excruciating round of exchanged pleasantries, during which I learned little of these newcomers, I at last finished my tea. Now I could truly speak my mind.

"Uemura-zul, thank you for your tea," I began, for to begin in any other way would've roused my ancestors. Only when he nodded in thanks for my thanks did I continue. "I shall not waste your time, nor the time of these honored generals. I come here today on behalf of the Xianese army, and I ask you, Uemura-zul—have you seen our barracks?"

"I have," he responded. "They are not our finest, regrettably. It seems all the time they stood empty has allowed the rats to find their way in. My apologies and those of Fujino—with luck, you've gotten enough rest to speak to the river today."

All the time they stood empty! As if we were cavalry and not infantry. As if we were told to arrive by a specific date! They wanted me to do a god's work, but they would not even treat my army as people.

"If I may," said Doan Taichi. "We of Dao Doan would be happy to clean your barracks out, O-Shizuka-shon. It is the least we can do to thank you for your assistance with the spirit."

Hm. He was the second one to bring up the spirit. I knew well enough what the message there was.

We have a use for you, and we will indulge you only so long as you fulfill it.

I found myself wishing I had more tea.

"Very well," I said. "While I am on my way to the river, then. We thank you for your service, Doan-tul."

"And we for yours," he responded.

We'd be stuck thanking each other all day if I did not forge ahead. "Where is this spirit, then?" I said. "Is there a temple nearby?"

Best to be over with this godly nonsense. Perhaps then they'd respect us. As if we hadn't already bled for Hokkaro . . .

It was Shiseiki Haru who answered me, to no one's surprise. "Five li away," she responded. Her voice was as delicate as a priestess's. "We of Shiseiki would be happy to accompany you."

That phrase was getting to be a chant. After so much time spent speaking Xianese with my army, I'd forgotten just how long-winded Hokkaran could be, how mired in its own etiquette.

"If you would be so kind, Shiseiki-tul, then Heaven would thank you," I said. "It is best we settle this matter as soon as possible. I understand we shall be building the bridge anew, once the spirit is placated?"

Uemura nodded. "Jeon-tul has brought with her a company of engineers. Surrounded as we are by Shiseiki timber, it should be a simple enough thing to reconstruct it."

Shiseiki Haru shifted at this. It had been her father's idea to destroy the bridge, after all. How did she feel about seeing it rebuilt?

"And the enemy?" I asked. I tried to keep my tone level. "We encountered a demon on our way here, and blackbloods besides. These fortifications you've built—how sound are they?"

"Secure enough, your Imperial Highness," said Shiratori's general. She did not have the drawl so many of her countrymen shared. "You encountered my soldiers when you entered last night—as you no doubt saw, they are well armed and well trained."

"We found them lacking," I said without looking at her. "Uemura-zul, I ask you again—what of the enemy? How often do they attack? There are villages in this area—have we sent patrols?"

It took him a moment to answer. I could hear Kasuri simmering with anger all the while, and this simmering buoyed my spirits.

"With your profoundest pardon, O-Shizuka-shon, I must beg your haste. The river grows angrier each passing day. We cannot begin to think of the enemy until it has been soothed."

More likely he wanted to discuss the enemy without me present. Without my army present. We were not needed, it seemed; they had everything *perfectly* under control. At last others were listening to me when I said I was a god—but even this they used against me. Divine though I may be, I was only a puppet as far as they were concerned.

A tool. Once their bridge was complete, we'd simply saunter over it and through the Wall, and there would be the Traitor waiting for us with tea and cakes. I'd have nothing to do with killing him, because I could not be trusted to.

To snap at him would have been to prove my uncle's assessment of me true. I took a heartbeat to compose myself. "How *foolish* of us, Uemura-zun. It is only—we thought a man of your renown would relish the opportunity to discuss his victories. We see now that we were mistaken. Shiseiki-tul, we shall be waiting for you outside, whenever you are prepared."

I rose then, bowed, and departed. If they wanted me to speak to this spirit so badly, then who was I to disappoint them? To disappoint a *nation*?

BUT I WAS through doing these things alone. I called for a camp messenger and sent word to Xianyu that I'd need a unit of eight to accompany me to the temple. Shiseiki Haku emerged from the barracks not long after. She, too, summoned a unit of eight.

"Sixteen warriors between us," she said as we gathered our forces. "Does this make you nostalgic, your Imperial Highness?"

She meant nothing ill by it. Now that I was next to her, I saw that we were of an age. In all likelihood, she'd grown up hearing stories of my mother, and we were near the Wall. I hadn't yet mustered the strength to look over the river, in case I caught a glimpse of it in its sorry state.

"You have miscounted," I said. "You and I make eighteen."

"A fine number," she said, and I knew then that we could never truly get along. "Although in truth, I am no warrior."

It was obvious from the difficulty she had walking in her armor—

but I did not say as much out loud. "You are here, and that serves well enough," I said.

We set off, then, the eighteen of us. Along the way, Haku explained her presence: she was the wife of Shiseiki Sora, who had perished only two months ago in an attack. This explained why I had never heard of her—they'd married while I was traveling with you. Shiseiki Sora I had met only once or twice, never enough to truly form an opinion, but enough that I did not hate him. That he had passed—and that the news had not yet been made public—meant things were worse than Uemura was letting on.

I HESITATE TO call the walk to the temple of the river goddess a march, as compared to the journey north, it was a sprightly little sojourn. The temple stood atop a hill surrounded by pine trees, with the gates and the doorway facing east. In better times, the sun would light it up each morning, lending an otherworldly air to the whole structure. Now the shadows clung to whatever surfaces they could find. On either side of the gates were marble statues of the Mother and Sister—strange choices so near a body of water. One would think the Father would make an appearance—but perhaps the Mother was well suited to a place where so many drowned.

There were only two acolytes present when we visited. One was outside sweeping, of all things, as if the only thing keeping the temple from its former glory was a thin layer of dust. The other—an older woman the size and shape of millet-sack—stood within the walls of the shrine itself. When she saw us, she hurried over and made her introductions.

"You are Her Imperial Highness, aren't you?" she said to me. "How long we've waited! Come, come."

I shared a long glance with Haku. The shrine here was tiny. There'd be enough room for only the woman and myself. What if she . . .

What foolishness it was, to assume the worst of an old woman!

I found my steel and followed her to the shrine. The moment I stepped foot inside, I made note to speak to Kenshiro of it later—the eons lent the air here a bittersweet scent, like almonds. On either side of me were shells, hundreds of them, their surfaces painted with flowers or poems or well-wishes. I had to be conscious of them with every move I made, for my elbows nearly brushed up against them, and something within me balked at defacing a shrine.

(You're laughing. I, with all my blasphemy, showing that sort of concern. What am I to say, Shefali? It felt like walking into someone's home and spilling plum wine all over their altar.)

The centerpiece of the shrine was a well, simply but artfully built, each block perfectly smooth, the joints of it like intertwined fingers. Over it was an eightfold thread of gold, red, and white—and around it was a waist-high fence.

"Pay no attention to that," said the old woman. "The fence is for mortals only!"

I wrinkled my nose at this. Was she mocking me?

"Oh, don't make such a face," she said. "You're safe here. So long as you do not displease Her, at any rate, but I doubt you will. She's friendly with her fellows."

She gestured for me to cross over the fence and I did, though it took me a bit of a hop. I wished that you were there to help me over.

I APPROACHED THE well. The water within was nothing like the water of the river, which to my eye looked a dingy gray. This was the blue-green of summer. Refracted within it were a hundred suns, shimmering and splendid. To empty one's mind is oftentimes difficult—but when faced with such natural beauty, it is reflex. Every ripple of the water smoothed something in my soul, until only a floating calmness remained.

The old woman watched with a serene smile. "Go on, then," she said. "If you want to speak to Her, you've got to dip your head in."

That this would be a prime assassination opportunity did not occur to me. The water, as I said, calmed me. You do not think of spending a night in the hunting grounds as dangerous until the tiger shows up. Or at least I didn't.

And so when this kind woman said "stick your head into that well," I did.

The water was as cool as it was calming, so cool that it sent shivers up my spine. For long moments, I held my breath and kept my eyes shut. That is what one does, after all, underwater—but soon the will to do even this left me. Against my better judgment, I opened my eyes and saw her.

Much is made of spirits in Hokkaran folklore. Much is made of the minor gods. You cannot cross a forest or a river or even a strangely shaped hill without encountering a shrine for the god that dwells within it. For most of my life, I paid these shrines no heed, as I had encountered no gods save you and me. The stories had never even interested me.

Thus, I was unprepared for the woman before me. For her hair like the reeds of a river, floating upward in this eternal blue; for her frog's-egg eyes. Rippling foam formed her robes, which floated like her hair; an impossibly long fish spine was her divine mantle. Blue her eyes, blue as a maiden's sorrow; blue her mouth, blue as the cry of the dying; blue her skin, blue as a weeping sky.

For one precious, eternal moment, she was more beautiful than the first day of spring.

There could be no doubt that she was divine—and when she spoke, there could be no doubt of her wrath. The calming waters soon plunged from blue-gold to deepest black. So, too, did her eyes change from their former human shape to glowing yellow spheres. Her mouth opened and opened, her teeth like needles puncturing through her gums—until, just as suddenly as it had begun, it was all over. There she floated before me in her near-human shape.

"At last you have come! I knew you when you were a child, O Dawn, and now look how you have come to me. Cloaked in Gold, cloaked in the feathers of the firebird, you have come to me! And for what? To beg for passage! You come to ask this of me without paying proper tribute. You ask this in spite of your army, your *people*, filling me with filth by the day. How bold you come to me, O Dawn, how commanding! But you forget that I am as divine as you, and older still. You *will* pay me tribute, or you will not cross. Am I making myself clear?"

In horror at her changing forms, I listened to this, and I wondered distantly what the old woman could possibly have meant by her being friendly. If this was a friendly spirit, then the serpent I'd met was an old lover.

"Is that any way to greet an equal?" I said. Bubbles rose from my mouth, but I could speak and hear. I decided that if I stopped to think about how any of this worked, I'd drown. "The Dawn bows only to Dusk, Mizuha, and you are no Dusk. Let us speak on equal terms: payment, and not demands."

The water around us darkened for a moment—but it passed with little fright. She lay one hand in the crook of her elbow, and the other by her lips. "If we are to speak on equal terms, O Dawn, then you must answer for what your people have done to me."

"My people are not your true enemy," I said, which I hoped was not entirely a lie. "For centuries, we left you in relative peace—for centuries we have honored this shrine and its god. You know as well as I do that it is the Fourth's influence that has polluted you. Were it not for his monstrosities terrorizing our villages, we would not have had to destroy the bridge."

She floated closer to me. For it to have been swimming, she would have to have moved, and she did not—only disappeared and reappeared right in front of me. I saw now that there were scales flecking her skin, iridescent in the golden light of the water.

I saw now the disgust in her eyes.

"Are you so naïve, O Dawn, that you truly believe in the mortals? When you march across the bridge with your toy army, the Octopus King will come for you. What will you do then? For I have met him, and I know well the sharpness of his blade."

"I will slay him," I said, for the arrogant girl within me at times got ahold of my mouth. "I swear to you that. I swear, too, that no more blood will stain the river."

Her lips parted. A low growl left her, and I saw again her teeth like needles. She raised her hands and I thought for a moment that she might strangle me.

"Do not promise what you cannot give," she hissed. Bubbles rose up around her; she jabbed a talon into my shoulder. "That is how this works between gods. If you make this oath and a *single drop* of blood enters my domain—"

"It won't," I said. I was so confident then. "I give you my word. I will slay him, and I will do it without polluting you any further."

The river laughed. It was not a normal laugh, full of mirth—it was a twisted and wretched thing. As she threw back her head, the waters around her went black for a second, her talons grew longer, her teeth grew and grew . . .

I swallowed.

She is kind to her fellows, the old woman said, but I was beginning to fear for my life.

Just as I started to back away, she raked one long talon down my cheek.

Out of instinct, I recoiled from her clammy grasp—but she held me by the hair. Terror took me then, for I wanted to leave and could not. I tried to kick my legs, but I could no longer feel them moving in the real world. In fear, I opened my mouth to suck in a breath. Instead I only swallowed more of that foul water; instead it flooded my nostrils and lungs and I could not breathe, Shefali, I could not breathe.

"I will have more than your word, O Dawn," she said. "I will have your tears."

I drew back my head to try to headbutt her—a trick that you had taught me after Dorbentei flung me one too many times in the wrestling ring. Perhaps she, too, had a Qorin teacher—she jerked back at the last moment. A cruel smile twisted her lips.

"Swear to me," she said. "Swear to me that you will slay any who pollute me—even a drop. Swear to me that I shall have your tears. Only then can you cross, O Dawn, only then."

Darker the water, darker, darker, like the mouth of the serpent where I lay bleeding—

Bright her eyes, bright as the coals flung at me by my own people—

Would it be a bad thing to lose my tears? For then I could no longer cry over you, then I could no longer spend my nights weeping, wondering where you had gone and why you had not yet written to me—

Tears and a vow.

I'd given those freely before.

"All right!" I said. "You may have the oath, you may have my tears!"

At that moment, she drove her nails into the corners of my eyes.

Water flowed into my mouth for the second time during that vision—I felt it flowing down my throat and into my stomach, felt the gold spreading within me. Just before she shoved me out of the well, I saw her holding two pearls.

Haggard, horrified, I stumbled backwards from the well. My hands flew to my face, to the wounds she'd left near my eyes—but there was nothing there. My skin was dry, besides. For long moments, I stood trying to catch my breath.

I wanted to scream. I wanted to crumple into a ball. I wanted to go somewhere far away from here, where I would never again have to lay eyes on the Kirin River. I wanted to weep.

But the Empress of Hokkaro must be as steadfast as the Kyuuzen Mountains; she cannot scream, or crumple, or run away.

And when, within the confines of my own rooms, I tried to weep—the tears never came.

Do Not Let Them See Your Fear

When I hear myself speak, it seems preposterous. Surrendering my tears so that an army could cross a river. What use had a river spirit for my tears, when she had more than enough water? There must be something powerful about the tears of an Empress. What sorrow for her, then, for I shed more tears in the days after your departure than I had at nearly any other time in my life. She'd missed out on most of them.

But not all.

We are so near to the thing now. The tiger lurking in the mists of my memory. Already, its mouth is slick with my blood; already, it has laid claim to me. For years, it has been following me, taking bites of me when it can. When I close my eyes, it is there, watching, watching.

Together we slew a tiger when we were children. Will we slay this one? I think not—some part of me lives in its stomach now. To kill it would be to kill that part of myself, as well.

But so much of me has already died.

You will think to yourself that I am speaking in circles, that I am avoiding the rest of the story. Surely by now you have heard the name of it. Ink-on-Water, my greatest triumph, my greatest sorrow.

Here is the truth: I am slowing now because there is precious little I remember between speaking to Mizuha and Ink-on-Water. In my mind, it is a story I've heard only once, a thing that happened to someone else that so transfixed me that for a time, I lost myself within it. The woman who crossed the Wall was not me. The woman who came back . . .

I wonder, at times, if I am still Minami Shizuka. Whenever I do, I hold the Daybreak Blade in my hand, and its warmth assures me I am the trueblooded heir to that family line.

It does nothing to assure me that what I did was right. But then again—what will?

My love, my dearest Shefali, I doubt that even you will say I did the right thing once you have heard the whole of it.

Stay with me. Please. I tremble to speak of any of this at all. Hold me?

The . . . the bridge. I suppose I should tell you of the bridge. When I returned from the temple, shaken as I was, it was Jeon Siyun who met me. Uemura had not been lying when he said she had an entire company of engineers—I saw them at the edge of the murky water, taking their measurements with instruments beyond my understanding.

"Your Imperial Highness, you have returned! You were able to talk sense into that spirit, were you not?"

Talk sense into the spirit. I remember this because it rankled me to hear such phrasing only moments after that ordeal.

"Heaven bows to no one," is what I said instead of reprimanding her. I did not have the strength to argue—and I had to project confidence, besides. "You may begin construction, Jeon-tul."

And so she did, with a deep bow and a promise for drinks later that evening. In honor of what I'd done, she said, as if I'd done anything worth celebrating at all.

I drank with her. I drank with her, and with Daishi, and with all the others. Every evening was spent in this way, Shefali, every single one—no matter what happened in the mornings. Ten giants could fling themselves at the camp, and after I had slain them, I would ask where we were drinking that night. Most often it was with Daishi or my own army—but Jeon-tul's army brought with them Two-Blessing Wine, and often enticed me away. Gathered around the fire, we spoke of everything under the sun, everything that came to our minds—everything save the enemy.

Everything save the enemy, and you.

For they would not discuss you here, not as my army had, not with Uemura prowling through the camp like a cat tracking its prey. Kasuri-yun had the temerity to ask why I wore my hair bound at all. Was I not unmarried? Was I not still a virginal young woman? Oh, she did not say "virginal," but it was there, lurking behind notions of purity, notions of youth.

UEMURA NEVER ANSWERED my questions. I had to discover the answers myself, and to do so was no easy task. The other generals were friendly enough with me—but none gave me any details on the campaign itself. When had Shiseiki-zul passed? Why? Was he not within the walls at the time? How often were we attacked? For I noticed on the third day how many memorial markers there were in each of the army's camps. Hadn't they each fielded ten thousand? The markers numbered a third of that, at least. How many had fallen to the river, and how many to the enemy?

How many now lurked in the forests, waiting for us?

In this, Daishi and Haku were my salvation. Neither had prepared for the position they now occupied—Daishi had risen to general only when a giant demon bit into Fuyutsuki-tun like a shoot of bamboo, as it happened. It surprised me how bad I felt for the man who had so insulted me. No tears came, of course, but I poured a drink on the fire in his honor all the same.

HERE WAS THE truth of the matter: this makeshift city was only a month old. Uemura had come up with the idea. Prior to this, they'd sent patrols along all the minor and major roads of Shiseiki, with the aim to cut down the enemy wherever they found them. For a while, this had been successful. To hear Daishi tell it, they slew a thousand of the enemy in the first month—this I did not believe, but accepted as an exaggeration of the real number.

The turning point had come at a small village named Rihima— one that I'd not heard of prior to this. Shiseiki-zul and his army, along with Fuyutsuki-zul and *his* army, were patrolling the road between Rihima and Kimoya. As they approached the village, the smoke grew thicker and thicker around them, until to try to see through it was like trying to see through stone. This despite it being the middle of the day.

Fuyutsuki called for lanterns—and that was his grave mistake. The moment they were lit, the army saw the enemy: grotesque human shapes mounted on puppet frames, unseen strings guiding them. Human heads impaled upon them, tongues like rope lolling from razor-lined mouths. Hundreds of these creatures had now surrounded them.

And now that there was light—the creatures struck.

Like hunters casting out nets, their tongues shot out toward the army. Whoever was caught by them was soon yanked back toward the puppet, so quick that there was no time to save them. The creatures' mouths opened wide enough to swallow every bit of the victim, except for the head.

The head they left untouched.

The head they reanimated.

Daishi survived this only because she broke rank. As soon as she saw their shadows, she abandoned the rest of the army—and she urged Fuyutsuki-zul to join her. He did, only for the two of them to encounter a giant farther into the mist—a giant that plucked Fuyutsuki right from his horse and bit into him.

Daishi fought the giant. She was careful to tell me this. Giants were not uncommon in that forest, and so a method for dealing with them had already been devised—cavalry ran between its legs with rope. When it inevitably fell over, the infantry would rush forward and behead it. Without a way to know the thing's name, it was a temporary solution, at best, but not an ineffective one.

She was lying, of course, but I accepted it all the same. If that was what she needed to tell herself to sleep at night—well. She was my cousin, and I wished her well. That no one had told Uemura the truth of the matter spoke to the horror of the incident; to escape alive was better than to stay for honor and die, no matter what centuries of Hokkaran folklore told you.

Nearly all the Shiseiki army had perished at Rihima. Of the Fuyutsuki army, only Daishi's unit was unscathed; they'd lost several thousand of the others. Thus to name Haku and Daishi generals was akin to naming them the mayors of empty towns.

After Rihima, Uemura declared that none of the armies would make any further patrols.

Which meant that the villages of Shiseiki would be unprotected from the dangers lurking within the forest.

Haku had been furious with him for this, but there was little she could do. The province was hers only by chance; she was neither warrior nor diplomat. She may well have been screaming at the Wall of Stone, for all the good it did her. Uemura and Kasuri told her that she must think of the army, and not simply of her province; that she must think of the body's survival now that one of its hands was gone.

And so she came to me with this request.

YOU KNOW WELL the sort of woman I am, Shefali. As horrified as I was by the darkness, as much as I wanted never again to be near a demon——I agreed to help. It was the right thing to do. It was the only thing to do, if I was to consider myself a ruler, a god.

Daishi volunteered to accompany me with her unit—but I saw the look in her eyes and knew this for politeness. I turned her down. I thought that I was saving her.

I thought a lot of things in those days.

When Uemura saw my army preparing to leave the makeshift city, he commanded me to stand down. He told me he did this on the authority given to him by my uncle, that it was Heaven's will.

"You, who hear Heaven's words from the mouth of another," I said, "you dare to speak against the woman who hears Heaven directly? Stand down, Uemura-zul, or else let us settle the matter with steel."

He could have dueled me. I would have won, as I had the previous time we crossed swords.

He could have ordered the Dragon Guard to surround us.

He did neither.

There is a good heart buried in the man's chest. He knew well this needed to be done. If I was volunteering to do it, with an army he considered expendable, well—who was he to stop us? So long as we returned in time for the march over the bridge, there would be no real problem.

One month after our arrival in the city, we set forth along the roads of Shiseiki Province.

My own army was so small that I dared not risk them for such an operation as clearing out Rihima—there was no one left in that village. I knew it in my bones. My duty lay with the people who remained, and not with those long gone.

And so we gave Rihima a wide berth, but we slew every black-blood we came across on our patrol.

Two months we spent along the roads. Two months I spent conjuring flowers and fruit in rebellion against the gray. Two months we ate rice and broth and plums, two months we spent painfully aware of every passing moment.

After the first weeks on the road, the fear that had sunk its teeth into us at our arrival to the North diminished with every skirmish. I do not mean to say that we were invincible, for we were not—we lost three hundred in the two months we patrolled—only that we were growing bolder. No longer did I have to ride up and down the line to pick out our scouts: we had volunteers for the job. The only screams I heard were war cries. For two days, it became fashionable to carve out horns and flutes and blow them as we approached. The music improved our morale—but so, too, did it give away our position, and thus I sadly put a stop to the practice.

And not *every* village we visited was in such a state.

We are so near to the beast now that I can hear it breathing. You will forgive me, I hope, if I delay our hunt. In truth, I do not know if I shall have the strength to face the thing when the time comes.

* * *

AND SO WE marched, Shefali; so we found success after reckless success. Having lost three hundred from our company—each loss mourned, each life honored—we circled back along the King's Oath Road to the makeshift city.

Only to find black smoke rising up from the place it had once been.

A cold terror seized my heart—this ashen plume was as wide across as my whole hand, seen from several li away. Such a thing could only be achieved by a great fire—and a great fire meant great losses. The faint shimmer I saw to the air only confirmed it. The reckless young woman in me wanted to charge forward, help those who needed helping—but the general I'd become, weary and wary, knew that might do more harm than good.

And so we sent the remaining scouts. Strict orders we gave them: See what had happened as well as they could, but return within a Bell's time.

Hours we waited for them, Xianyu and myself, huddled in our tent with our captains. Hours we spent in quiet anticipation. When I offered Xianyu a drink to ease her nerves, for the first time she did not refuse me. Of the eight we'd sent, only one returned, streaked in black and soaked through besides, bruise-violet circles visible on his skin.

"They tried for the bridge," he said. When he spoke, he did not look at us—he looked somewhere over our shoulders. Beneath the black and violet, he was sheet pale.

"Who did? The enemy?" said Xianyu.

He shook his head. "The northerners. They finished the bridge, and they tried . . . they tried to cross it . . . General, there were bodies like fallen leaves . . ."

Xianyu embraced him. Never had I seen her make such a gesture—

heedless of the evil ink on him, heedless of the potential danger, she embraced him. He stood a head taller than her and yet he crumpled against her like a babe. Soon he broke out weeping. She patted him as he did. It struck me then—she was old enough and he was young enough that she could have been his mother.

I thought of your mother holding you. I thought of the anguish on her face when she'd exiled you. Were you safe? Had you gone to her after you'd left, had you begged for a place with the clan? But you had not written me, you had not written. . . .

I could not die. Not until I saw your familiar scrawl.

But that city was not going to investigate itself.

While Xianyu comforted the boy, I returned to the other troops. Advancing on a fortified city like this, with little idea what lay beyond the walls—we would need Linked Crescents for this. Chen Luoyi devised it two hundred years ago—I was certain it would meet with Xianyu's approval, since she approved of nearly everything Chen Luoyi had done. I called the formation, and the messengers signaled it down the lines, until one by one my brave farmhands formed two crescents slightly offset from one another. One company of archers led, with another directly behind the last sweep of the crescent, allowing us to get at least a single volley on any of the enemy if they appeared before us.

Xianyu found me after I'd mounted, just as I put on my mask.

"He said it was the Octopus King," she said.

"The river mentioned him," I said, frowning. "A demon, then?"

"From the sound of it," Xianyu said. She, too, pulled on her war mask: a bear. "He says he caught a glimpse of it across the river— a man in old robes, with eight tentacles floating up in the air behind him."

An uncreative name, then, but it was good to know something of him. "And the camp itself? Did he see any survivors?"

Xianyu shook her head. "None, though there may be some over the river. He saw banners and pikemen, but he's not certain . . ."

Did the enemy field banners and pike now? It had to have been our army. That was the only explanation. There was no way that they could have hollowed out the city itself, not with all the soldiers within it.

"We must be certain, even if he is not," I said. Then I squared my shoulders and turned to the ranks. "Xian-Lai!" I called to them. "Remember why we have come: the Emperor has abandoned us. My uncle sits atop his throne without a care in the world for us or the land we now fight to hold. Every blackblood we strike down, every life we save, is a needle beneath his nails. Though the Hokkaran banner now waves atop the Bronze Palace, you have never bowed to the Emperor's will. Fight, and live, and let our triumph herald the return of your nation!"

It was a good thing I'd spent so much time practicing my Xianese— that speech would've gotten the better of me a year ago. I was a little uncertain how they'd receive it. I was, after all, the very symbol of their oppression. It was I who had taken them from their homes and I who led them through the bamboo forest. They had no way of knowing that I meant what I had said—that the moment the throne was mine, I was going to sever the threads.

They had no way of knowing.

But here was what they did know: I'd served with them every step of the way. I bled with them, I ate with them, I slept on the cold earth with them. My uncle had taken me from my home just as he'd taken them, and he'd taken my wife besides.

I had every reason to hate him, and every reason to care for them.

Still—when the cheer broke out, I admit I was relieved. Tension unwound in my chest. In spite of the coming danger, looking on the vanguard, I liked our chances. "We will not bow!" was the answer.

To hear it from their thousands of mouths bolstered my spirits some—and I would take whatever fortifications I could find for the coming battle. The air tasted wrong.

And so we marched on the city. Slowly at first, cautiously. Though the lookout towers lay in ramshackle piles, we paused some distance from them all the same, and called out to any who might yet lurk within. The air tasted wrong.

A quarter hour we waited, but there was no response.

Within the gates, then, after our archers tore it open. Before us a grisly sight: bodies facedown in the dirt, the barracks collapsed in on themselves; a thin layer of water and blood that turned the soil to mud. The storied horses of Fuyutsuki now ran wild around the encampment—they were the wisest of the animals. Dogs and pigs and even chickens feasted on the bodies as we watched, their eyes glowing a faint red. A distinct web of black appeared on their skin and fur.

The bodies, after all—there was no red to be seen save for their uniforms. The pools of blood they lay in were as black as their eyes, as black as the veins at their temples, as black as their tongues.

What had done all this? For there were so *many* bodies that it was difficult to move without treading upon them, and not all bore the same injuries. Here lay a company in Oshiro Tan with arrows jutting from their backs; there, brilliant Doanese Red adorned a hundred corpses with gaping chest wounds. There was no reason to where they lay, no formation, no *sense* to any of it, only death everywhere we looked—

"Sever their heads," I said, "and pray the Mother is kind to them."

And so we went, our boots squelching in the mud, slicing the heads off our former comrades with every step. With every body I approached, my heart sank into my stomach, for I feared I'd find Daishi among them—but I never saw the violet of Fuyutsuki, and that was worse.

For if she was not here among the dead, then where was she?

We'd gotten halfway to the camp when we first caught sight of the river. Gone was the murk, but gone, too, was the gold I'd seen at the temple—this water was clear blue and all the more terrifying for it. No one has been to the bottom of the Kirin—but we that day saw what lay beneath. The bodies were the least of it. If you were to look on a carp pond, you'd see pebbles at the bottom; these bodies were no larger than those pebbles. We recognized them only from their plumed helmets.

It was the depth.

Have you ever been to the top of Gurkhan Khalsar? I know not if your mother permitted you to climb it. If you have, when you reached the summit—did you look directly at your feet? For to do so is to confront height at its most dizzying. When gazing upon the horizon, you may imagine yourself safe—but when gazing at your feet, your whole body longs to jump.

So it was to stand on the edge of the water. So clear was it that you could imagine sinking to the bottom as gently as if you were falling through the clouds. So cool the water! So *inviting*!

At the sight of the river, I felt the tension rise within my ranks. Their throats were as dry as mine. To sip from those waters would surely quench our thirst—but we had to remember why we'd come. How strange that a simple thing like the water could entrance us.

"Keep at the work," I said. "There will be water when we're done."

"And the signal flame?" said Xianyu. Startled, I followed her pointing hand. The river so preoccupied me that I'd forgotten to look at the far shore. Indeed there was a flame there, and indeed there were banners and pikemen surrounding it. When I squinted to get a better look—I saw the banner was violet.

Fuyutsuki Violet.

Just as I raised my hand for the order, Xianyu let out a sharp sound.

"Be certain of what you're doing," she said. "That may be your cousin. It may be this Octopus King we've heard of."

I clenched my jaw. Though I was loath to admit it, she was right. Charging in would do us no favors. "Your recommendation?"

"Clear the camp first," she said. "Whatever's lurking here—we need to be certain we won't be attacked from behind when we cross the bridge."

That we would cross was a foregone conclusion, it seemed.

I set my jaw. In the distance, the banner flapped in the wind. Was that my cousin, riding her dun among the pikemen? I could not see her armor.

"Very well," I said. "We will continue through the camp."

And so it was. We divided our army into two segments, one each for the western and eastern sides of the city. One by one, we searched the barracks as well as we could for any sign of survivors. All of us together were only waiting to exhale.

At the end of an hour, we'd learned little of what happened, and we had not yet found our scouts. We had, however, found the Jeon army and Jeon Siyun, all within their barracks, piled atop one another like discarded game tiles. Doan-tul must have been among his army, for I saw no sign of him, and no sign of Haku, either.

The sun was beginning to hang low in the sky, casting shadows on an already grim view. In the center of the camp, the Fujino barracks had been lit on fire. With no safe way to examine it, we could not know if the army lay within—so Xianyu said.

She was not amused when I dismounted and walked into the building.

Have you ever been in a burning building? The light there is brighter than you can imagine, but only where the smoke has not become overwhelming. The fire itself did not bother me—but the smoke forced me to crawl on my knees. Two breaths of it was enough for a lifetime.

I saw plenty from that low vantage point. The army had indeed been in the barracks during whatever tragedy befell the camps. Little was left of them now—flesh already sizzling, armor glowing white-hot. Still I crawled.

I wanted to know if he was dead, you see.

I liked Uemura only as much as anyone likes a lukewarm meal, but I'd known him for years, since childhood frolics. To leave him to die in this barracks without even confirming he was there—I could not do him that disservice.

It took me ten minutes to find him. He lay in his bed, his armor on its stand less than a horselength away. He slept curled up on his side, like a child, and somehow that made the sight worse: whatever killed him had torn him open at the stomach.

Amidst the flames and the smoke, I sat in the court style, and I watched him burn—this man I'd known since he was an over-confident boy. Within me, I felt a storm of emotion—but to beat my fists against the ground would be more than he deserved. To weep would be proper, but . . . My chest ached. Pressure was welling up from deep inside me, looking for some way to leave, finding none. All I could do was gape and whimper. The tears never came.

All the things I had seen this day, all the bodies of those I once knew, all the death, and there I sat alone with the corpse of an old acquaintance—and I could not cry?

Was I so inhuman? Had I really lost so much of myself, and for what? To cross a bridge that did not need crossing, to fling myself at destiny and hope for the best.

Only when I heard Xianyu calling for me did I abandon these thoughts. I crawled back out of the barracks, and I told her what I had seen.

She narrowed her eyes at me.

"You knew him well, didn't you?" she said.

"I did."

Her brows came together. "A leader must be stoic, I suppose."

I hadn't told her about the river. I hadn't told anyone. Inside my chest was a glass jar about to burst—and I told no one.

"We can use the building for a pyre," I said. "There aren't any of the enemy within. Whatever killed them struck in the night while most of them were sleeping."

"That does not explain our scouts going missing," said Xianyu.

In the distance, the cry of a nightjar. The sound reminded me of my summer nights with you. The last time we'd been in this forest, we slept beneath the stars. You pointed to them, one by one, and told me all their stories. Knowing that the Kharsaqs and Kharsas, the great hunters and runners and wrestlers, watched over me—there was something comforting to it. All of them were in you, after all, and you were in all of them.

Do you remember? I asked you if you thought my mother had a star.

"If she doesn't," you said, "Burqila will craft her one."

We heard the nightjar then as you pulled me close. When you kissed me, I thought to myself that I would craft you the brightest star anyone had ever seen. A star that burned as I burned for you.

All of this was so much—how I longed for the days of our youth.

I hadn't told Xianyu about the river, and the threat I'd felt beneath the surface.

"FUYUTSUKI AND SHIRATORI are yet unaccounted for," continued Xianyu. "The army across the river—that is large enough for Shiratori, I think, but why are they the only ones who made it across?"

I thought for a moment that she was testing me—that this was a tactical quandary she'd already slain. When her pause stretched into a silence, I knew she was as lost as I was.

"Daishi-zur knows the better part of valor," I said. "Perhaps she convinced Kasuri-zul?"

"Perhaps," said Xianyu, and left it at that. "We must cross if we're to find out."

I looked to the bridge. Jeon Siyun had done a fine job reconstructing it. The pathways themselves were mahogany and cherry, lending them a stately look; the posts on either side featured all eight gods, each to a single outward-facing facet. Among her engineers, there must have been artisans: the whole arc of the bridge was decorated with a triumphant army in gilt leaf.

Yet a mist hung around the bridge like a veil over a singing girl, gauzy and pale green. We could not see the peak of its arch.

I looked behind me, at the army, at these farmers and smiths executing their comrades.

I thought of Rihima, and the other villages we'd seen. I thought of Uemura, dying in bed; I thought of Fenglai on his pyre.

My father used to say that poetry came to him from silence—but not just any silence. Only perfect silence would do. The moment between a dew drop's fall and impact; the moment a flower first unfurls; the space between two heartbeats. These things are perfect silences. Within them he heard whispers of the truth.

As a child, I believed every word of this.

As a young woman, I thought it sentimental nonsense.

As a woman grown, as a general—I heard the perfect silence then, and I heard the truth's whisper.

I would cross the Reforged Bridge. I would slay the Octopus King.

And I would rebuild the Wall of Flowers with my own two hands.

How else to keep the Empire safe? How else to prove to the nation that I was the better sovereign?

"Ready the army," I said to Xianyu. "We will put an end to this."

The Flowers You Loved—

My father loved the morning fog. Every day he would rise before the dawn and step out onto the veranda to watch the light filter through it. Often, I was awake, and I would sit on his shoulders. The two of us would watch as the sun painted the world gold.

I used to love the fog, before all this.

The fog covering the Reforged Bridge was not a golden one. It was not the white of early-morning whispers. It was not even the gray that had so often overtaken us in Shiseiki.

It was the pale green of a bamboo forest. It did not billow in the breeze, it did not curve, it did nothing that fog should do. Like a veil it sat there and waited for us to part it.

"No torches," said Xianyu. "You're certain of this?"

"We'll not have another Rihima," I said to her.

The army seemed less certain. When I looked back on them, I saw many struggling to conceal the fear in their eyes, I heard the rattle of their armor and their weapons. Would they hate me for leading them here?

So long as they were alive at the end of this—I could withstand their hatred.

I stood in the saddle again, and seized the banner from Captain Lu. So armed, I faced the army and began to speak.

"Xian-Lai! We march over the Reforged Bridge, to the far banks of the Kirin! We cannot know what awaits us there—but we can know our own hearts. Our heartbeats sing the story of our valor—and with every beat, they become more and more eternal. When at last we cross the bridge once more—we will return to Fujino, and the Empire shall tremble to hear our elegy. This I swear to you, not as the Imperial Niece or General Dog-Ear, but as the Phoenix Empress!"

The cheers that followed were not as strong as they had been in the past—but they were cheers.

I tossed the banner to Captain Lu and sank into the saddle. With my heart pounding like the beat of a drum, with the hairs of my neck standing at attention, with my tongue stuck to the roof of my mouth—I urged my red into the mist.

The air near the sea tastes of salt, the air near a mine tastes of coal—the air within the mist tasted of moss, of mold, of the prickling woods. Thick, it was, so that you felt it sinking into your lungs with every breath; warm, it was, as if you'd emerged from the hot springs. Within the mist, the sounds of the forest fell away—we could not even hear the rush of the river beneath our feet. Only the creaking wood of the bridge, only the falling coins of our armor, only our own haggard breaths.

Up ahead—only more green. No sign of the forest. No sign of the Shiratori army.

My heart stuttered. What if the enemy waited for us on the other side of the bridge? For Chen Luoyi had done such a thing once, during the War of Golden Favors, and he had won his battle with ease. We marched in Linked Crescents, an excellent formation for fending off surprise attacks, but what help would that be if we could hardly see two horselengths in front of us?

Well—if the enemy awaited us, then I would send my army back over the bridge. *They* would retreat to safety. To Horohama, perhaps, or even to Fujino.

But I knew what it was I had to do. Silently, I begged your forgiveness. This idea of mine—I had no way of knowing if it would work. If I died on the banks of the Kirin, would my body ever find its way to you? Or would the river take me—would I sink to the bottom of a bottomless ravine, my Imperial bones indistinguishable from those of merchants and fishermen?

As the planks of the bridge beneath us began to slope downward, I called for the archers to ready.

When at last we saw what lay beyond—many of them dropped their bows altogether.

Where once stood the forest, now there were fields of flowers, tall as my knee, each one a different color. Peonies. Chrysanthemums. Violets, orchids, lilies, plum blossoms—every flower in existence swaying together in an unfelt breeze, far as the eye can see, with no sign of the towering pines for which Shiseiki was so well known. Houses in the old Hokkaran style, before we had to reinforce everything against attacks, dotted the rolling countryside. In the distance were four mountains, taller than the Kyuuzen and broader than the wide-shouldered Tokuma. Just behind us was the Kirin—but it ran west instead of north now, and its water had gone the impossible blue of a blacksmith's flame.

There were people—but no army. We saw fishing boats manned by warm-faced Hokkarans, washerwomen surrounded by laughing children, scholars who sat outside on benches practicing calligraphy, students waving wooden swords in familiar strokes.

If my father painted a picture of ideal Hokkaran life, it would look like this.

Except for one thing: the sun. For this idyllic scene was not bathed in gold or yellow or even pale amber. No.

Everything was violet. Up in the sky, where the sun should have been, was a yawning violet pit, clouds surrounding it like gossiping court ladies. The light radiating down from it made me sick. Whenever I blinked, I caught glimpses of massive teeth on its brim.

One moment you are walking through the hunting grounds, wondering why you cannot help but smile around a certain Qorin, and the next all your hair stands on end. Something inside you spots the tiger before you ever do.

That pit was watching me.

"Halt!" I called.

Xianyu sent the order down the line—but she did so while narrowing her eyes at me. "General," she said, "we cannot stay on the bridge. There's no sign of the enemy here; why not at least let the army put their feet on solid ground?"

"No sign of the enemy?" I said. "Xianyu, look at the sun! Do you not see that pit?"

So rarely did I use her first name that she flinched for a moment. When her eyes flickered upward and back down to me, I saw concern within them. "General," she said carefully. "There are many strange things about this place. The flowers, the disappearing forest, these people. The sun, however—the sun remains as it's always been."

Up ahead, the army shifted on their feet. The fishing boats on the Kirin were heavy with meals. How long had it been since we last had meat? How long could I deny them the ability to at least make camp in this strange new world? They did not see things as I did, and if I continued to protest, they might think me mad.

You'd have to be mad to walk into a burning building, you'd have to be mad to duel a giant serpent. I suppose this would only be confirmation.

One of the fishermen caught my eye. He was fishing with his bare hands, the way my mother used to when we went to the Jade River. As I watched, he leaned over the water and thrust his hands in. For long moments he struggled and struggled, until at last he pulled a massive carp from the water, the largest I'd ever seen, gold with orange spots—

No, no, it wasn't, it was a festering leech with a woman's face, and it was reaching for him—

No. It was gold with orange spots.

I pinched my nose. What if I was seeing things?

"Go forward," I said, "but do so slowly. Do not trust anything you see. Lest you all forget, this is the Traitor's territory, and his armies lie in wait for us. Be vigilant."

And so we rode farther in, though the pain in my chest only got worse and I wanted to vomit every time I looked at the sky. We'd no trained scouts remaining, but volunteers were found. Strict orders we gave them—do not wander too far, do not engage with anything that attacks you, and above all, to trust nothing. Eight blessings I wrote for them, the awkwardly worded benedictions of a blasphemer.

Eight we sent out, while the rest of us rested near the river.

I avoided the people. Even the kindest grandmother transformed, whenever I blinked, into a four-headed monstrosity. This does not mean, of course, that everyone avoided the people. Many didn't. Many called out to the long-haired washerwomen, many called out to the fishermen with their rippling arms. Whenever these illusions

responded, they did so in Hokkaran so old, even I struggled to understand them—but the soldiers were happy to carry on.

So long as they did not move, I told myself. So long as they did
not go to these creatures.

I was not seeing things. I knew I was not. The others were—that
was the only explanation. Never in my life have I looked on a thing
and not seen its true form. Court magicians hated me. Forgeries stood
out to me, counterfeit cash seals, even the white lies that fell from the
lips of courtiers.

I knew lies, Shefali, and it seemed we'd ridden straight into a web
of one.

But even I know the value of a lie—and after what my army had
seen today, perhaps allowing them an hour's rest in this one was a
mercy.

For an hour was all it took.

To my relief, this time, all eight scouts returned, and most looked
no worse for the wear. Two told me of a castle farther to the north—
one they had not approached but had both seen. Two told me of a
massive road to the east, wider even than the Three Kings, which
led to a city of spires. Two told me of the west, where they'd come to
an ancient valley filled with statues of unknown Kings.

But it was the final two who concerned me. One had gone to the
northeast. There, she'd come across an encampment flying the Shiratori banner. She had not ventured inside—having hewn close to
my instructions—but she had concealed herself among the flowers.
So it was that she waited until she'd seen the enemy to report back
on them.

And sure enough, they *were* our enemy, for the woman reported
that shadows now wore Shiratori armor in place of people.

The final scout had gone to the northwest, over the largest hill
visible. For the best view, he'd argued, and he showed me a spyglass

he'd made back home in Xian-Qin. Amidst all the flowers, he had
seen a single square of muddy violet perhaps two li to our north. Next
to the square had been a fire no larger than his thumb in his view,
and a single soldier resting near it.

Daishi.

In my bones, I knew that it was her.

The encampment was twenty li away, far enough that they might
not have noticed our arrival yet. I doubted that—something told me
this Octopus King, wherever he was, knew well enough when someone entered his domain. They had not yet marched against us. Our
scout told us that they had not sent anyone forth the whole time
she was watching. That they would give up their fortified position
was unlikely—and yet we could not strike down these aberrations
without marching on them.

So Xianyu argued, anyway.

But I knew how we would send them coming to us, and I knew
how we could attack them.

"While I rebuild the Wall of Flowers," I began.

"I'm going to stop you there," said Xianyu. "*You're* going to rebuild the Wall of Flowers?"

"Yes," I said, "unless you mean to wait eight hundred years for
the Daughter to rise from the dead."

"You're going to rebuild the Wall of Flowers," she repeated.

"What?" I said. "Is that meant to be difficult?"

She pinched her nose. "You cannot be serious. You *must* consider
proper tactics, General; this grandstanding will not keep us safe from
the enemy."

"But it will!" I said. I called for a daffodil then, just to make the
point. "How often have you seen me do this? And you *doubt* me,
Xianyu? I, who swallow fire like wine? Do you doubt the moon and
stars as well, or only my capabilities?"

Was I speaking to her, or to myself? For a sliver of me doubted I could raise the Wall. Hearing the words from my own mouth made the idea real—and hearing your mother's famous tournament boast in particular.

Burqila Alshara must have heard the same thing from her clan-mates when they said she could not breach the Wall of Stone. Her response? Selling dragon bones to the Surians, returning with carts full of Dragon's Fire, and carving her own path. And she was younger then than I was at the time.

If she could break a wall—I could build one.

Xianyu waited before answering, the planes of her face moving as she thought over her options. Finally, she sighed. "You're certain—"

"I'm—"

"Always certain," she finished. "Of course you are. Well. Let's hear it, then."

A grin came to me then, in spite of all I'd seen. Xianyu's recognition was so hard to earn! "When I raise the Wall, I will send it through their encampment. By splitting it in two, we split their numbers in two—and with nowhere to go, the enemy will come south toward us. In anticipation of this, we shall place our archers on those two hills—do you see them?"

Xianyu nodded. They were close enough to create a small valley. "And if the enemy does not come through that passage?"

"They will," I continued. "For we shall send what cavalry we have to harry them."

"We have fifty horses," said Xianyu.

"Did I stammer?" I said. "We send the cavalry to harry them briefly and then retreat—and *they* will go through the valley. The enemy will surely follow."

I saw her eyes light up. "And we shall be waiting in Keyhole formation on the other side. You *have* been paying attention."

"You never let me drink when you're around; what else am I to do but pay attention?" I said. In truth, I found her lessons invaluable—but I could not resist the urge to needle her. It was three days since I'd had a drink, which was two days too long, by my reckoning.

She scratched at her cheek as she considered the plan. "General, my only question is this: If you can conjure the Wall anew—"

"I can," I said.

"When you conjure the Wall anew, then—why not simply cut off the encampment entirely?"

The thought had occurred to me, yes. That would be the safest thing to do for all of us—and yet it would not be *right*.

"The Octopus King is within that camp," I said. "And so, too, is Kasuri-yun. I mean for them to face Imperial justice, or at least to know what became of the other armies. The scouts have given us enough information—I think I shall be able to keep them on our side of the Wall. They'll funnel in between the two hills, where we will strike while they are confused. If it seems we are losing the battle, I shall call for a retreat over the bridge—but we will not leave without learning the truth of what happened here."

I worried she might chide me for being selfish. Again she nodded. "Very well. I'll give the orders."

With that matter settled, all that remained was fetching Daishi from where her army had gone. It would take time for the army to fall into place, and she was camped only five li away. I longed to get her myself—but I could not shake the gnawing fear that something might happen while I was away.

And so, though it pained me, I sent a company of eight. Every moment they were away was a moment of cruelest anticipation—would it truly be my cousin they brought back? Would she be herself, or would the enemy have gotten to her? What if it were some other

Fuyutsuki captain, and not her? These questions ate away at me as I watched the army ready itself.

And then I decided that it was better to take action than to let my fears consume me.

When you set your mind to do an impossible thing, Shefali, do you ever have any idea what you are doing? For you, it seems such a natural thing—you do not think about drawing back your bow, you hardly aim at all. You simply draw back the bowstring and let the arrow fly. Often it is like that for me—I do not consider the impossibility of a thing before I resolve myself to do it.

But there are times I wish that I did. There are times I wish I had a tutor for miracles alongside my zither tutor and my acting tutor and my singing tutor. Of all the teachers my mother saw fit to fling at me—was there no one in the Empire who could teach me what I really needed to know?

No.

No, and I knew that.

How would I do this thing? I needed to be closer to the earth; this much I knew. I pulled off my gloves and stepped out of my boots. The captains stared at me as I tugged off my socks.

"No need to worry," I said. "Only getting us prepared."

Xianyu was at my side in an instant. Was there a signal fan for "the general is doing something foolish"? She always seemed to know. "General," she began, and I waved her off.

"I don't know how long it will take to regrow the Wall, and this waiting for news of my cousin grates on me. I thought I would start out early."

Now there was the familiar narrowing of her eyes, the ever-present pursing of her lips. "You should have told me," she said. "I'll send out the cavalry."

I nodded. "And see to it I'm not disturbed," I said.

This did not earn me a nod or even an acknowledgment—only a brief parting bow. Soon the others cleared the space around me, so that for ten horselengths all around, I was the only living person.

There were the illusions, of course, but it was simple enough for me to ignore that which did not deserve to live.

Among the false flowers I sat, the flats of my bare feet against the cool grass. I allowed myself to focus only on my breathing—only on air passing up through my nose and down into my lungs. With my eyes closed, the whole of the awful world fell away. It was simply me and the flowers.

In and out, in, and out. Soon I'd fallen into a duelist's clarity of mind. These flowers were not real—they did not sing to me—but I could make them real.

I could make whatever flowers I wanted.

My blood began to hum. I heard it, yes, but I felt it more than anything, the way you might feel a drummer's rhythms a li before you heard them. With every breath, the fire within me grew brighter, hotter, until it dwarfed the signal fires of Fujino, until I tasted the starburst orange of the sun on my tongue—and it was then I knew I was ready.

Fingers spread, I drove my fingers into the dirt. What I felt there so shocked me that I nearly drew them back.

Let Them Be Your Armor

How to explain it?

As if you are riding your fastest horse down an impossibly steep hill, wind whipping through your hair, your knuckles white on the saddle horn.

As if you are staring the Emperor in the face and telling him you will not bow to him, your fingers entwined with your wife's.

As if you are an arrow hurtling toward its target, as if you are a brush in someone else's hand.

I felt *everything*. The footsteps of the army as they meandered into formation, the roots of the great trees of Shiseiki this illusion now concealed, the rush of the water over the riverbed. I felt the wind through my hair and through the grass, I felt the earth as my skin, I heard the secret sighs of the pine. The splendors that danced before me! For I was no longer my own, Shefali, although I never truly had been; here I was no longer the Empress but something entirely new and different, a thousand-faceted crystal of a woman, a queen bee with hundreds of eyes, a dozen flowers growing together in spite of their season! I was all these things and more. If I allowed myself to think of it for even a moment, I would be lost in the stream of it all, a stone sinking to the bottom of the Kirin.

And the riverbed! How far down it was, how alien! As if I stood at the top of the Grand Temple and looked down now at the ants crawling along a blade of grass!

To speak of it is to rob it, Shefali, for I cannot convey to you the cacophony of it all: the chirping crickets and the singing nightjar, the rough voices of soldiers and the murmuring of the water, the voices crying out all at once: *Hear me.*

And theirs were not the only voices. Among them I heard, too, the drumbeats of Hokkaran. More requests from unseen supplicants.

Watch over my son, wherever you have gone.

Has my wife been lying to me? I know you do not listen, and yet I ask you all the same, what a fool, what a fool . . .

They say my daughter's fever has put her in the Mother's arms, but I know better. You do, too, I think. Save her.

Like threads these requests, wrapped around me so tightly that I could scarcely move. If I wanted to, I could follow the thread to its source—I could see the old woman kneeling before the Fallen Son; I could see the woman painting the letters of her prayer onto a piece of discarded hide. How far were they? Hundreds of li, thousands, and so to see them should not be possible—

Hear me. Grant me my prayer.

So—that was it.

I was hearing prayers.

What was I to do about them?

I reached for the threads with my self that was not my self, with the body I'd shucked away. I saw myself then as if my skin were silk gauze—and yet this did not frighten me.

I felt . . . I felt as if I were seeing myself the way you always saw me.

What did I do, now that I'd left behind my mortal form? I grasped the threads around me, and I unwound them one by one. When I held the end of a thread in my hand, I listened again to the request that had spawned it. If I found it worthy, I pinched the thread between two fingers. With a thought, I spread some of the fire to it—not enough to burn, but enough to light the way. And so the fires consumed the string all the way back to their owners.

If I did not?

If I did not, I simply cut the thread.

I could have spent an eternity among those threads. Later, when I returned to Fujino, I spent whole days among them rather than face the court. Still—though I'd shed my mortal form, I had not shed my mortal determination.

And so I stood as a spirit in the forest of Shiseiki, and I saw before me the abandoned watchtowers, the barracks now torn asunder. I saw the bodies of the fallen, and I saw the enemy stooped over them, feeding. Though I searched and searched for the brightness of villages, I saw none, only the dark, only the enemy creeping farther south with each passing moment.

They would stop here.

I sent my consciousness into the earth, and I commanded it: *Grow*.

To the white camellias, to the black lilies, to the white chrysanthemums, I said: *May you stand guard for their evil.*

To the peony, to the hydrangea, to the daffodil, I said: *May they fear you.*

To the iris, to the jasmine, to the lavender, I said: *May you protect us.*

To the red spider lily, to the primrose, to the yellow tulips and the violets I spoke; to the sagiso, to the gardenia, to the dahlias and the daisies.

And as I named them, I shaped them, I wove them into being. Taller and taller, until the castle walls could not hope to match them; wider and wider, from the base of the Tokuma Mountains over the hills of Shiratori, all along the river. As the flowers I saw them, Shefali, as the flowers I looked on the beauty of the world.

Yet amidst the beauty there, too, was ugliness, and its center was the encampment.

Grow, I said to my creation, and so it did: hungry cavern mouths and vine hands it grew, root claws and petal teeth. As the new wall exploded up from the earth, it seized whatever enemies it found. Wriggle and twist, change shape though they might—it was their will against mine.

And I would not falter.

Into the mouths they went, crushed and strangled by the vines, screaming and screaming they went, until at last their comrades ran with fear in their hearts. They ran from me. They ran from the flowers.

Grow, I commanded my creation, and so it did, unfurling toward the sun and the Kyuuzens.

When it said at last that it was done—when it said it had grown all it could—I told it to be strong.

For I had two flowers left to call.

To the plum blossom, I called, and to the wild flowers of the steppes, who knew my tongue only through you.

Grow, I said to them, *and keep her safe for me.*

And so they did.

How beautiful it was, Shefali, this new Wall of Flowers! How my heart swelled with joy to behold it! Transfixed I stood and marveled at this thing that I had created, this impossibility; my mouth opened into a trembling grin and . . .

Oh, the tears would not come. But they were there in my chest, they were there in the swelling of my throat, they were in the crack of my voice when I spoke: "I did it."

When it occurred to me to look back on my body, I saw that the others were trying to shake me awake.

I considered, for a moment, whether I should return to my flesh. Could I not fight in this state? How acutely I felt the sun, the fires within. Surely I could fight like this.

But I could not hold you with these arms of wind; I could not feel your lips against mine. And so what use was godhood to me?

Step by step, I approached my body. Xianyu had taken off my mask. I saw my own face staring back at me, wan and glassy-eyed, my mouth open and a froth forming between my lips. There was the scar Nozawa had given me, there were the brows you so adored, there was my dog ear.

Had I always been so small?

Slowly, slowly, I kneeled down in front of myself, and I slipped back into my own skin.

I WANT TO tell you that it was like being pulled from a lake, drowning, and having someone punch you in the stomach so that you spat up all the water.

But I won't tell you that, because drowning . . . drowning feels nothing like that. Drowning feels . . .

I will tell you. Soon, I will tell you.

But you are welcome to think of it as such, if that will help your imagining. Certainly, it looked much the same: I sat up coughing and sputtering, pale as Akkino snow. Xianyu was beating my back as if I were her clothes and she was a peasant woman. My ears rang with silence—not because it was quiet, but because nothing could compare to the sounds I'd heard once I left my body behind. In comparison to the singing of the world itself, the panicked cries of the captains were like two drops of water falling on a distant lake.

And so it took some time before I heard them. After I vomited, I think—that was when I first began to make sense of what they were saying.

"Get her water!"

"Where are the surgeons? I asked for a surgeon!"

"She's cold as ice, Zhou, a surgeon isn't going to help with that—"

So much noise—and so little music. How empty I felt now that all of that was over with. As if someone had reached inside my body and torn out part of my soul.

But they thought I was dying, and I could not let them suffer that delusion much longer.

"I'm fine," I sputtered between coughs. "Don't worry about the surgeons. I'm fine."

All at once everyone took three steps away—everyone except Xianyu, who knew well that I would not be chopping hands off those who touched me. She knelt in front of me with a warm rag and a look of honest concern. Where she'd found a warm rag escaped me—but I was grateful for it all the same. I really did feel cold. Now that I was awake, I was shivering even in my armor.

"Are you truly well?" she asked me. "Do not lie. If you aren't, we'll retreat, and no one will question your bravery."

"Did you see it?" I rasped. Someone handed me a skin of water. When I tipped it to my lips, it was sweeter than any wine. "The Wall. Did you see it?"

Xianyu's smile was gone the moment I realized it'd been there at all. "General, I doubt there's anyone in the army who missed it."

"I did it," I said, for I was still giddy. "I raised the Wall of Flowers."

"So you did," she said. "And there will be time to sing your praises for it later. The forward scouts have already sighted the cavalry."

Already? This was happening so quickly. Didn't we have time to admire the flowers?

What a foolish thing to hope for.

I pinched my nose, shook my head, tried to will myself into coherence. Words came to me only in petals and stems—I had to shape them into sound. "Right," I said. "Where's Daishi-zul?"

Xianyu stood, and I took that as my cue to join her. I was wobbly on my feet, and still shoeless besides. I set about remedying that as she spoke.

"With the surgeons and the support troops."

"Not fighting?"

"No," said Xianyu. "Not fighting. If you mean to speak to her, you've only a few minutes to do so."

I stomped back into my boots. Part of me was sad to be so parted from the earth—but it was easier to think this way. "Lead the way."

Xianyu was right—the whole army, anyone left to ride alongside us, had seen this new Wall spring into life. As we made our way to the erected support camps, we heard cheers with every step.

"General Dog-Ear!" they'd call. "May you reign a hundred and one years!"

I did not fault them for calling me such a thing. In its own way, it was comforting to know they still thought of me like that, in spite of what I had just done.

Here is what I saw when I entered the last support camp: my cousin, hiding in a tent, with her knees to her chest and her head resting atop them. The monkey mask she'd worn so proudly lay beaten and misshapen at her side; the top half of a broken glaive was at her feet. The cloth parts of her coat had been torn away, leaving dangerously bare her skin; my breath hitched when I saw there was a wound on her arm. Stitched and cleaned, yes, but a wound still.

Though I could not see her face, I heard her sobbing.

My cousin, who was so fond of jokes—sobbing, wounded in this strange place, where we were not safe.

Whatever pride I felt at building the Wall crumpled at that sound.

"Daishi?" I said. Slowly I approached her, for I did not want to scare her. "Aki-lun, it's me."

She looked up only long enough to recognize me, and then turned away.

"No, it isn't," she said. "My cousin wouldn't be stupid enough to come over the bridge after seeing those ruins."

"You mistake how stupid I can be," I said. Another step forward. I wanted to touch her shoulder, but she might strike my hand away if she thought I was some sort of illusion. "If you'd like, I'll draw my mother's sword. Would that convince you?"

A furtive glance. True to my word, I drew the sword and made it flash for a moment. Only then did she throw her arms around me. I was shocked at the strength of it—she held on to me as if she were trying to absorb me into herself.

"Shizu-lun," she said. "Oh, Mother, it really is you. It's really you!"

Behind us, Xianyu clapped her hands. We had only just begun, and yet it was almost time to leave. Perhaps I shouldn't have returned to this body; time did not seem the same as when I'd left it.

"It is," I said. I held her at arm's length. It'd been only two months since I last saw her, but her cheeks had gone hollow, her hair limp. I was reminded of Uemura—and then reminded of his body. "Aki-lun, I don't know what it is you've seen, but once this battle is through, you won't ever have to take the field again. I swear."

"You couldn't make me," she said. She was trying to make it sound jovial—but she failed.

"I know," I said. "Your wound—"

"It's clean," she said. Then a wild determination took her, and she seized me by the shoulders. "Listen to me. When you see Kasuri—that's not her. I saw it with my own eyes, she peeled off her skin—"

"The Octopus King?" I said. "It was . . . it was wearing her?"

"I don't think there was a her," she said. "Middle of the night, she told her army to march over the bridge. Ordered them to. I was up drinking with the Doanese folks, and I thought it was weird, so I followed her. The minute they crossed the fog, Shizu-lun, they *changed*. Became those things."

Like drinking ice water. Twice, now, I'd been fooled by that trick of the enemy. If only I'd come with you—your nose would have picked it out immediately.

All of this was my fault. I should have known, Shefali, I should have known it was not who it claimed to be.

Daishi shivered, as if she, too, could feel the chill in the air.

I didn't ask her if she was certain—but I did want to ask her how the Octopus King had done it. Was my army in danger of changing, too?

"I hid. I was . . . I was a coward, but I hid, because I didn't want to die to those things. I've seen what happens when they get to you, Shizu-lun. I've seen how your body changes. If there's any body left at all. If they haven't just eaten you," she said. My cousin licked her dry lips. She was shaking, and I wanted to tell her that she had no need to keep going, but she could not stop herself. "The Fuyutsuki army, when they realized I was missing, they decided to cross, too. But they didn't change.

"I saw it, Shizu-lun. All of it. Kasuri, the thing in her skin, was waiting for them on the other side on top of her horse, the army fanned out behind her. The normal-looking ones. With the war masks on,

you couldn't tell they'd changed at all. My lieutenant, Usami Yuuto—
he rode up to her and demanded to know the meaning of all of this.

"Kasuri told him to follow her deeper in. Said she'd found
the enemy, and if the two armies struck now, they'd get all the
glory. Yuuto-zun—he's young. He loves—loved—glory. So he
followed.

"I followed them for three li. How Kasuri's army didn't notice me,
I'll never know, but my heart was in my throat the whole time. Kasuri's abominations flanked the Fuyutsuki army, so I had no way of
signaling to my people.

"I told myself that if I was going to be a coward, the least I could
do was see what happened. The least I could do was scout. I owed
you that much—"

"Daishi—" I began, reaching for her, but she struck away my
hand. The cold fury in her eyes told me there would be no more in-
terruptions.

"When they had gone three li, I saw Yuuto-zun call for a halt. I
couldn't hear what he said—I was hiding in a tree—but I got the gist
of it from his gestures. He wanted to know why they'd gone so
far out.

"Kasuri lifted her war mask. She got off her horse, even, and
walked up to him. He did the same. What else are you meant to do?
Kasuri outranked him. So she patted him on the back, and she said . . .

"Something. I didn't hear it, but I saw the look on her face, and
the way the light fell on her skin. She looked almost like a frog, Shizu-
lun, all pale and clammy and *wrong*.

"I . . . I think Yuuto-zun realized what he'd gotten himself into
then, because he drew his sword and lunged at her. She didn't flinch
at all—not even when the sword sliced right through her neck.

"I saw it, Shizuka. The blood black as ink bubbling out of that pale
gash, the smile spreading across her face. She laughed once, and drove

her fingers into the wound. Hooked them on the edges and pu . . .
pulled . . .

"Its face . . . I couldn't . . . there was so much blood, and the tentacles burst out of the place where her head was, and they pulled
him in and swallowed him up, and there was this sound like crushing a fish beneath your boot, and the army, Kasuri's army, they
charged. . . ."

My cousin's voice cracked as the tears at last forced their way out.
I pushed my own horror, my own discomfort aside, to hold her as the
tears came. What was I to say? What could I say to this?

My bravery spoke before my sense could stop it.

"I will slay that demon," I said. "I'll bring you its head, Aki-lun,
I swear I will."

Xianyu clapped. We were out of time. I bit my lip and hugged Daishi close. When at last I pulled away from her, she looked on me as
though . . . as though I were Minami Shiori, Shefali. As if I were my
mother.

"I don't want you to swear you'll kill it," Daishi said. "I want you
to swear to me you'll live."

"I will," I said. There was no doubt in my mind of that. "And one
day, we'll go out drinking in Fujino together, and forget about all
this."

"Shizuka-shal," she said. "Promise me you'll be safe. For me. For
your wife. For your people. Please, promise me."

I couldn't see why she'd make such a demand of me, when she
knew what I was about to do was dangerous. When she knew . . .

I swallowed. I couldn't allow myself to die so far away from
you—and yet none of this felt right. I'd raised the new Wall without
you. I was facing down a Demon General without you. All those
years ago, when I first heard the call to go north, I thought you would
be at my side.

What if . . . what if without you, I was bound to fail?

I couldn't allow myself to have that thought.

"I promise," I said.

I ROSE, AND walked to Xianyu. We closed the tent flap behind us. Someone had brought out my gelding for me, and so I mounted him, and together we rode to join the rest of the army.

We rode to Ink-on-Water.

Petals Upon the Dark Water

Have you braced yourself, my love? I know what you are expecting: a tale of heroism and bravery. The enemy rides into our ambush and we riddle them with arrows. They die in droves as they crash against our unwavering line of pike and sword. Toward the middle of the battle, when all seems lost, I ride in and turn the tides by calling their general to duel. In two strokes I end him, and the illusion around Shiseiki fades, leaving us to cross the river at our leisure. We return to Fujino in only a month, and my uncle abdicates in shame for what he has put me through.

That is the story you would like to hear.

But life is not a story, Shefali, as much as I wish it were.

Stories fool us more than anything in this world. Emperor Yusuke does not drink himself to an early grave in the legends—he dies wrestling a dragon. When his sister takes the throne after him, she erects a statue in his honor, she prays for eighty days and eighty nights for his guidance. She does not try to write him out of the

Imperial Lineages. She does not declare it illegal to speak of him for a generation.

The stories you may have heard of this moment are like the one I told you above: a glorious battle.

In reality . . .

In reality, I sat atop my gelding and I watched the enemy charge toward us, five thousand shadows wearing the blue armor of our own kingdom. In reality, when the arrows rained down on them, they found no purchase on their ghostly flesh, plummeting uselessly to the ground.

They did not stop their charge. A stampede they were, trampling our arrows beneath their boots, and though their footfalls quaked the earth, they made not a whisper of noise. Without faces, without bodies, without mercy, the suits of armor advanced on us.

In the moments before our armies collided, I heard Xianyu curse for the first time in the awful eternity that I'd known her. She was not alone. All around me, the army's bravery gave way to confusion, gave way to fear. That they did not break formation and run—was that a triumph of their training, or a tragedy of it?

Oftentimes I wonder if it would have been better if they ran. Knowing what happened next—should I have ordered the retreat then and there? Would I have saved any more of them if I had?

BEAR WITH ME, my love. Long have I tried to bury these memories. I have exhumed them for you—but the soil clings to them still.

I LOOKED AT the soldiers around me, their names emblazoned in the air so near to them, and I thought to myself that perhaps pike and sword would prevail where bow and arrow had failed. Not all was lost. They had me, after all, and I'd just raised the Wall of Flowers. So what if I was swaying in the saddle, so what if I was light-headed? All that mattered was this battle. These suits, these creatures—though they had once been soldiers, the Octopus King had consumed them. If I killed him, then the wind would scatter their foul essence.

Xianyu did not agree with me. I remember still how she turned to me. Her mask hid much of her face, but there was no mistaking the panic in her eyes. She held her reins in hand and jerked her head behind us. Despite all this, she did not voice her wishes—she did not *say* "retreat," and if she had, I wonder . . .

Divinity's cloak clouded my judgment. I saw her, this woman who had guided me through so much of this campaign, and I said to her: "Heaven rides with us."

There is a certain beauty to the terrible. Have you seen the great waves rise off the coast of Nishikomi? Tall as castles they rise, tall as palaces, taller than human ambition. How slow they move! You have time to observe them before they crash against the rocks, time to see them grow from bumps on the horizon to those towering waves.

When I was a child, I stood on the shore and did just that: I watched the waves rise and rise. I wondered to myself how such a thing could be possible. I wondered just how tall the wave would get, and whether it would touch the sun. Would it swallow me up? For so hungry it seemed, so ravenous, and when the sun pierced through, I saw so many fish already within its grasp.

What would it be like to swim among those fish, suspended in the wave?

My mother plucked me from the beach only a few minutes before the wave crashed against the Father's Teeth. To this day, I remember the spray of the salt against my skin.

Such nightmares I have about that wave. About the waves that followed.

In that moment before our armies met, I was again a child on the shores of Nishikomi—but my mother was not there to save me.

Pikemen lowered their weapons. Archers drew back their bows. My tongue stuck to the roof of my mouth and I prayed to myself—*let this work.*

And then—impact.

The first company of the enemy crashed against our front line, but we were no Father's Teeth, and they did not scatter before us. War cries filled my ears alongside the crush of metal and leather and horse. From my position at the rear, I watched them build up against us, more and more coming, this endless blue-black sea.

And I saw, too, what little effect our weapons had on them. First Company had dug in their heels to fight back the onslaught—but they could do nothing to truly dispel it. Here a lieutenant swung her glaive for a decapitating blow, only for the blade to arc through the enemy and stop just short of slicing her comrade. Here a pikeman charged, convinced that the additional force of his charge might be the thing to wound these creatures. He succeeded only in wandering farther into their ranks. Watching him, my heart clenched—he was so far in that there were two rows of shadows between him and our soldiers.

Birds descending on a corpse—that is what I expected.

Imagine my shock when they did not strike at him! For twelve steps he took into the enemy before he realized what he'd done. With dull horror, he raised his pike again and ran to his former place in the formation—and the enemy did not stop him from doing this!

"What?" said Xianyu next to me. "Are they . . . General, are these illusions?"

Something in the air had changed. The other pikemen were raring to try to push forward—I saw it in their footing, I saw it in the lean of their bodies. The shadows pressed against them—but the pikemen were uniting now, as one, to force them farther back.

Or to pierce their ranks. It was difficult to tell their intent. My eyes flickered to the war fans—both Imperial Gold, both pointed straight ahead.

Like reeds against the current, their pikes.

"They're pushing them," I said. "You can't push an illusion."

"Then why are they letting the pikemen through?" Xianyu asked. She wheeled around in the saddle to look behind us—the second company of archers looked as confused as we were, their bows half-readied in their hands. Behind us only the swaying flowers, behind us only the uncanny residents of this place, going about their business as if we weren't there. No sign of a flanking force.

But then again—we could not see over the bridge.

"General," said Xianyu. "If they aren't an illusion, then they must be a trap of some sort. We have to pull them back."

The pikemen were four ranks deep into the enemy now. The swordsmen continued to swing uselessly at the shadows—but if we did nothing, then they, too, would charge ahead.

Would that be the right thing to do? For doubtless Xianyu was right—if this was no illusion, then it must be a trap. But to what end? And what if the enemy knew we'd see through the tactic? What if the trap awaited us only when we drew back?

It was a risk I was willing to take. Whatever came before us, it would be best if we faced it together, and not with our pikemen out so far ahead.

"Call them back," I said to Xianyu before my fear could get the better of me.

This battle was not what I had expected—but it was not yet over, either.

Fans turned up and down the lines, heralding shouts in clipped

Xianese. As one, the pikemen began to retreat, taking wide steps backwards, their weapons out in front of them.

One step.

A raindrop fell on my shoulder.

Two steps.

I tasted salt—and it could not be from tears.

Three steps.

Was it my eyes, or were the shadows now solidifying?

Fourth step.

The sky opened and wept upon us. Rain thick as we'd seen back in Xian-Lai came down, each drop as fat as a cherry pit, thousands of them all at once. The sound alone was overwhelming—and soon the good soil beneath us would turn to mud.

But that was the least of our worries.

For as the rain fell down, it filled the smoke—as if the smoke had been a waiting bladder all along. As we watched it solidified into something like eels. Slick and dark they were, with one mouth in the center of their otherwise featureless faces. They laughed, then, and we saw the teeth lining their throats all the way down.

Five steps back.

"Four-Petal!" boomed a voice behind us in Hokkaran. "It is impolite to bring an army into the domain of a King!"

I unsheathed the Daybreak Blade. I did not look behind me—to do so would be to look away from my army as the eels now advanced on them.

For they were advancing, and the wounds they now bore did not seem to slow them. My pikemen were happy to give them more—but how many would it take to kill one of these things?

And why had they not yet attacked?

"Four-Petal!" again. "So, too, is it impolite to ignore your elders. Have you forgotten the teachings of your parents?"

Now—now I flinched. To hear the enemy mention my parents even in passing boiled my blood. Now I looked back, the Daybreak Blade burning like the dawn in my hand.

Three li behind us, a spot on the river, too, was boiling like me. Great bubbles rippled its surface; clouds of steam rose from it amid the rain. Though I saw no source for the voice, I knew that it sprang from the river's depths.

Yet that voice was nothing like Mizuha's had been—this was a demon's voice. It chose to sound like the sort of man who chides you for wearing Camellias-at-Dusk because he once saw a singing girl wearing the same combination. That decision boggled my mind—but perhaps it wanted to sound authoritative, and this was the closest it could get, plucked from the minds of mortals.

"I shall ignore whomever I please," I called, "and my mother would be thrilled to strike you down."

I was about to level my sword at the river when Xianyu called for my attention. When I turned toward the army again, I saw why.

The eels had slipped out of their armor—and now they'd wrapped themselves about the bodies of my soldiers. Cold seized me by the throat as I saw it: the eels had torn off the masks of the pikemen, and were now pressing themselves into the mouths of the horrified soldiers. The archers could not well fire to try to free them without killing the victims—but they fired now on the ranks of eels still filtering through the valley. Our swordsmen withdrew—but there were two ranks pressed right up against them still, and the eels were hungry.

Against a hundred of these things we might prevail. Against two hundred, perhaps, if we positioned ourselves well.

But there were four thousand of them at least. Valley or no—if these things meant to eat us, there was only one option open to us.

"Full retreat," I said to Xianyu. "What are you waiting for? Call a full retreat!"

Xianyu sent up the orders, and the army soon followed—we did not need to tell them twice. The rear of the army was already well enough away—but the vanguard was collapsing in on itself as the eels pushed their way forward. Each one grabbed a soldier, each one forced itself into their mouth. Their bodies fell wriggling to the ground.

And then they rose.

Ah, Shefali.

I knew all their names.

Chen Qiuli was the first to rise—a woman so frank and honest that she had told me when I got seaweed stuck between my teeth during the Jubilee. She rose now, her eyes milky white, her veins pulsing black. An eel's mouth had replaced her own. Within moments, she dived for Lu Shuying, a hostler's son who had fed my gelding on more than one occasion. What misfortune he had to be so near to her! For she tore off his mask and sank her teeth into his neck, and that was the end of his dreams of riding a Qorin horse.

I knew them. I knew them, and I'd led them here to die horrible deaths.

I should have enclosed the entire encampment. That I did not . . . oh, all of this is my own doing, all of it caused by my own hubris.

"I have to help," I began, for I could not bear to see my own army being pulled down like this, and already we'd lost most of our first company. Just as I lifted the reins, Xianyu grabbed hold of me.

"You want to help?" she said. "Strike down whatever it is that's taunting us. That's the enemy."

What was she saying? Had the enemy gotten to her, too, that she should be saying such a thing?

"Don't look at me like I'm speaking Surian!" she snapped. "Kill the Octopus King, and his minions will fall, too. Go. It's only a few li!"

"But—" I began.

She shook me. No one had shaken me since I was a child. "You've already called for the retreat—let me handle it. Go!"

There was a knife in my throat. I wanted to say that I should stay with my army—that it was my decision that had gotten them into this mess, and so I should see it through. I wanted to tell her how afraid I was of seeing the rest of them die.

But to falter when there is a decision to be made—that would be worse.

And so I nodded. "Stay safe," I said to her.

"Nowhere is safe in a war," she said, "but don't you die before my little sister gets to see our faces again."

In all our time together, she had not once mentioned Baozhai. To do so now—things truly were dire, weren't they?

"An octopus cannot kill a phoenix," I said.

All around me the cries of the fallen soliders, all around me the fog of panic and fear. The rain bearing down on us only added to the cacophony—but I told myself that all of this was Xianyu's now.

A hollow reassurance it was—but it drove me to send my horse into a gallop toward the river. I passed the support camps as I went, shouting for them to evacuate—but I did not stop. There was no time for me to stop. Each heartbeat I wasted was a heartbeat ended. All I could do was hope that Xianyu got Daishi to safety—the look in my cousin's eyes haunted me still.

"Four-Petal!" came the voice, and I saw then that when the demon spoke, the river flashed with red. "Coming to pay your proper respects? What insolence it was to avoid me!"

At last I arrived at the riverbank. You will call this folly, but I dismounted—fighting in the saddle has always been your talent and not mine.

How it taunted me, this voice. How it presumed to have my attention. That I had to indulge it at all was a yoke—my place was with the army.

"The only insolence here is your refusing to face me," I said. "Hiding in the river, Amari?"

A wordless flash of light. Had it expected that I knew its name already? I saw it written on the shimmering surface of the water.

I drew the sword. "What have you done to Mizuha?"

The bubbles now gurgled in time with the thing's laughter. "I have done only that which you have done yourself," it said. "I *negotiated*."

I somehow doubted that the Octopus King surrendered its tears, or that it had sworn to keep blood from touching the water. Part of me feared for the river god—but the larger part remembered her assault upon my body, her taunting laughter.

If she was truly gone—well. I'd feel only a little sorry for her.

"Then let us begin negotiations of our own, you and I," I said. "Surrender now, and your death will be a quick one."

"As if you could strike down a being as old as myself!" it said, which was no proper boast at all. The gurgles again. "Pah. I do not fear a chicken in phoenix feathers."

So that was what it thought of me—that I was not truly a god?

My head hadn't quite recovered from rebuilding the wall. Heavy my limbs, heavy this flesh I'd trapped myself in.

But it would serve.

YOU SAY I always seem to know what I'm doing. I hope that by now you have learned better. I don't. Sometimes I set my sights on an end goal and walk toward it, hoping the rest will fall into place as we go. Now, that usually works. I am Minami Shizuka. My destiny is my own.

But at that moment, I was staring at the babbling hideout of an octopus demon, while my army was being slaughtered only three li away, and I had determined that I was not going to swim. The thought of being submerged rankled me—it was too close to the hell I'd lived within the serpent's mouth, except that I could not swing a sword underwater.

Which left walking.

You're thinking to yourself: *What foolishness my wife is feeding me.* You are right. I don't have anything to say to defend myself. The smallest child in Hokkaro knew I'd sink if I tried what I was going to try. Yet not twenty minutes before, I'd raised a new Wall of Flowers, and so everything now seemed within easy reach.

So I took my first steps onto the dark. Lifetimes passed. I thought I saw a stone floating, and so I aimed my next step for it. If you've ever stepped on a washerwoman's rags, you know the feeling of something wet and cold and not quite solid. Yes, I was standing on something, and I was not going to stick to standing for long.

"Do you think your little trick intimidates me, Four-Petal?" rumbled the water beneath me.

"It surely does," I snapped. "If you were not afraid, you'd challenge me in person."

A clap of thunder, a flash of light; the surface burst beneath my feet. Then I really did leap, scrambling for the next good foothold.

Laughter.

"Do you think me a fool?" it said. "A child always leaping to defend itself—as you do?"

"Amari," I said, "you will notice—I walked here."

Another burst of lightning. This time I anticipated it. As I finished speaking, I hopped away. Though I wasn't struck, I felt hot all the same, my cheeks and hands burned, my spine tingled.

"I could smite you where you stand."

How considerate this demon was, to make my job so much easier. As if it knew I had better places to be.

"Then it is a good thing I am running, isn't it?" I shouted. "Come and face me, if you are so fearless, if you are so powerful!"

This time the hairs on my neck went stiff a split second before the lightning hit. Now, I could've jumped away. I had before. But this demon wasn't going to come out until I intimidated it properly.

So in that split second, I raised my sword.

If twenty giants heaved their clubs and smashed them against my arm, it wouldn't have hurt as much. My bones rattled, blisters popped all the way up to my neck, my mind itself sizzled. My teeth rattled in my skull with such intensity, I worried they'd fall out.

And yet I stood, mostly unharmed, when the bolt passed. Every breath I took tasted like cinders.

I forced myself to stand straight, to look into the water and grin.

"If that is the best smiting you can muster," I said, "then your dueling cannot possibly be worse. Come here, Amari! Face me!"

Did it matter that I sounded awful, that my voice was sackcloth rough? No—for he had tried to kill me, and he had failed.

Let him think me less than a god now.

The surface beneath me broiled and bubbled. Not far away, perhaps two horselengths, a vicious violet light took the shape of a person. Soon the surface gushed up, the air thick with mist, and a man stood in front of me.

A thing that wore a man's shape, at any rate. It was short, with a flowing black beard and long hair piled into a topknot. Its face was long—very vertical, very narrow, like a stone wedge shoved beneath an uneven table. If it were not for its awful clothing, the gray color of its skin, and its black sclera, it'd be right at home in the court.

I will not bore you with the details of its dress; I have already spoken too much of Hokkaran fashion. But the whole outfit was so outdated, so ridiculous that it was comforting, in its own way. How could I be terrified of something in such an outfit?

Amari wore fury. When it spoke, it roared, its huge sleeves swaying with each word.

"You come to my kingdom and mock me?" it sneered.

"No, I've come to kill you," I said. "Now, conjure your weapon."

Solid black eyes flashed with rage. It held out one hand. The dark sprang into it, solidifying into a broadsword.

It wasted no time with words.

Dueling is the opposite of war, in many ways. In the thick of a battle, with steel coming at you from all directions, your body thinks more than your mind does. Your years of training manifest in this way: a vertical stroke comes at you from the right, and in the instant before it meets you, you slash the attacker's hand off. At the same time, you sway away from a punch; at the same time, you count the seconds between the archers' volleys.

But dueling is nothing like this.

Well, no, that's not quite right—steel is flying at you, yes, and you do not have much time to think. But the time is there. When you face only one opponent, that split second you have in which to think must, at once, be decades long and quick as catching fire.

Amari compressed that time into an instant, at best. All at once, it came at me with vicious swings, each cutting a wide arc through the air. The first, I barely avoided by swaying away at the last moment. The harsh whip of air in its wake nearly threw me off my balance— I reached for the ground to steady myself, only to find water instead. Before I could reorient myself, another slash came down toward me, and another, and another, until I was wheeling backwards simply to keep myself from getting hit. The lightning had hurt me more than I thought; I was struggling to get my arm up long enough to counterattack.

Yet even as I danced away from the demon, I did my best to study its technique. If you can call "wildly swinging at everything in front of you" a technique. Amari was accustomed to mowing down its enemies, accustomed to wading into a melee, where there would be no space to avoid the wild slashes. A plan was forming in my mind—at last the fire was beginning to catch.

Like a farmer scything through his crops, it continued cutting arcs, continued plowing ever forward. I counted to five—and then ducked to its side instead of going backwards. An small opening there, on its off side—but I'd need to strike, and not simply gawk! Heaving up my blistered arm, I thrust my sword toward it. A jolt of pain shot up my arm as I did—but pain was a small price to pay for a wound on an enemy like this. When the first drops of black fell onto the water, when it let out a grunt and flinched away from me, I knew I could kill it.

Of course—that was when the river began to well and truly roil. Between the battle and the duel, I'd forgotten to drag the demon back to shore before I fought it.

As the realization took me, I stood there for a moment looking straight down at my feet. One would have to be an absolute novice or else an honor-obsessed Hokkaran not to take advantage. Amari was neither. I was rewarded for my mistake when it drove the pommel of its broadsword right into my temple. Instantly my vision swam with black, instantly I was reeling, my mind somewhere several li away from my body and not even in the pleasant sense. My ears rang, and I raised my hand to it.

And again, it took advantage. Before I could put together the pieces of the world, it slashed at the back of my left leg. Fortunately, Baozhai had excellent taste in armor and the blow did not break skin. Less fortunately, I'd still gotten hit in the back of the leg with a steel rod, and so I still staggered.

By then my vision had almost returned to me—but the river's furious waves now rocked me before I could stand. The water was steaming now, and getting into my eyes. I didn't know how much more of this I could stand—especially when Amari had no trouble at all standing atop the furious river.

What sort of deal had it made with Mizuha?

There'd be time to sort it out after I'd killed it. And time to figure out the ramifications of my broken oath, too. Surely she would see the righteousness of what I was doing, though it would have gone against the specific promise?

I stood as well as I could to face it, my face already swelling, my arm screaming in agony from the burns. Before the river could topple me, I lunged toward Amari. Passivity won me nothing when it came to the demon.

Still, in the moment I'd waited, steel bit into my skin, steel bit into my bone. Blood seeped from the wound like juice from a cut plum, seeping into my jacket and dripping onto the river. How fortunate I was that I could not cry, for I surely would have if I'd the ability—a cut across the collarbone is a wicked thing indeed.

I stooped over for a moment, bleeding. I half expected another punishing blow. Instead, it chose to speak.

"We want this no more than you do," it said. "It is your own fault that you refuse to listen to us. To all of us."

Had I been hale and hearty, sitting within my throne room, I would grin and bear this sort of talk. With blood seeping through my fingers, with cold sinking into my bones, with my army dying by the second—I had no time for it.

Again I attacked—a thrust that I knew it would parry. There was something off about his parrying. If I got a better look, perhaps I might find another opening. I knew the counterattack was coming, and just as I would expect from an uncreative hack, it was another pommel strike. I ducked just in time, and it was there that I saw the opening—it favored its unwounded side, even when it meant it had to turn to do so.

"Even now you refuse to listen," it said. A soft laugh. "All this fighting, all this struggle. If you allow the Eternal King into your mind, Four-Petal, he will take your pain from you."

I did not *like* my pain, but it was mine. I'd earned it. In fighting this demon, in fighting this war—I'd earned every scar I now bore. If the Traitor wanted to take it from me, he'd have to track me down himself.

I staggered to the left, made a show of holding my wound. It did not take much acting—I really was feeling colder and colder.

"He knows you. He has always known you. And he knows, too, what awaits you if you do not heed his call."

Left, left, left. All I had to do was bait its parry. Once I struck, I'd have all the opportunity I needed to lop that sanctimonious head from its shoulders.

"The weight of an Empire is a heavy one to bear, Four-Petal. Let us help you."

So it was. But the weight of the Empire—that, too, was mine.

What a mistake the demon made to mention the Empire then. For I myself was an Empire—and Empires do not fall at the behest of a single soul. Within me burned a new confidence, a new determination, and it was that which pushed me to strike. I feinted for its right, knowing it would turn.

It did.

And then, quicker than the lightning Amari shot me with, I drove my sword down into its thigh, piercing through it and its calf down into its foot. To the hilt, Shefali. To the hilt I ran Amari through.

Its leg buckled beneath the weight of its agony, blood spraying from the wounds as it tried and failed to level itself. Yet there are certain wounds that end a duel straight out. I'd taken two, over the course of this fight, but this one was a horrific thing to see. How it howled!

Just as I approached it to lop off its head—

I blinked. That must have been it. I must have blinked, and in the time it took my eyelids to open anew, it had disappeared. Or—no. No, it hadn't disappeared, for I saw beneath me a massive shape with tentacles curling, and I knew it to be Amari. The Octopus King.

No sooner had I spotted its new form than a tentacle shot at me from the depths. Luckily I was quick enough to avoid it—a single slice sent ink spilling into the river, a single slice severed it. Would that there had been only one! For from the depths I heard the screech-ing of the demon, and when I looked down, I saw its head split down the middle, its beak and mouth yearning for my flesh! All at once, seven more tentacles broke through the surface like the ropes of a Qorin hunting party—each aiming straight for me.

With light steps I ran across the surface of the lake. Two on either side swung down for me, and I bent backwards, backwards, my ar-mor skimming the surface to avoid them. It was all I could do to twist away from it before I slashed. Two more tentacles fell to the water, the resulting waves rocking me to and fro. The hot rain of blood coated my hair, my neck, leaving an awful dampness that was not soon to disappear.

I managed to get back to my feet only for the river to take matters into its own hand. As if pulling a carpet out from under me, it re-treated beneath my feet, leaving me to sink straight into one of Amari's waiting tentacles. It clamped down around my middle, threatened to squeeze the air from my lungs.

A moment of panic seized me—but I looked to the sword in my hand and remembered who I was. I would have only one chance.

Higher the demon raised me as it emerged from the water, the vio-let light lending its body a mucosal sheen. A rumbling laugh shook its body, sending me bouncing up and down as it slowly lowered me toward its mouth.

It wanted to eat me?

Well. How kind of it to bring me closer.

"Amari!" I shouted. "You think to kill me? I am a nation!"

Lower I went, lower and lower, until I was only two horselengths from its mouth, until its bulging eyes were so near that I could see the striations of its irises.

"I am the Daughter of Hokkaro and Xian-Lai, I am the Grand-daughter of Hanjeon and Dao Doan!"

As it brought me closer, I severed the tentacle with a single slice. Tumbling through the air, I thrust my sword into the filmy skin of its body, landing at the base of the severed tentacle. A roar of pain heralded the careening of its body; I dug the sword in deeper and used it to anchor myself as I ran to its eye.

If I wanted to be certain I'd killed it—that was the best place to strike.

The gold in my blood lent me fire. I held aloft the sword.

"You cannot kill an Empire, and you cannot kill me, Amari!"

And down I went, my blade piercing its cornea, gore pouring all over me as it began to bubble and boil. Like a ball of spices dropped into a waiting pot, the demon's flesh began to dissolve into black, chunks of it falling away until I fell, at last, exhausted and triumphant upon the river.

But as I caught my first breath of the entire duel, Mizuha reappeared. Before I had even finished breathing in, two watery arms seized me around the chest and pulled me backwards into the abyss.

And it is this, above all, that I hate to speak about.

The river.

I HAVE NEVER liked the dark. When we were young, it was no worry at all, for I'd spend my time with you, and you were so at home in it that I thought it must not be so horrible. When we were apart, I stayed with my parents until they put me to bed. And when my parents left—when my parents left, I'd light all the lanterns I could.

It was not that I was afraid, precisely. More that I felt the dark watching me. I knew, on some level, that it hated me as I hated it; I knew that if I closed my eyes, it would close its hands around my throat and squeeze.

And so—lanterns.

But there were no lanterns in the darkness of the river. My parents had been dead near ten years by then, and you gone for three. As the river pulled me deeper, deeper, where the light dared not to dwell, I felt the touch of the dark.

I struggled. Oh, Shefali, how I struggled! Kicking and squirming against unseen bonds, slicing with my mother's sword at the water itself. But struggling only made things worse, for I grew more tired, and without thinking, I tried to breathe. Water filled my mouth and nose. I felt it flowing down into my chest, I felt the crushing weight of it against me.

How cold it was in the depths.

How heavy I felt.

And yet I could not close my eyes as the water filled my lungs, Shefali, I could not. The water stung at them and kept them open, and so I saw the bodies, bloated and fetid, their skin sloughing off, their Imperial armor gone to rust, but their eyes, their eyes were still there. Death was no barrier to those eyes. They saw me, they knew me, they knew it was I who had put them there.

So *many* of them! And not only soldiers, no—what a mercy it would have been if there had only been soldiers, who at least knew they might die when they took the field. Old men and women who had never stood a chance of running from the enemy, with their stomachs torn open and their entrails floating behind them; plump baker's sons; hunters with their bows still in hand.

Blackbloods, too, filled the river, their grotesque shapes rendered all the more nauseating when their bodies began to bloat.

There were dolls, Shefali. Small shoes coated in barnacles.

I screamed.

For an eternity I screamed, for I could think of nothing worse than this, nothing worse than being bound against my will in the depths and staring at the bodies of those I'd failed, and I kept expecting to see you there, I kept thinking the next body would be yours or the next or the next . . .

"Scream all you like. Once I've killed you, this is where you'll rest, Four-Petal."

Mizuha. I felt her now, her slimy body pressed against my back.

I wish I could tell you that I grabbed at her immediately. I wish I could tell you that I was brave enough to do so, that I summoned some hidden well of courage.

But I was not. All I could do was thrash, for even thinking was too much when surrounded by such horrors—even thinking meant I might think of you, and if I thought of you, I was going to see your face.

For once in my life, Shefali, I did not want to see you.

Not here. Never here.

"Do you see what your people have wrought?" she said. "And you wonder why I am so angry!"

She grabbed me by the hair and forced my head back. There, before me, was the body of Mei—the woman who had told me so long ago of the Lightning-Dog.

"You think a righteous cause means you can do what you please, but you do not consider us. Your kind never do."

I tried to turn away, but she forced me to look; I tried to close my eyes, and she with her nails pried them open.

"The demon said it would kill you. It swore to me that when you were dead, your people would at last leave me be. But I see now— what use has a god for a demon? I shall finish this myself."

In desperation, I tried to look anywhere but at Mei's body—and so it was that just over her shoulder, I saw someone else approaching, too far away for me to make out their shape. They were swimming toward me.

Who would be foolish enough to leap into a wrathful river?

Mizuha tightened her grip around my throat—but so, too, did I feel us rising. She pushed Mei's body away like a leaf, and closer, closer we came to the descending figure.

"Look what you've done now, Four-Petal," said the river. "You've brought *more* pollution. Ugh. Her blood tastes as awful as yours does."

Her blood?

A spear of ice through my body. All at once, I was hyperaware of the shape, hyperaware of her long limbs, the barely there violet of her uniform. I knew that shape. I'd seen her swimming before, in the Jade River, all our families together. She'd held my head underwater as a joke—and when I came up pale and terrified, she had spent the rest of the day comforting me.

Akiko.

What was she doing here? She'd run from Rihima, she'd run from the shadow army—but she dived into the river *now?*

What was she thinking? The blood in this water—it was going to get in her wound, and . . .

She was throwing her life away for me.

All she'd wanted was for me to keep myself safe, and . . .

I wanted to kick, I wanted to push away from Mizuha, I wanted to signal to Akiko somehow that she had to leave, that she had to leave *right now*, that the river itself was going to kill her if she did not leave, that she had to live because her youngest sister had just gotten into the Academy—

But the water filled my lungs, and she could not hear anything

I had to say, and Mizuha held me fast, and oh, Shefali, I should have . . .

I tell myself there is nothing I could have done.

But I know that is a lie.

Closer we came, until at last Daishi threw her arms around me. How scared she looked! And yet I knew she did not see the spirit behind me, for if she had, she would have turned away.

And that is the worst part of all of this. Akiko did not see the spirit. She only saw me. All of what happened next—in her eyes, I chose to do it of my own free will.

She threw her arms around me, this woman who had not eaten in days, the last time I'd seen her, and she began to swim. I saw the desperation on her face, I felt her heart thundering, and still, Mizuha held me tight.

"You've broken your oath, Four-Petal, but you're going to pay me all the same."

No. No, no, no, anything but this—she was pulling my hand— the hand that clutched my mother's sword still—and Akiko wasn't looking toward me, she had her eyes on the impossible horizon. She wasn't going to know until it was too late. The water sapped away what little will I had; I was too weak to fight, too weak to stop her as she grabbed Akiko's hair with one hand. Cruel, how cruel she was! She pulled Akiko's head back, and she turned toward me and met my eyes, and hers were so like mine, Shefali, they were so like mine. . . .

Like falling from a saddle, like plummeting through the air and waiting for the ground to hit—the tip of the sword nears her back.

How many times have I run someone through? How many times? And yet my soul rested on the tip of the sword now. All of creation fell away, and I whispered in the palace of my mind: *Don't do this*.

But no one heard.

When Mizuha thrust my mother's sword through Akiko's back, it felt the same as running through the enemy. The shock of her body against the metal echoed up my arm, and I felt it, I felt it in my heart, the whisper of her bones. Metal slicing through meat, that was all it was, that was all it had ever been. If I'd closed my eyes, I could not have told my cousin apart from anyone else. As she curled back toward me, as the light drained from her eyes, as her last breath left her in bubbles—she was no different from anyone else in the act of it all.

But she was my cousin, Shefali. She was my childhood savior at court, and the only one left who remembered my youth.

Aki-lun.

And now there was a sword through her heart. There was no surviving a wound like this. Even less of a chance if the attacker withdrew their sword and left the wound to weep.

LIKE INK. The cloud of blood that spurted from the wound—it looked like ink.

The last thing my cousin ever saw was my floating form, my mouth open, her blood on my sword.

Misery welled in my breast like a geyser. I could not even hold her as she went! I could not even . . .

After she'd traveled from Fuyutsuki to Xian-Lai just to be there in time for Sakura's party. After living through Rihima, after living through the destruction of the camp—why couldn't she have stayed in the tent? I told her to stay in the tent!

I wasn't worth saving. I wasn't worth all the lives given for me. I wasn't worth *any of this*.

"There," said Mizuha. "Was that so difficult?"

Soon, my cousin would be as bloated as the others; soon, they would dredge the two of us from the river and lament the death of our Empire.

But Daishi died to save me. Daishi, Uemura, Fenglai, Mei, all the others—I could not let their deaths be in vain.

The misery within me kindled the flame of my godhood. The sword in my hand burned with righteous fury, its light cutting through the dark. So, too, did the blood in my veins shine with gold.

This river god thought she could contain me, and perhaps, for a time, that had been true.

But no more.

Deep within me was a sliver of will. As I closed my hand around it, I found the strength to seize control of my arm. I didn't have it in me to pull away from her—but the quickest way to her . . .

Before I could begin to doubt myself, I plunged the blade into my own waist, aiming for a spot between the folds of my armor. You will think it strange when I say that I did not feel the injury then, I did not feel the bite of it. The fire was too strong in my veins for that. All I felt was a pressure, as if someone twice my size had punched me square in the stomach. All my focus went to thrusting through my own body and out the other side—it took near doubling over to do it. The hilt of my mother's sword jutted out from me like a nail from a split piece of timber.

And the rest of the sword punched into Mizuha. Her howling filled my ears; the river boiled around us. In agony, she pushed me away— but I withdrew the sword from my aching stomach and whirled on her. One cut was all it would take.

I always said I would one day kill a god, didn't I?

Aching, I raised my sword. Mizuha was already swimming away.

In a moment as brief as a lover's last night, I sliced. Her throat opened, and the river . . .

Have you ever left a covered pot to boil only to find it throwing off its lid and bubbling over?

Imagine this, but worse.

The river itself boiled over, bubbles buffeting me up and up until I once more broke the surface. I was too weak to swim—but Xianyu was on the shore, waiting, with rope. As she and the troops reeled me in, the river rose and rose and rose . . .

They dragged me ashore, and we saw it all from there.

HERE . . . HERE IS the death of Shiseiki. For the wave that rose was no ordinary wave—it was a towering Wall of Water, taller than Stone and even Flower, its glossy surface pockmarked with fish and corpses and the detritus of life. So high did it rise that the sun itself shied away from it; a moonless shadow swallowed us as we stood on the shore. A thing this massive could not be water, could only be glass worked by ten thousand artisans. A mad Emperor could not have commissioned a thing like this, ten mad Emperors could not have commissioned a thing like this, as great and horrible as an island-swallowing storm.

We watched this wave rise up.

Some fell to our knees and prayed, though the gods had not listened in centuries.

Some embraced each other, for no one in their final moments wishes to be alone.

Some—and this haunts me—chose to end their lives there, rather than let the sea take them.

For my part?

For my part, I was too horrified to look. Like a child, I buried myself in Xianyu's lap, and I thought of you, and I hoped that you would forgive me for this last thing that I had done.

When the wave at last crashed south, swallowing the encampment and everything we'd known for months, swallowing what few survivors we encountered—the sound was no different from the waves of Nishikomi crashing against the Father's Teeth.

Claim Your Ancestral Crown

I did not know, Shefali.

You must trust me when I tell you that I did not know.

If I *had* known that slaying Mizuha would summon a wave tall enough to swallow Shiseiki Province, a wave that would burst dams and send the Jade River into overflow—well. I cannot sit here and write to you that I would have chosen not to kill her. I have sworn to tell you the truth in this letter, and the truth is that I wanted Mizuha dead. In the broiling belly of my rage, the consequences of my actions did not occur to me.

Then again, when have they ever?

In all my life, Shefali, when have I ever considered the consequence of a thing before I did it? Over and over, I make the same mistakes. Over and over, I charge headlong into danger and I think, "This time, this time shall be different."

But it never is—and I am never the one who pays for it.

You wrote to me of your mother's oath. Before I read your letter, I didn't know the circumstances. Now that I do, I find myself wondering if I should not swear a similar oath. To have your best friend's tongue put out because of a thing *you* said—what uniquely royal punishment, what uniquely royal misery. It is no wonder your mother seized power soon afterwards; I would have done the same in her position.

I *did* do the same in her position.

Except—an entire province had been mutilated in my stead, and not simply a friend.

This is not to say that I was not injured following Ink-on-Water. I was. The blisters left by the lightning soon cracked, the burns began to truly torture me once the heat of battle left me. I'd stabbed through my own liver to get to Mizuha, as our surgeon explained to me, a thing which took me the better part of two months to recover from. That it took only two months astounded the surgeon—but I found little astounding about him tearing me open to stitch the wound shut. It all seemed counterintuitive—if he meant to treat the wound, then why was he creating a newer, bigger one? But at least I was given wine for that.

No amount of wine could have prepared me for what happened to Shiseiki.

The waves, they . . . they swallowed it. The first we saw was the encampment across the river, its sturdy walls now bowled over. The thick columns of wood had been snapped like twigs; the barracks now river-trampled ruins. Pine and maple were as flimsy as bamboo husks before the might of the Kirin. The bodies we'd left in the pyre now lay scattered among the wreckage. So, too, did the fish.

And the barracks got the best of it. Of the shrine we visited, only the well remained—the rest had been carried off downstream.

It would be a month before we saw the rest of the province, for when the river rose, it took with it the short-lived bridge of Jeon Siyun. We thought of making our own, but the land by the Wall was worse than it had been across the river. The fantastic visions of idyllic villages had faded now, revealing the decrepit needles that passed for trees, the ash-gray gristle of the ground—and the river. We had no hope of finding proper timber. Had you been with us, we might have been able to shoot arrows to the far bank and create a rope bridge, at least, but someone would have had to swim across, and that was not a risk we were willing to take.

For without Mizuha to rein them in, the blackbloods on both sides now took to the river as their home. Soon the blue-gold water turned a foul, murky black. None of us dared to venture near it.

Myself included.

But with no timber and no way to form a rope bridge, our only option was for me to grow one.

It should have been a simple thing to do. The Wall was far larger, spanning hundreds of li across two provinces. The Kirin was a wide river—but it was not impassable.

Yet it took me a month to grow the bridge.

It was . . . How was I to enter that state of duelist's calm when I'd lost my cousin? When only four thousand remained to me of the ten thousand with whom I'd departed, when I knew in my heart that I'd drowned half the province at least—how was I to find any calm at all? Worse, being anywhere near the river triggered a dread in me. The sound of water, the smell of it—within moments, I'd find myself back beneath the surface with Mizuha's hand around mine, with Daishi before me, and . . .

What a hypocrite I am. I have made my fortune facing my fears, I have made my name conquering the unconquerable and doing the impossible—and to this day, the idea of being submerged leaves me in tears. The sight of open water, even. Did you notice, my Shefali—the windows in my chambers no longer look out on the Jade River, or the Sound of Stone River? I've covered them. I cov-

ered my windows like a child because to see the river is to remember
and to remember is to . . .

I found no calm near the Kirin. Instead I had to use my own force
of will, a process far more exhausting. Never have I left my own body
behind, Shefali, never since the Wall; to grow the bridge required me
to assert myself over the elements, and that required my flesh. It
required my pain, it required my shame, my hope of returning to
you, my hatred for my uncle. All these things I wove together into a
banner of flame, and with this banner I called forth the flowers.

Marigold, I called, whose color belies the sorrow in her heart. She
formed the path of this bridge.

Gladiolus and violet hyacinth I called, stout-backed in spite of their
own regrets. Standing in remembrance, they formed the supports.

White oleander and white tulips I called, in a plea for forgiveness,
in a cry of warning. Reaching for those who'd dare to cross, they
formed the rails.

So rose the Bridge of Ink's Regret.

We crossed it, the Inkblots and I. I want to tell you that I put aside
my fear long enough to march across a bridge, but this, too, would
be a lie—I spent the whole while trembling. Only a conjured blind-
fold of hydrangea kept me calm. What the others might think of seeing me in such a state did not occur to me. Perhaps I should have
presented a stronger front, but I was too exhausted. I'd burnt funeral
prayers for my cousin, I'd spent weeks in frightful misery; I'd lost
six thousand sons and daughters.

I was too exhausted for much of anything.

And yet the march south continued.

A young Qorin woman dances near the fireplace, her cheeks ruddy
with drink. Her mother watches her as she feeds the dogs. She does
not dance, for tomorrow they will eat the last of their food stores;
if the dogs return empty-handed they will have to go hungry.

Watching them both is the matriarch of the family—a wizened old woman, her hands swollen and stiff, a woman who has survived the plague my people wreaked upon yours. Her years have taught her the lay of the steppes. There will be no food tomorrow, no food the day after. She will die here in this ger. She does not know whether or not she is afraid—but she watches her granddaughter dance and dreams of better days.

The three Shiseikis together in a ger.

For the Shiseiki we returned to was a different province altogether. The Great Wave had battered the province for li, reaching as far south as the Jade River. The Jade then overflowed and flooded anything directly around it.

But these things—they are statements, they are history. Useful to your brother perhaps, but not . . .

There were people in Shiseiki once. There were houses. As we marched, we passed the villages that had been so cruel to us, only to find houses leveled, only to find paddies ruined, only to find bodies like driftwood floating along the highways. The people who had named us foreigners and criminals now called to us for aid.

And what were we to do? Leave them to die? For they would die if we left them, waist deep in water with no food to speak of, trapped within their collapsed homes like fish in a cage. When we heard them crying out—what were we to do but help them?

What was *I* to do but help them?

Already the weight of what I had done bore down upon my soul. All of this had been my fault. If I had not struck down the river, then . . . then they might still be starving, I told myself, then they might have been attacked by the enemy, or all sorts of other foul ends.

But it was no comfort. I'd done this. I'd caused all this flooding. The least I could do was wade into the waste-streaked water and carry them from their cages. The least I could do was assure them that I'd find a place for them in the capital. The least I could do was feed them.

So long as they could march, I would feed them. Though it drained me, though it left me shaking and cold and frothing, it was the least I could do.

When they asked what had happened, when they asked why the Kirin had betrayed them—my guilt pierced my tongue.

It was Xianyu who answered instead.

"Who knows the whims of gods?"

She did, of course. She knew what had happened in the Kirin. Since that day, she's scarcely said a word to me, Shefali, and I did not have it in me to blame her.

Will you do the same, I wonder? Now that you know the truth of the matter, now that you know it was I who flooded Shiseiki—that you are still sitting here at all mystifies me.

All told, by the time we reached the remains of Horohama, we'd picked up three thousand destitute souls—and these only the ones we could save, only the ones who could march. There were twice that at least that either could not or would not make the journey, and twice *that* among the dead. And this without us wandering too far through the province.

We should have walked the roads. We should have tried to find more survivors—but, Shefali, all we wanted to do was to go home. All I wanted to do was . . .

Where was home? Fujino? For I'd been raised there. Was it Xian-Lai, where I'd last been happy with you, and where I'd found new happiness?

No—home was wherever you were. Over the Wall of Stone and out amidst the Golden Sands, or within the thousand-splendor palace; in a ger or in a bedroll; in the rain and in the sunlight, on the brightest days of summer and the coldest nights of winter—home had always been with you.

And so even to return home was denied me—but taking Fujino would have to do.

Horohama provided us some opportunity to regroup, some opportunity to learn of what had happened to the Empire while we were at war. When we arrived, the governor refused to believe we were who we claimed.

"The Emperor's army perished," he said. "Even before the wave, we had not heard from them in months. You may wear the phoenix, but I will see your blood with my own two eyes before I believe that you are Her Imperial Highness."

You will think I said something biting to him. I did not. I pulled off one of my gloves, rolled up my sleeve, and cut myself lightly along my forearm. Only when the red began to run down my skin did he relent, only then did he fall to his knees and ask for my forgiveness.

I granted it to him, of course. He was only being cautious.

They did not have much in the way of space in Horohama, as many of the smaller southern villages had gone to them for shelter. An open field was cleared for us instead. For food, there was only rice and broth and millet, and we ate these things without complaint, for they were treasures given the circumstances. Governor Atsuki invited me to a feast at his manse, but I refused the offer. Rice and broth and millet were more than I deserved.

"If you will not eat with me, then I beg you at least to use my writing desk," he said. "The Lady of Xian-Lai has sent messenger after messenger to us, asking for news of her sister and you. If I tell her I saw you and did not insist you wrote back, I fear the letter that would await me."

She counts the minutes while you're away, Sakura had said. I thought she'd been foolish for it then—but now I saw how right she'd been.

Part of me did not want to write her, for I did not know where to begin with this tale, but I knew that leaving in silence would be worse.

And besides, I *had* learned something of warfare from Xianyu. Three thousand farmers had little hope against the Dragon and Phoenix Guards—but the Bronze Army? Xian-Lai had surrendered before the Bronze Army took to the field. Many of my soldiers believed the Empire would be bowing to Xian-Lai now, if they had.

We were going to make them bow.

And so I took the governor up on his offer, in spite of the fact that I had my own writing desk, my own ink and brush. The man wanted to say the future Empress had used *his* desk, his ink and brush, and who was I to deny him that? I did not care enough to fight it.

Yet when the moment came to put brush to page, I could not think of words. It was too quiet, you see, in the room. For the first time in three years, I was kneeling on good bamboo mats, surrounded on all sides by rice paper screens and wooden doors. Atsuki left his rafters undecorated and unfinished, in the style my mother had favored. No chatter surrounded me, no water, nothing but . . . nothing but silence.

I knew silence. All my life I had known it, but in that room it pricked the hairs at the back of my neck. I kept expecting to hear an arrow.

In the end, I summoned two women to play the biwa for me so that I would not be alone, so that I would not have to deal with the oppressive silence. And I wrote.

To the Queen of Xian-Lai, Xian-Qin, Xian-Lun, and
Xian-Ru, Lai Baozhai,
    Your mask has served me well—in spite of what you may
have heard, I haven't yet died. Your sister is likewise well,
if you can call it "well" to have survived what we have
survived. You may hear rumors of what happened. I do not

know how much has already reached you. Some of it is true,
and some of it is false, and there are days I myself cannot tell
the difference.

Know that it is not your friend who writes this, nor your
sister-in-law. These are the words of Empress Yui.

It is time to sever the threads.

We march to Fujino to reclaim what is ours. Send the
Bronze Army—we will meet them in one month's time.

> *Empress Yui, Twenty-First Descendant of Yamai,*
> *Daughter of Heaven, Mother of Hokkaro.*

So the words left me. How it had pained me as a child to write the name Yui, and how easily it came to me now. My uncle failed at many things in his life—but he had not been wrong about this name.

Despite the women playing their music, I was alone.

I had always been alone.

You will want to know the details of how we took Fujino. Again I must disappoint you. The farther south we went, the easier it was for me to find something to drink, and the more I drank, the harder it is to remember. No longer did I bother waiting until night fell to start. It did not matter, after all. Nothing did. I'd killed thousands because my cousin had died, I'd raised a new Wall of Flowers and Bridge of Regret, fire did not burn me, and in the mornings I heard the prayers of a nation that did not truly know me. I could not die until you returned to me, and I needed to seize the throne—but besides that, little mattered to me.

To *me*, you understand. To Shizuka. No one cared if she was drunk in the middle of the day; they cared if the Empress was. So long as I kept my war mask on, so long as I was coherent enough to give orders, so long as I did not sway in my saddle—no one cared.

And so I do not remember much of the journey, I am sorry to say, only that it happened and that I spent most of it wondering where you'd gone. When I got far enough into my cups, I forgot that you'd left at all. I kept searching the crowds, looking for your mop of white hair, I kept searching for your mare, for your soft green eyes and the dimples in your cheeks.

And then, inevitably, I remembered all that had happened, and I spent the rest of the day in silence.

One of the few things I can tell you with certainty is that we went around the bamboo forest instead of going through it again. I was insistent on this, though it added a week to our travel time. Xianyu was less than pleased with the decision, but I was too drunk both to notice and to care even if I had. We were going around. I refused to march on the soil that drank so deeply of my army's blood.

I told Xianyu of my plan to sever the ties, and she told me she'd only speak to me sober, something that infuriated me but in retrospect was likely for the best. Huddled in a tent one hundred li north of Fujino, we drew our plans in the dirt. Here was the Jade Palace, around it the hunting grounds, and at the foot of my father's favorite hills was the city itself. We were coming from the north, which meant we had to ford the Jade River, a prospect that excited me about as much as sticking my hand into a bear trap.

"The Jade River is hardly a river at all," said Xianyu. "Don't concern yourself with it. Our focus should be the patrols, instead. If one of them sees us, we'll lose the element of surprise."

Don't concern yourself with the river, she said. I clenched my jaw, dug my nails into my skin. Don't concern yourself.

"Our best course of action is to dispose of them when we find them," she said, and like oil on flame, I roared at her.

"We aren't killing any Hokkarans!" I said. "We've spilled enough blood already. Capture them if you must, but let them live. I won't have any more lives on my soul, Xianyu, I won't. Do you hear me?"

"I do," she said. "But a sovereign's life belongs—"

"I know to whom my life belongs," I snapped.

She raised her brows at this. Then, slowly, she nodded. "Very well," she said. "Capture only, Your Majesty."

She'd meant to rile me, and she had. I sat there stewing for the rest of the strategy meeting. The moment she left, I reached for the bottle of rice wine in my pack just to forget any of it had happened—but that only served to make me angrier. That night, I threw my own belongings around my tent, screaming in a fit of rage that I did not understand. If I'd thought for a moment about what had caused this, if I stopped to consider why I was angry—I would have realized that none of it made sense.

But that poison had already seeped inside me, and maybe at the time, throwing things made me feel better. Maybe it gave me some measure of control.

To be entirely honest with you—I don't remember if it did. Only the headache the next day, as Xianyu woke us all before dawn to hide on either side of the road. Like bandits, we hid, Shefali—like bandits and murderers. I suppose that technically we were usurpers—my uncle had not abdicated, and thus the crown was not *really* mine—but still, these tactics felt underhanded. We dug a pit in the middle of the Weeping Road, which we covered over with thatch and a thin layer of dirt. Two companies waited for the patrol to come.

They did, of course, and promptly fell into the pit. Xianyu told me to address them then, and I did, pulling off my mask so they might see my scar and mangled ear. The sun hung high over my head, leaving me in shadow; I angled my mask so that they wouldn't mistake me for an impostor.

"Empress Yui has returned from the war," I said to them. "We have tired of Yoshimoto's follies, and so we march on Fujino to take what is ours. If you are loyal to Hokkaro, then join me and mine."

Five times I did this, ten times I did this. All of it blurs together. To my surprise, most did not fight us. My uncle's popularity lay with the lords and not the people—who were starving, thanks to his lax taxation policy. Sending the Empire's fighting youth north only to have them die as the Sixteen Swords had died—many saw that for what it was.

A mistake. An execution. A trail of corpses. An all-consuming fire that had birthed the woman who now stood before them.

Those who did not agree, we took prisoner. It is not something I am proud of, but neither did I want to kill any of them. If I was going to free Xian-Lai, if I was going to improve the lives of the people as I swore to you I would—then my uncle needed to be deposed. And if he knew I was coming, we'd face a siege.

No one wanted a siege.

And so we bound those who did not swear fealty. But we did not deprive them of food or drink; we did not force them to break ground for us. We merely saw to it that they did not wander far.

The nature of this march meant we did not stop at any major villages along the way. By extension, we did not stop at most of the villages frequented by messengers. The exception to this was Kikuma, a furrier's town often visited by merchants. We needed to get some sort of word from Baozhai, and we'd agreed before we left Horohama that Kikuma was the place to do it—patrols didn't often stop there, since most of the population was so heavily armed to begin with.

And Baozhai had indeed sent two messages to us there, on perfumed paper tied with silk cord. Even her declarations of war were impeccably presented. I presented Xianyu with hers and unrolled mine.

To Empress Phoenix, Empress Solitude,

Queen Lai addresses you now, for you have summoned her with your previous letter.

You have asked me to sever the threads, and so we lend you our scissors. The Bronze Army will meet yours. We lend you twenty thousand infantry and ten thousand horse; the remainder of the army will stay within their own lands. Though our faith in you is as unshakable as ever, one must prepare for every eventuality. Details of our plans are included in the letter to Captain Lai. Once you have reclaimed what is yours, and once we have reclaimed what is ours, we hope to once more have peace between our nations.

And that is what the Queen has to say. Let the woman speak now, and let the woman hear her.

Lady—I cannot know what you have seen. I make no assumptions on that, and I take no stock in rumors until I have heard from your own mouth what happened over the Kirin.

Whatever has happened, however it has changed you—you shall always have a home in the Bronze Palace.

Yours,

Lai Baozhai

I held this paper in my hands, and I read it over and over. Home. How long ago that had been! How I wanted to sit by the orange trees! I saw it so well in my mind: green everywhere, without a trace of river or lake; flowers that had grown without me turning to greet us. The gentle melody of the zither in the evenings as she read me poetry.

An impossible dream—and yet one presented to me in ink.

Air came to me only in gasps, only in gulps; my chest grew tight; my tongue stuck to the roof of my mouth and I sank to my knees under the power of that image—of orange blossoms and gardens, of silk and safety.

And still—still the tears did not come to me.

Soon the hills of Fujino rose up before us, soon we saw the spires of the Jade Palace.

Soon we came to the Jade River.

Xianyu is right, as usual—it is far smaller than the Kirin. As cats and tigers, the two of them. Despite their size, cats still have claws, they still have teeth. When I first heard the rushing of the river, I began to tremble. Without realizing, I'd begun to move slower than the others. It was Captain Lu who pointed this out to me, and not Xianyu. For that, I was grateful. Captain Lu only asked if we should slow—Xianyu would have told me to quicken.

I told him no, that we would not slow, that I was not afraid. With my own two lips and my own tongue, I pronounced that lie. I do not think he believed me. I did not believe myself, in hearing it—but I quickened my pace all the same, and when we crested the hill, there it was.

The river that I'd floated paper lanterns down every Sixth of Tokkar; the river where my mother tried to teach me to fish. The river where your mother learned to swim, the river I played in until my fingers looked like sun-dried plums.

I knew this river.

And yet I did not.

Seeing the water was seeing the bodies again, was seeing Daishi's horrified face again. Sweat trickled down my brow; my hands shook, my teeth rattled in my skull. The air left my lungs, and I felt again the water filling them, I felt again the ache in my liver and the shooting pain of my arm.

I sat there in the saddle, attempting to face my fear—only to be slain by it. I could not move, Shefali, I could not break the spell the water laid upon me. The eyes of the captains turned to me and I felt them, too, I felt the weight of their judgment but I could not move.

If I moved, I'd fall into the water.

In my fear and shame I called the hydrangea again. Only when I was safe in its embrace did I cross the Bridge of Imperial Splendor into Fujino City.

The Taking of Fujino, if you can call it that, happened quickly. We did not enter Fujino as an army, but in groups of twenty, with our rags on over our armor. Given the flooding of Shiseiki, there were many migrants entering the city, most of whom were from Shiseiki. We looked no different from them—horror colored our faces and weariness bent our shoulders. The guards asked us only from whence we'd come—and Xianese though the Blots are, most speak at least a little Hokkaran.

Will it amuse you to know that I slipped by the guards the same way? With a farmer's hat low over my brow, there was little to differentiate me. My eyes might've given me away, but Xianyu was in my group, and she handled all the talking for us. The rest of us hardly merited a look.

And so we entered Fujino in the early days of Nanatsu, with the summer sun bearing down on us.

We reached the Imperial Hunting Grounds without much incident—and it was there that some subterfuge became necessary. Only Imperials, nobles, and the Dragon Guard could freely walk through the hunting grounds by law. Anyone else foolish enough to try would be executed on sight if the dangerous game within did not find them first. Therefore, at the borders of the hunting grounds, the city guard gives way to the Dragon Guard—and we did not want to have to fight them.

Thankfully—we did not have to. Once the bulk of the army was near the hunting grounds, Xianyu pulled a flute from her sleeve. The five notes that sounded from it began an old Xianese song Baozhai liked to sing as she dressed: "Four Seasons, Four Loves." I'd not once heard it in the Northern Provinces.

But I heard it then. In the distance, I heard the next five notes, and the next five, gently fading as the signals carried all the way to the outer walls, where our scouts lay in wait. The Bronze Army hid five li from the city, nearer to the Sound of Stone River. When our scouts reached them—that was when they began their march.

As word began to spread of an army advancing on the city, panic took hold of Fujino. The crowds I saw before now became stampedes as everyone shoved everyone away in search of safety. The hunting grounds, once seen as dangerous for the trespass penalty and the creatures within, now seemed the best place to hide.

For the second time, I found myself swallowed by a great wave— but this time, it was a wave of people. There were only a hundred or so guards around the perimeter, and thousands of us, thousands of desperate peasants pushing forward. Concerned murmuring gave way to shouting, gave way to shrieks, and suddenly everyone, everyone, was running into the grounds, and trampling whatever stood in their way.

The army had planned for this, of course. While in the forest, we changed into our armor and fetched our weapons from the wagons. With my war mask on and my sword in hand, I felt powerful, I felt myself, I felt *right*.

In Crane's Wing, we gathered; in Crane's Wing, we advanced through the forest. By then, the bulk of the Dragon Guard had taken off for the Southeast Gate, where the Bronze Army was entering. Thus we had already split their forces. The last thing they expected was an army to emerge from the forest—and for them to unfurl the Imperial banner.

Alarms rang throughout the palace—I heard them even from the gates. They cried for us to identify ourselves, to show ourselves.

I stood once more in the saddle. With the Imperial banner behind me and the palace before me, I raised my sword, I raised my mask.

"I am the woman my uncle could not kill," I said. "I am the Eternal Flame of the Empire, I am my father's daughter. You have asked who I am, and I tell you—I am the trueborn blood of Yamai, I am the trueborn blood of Minami Shiori. Empress Yui stands before you!"

And, in truth, I half expected an arrow to the face for this boldness. Certainly, I expected arrows to fall upon the army, but the telltale whistling darkness never came.

Behind me, I heard the rustling of my men and women; ahead of me, I saw the eyes of the Phoenix Guard go wide beneath their plumed helms. Wind whipped through the courtyard, jostling our banners and theirs.

A father is visited by the local lord's retinue. Demons are coming from the North and it is time to muster an army; the man must provide one of his children. He has five, a blessing for which he has offered incense and prayers at the local shrine. The lord allows him a moment to decide which child he will offer up. Will it be his eldest daughter, stronger than any of the boys in the village, whose talent for wordplay astounds him? Will it be his eldest son—a sheepish boy who taught himself to read by listening to the Imperial criers and comparing what he heard to the posters they'd leave behind? Perhaps the middle child, a girl scarcely fifteen summers? She has always had a way with horses—but she is a child, a *child*, and the thought of her getting hurt brings the man to his knees.

The horror of that decision was one well known to the Phoenix Guard.

Their sacred duty, their oath, was to protect the Jade Palace. To do so, they'd have to strike down me and my army—and in so doing, they may well kill the only remaining heir to the throne.

If they allowed me entrance, then I might well kill the Emperor to seize the throne. That would be the wise thing to do, the safe thing to do. If I let him live, I was going to have to deal with myopic nobility claiming our lives were better under his rule. Seizing power this way was bound to earn me a few enemies. And so, obviously, I was going to have to kill him.

Yet if I did—would that really be so terrible for the guard? A new ruler meant new rules. My uncle was unwilling to raise taxes on Shiratori and Fuyutsuki, and so we did not have the funds to feed the Inner Empire. My uncle conscripted armies to travel over the Wall, knowing well and good that it would never work. My uncle, who had not even managed to recover the bones of the last dragon from the Surians.

Would it be so terrible if he left?

For then, they'd trade assignments with the Dragons. No longer would they be forced to patrol the palace, no longer would they be bound to Fujino, to guard a man who gorged himself while his Empire starved. They might travel the whole Empire in my service. They might actually *help* those who needed it.

The Phoenix Guard, after all, is the personal army of the *Empress*. And it was the *Empress* who now stood before them.

Again the wind. There are no trees at the gates—my ancestor Yasaru despised the old maples that used to stand at either side—but there are two near the steps. Summer camellias, both of them, their bark a motley of brown-orange-white. They weren't true camellias, you understand, only imitations. Legend has it the tree flowers best when you plant it across from real camellias, for jealousy will encourage it to be more beautiful. As a child, I hadn't liked them.

But to see them now swaying in the summer breeze, to see their bark and know I'd come the closest I could to home—now, the sight brought me the peace to speak.

"I've no great thirst for blood," I said. "And neither do my soldiers.

Many of you have known me since I was a child; many of you had the honor of knowing my parents. You know I keep my word. Stand down, and I will call for the Bronze Army to stand down; we need not stain the tiles red."

"How can we be certain it is you?" called one of them. Isshikawa. Of all the guards in the palace, it had to be her.

"When I was twelve, you caught me running drills with the Daybreak Blade. It was First Bell, and I was convinced no one would see me," I said. She was already flinching, but I had already begun the story. "You fetched my mother although I begged you not to."

"I did not know she would hurt you—" she began, but I raised a hand to cut her off.

"You knew my mother," I said. "And so you know me. Stand down, Isshikawa-zul."

A moment of hesitation. Her eyes flicked up to me, landing on my shoulders instead of my eyes. An old trick for anyone who dealt with Imperials. Slowly the eyes of the entire courtyard came to rest on her.

And slowly, she bowed.

Like the wind through the reeds of Nishikomi, the sight before me—one by one, the Phoenix Guards bowed to me and mine. I let out a breath that I did not know I had been holding.

With no more bloodshed, I'd already taken the throne. All that remained was to drag my uncle off it. We sent our scout along with the Phoenix's down to the Southeast Gate—and me and my army continued into the palace.

It is strange, isn't it? As a child, I thought the palace was endless. One wrong turn, and I'd never be able to find my way out again. Everyone said Ancestor Yashin was killed by the Qorin on his way to Sur-Shar—but I knew better. He'd gotten up in the middle of the night to find a cake, and he'd made that wrong turn, and somewhere in the palace was an old man begging to see the daylight one last time.

As a woman grown, I knew there was an old man in the palace, and I knew he'd be begging for his life.

Would he fear me, when he saw me?

As I took those steps through the palace, as I walked the path so familiar to me, as the guards bowed one by one—did I look fearsome?

I cannot answer—but I will tell you this.

When I came upon my uncle, he was alone in the Imperial chambers. When I came upon him, the room was open, the only walls being those provided by the foundations themselves. Behind him, a screen of General Nozawa conquering Xian-Lai left the room awash in green. He, sitting in the proper style in the center, wore all white. His hair—thick as my father's and streaked with gray—was unbound. At his side, a sword that my grandfather had given him; before him, my father's writing desk, with a half-finished poem written upon it.

As I entered, he sat with brush in hand, trembling like a branch in a storm, his eyes bulging from his head, sweat coating him like an eel. Drops of ink fell from the brush onto the paper.

"Uncle," I called to him, and he dropped the brush with a clatter onto my father's desk. Frantic, his hair flying up like feathers, he scrambled for the sword. I did not stop it. He leveled it at me, and I did not fear. He hadn't had the presence of mind to unsheathe it.

I had the presence of mind to take off my shoes.

"Uncle," I said again as he wheeled backwards, as he knocked against the screen. "You tried to have me killed."

"You should be *dead*!" he wailed. Now he remembered to draw the sword. "They told me you were dead!"

Behind me Xianyu drew hers, behind me the archers readied—but I waved them off.

We would settle this alone.

"Who told you that, Uncle?" I asked. Now I was within two horselengths of him. The rattle of his sword filled the room. "Who told you that I was dead?"

The screen fell onto him. With one arm, he tossed it up. Soon he was standing—soon he was walking into a corner. "Kasuri-zun," he said.

As a drop of water onto a mountain lake—the purity of my mind in that moment. *He'd* spoken to Kasuri. *He'd* put her in charge of the Shiratori army.

When had he spoken to her? Was Kasuri ever a real woman, or simply a creation of Amari's?

I lunged for him. He swung at me, but I batted the blade away with my forearm. A swift stomp on his instep sent him crumpling in pain. I grabbed hold of his wrist, turned, and flipped him over my back. He fell like a sack of millet to the ground—and then my foot was on his throat. I did not drop his wrist, either, but twisted it until I felt it snap.

"You knew, didn't you?" I said to him. There was more black to his eyes than amber. I felt him try to swallow. When he stared at me rather than answer, I twisted his wrist further. Beneath his skin, his wrist was like snapped bamboo. "You *knew*."

"Sh-she said she could rid me of you," he said. "She said I'd never have to worry about you again—"

My vision was going red. I stomped on his throat. "And you believed her? You sent thousands to die, just to kill me?"

He was turning blue. "There wasn't . . ."

"There wasn't what, Iori?!" I roared. I lifted my foot from his throat long enough to kick him in the crook of his shoulder. The wordless sputter that left him, the dry retching sound he made only infuriated me more. "There wasn't any reason to treat with demons? No, there wasn't. There wasn't any reason to send us north, no reason except your own petty grudge? No, there wasn't. Come on. Say it!"

Again I kicked him. Faintly I heard Xianyu calling my name, and I ignored her. "Say what you mean, Iori!"

I could see the veins at his temple, I could see his bruises forming. My father told me that he and my uncle once rode into battle—but I found that hard to believe.

His eyes met mine, and he said the words, Shefali—he said the words that taught me how to hate.

"There wasn't enough food to feed them all," he said. "What was I supposed to do?"

I THOUGHT I knew horror, Shefali. I thought I knew rage.

Now it was my stomach sinking, now it was my soul leaving my body in a glimmer. I could not have heard him correctly.

He sent us all north because he could not afford to feed us?

Fire, crackling in my veins; anger and agony a storm in my chest.

"They said you'd die," he said. "They said no one would know. They said they'd leave my throne alone if I sent you north—"

I punched him. As hard as I could, Shefali, I punched him. In the way you taught me—thumb tucked and wrist stiff, my legs and hips providing the momentum. I punched him over and over, until the right side of his face was too swollen to recognize.

"Was it worth it?" I asked him, over and over. "You can't kill me. You could *never* kill me. Do you understand who I am?"

Sputtering was his answer, blood spittle on the mats was his answer. I stood astride him and grabbed hold of his robes. "Do you understand who I am, Iori?" I asked him again.

His eyes glassy, two of his teeth missing, he answered. "A god," he said. "I . . . I see it now. A god."

I drew my hand all the way back this time. When my fist met his nose, when I felt the pop of his broken nose, I am ashamed to say I was thrilled.

"Wrong," I said. "I was Shizuru and Itsuki's daughter before I was a god."

He was staring at me now, too weak to fight me off. The sword he'd dropped lay right by us—but I had no need of it. I drew the Daybreak Blade instead and pressed it to his sweat-slick throat.

And . . .

And he changed, in my view. My mother's face stared back at me, just as swollen as his, her teeth missing and her nose broken, the same desperation in her eyes. I heard her in my mind: "Itsuki, Itsuki, bring me Itsuki. . . ."

But I couldn't bring her my father. I'd never seen him after he left on the ninth; I had no body to burn.

She kept calling for him, and I could not bring her peace.

And so I'd pressed the sword to her throat and I'd made my cut.

I saw Daishi within him, her eyes wide with fear, the water lending her face a cruel darkness. I saw her swallowing water instead of air, I saw her reaching for me, I saw her floating. I saw her, three days later, when one of the soldiers had found her body on the riverbanks and seen fit to call me to see it.

I saw her.

Mizuha had forced my hand to run her through—but it had been my hand. I'd killed her.

When I blinked, it was the Toad before me again, with my sword at his throat.

The man who had killed thousands rather than try to feed them. The man who had treated with demons to try to kill me. The man who had commanded my mother to fight forty blackbloods on her own, the man who burned down the gardens because I had changed the flowers.

The man who exiled you.

His tears fell on my bruised hand.

"You are, without a doubt, the most pathetic human being I have ever met," I said. "If I killed you, the world would name me a hero for it."

My eyes went dry. I pressed them together, opened them again. "But I have shed too much blood, Iori. I have killed too many already."

Before he could gawk too much, I shoved him into the ground and pressed the sheath of my mother's sword against the base of his neck.

"Death is what you deserve. My mother would have killed you, and we both know that to be true. You are fortunate indeed that there is too much of my father in me."

I gestured for Xianyu and the others to enter, and they did, albeit eyeing me as if I'd grown a second head. They bound him as I sat before my father's writing desk. The poem my uncle had attempted to write was by now illegible; I picked it up and burned it with a thought. The paper beneath, thankfully, was free of his influence.

"You shall live," I said, "but you shall not enjoy your life. You have shown that you wish to stay in the palace while the world burns around you, and so you shall."

I wrote an announcement of abdication—this I kept as simple as possible. Without looking him in the face, I took the seal from his robes and stamped the paper.

"I will build a pit in the gardens," I said, "with steep stone walls. We'll lower you down into it with a bucket, and then we will close it off, leaving only a hole wide enough to accommodate a bowl of rice— and then I will cover it with flowers, so that the demons shall never be able to reach you. You shall be alone for the rest of your days."

I rose, the paper in hand.

"You shall think on what you have done, and when the Mother takes you, you shall tell her your name is Solitude," I said.

I called for the guards to come in—they answered to me now—
and I called for them to keep a close eye on him until the well could
be finished.

And with that—it was done.

That part of it. The exciting part, if you can call it that. The rest of
it—like clouds passing over the sun. Hokkaro has had enough mon-
archs that transitioning between the two is a simple enough business;
most of the servants have had at least one generation of practice. Of
course, since my uncle had treated with demons, I could no longer
trust any of his servants. I required each of them to shed a single drop
of blood in my presence before I would allow them to return to my
service.

And when you do a thing like that, people naturally ask why.

But they were asking me a lot of questions just then. How had I
lived? Why had I gone north with only a farmers' army? Why had
I not taken the Bronze Army instead? Where had my uncle gone?

And these questions all had their answers, which I gave to the waiting courtiers. I conscripted farmers because I was forced to. I went
north because I was forced to. My uncle? My uncle had tried to sell
us to a Demon General.

What proof did I have? My word. The word of all the soldiers who
had seen the ruins of the encampment. Did they mean to challenge
me? Let them.

And so where had I sent him, how had I punished him? That was
for me to know—but safe to say, he would never again trouble the
Empire. I insisted on being coronated before the Jubilee, and so I
summoned the lords to court so that I might have witnesses.

I shaved my brows, I painted my teeth black and my face white, I
buried myself beneath eight layers of robes, and I pretended to be
the thing they needed me to be. Traditional, unwavering, made wise
by my time at war. Gone my fashionable silk robes, gone my fiery

demeanor. The Empress at last and no longer the headstrong girl. The Phoenix, though my crown lacked its feathers.

To my rooms I went, where I might be alone with my guilt; to my rooms I went, where I had my liquor to keep me company. As the voices of the army echoed in my mind, as the memory of their faces rose before me, I drank until they began to fade. I drank until the world spun, I drank until my sense left me, until sleep embraced me.

But even sleep's embrace soon turned on me. In my dreams, I returned again to the serpent's mouth. Desperate and panicked, I tried to climb out, only to find Daishi waiting for me when I reached its lips. Yet this was not the Daishi I'd grown up with—it was the bloated corpse we'd taken from the river, barnacles coating her skin, her eye eaten by some passing opportunist. When she smiled at me, her teeth were needle sharp.

"Cousin," she said. "We both know this is where you belong."

She clamped the serpent's mouth down. I woke up still screaming for her to leave me be.

It was not the first time I'd had such a dream, and it would not be the last. You, my Shefali, have seen me through a few of them already. In the days since I returned from Shiseiki, I've forgotten what it feels like to wake rested. I thought—I hoped—that when you returned, I'd at last know proper sleep, but . . .

The corruption that poisons your blood is not something you can cut out—no matter how I wish it were. If it took every drop of blood in my body to cure you, I would give it, and happily, to see that you are well. You have lived a life of such suffering already, Shefali, this disease is not something you deserve.

But diseases aren't demons. You cannot challenge them to a duel. You cannot lead an army against them. All you can do is learn what you can about their treatment and work toward a cure.

And so you—the only person to have survived infection—continue to stare at the Mother and tell her to wait.

My nightmares, my memories, my bone-deep fears—these things cannot compare to your condition. Sleep is furtive for me, but attainable; I have not lost the ability to taste sweets and plum wine. Only my own maudlin emotions keep me confined to the bed—do not think I have not noticed the stiffness in your movements of late.

But you can no more cut these memories from my mind than I can cut the Traitor from your blood.

I see that now.

I had such hope, Shefali, that when you returned, I would be better. So much of my life in your absence was predicated on that thought. It did not matter how much I drank—when you returned, I'd lose the taste for wine. It did not matter what I'd done in Shiseiki—when you returned, your love would wash me clean of my impurity. It did not matter whom I took to bed—when you returned, my heart would beat only for you.

So little of that has come true.

I lose myself in these emotions.

I haven't finished the story, have I? In truth, there isn't much left to tell.

You will want to know about the coronation, but you will have to ask someone else who attended. Because of the nightmares, I spent the morning drinking myself into half a stupor. I hardly remember the ceremony itself, and if I hadn't written myself a speech, I would've forgotten all my planned proclamations. Baozhai can tell you, or your brother—if you are keen to speak with either of them—how I slurred through the speech, how I had two servants sitting on either side of me just to keep me up.

What an impression I made my first day as Empress.

All I remember are the proclamations themselves. That my first proclamation as Empress was that you were no longer exiled, and your name may again be spoken. With drunken ardor, I referred to you as Empress Wolf. I remember *that* part because no one has let me forget it; the name unfortunately caught on. Soon I was inundated with portraits of "Empress Wolf" to try to win favor, all of which rendered you either pale as snow or dark as coal. I received new word of you every day, it seemed, from twenty people who had all seen you in different places. You were in Axiot warring with the heathen gods; you were in Ikhtar, kept as their Queen's pet; you'd become a pit fighter in Sur-Shar.

I entertained these stories because they entertained me—yet for each one I heard, you seemed farther and farther away. Surely, if you were the Queen's pet—you would have found the time to write.

And yet I hadn't heard from you.

I thought that perhaps my uncle had been intercepting your letters to me, or mine to you, and so I redoubled my efforts. Every day I wrote you. *Every day.* Somewhere in Sur-Shar, there's an entire company's worth of messengers too ashamed to return to me, who have read the words of a vulnerable heart. I shudder to think where the letters ended up if not with you.

The second proclamation was far more important to most people.

Effective immediately, the Empire freed Xian-Lai to its proper Queen, Lai Xian-Lai, with Lai Baoyi as its Crown Princess. In the coming years, the Empire would also free Hanjeon and Dao Doan, should they so wish to be freed. Xian-Lai had been in our possession only sixty years, and thus many of its independent bodies could be reappointed with little delay. This, combined with Baozhai's family line being undisturbed, meant independence could be accomplished with relative quickness. Dao Doan and Hanjeon had remained under Hokkaran rule for five hundred and three hundred years respectively—and of the two, only Dao Doan had a monarchy.

Hanjeon functioned as something called a "republic," a thing that I have never bothered to understand but they seemed to enjoy very much before we came along. In cases like that, a little extra time would be necessary, I thought.

You can imagine what the reaction to that was like.

Because I'd been obviously drunk when I read it aloud, the first assumption was that I'd been joking. Shiratori had the temerity to ask me if I was serious before the other gathered lords, I remember, and I told him I was as serious about this as he was about running a mob-infested den of sin. He did not take well to that, which I suppose I cannot blame him for, and stormed off. The rest assumed I'd come to my senses later in the evening, when the liquor wore off.

They were mistaken there—I was still drunk in the evening.

But the next morning, I was sober, and I reaffirmed what I'd said. Xian-Lai was free.

The nobles acted as if I'd torn off the heads of their firstborns. How was the rest of the Empire going to function without Xian-Lai, they asked, as if we had not done so perfectly well for over a thousand years. Yes, things were more difficult now, and the North's crops were failing—but with the new Wall in place, we'd have a few years to re-plenish ourselves at least.

I had it all thought out, you see, in the way that a drunkard has everything planned out until you ask her for details. The absurd taxes we'd levied from Xian-Lai would now be levied from Shiratori and Fuyutsuki—the two provinces least affected by the blight, given their chief exports of gem and stone. We'd get less food from Xian-Lai, certainly, but Baozhai wasn't about to let us starve—and with more money in the Imperial coffers, we could trade with Sur-Shar via the Qorin to make up the difference. Nishikomi's port would continue to take in food from abroad, as well.

It would all work out.

Well.

I haven't been entirely unsuccessful. The people, I'm told, are pleased with the changes I've made, although freeing Xian-Lai is sometimes seen as a weakness.

A weakness from the woman who raised a new Wall of Flowers— but I digress.

The nobles are different beasts entirely.

Part of this is because I've taken Baozhai's (continued, and very well reasoned) advice. I've shaved off my eyebrows, I've painted my teeth black, I've endeavored to be as traditionally Hokkaran as possible. Soon all this nonsense spread, as fashion is wont to do, until the whole court now convenes in clothing our grandparents would've deemed antique.

But fashion was not enough. I had to convince them we could be Hokkaran without owning other nations—and that meant returning to all the older pastimes. I took to playing zither concerts, I took to practicing my father's calligraphy. I commissioned a Book of Imperial Poetry for the first time in two hundred years. *The Gilt-Petal Book*, I called it, as I have never been as creative as my father. Throughout the Empire, I called for more painted opera, more storytellers, more musicians. Anything to remind us of who we'd been before we got a taste for other people's food.

How has it gone?

Your father's pleased with me, for once. He sent me a detailed Imperial genealogy for my last birthday, which is the first gift I've received from him since we were married. It's not a very good gift, but he wrote the whole thing by hand. Earlier this year, he sent me new sticks of ink, too.

Shiseiki, Dao Doan, and Hanjeon—I am friendly with these lords. Even Fuyutsuki, though displeased with my taxes, is willing to sacrifice for the greater good of the Empire.

You and I are two pine needles, Shefali. So we have been since the moment of our birth. Our love is as immutable as the stars, as unconquerable as the sun. The days I've spent with you are more valuable to me than my mother's sword. No matter the distance, our hearts beat as one. Our love is a *power*. To run amidst the wind and rain during the heaviest monsoon of the year, to swallow lightning, to laugh in the face of the gods we've usurped—that is what it is to love you.

You have asked me for the truth of the matter. As best as I can recall it, I've shared it with you.

All that remains is the decision.

It is yours to make, my wanderer, my great love. Should you choose to leave having learned what you have learned—I shall not say that it will be an easy thing to accept, but I will accept it all the same. You are no woman's to tame; you ride where the wind will take you. This I have always known. That you have remained at my side through so many years is a priceless gift.

If . . . if you choose to stay, in spite of all this, then you know now the woman I have become. You know the blood that stains me, you know the decisions I have made, you know what lies in my heart. I have laid myself bare for you in ways often uncomfortable. Will you stay?

BARSALAI SHEFALI

FOURTEEN

By the time Shizuka has finished speaking, her voice is little more
than a whisper. Curled in Shefali's arms like a child, she stares at
the crescent scar on her palm instead of looking at her wife. From the
slump of her shoulders, from the tremble of her lips, it's clear—she
doesn't have the strength to continue.

There is a pain in Shefali's chest, a feeling like swallowing glass,
as the story settles in. The wave swallowing Shiseiki; the water
spirit guiding her murderous hand; the Toad's heartless admission. All of this her wife has endured, and all of this she has endured alone.

If Shefali had refused to leave—if she'd returned sooner—how
much of this could have been averted? If she had been with Shizuka in Shiseiki, would the river have betrayed her in such a way?
For if the god were not dead, Shefali would've hunted her down. If
she had been with Shizuka in Shiseiki, then she could have torn
apart the Traitor's army with her teeth and claw. If she had been

with Shizuka in Shiseiki, Amari's deception would never have continued so long.

But she hadn't been.

"Will you stay?" she asks her.

As if they are children again and the dark is frightening her.

Words fail her as they so often have. How is she to convey the guilt in her heart, the shame? How can she tell her how grateful she is to hold her wife in her arms, knowing what she knows now?

All she can think of is to show her.

To promise her, without words; to swear an oath to her.

Yes. She shall stay. She shall stay until the Silver Steppes shine violet; she shall stay until the seas dry; she shall stay through the fires and the flames and the coldest breath of winter.

When Shefali brings their lips together, it is more than a kiss. The star she swallowed their first night together once more warms her, warms them, envelops them. Their hands are joined now, the blood staining them both only an afterthought.

Together, they swore.

Shefali swears it again and again, her unspoken oath an unspoken prayer; Shizuka's lips the altar.

When they part, there is something of the Phoenix again in Shizuka, something of the fire she once commanded. Her slender fingers fly to her mouth. She looks down, and then again at Shefali, expectant, hopeful.

"Shefali," she says. "After all you've heard . . . ?"

How can she tell her?

How can she tell her there are no words that can keep them apart? How can she tell her that she has loved her since her first breath, and nothing will come between them?

What happened beneath the Kirin shall not sway her. There was no way Shizuka could have known the wave would follow.

And if Shefali had been in her place, she would have done the same.

Whatever path the two of them walk—the crows will follow them both.

So be it.

Shefali pulls her closer. Shizuka is atop her now, her hair pooling on Shefali's thighs, her mouth open, her cheeks red beneath the line of her scar.

Shefali places her thumb right between Shizuka's brows. "Like two pine needles," she says.

"But I'm not . . . I've . . . Shefali, Shiseiki is in ruins because of me, and—"

"You didn't know," Shefali says. She strokes Shizuka's cheek, stopping at the scar, running her thumb across it.

"I should have," says Shizuka. "Every night I wonder what would have happened if—"

"The man who only dreams of hunting starves," Shefali says. Something Otgar told her once, when she needed to hear it. "You raised a new Wall, Shizuka."

"It didn't save them," she mumbles. That she can mumble about so wondrous a thing!

Shefali kisses her eyes. "Without it, they'd overrun the North."

"But I couldn't save Daishi," Shizuka says. Her voice cracks. "I couldn't save the other armies; I couldn't save Shiseiki. I'm not the woman you fell in love with, Shefali, I'm a broken—"

"Don't say that," Shefali says. The words well up inside of her and she cannot stop them from pouring out—only with Shizuka does she feel this comfortable, to speak at such length. "Who else could have done what you did? Your uncle sent you north to die, and you returned an Empress. More than that! You raised a Wall of Flowers across the whole Empire with only your own will—and you say you are broken?"

She cups Shizuka's face. Gone, her stoicism; passion seizes her now as she speaks, written plain across her face.

"The woman I see in front of me isn't broken at all. Who can break a storm, Shizuka? Who can break a mountain? All your life, fate has *tried*, and yet you stand defiant. You remain. The sorrow in your heart does not lessen you. How could it? What is a storm without rain? That you yet breathe is proof that you are unbroken, my Shizuka, my mountain of faith, and I will be by your side until I draw my last."

Thousands of li away, the great mountain Gurkhan Khalsar stands as a testament to all Qorin of Grandfather Earth's majesty. At its base, the mighty Rokhon River grants succor to the gathered clans once every year. Fifteen summers Shefali spent at the base of the mountain, fifteen hundred mornings spent watching the sun rise to crown its storied peak. She knows the colors well: Grandmother's scarlet blush as she draws nearer to her husband; the violet of the fading night; the roan of the mountain itself. Most regal of all: the gold of the sun.

Fifteen hundred times she saw this sight.

Fifteen hundred times, her breath caught in her throat.

Shizuka's eyes have gone that same gold.

How holy, how holy—to hold such a woman in her arms.

And this time, it is Shizuka who will come to worship.

TOGETHER, THEY'D SAID.

And they needed each other now more than ever. Shefali is sure of it. That is why she spends the night holding on to Shizuka's hand, even after the Empress has fallen asleep. In the rise and fall of her wife's breast, in her dreamy exhalations, Shefali hears that word: "together."

She cannot remember the last time she weathered a night so long as this. Every passing moment, she worries that the Scholar is there, lurking, waiting for the chance to spring his foul influence upon her anew. It had happened so quickly earlier. What was to prevent it from happening again, save her own will and the woman asleep in her arms?

Is her own will even enough? She isn't certain anymore. Not after . . .

Sky, she hadn't even been speaking Hokkaran. What was happening to her?

When she catches the scent of the servants in the morning, bringing Baozhai's carefully selected breakfast, Shefali is thankful for her nose. If they'd knocked on the door instead, she would've leaped half out of her skin.

"Empress Phoenix, Empress Wolf," comes the call. "Her Most Serene Majesty the Thorned-Blossom Queen has graciously provided you your morning meals."

A youngish woman, one Shefali has not taken note of before, is doing the speaking. Shizuka hasn't yet awoken, and Shefali is hesitant to blaspheme her sacrosanct slumber. If she wants to tell the servants to leave the tray, she will have to rise and tell them herself.

And that means letting go of her wife's hand—for surely if she picks her up, Shizuka will wake.

Shefali swallows. She is the Kharsa's daughter—she cannot let her fear rule her. With a quick kiss on Shizuka's brow, she rises to her feet. Withdrawing her hand is like cutting off a limb.

But she makes the cut all the same.

Her chest flutters. Yes—there is a darkness around her now, quickly encroaching, but it is only a passing shadow. She tells herself this because if she does not, she will falter, and if she falters . . .

I am Barsalai Shefali, and I have twice earned that name, she mutters to herself.

But as she makes her way to the door, she reaches for her mask, and as she tugs on her deel, she reaches again for the feather O-Shizuru gave her. With her mask in place and the feather in hand, she feels ready to face the world.

Or at least these servants.

They do not start when they see her, and they do not question her when she asks to take the tray. As they politely bow and turn away, Shefali takes a deep breath.

Maybe she can handle this. For now, anyway. The moment she sets the tray down, she once more takes Shizuka's hand.

Two hours later, when Shizuka at last awakes, she is smiling and full of wonder. It is as if this is the first time she has laid eyes on Shefali.

Her first words of the day: "Beloved, take off that mask."

Shefali smiles beneath it. She'd forgotten she was wearing it, in truth, as worried as she was about the Scholar. After a while, the bronze warms enough that she cannot feel it at all.

But she takes it off now, for her wife has asked her to. Shizuka traces the hollows of Shefali's cheeks, the hard line of her jaw. For not the first time, Shefali wonders how her wife still finds her attractive—this condition has ravaged her.

"My warrior," Shizuka says. "I don't think I'll ever tire of waking up to you."

"I'm terrifying," says Shefali.

"Only to people who deserve to be terrified," says Shizuka. "To me, you will always be the girl who was too nervous to kiss me."

Shefali's cheeks go hot. Embarrassment and bashfulness swallow her anxieties; she allows herself this brief peace, and in so doing, allows it to Shizuka.

And yet peace is as fleeting as a winter flower for them. The tiger in the room remains to be addressed.

"How are you feeling?" Shizuka asks. "Is he . . . ?"

"Lurking," Shefali answers. "I'm myself, for now."

Shizuka nods. She sits up, the blankets peeling away from her. Where the morning light caresses her skin, it turns her to gold. Shefali tries not to stare, and fails.

"We don't have much time before my handmaidens arrive," Shizuka says. "If that shadow-clock is right, it's nearly the Hour of the Buried Axe; Baozhai will be expecting me for morning tea."

"Buried Axe?" Shefali says. She cannot keep all these systems straight.

"Third Bell," Shizuka says. She covers Shefali's hand with her free one. "Do you want to come to tea? If you aren't feeling up to it, my love, that is perfectly understandable—you've been through so much already."

"With Baozhai, or with the Queen?" Shefali asks, for they are two different women.

Shizuka winces. "The Queen," she says. "I should have mentioned that. We're discussing tea, actually; the South grows most of it, and they're thinking of increasing our tariffs—it is a business meeting."

While Baozhai no doubt selected something wonderfully fragrant for such an important meeting, the thought of listening to the Thorned-Blossom Queen and the Phoenix Empress discuss trade agreements makes Shefali grit her teeth. She has had more than enough trade agreements for one lifetime.

And yet, if she leaves . . .

"If you'd prefer," says Shizuka, "you could speak to Sakura-lun and your brother about . . . about what happened."

Shefali stiffens.

"I know—you are not fond of him and you have not forgiven him," says Shizuka. She squeezes Shefali's hand. "But if there is anyone alive who might have some idea of what is going on, it's them. He's been researching the blackblood like a man possessed, and Sakura is the only one who really knows the extent of it."

The handmaidens are coming. Shefali can smell them in the hall already. She lets out a long, labored breath.

Speaking to her brother.

"Beloved," says Shizuka. She cups Shefali's face now, and Shefali turns toward her—a fly trapped in amber. "I am worried for you. I swore to you that I'd do whatever it took to slay this beast, and . . . and perhaps this is it. Perhaps the best I can do is ensure you speak to them. But seeing the way you were last night . . . we must do *something*."

She's more right than she knows. They don't have much time, if they are to do something. Shefali's convinced there's nothing to be done, but . . . it really is difficult to turn Shizuka down when there's such plaintive worry in her eyes.

Shefali sighs. It was going to happen eventually, wasn't it?

"All right," she says. "But I won't go alone."

"Of course," says Shizuka. "I'll go with you. Are you coming to tea?"

Shefali shakes her head. "If I'm going to deal with my brother," she says, "I'm going to fix some of his mistakes first. Baoyi needs someone to teach her how to ride."

She can see the argument forming: *She already knows, she has very fine tutors, your brother is part Qorin, too.*

But these arguments do not leave Shizuka's lips. Instead: "Will you be all right?"

I don't know is the genuine answer. If the Scholar comes over her while she's around Baoyi . . . Shefali does not want to imagine what might come of it. But that is all the more reason to go. If reinforcing her will is the only way to stop this, then nothing will motivate her like keeping her niece safe.

"Yes," says Shefali. She picks up her mask. Shizuka stands, and Shefali pulls her closer, kissing the soft skin of her wife's stomach.

"Shefali, I'm serious!" she says. "Are you absolutely certain you'll be okay?"

"I'm always certain," Shefali answers her.

Shizuka puffs in mock offense. "Now I've half a mind to drag you along."

"But only half," says Shefali. She stands, holding Shizuka by the shoulders and admiring her as long as she can. Perhaps holding this sight in mind will help later.

"Fourth Bell, then?" Shizuka says. "Outside the library?"

Shefali nods, and Shizuka kisses her.

"Stay safe," Shizuka says as Shefali leaves her.

And Shefali says that she will, though she reaches for the feather with a trembling hand.

SHEFALI NEVER VISITED the libraries of Xian-Lai in her youth. She had no reason to, as Xianese and Hokkaran shared scripts. Without someone to read to her, there was nothing for her beyond the heavy doors. In truth, she cannot remember ever seeing these doors before; she would've remembered the engravings. Inlaid upon the black doors to the library are two horned creatures, both taller than Shefali, both standing with one paw upon a scroll. The one on the right wears a crown; the one on the left, the small square hat she's seen on White Leaf scholars. Though their horns are as long as Shefali's forearm and their teeth fanged, their expression is serene. Were these the lightning-dogs Shizuka had mentioned in her story? For they looked a little like wolves, but there was no lightning near them at all.

Shefali looks on them and wonders what their voices would sound like. Something about them reminds her of well-bred mares.

The guards—there are always guards—open the door for them, and a servant runs ahead to try to announce them before they can finish stepping inside. It's a fool's errand; they are only steps away. Had something more pleasant brought them to the libraries they might've stood and gawked at the hallway opening before them: at the aisles full of scroll cases like the trees around the Three Kings Road; at the bright green of the walls and the violet of the carpets; at the statue of a King neither of them recognized in the center of the room, six scrolls tucked under his arm; at the pure size of the place; at the scent of ink and paper and old things.

But they did not have time to gawk, and so their eyes only fell on the messy table near the entrance: the desk piled high with papers and half-forgotten cups of tea, the woman in expensive robes a little rumpled from sleeping in them; the man speaking of missing punctuation as a bard recounting the deeds of Minami Shiori.

Kenshiro, in the middle of a rant; Sakura indulging him as she studies a scroll as thick as her wrist.

"Presenting Her Majesty the Empress of—" begins the crier. The two of them snap to attention—or Kenshiro does, at least. He stops mid-sentence to look up at them. The bags under his eyes suggest he's gotten about as much sleep as Shefali has.

Kenshiro bows to the guards, dismissing them. "I think we shall be safe here alone with Phoenix and Wolf."

Did he have to call her that? Shefali'd be more bothered by it if she had the strength to be bothered by anything. There is a laugh hiding behind his eyes at his own cleverness; she will not be the one to ruin it for him.

The guards leave. The doors shut behind them—there are horned dogs painted on this side, too, although they have forsaken their scrolls. Kenshiro reaches for his tea tray, only for Shizuka to stop him mid-motion.

"Forget the tea; I'm in no mood for niceties."

"Are you ever?" sighs Sakura.

"I'm not in the mood for sarcasm, either," says Shizuka, a little too harshly for Shefali's taste. Still, she cannot quite blame her, given the circumstances.

Sakura and Kenshiro exchange a glance. The laughing green in Kenshiro's eyes dies out; his jaw goes tight as he studies the two of them. How severe he looks. Shefali wonders how his face will change over the years, but the exercise only pains her.

"Sister, are you well?" he asks her. That he asks her directly endears him a little. As much as Shefali loves her wife, this is her brother she is speaking to.

The man who told the Emperor where she was hiding. The father of her perfect niece. Halaagmod Kenshiro; tree-minded, who could never quite decide which nation to call home.

Her brother.

"No," says Shefali. It surprises her how good it feels to admit it. There is no sense in hiding it anymore; no sense in pretending.

In that moment, she knows there will be no more avoiding it, no more running from it. Four months of peace.

She'd gotten one and a half.

Shefali takes Shizuka's hands, both of them.

Amber eyes meet green and steel.

This . . . It is best to say it quickly, to make the cut, and yet she cannot. She opens her mouth, and the words do not come out. How can she say it?

A hunter stands before the doe she's killed. Blood coats her deel and the lower half of her face—she hesitated, and the wound is a jagged one. It will be some time before the doe finally succumbs. Transfixed by shame, the hunter watches the blood gush from her and thinks: *Today I have slain a mother.*

"I'm dying."

A small, choking sound. Eyes, near white and glassy. A strained, trembling limb extended out for help—

Shizuka, and the deer.

"How long?" she says.

"Two months," Shefali says. Half her remaining days she's spent traveling with her wife—at least there is something Qorin about her still. "The double first."

"Your *birthday*," Shizuka says. Like sharp glass, her voice. She sniffs. Shefali keeps expecting the tears to come, but they never do—her nose starts to run and her lips tremble, but the tears never come.

"The Mother doesn't care about birthdays," Shefali says.

"She's the goddess of birth!" Shizuka says. "Couldn't she—couldn't she give me more time with you? Two months. Two months, Shefali . . ."

Shefali wraps her arms around her. For a long while, she simply rocks her back and forth as she repeats: two months, two months.

"Can't I give you some of my time?" Shizuka argues. "You spoke to her. What if I go to the Womb, too? I've half a mind to duel her. There must be *something* she can do; it's her job to claim you, isn't it? Can't I . . . What if I convince her . . ."

"It's out of her hands," Shefali says, though it gives her no pleasure to say it.

"What do you mean, it's out of her hands?" Shizuka protests. She breaks free of her wife's embrace, her hands balled into fists, the air around her shimmering with her fury. "She's a *god*. If you call yourself the god of death and you cannot even prolong someone's life—the most deserving person I've ever known—what are you? A coward! If she showed her face to me, I would cut it off her shoulders, I would—"

"Shizuka," says Shefali. "Please. It's never been that way for us.

"All I want is to spend my days with you the way we dreamed. All I want is peace, Shizuka. With you. With my family."

Shizuka hangs her head. "Your clan. I moved us all the way to Xian-Lai, and you wanted to see your family. . . ."

"They're coming," Kenshiro says, quiet and still, seeming to have already known what Shefali thought she'd been hiding so well. "Along the Three Kings, from what I hear. They'll arrive in time for the Jubilee."

"OH, SHEFALI," SAYS Shizuka. She takes her hand. "Oh, my love. I'm sorry. I'm so sorry. What have I done?"

"You didn't know," says Shefali. Her cheeks are hot; her vision is going a little blurry. Is this . . . is she . . . ?

And it is only then, after a year of feeding herself through the wringer, that Barsalai allows herself to weep, and take comfort in the family that surrounds her.

HOW LONG DOES she spend weeping?

How long does it take a single raindrop to fall from Heaven?

The time is all too brief. Much as she wants—needs—to let these tears fall, every moment she gives to her sorrows is one she cannot give to her family. Though she does not cut the moment short, nor does she languish in it—when she catches her breath, she sits up once again.

The entire time, she holds her wife's hand.

Kenshiro riffles through the papers. He says something under his breath in Xianese, something Shefali cannot hear; Sakura answers him. When had she learned the language? It seemed everyone now in her family spoke it except for Shefali, and she wasn't going to have time to learn. He'd better be teaching Baoyi Qorin.

"You've been losing your shape?"

"Only sometimes," Shefali says. "The medicine helps."

The medicine. Shefali cannot thank Ren enough for it—even in the daylight, she feels nearly her old self. Perhaps it took a few days to settle into her system; perhaps the incident with Kenshiro had been a fluke. It's true that she hasn't lost her shape since they arrived in Xian-Lai; only the Scholar has tormented her.

"Shefali," says Shizuka quietly, her voice full of concern.

Shefali shakes her head. "It wasn't that," she says loudly enough to catch Kenshiro's attention. "I kept my shape."

"There's a document we found," he mumbles. "I was in the middle of translating it. An early record of the very first blackblood outbreak, just after the last gods took their places. . . ."

"While he looks," says Sakura, side-eyeing him, "what was it that happened?"

Shefali opens her mouth, but it is Shizuka who answers. "Something came over her. Someone, maybe. All at once, she started speaking to me in Old Hokkaran, in a man's voice at that—there was such *hatred* in that voice, but it sounded so familiar to me."

"Dearest, most Imperial cousin," says Sakura, "I asked your wife."

"Right," Shizuka says. "My apologies."

Sakura raises a brow when Shizuka apologizes, but she has the sense not to draw attention to it. She waits as Shefali gathers up her thoughts, as she whittles them into phrases she can say.

"There have always been voices," Shefali says. "This one—the man—is louder than the others. I've never *seen* him. I've seen the others; I've killed them over and over. This man is new. Earlier, he . . . he used me. It was as if I were a cup, and he poured himself into me, and even after he'd left, I felt . . ."

Shizuka squeezed her hand. Together.

"I lost myself. I forgot who I was."

Kenshiro stops going through the papers. The fear is coming off him in waves. Shefali worries she will feel hungry—but all she feels is a distant disappointment.

"Do you remember anything you saw?" says Sakura. "If you saw anything, I mean. I'm not certain how these things work."

"It wasn't a vision," Shefali says. "I *was* him, I think. Everything looked the same."

Shizuka is squeezing her hand so tight, it hurts a little. She's afraid, too—the ragged cut of the light around her gives her away. "Whatever is going on, whoever this person is—we need to find him. We need to *end* him."

"How about we get more details before you go waving your sword around?" says Sakura. "There's an order to this sort of thing. We need to know where to start."

"You've only been doing this for four years," Shizuka says.

"Yeah," says Sakura, "and I'm good at it. I know you're upset, but just trust us a bit. Ken-lun, what do you think? Doesn't sound like anything I've read, but—"

"It sounds like something *I've* read," says Kenshiro. His voice is low. He picks up one of the papers and stares down at it, his jaw working, his brows nearly meeting over his eyes. "But that doesn't bring me any comfort."

"What is it?" Shizuka says. She sounds as if she will pluck the page right from his hands. That she hasn't is a minor miracle. When he passes it to Sakura instead, Shizuka's anxiety only grows.

"Sakura's already told Shefali about this," says Kenshiro. "I'll keep it as short as I can for you, O-Shizuka-shon. You two are gods, but you aren't the only ones, or the first. There've been at least four sets before you. Always eight, and always appearing in the face of a great cataclysm. The heroes gather together and save us all—and for their trouble, we forget who they were. Their identities blur together. Grandfather, Grandmother, Father, Brother, Mother, Sister, Son, and Daughter—they never wore these names in life. We don't even think they were related in most cases. Not the later gods, at any rate.

"Sakura and I have been trying to learn about the *last* set of gods. I thought that if we learned a bit about them, we might learn about the blackblood and how to overcome it, you see, and she showed such interest in the subject—"

"In learning to read," Sakura says. "But I like to help."

"The first mention of the blackblood comes to us one thousand five hundred and seven years ago," Kenshiro says. "Half a millennium before the Daughter raised the Old Wall, only two generations removed from Minami Shiori. Paper being what it is, most of these documents have degraded to the point that we can no longer read them, although there are rare exceptions. That scroll is one of them, and it is older than the blackblood itself."

He hands Shizuka the scroll he'd been reviewing, although it pains him a little, if his face is any indication. When Shizuka unfurls the scroll, he sucks in a worried breath.

Shizuka's brows come together.

"You said this was from two generations before *Minami* Shiori's time?" she asks. "The author of this is *Tsukizake* Shiori. You aren't telling me my family bad habits go back that far, are you?"

"This is Shiori written differently," Kenshiro is quick to say.

"She spelled it 'bookmark,'" Shizuka answers flatly.

"Probably a pen name," says Sakura. "Shiori was a popular name back then, like Keichi is now. Everyone wanted to be named after our great-great-grandmother."

"*Bookmark*, though," says Shefali.

"The woman knew what she was about. You'd like her if you read more about her. Spent her whole life claiming she was married to a woman named Motoko. Apart from being a scholar she was a woman after your own heart," says Sakura. "We're lucky to have Tsukizake-kol's contribution."

Shizuka doesn't seem likely to believe either of them—but she studies the rest of the text all the same. At last, with a huff, she hands it back to Kenshiro.

"Old Hokkaran never made much sense to me," she says. "I don't know most of those characters."

"What, didn't you pay attention to your tutors?" says Sakura with more than a touch of pride. "Ken-lun just handed you *A Treatise on the Eastern Plague and Its History*."

"It is our only record of the cataclysm that prompted the *last* ascension."

"Ascension?"

"That's the word Sakura and I have settled on," says Kenshiro, "for what is happening to the two of you."

"So lovely of you to have that decided for me," says Shizuka.

"I like it," says Shefali. "What was the cataclysm?"

Sakura winces. Shefali's hackles rise—whatever is on that paper is enough to shake her, and Sakura seems a woman to take near anything in stride. "Well," she says. "It says here that the Sun fell from the sky."

Shefali nods. "Batumongke forged a chain, and Tumenbayar threw it around the sun. She hitched the chain to her horse and rode her mare across the sky for twenty days."

"A story our uncle told with surprising ability," Kenshiro says. "As a child, I never questioned the details. How can we qualify a 'day' if the sun is falling?"

"The sun went down, the sun came up," Shefali says. "Tumenbayar made certain of that." Sky, how did she not realize?

"Whether or not she did ride her horse across the sky," Kenshiro continues, "we do know that the sun hung in the sky for twenty days. This incident was known as the Undying Dawn. To set the sun back in its proper place required all eight of the new gods, only four of whom shared a language. Two were Axions, if you can believe that."

Shefali had met two Axions. If they were any example to go by, then Shefali had no doubt their predecessors were fierce companions.

"One of our gods had a particular talent. He could link the minds of those around him, so that they might communicate without words. Given that the plan to keep the sun from crushing us relied on precise planning and misdirection, this was an invaluable gift. But from the early legends, it also had its . . . drawbacks. An afterimage. The water still clinging to the cup, to use Shefali's metaphor."

Shefali's skin starts to crawl. She knows the words her brother will say even before he says them.

"The god who did this came to be known five hundred years later as the Traitor."

The words pour into her ear and settle into her stomach like milk left out in the sun. She wants to vomit. Is it not enough for him to pollute her blood? Is it not enough for him to change her shape and her body, to warp her into this horrible creature? He is *killing her*. Is it not enough for him to kill her?

"You're saying *he* was the one in Shefali's head?" Shizuka says.

Shefali staggers, looking for a chair; she does not trust herself to stand in the face of this news. Sakura is the one who hands it to her.

"I am saying it's likely," says Kenshiro. "Sakura can read the document I've handed her; you can ask her what she thinks."

"He's right," says Sakura. She sets the paper down with care far away from the tea tray. "They called him the Stitcher of Minds back then. I'm sorry, Shefali."

Shizuka's eyes have gone the color of cinders. "If he's in her head, then we need to get him *out* of it," she says.

How like her. Strange. Shefali knows in her heart it will be impossible, so long as her blood runs black, but Shizuka's determination is almost enough to convince her.

Almost.

She stares at the backs of her hands, at the black veins beneath her gray skin.

"We don't have any record of that being possible," Kenshiro says.

Shizuka stands, storming toward him. Soon there is only a handsbreadth between them. The muscles in her neck strain to contain her frustration. "Then we will *make* it possible," she says. "Are you telling me you've spent *years* researching all of this, and that is all you have to show for it? 'We have no record'?"

Kenshiro does not flinch. He has nothing to say for himself—but he stares down the storm before him and he does not flinch. In that moment, he looks something like Burqila Alshara's son.

"We're dealing with something that's never happened before," says Sakura. "We haven't even found anyone else who lived through the blackblood, Cousin, not in all our years of searching. That doesn't mean there isn't a solution, but it does mean you shouldn't jump down his throat about it."

"What would you have me do?" says Shizuka. "Sit idly by and let this happen? Lose myself in a book?"

She is furious. Shefali knows she is furious, and knows she is striking out only out of her fear.

But she cannot keep shouting at her family like this.

Shefali takes her hand. The moment skin meets skin, Shizuka's manner changes; she drops the anger all at once in favor of throwing an arm around Shefali. "Are you all right?" she says. "Is *he*—?"

"I'm fine," Shefali says. She isn't—but *he's* not here, and she's not in any pain. It's true enough.

Understanding dawns on Shizuka's face. She looks down in shame. "My temper's gotten the better of me again," she says.

Shefali only nods.

"Where were you for the past four years?" Sakura says to her. "Never seen her calm down so quickly."

"Sur-Shar, mostly," says Shefali. She doesn't want to think of Ikhtar at the moment. She doesn't want to think of *anything*.

"Right," says Sakura. "You mentioned you'd gotten yourself tied up in contracts."

Wait.

Wait.

That was it, wasn't it? The idea springs into her mind like a marmot darting through the brush; she must act quickly if she is to catch it.

"Ken," she says. "Kumaq?"

Kenshiro furrows his brow. "I can send for some, if you'd like," he says. "I thought you said you couldn't taste—"

"Not for tasting," Shefali says. Well. She'd have to use her own, then, which was fine—although she'd need to visit the stables later and see if she couldn't start making more. She was running low, and it seemed as if she'd need to keep some on hand for the foreseeable future.

"Shefali?" says Shizuka. "What are you planning?"

"I need a bowl," Shefali says. She's gotten the skin out already. Shizuka is the one who gets her the bowl, plucking it from the tea tray. Shefali scoops out the rice and squeezes it into a lump, which she sets down on the ground. Can't go spilling rice all over a library. With the bowl half-full of kumaq, she sets the skin down on the ground, too, and reaches for her boot knife.

"Shefali," says Shizuka again. "My love—what are you doing?"

"It's like a contract," says Shefali. "Both people are bound by it."

"You're going to . . . You're going to spy on him?" Shizuka says. She sounds incredulous, which, really—Shefali knows for a fact this isn't the strangest thing she's heard. "Are you certain?"

Shefali finds herself smirking. "I'm always certain," she says. When she drags the knife across the back of her forearm, she hardly feels the cut—but it starts bleeding at once. Thick black oozes out of the wound, falling into the waiting bowl. Shefali allows herself to reach for the cold she'd felt earlier, to breathe it out onto the bowl. Only when she sees the crystals forming atop it does she feel ready.

"You can't be serious," says Kenshiro. "Shefa-lun, what if something goes wrong?"

Does he think he has the right to call her that? Oh, she has only two months left; what's the use of getting angry over it?

"Bind me," she says. She looks to Shizuka, wrought with worry, but too trusting of her to say so. Perhaps Sakura is right—perhaps she's taken on some of her wife's foolhardy tendencies. "I'll be all right."

"See that you are," says Shizuka. "If . . . If anything were to happen—"

"It won't," says Shefali. "It's not my birthday."

She kisses her wife. She kisses her long, kisses her sweet; in spite of her determination, she is not certain that this will work.

But she must try, all the same.

Barsalai Shefali tips the bowl to her lips, and drinks of something like divinity.

THE ETERNAL KING

It is night and the sea stretches before him. The gleaming stars, the silvery moon, the crisp air—these things do not interest him. Only the sea does. Only the sea ever truly has.

Hear its rise and fall. Yes, hear it—the soft crackle of it, like crinkled paper; the low drum of its approach; the final, triumphant roar as it crashes upon the Father's Teeth and sinks, defeated, to a whisper. When he breathes, he tastes salt and he imagines, just for a moment, that the waves will swallow him. In the hiss of the retreating water, he hears the call: *Come and meet the King Beneath the Waves.*

The King Beneath the Waves.

He knows that name.

He knows the trappings that come with it: the robes woven from seaweed, with barnacles for embellishments; the fish-bone crown. How often has he imagined himself in them?

He takes three steps into the water. Their mother always told him he should be careful wandering into the sea at night, but he knows it will not hurt him. Twenty years ago, he fought the sea and won; it serves him now, as it always has. It loves him, as it has learned to. Warm water laps at his ankles. He thinks of his brother.

A gust of wind.

The waves are crashing into one another now, before they can truly envelop him.

"No, no," he whispers. "Listen to me."

For he can feel his heart beginning to thump against his chest. He *is* meant to be here. He was always meant to be here. He tells himself this over and over as he takes his next steps into the water, as his robes float around him like petals, as his stomach starts to twist.

This is where I belong, he thinks.

And the shore has always been the only place he could truly find peace, but there is no peace in him now. The whisper of the ocean grows louder, louder, into that crumpling din that is not yet a roar: *This kingdom is not yours.*

But that's not true.

It's always been *his* kingdom. Born in the sea, his first breaths filled his lungs with salt water; his mother left him there on the shore in her anguish. It was his brother who had discovered him alive and well the next day, floating amidst the sea spray, a strand of seaweed clutched in his tiny hand.

His *brother* found him. He knew. He'd known, all these years, and yet . . .

The water floods into his mouth. He lets it. Perhaps the salt will drown out all the bitterness, but his hopes are not high. These days it feels as if his blood never ran with seawater at all, as if he is doomed forever to walk upon the dry land.

So he has come to the ocean, to prove to himself that it will listen. He takes a breath. Heavy, heavy—the water shooting up his nose and down his throat, settling once more in his lungs. It *hurts*. It shouldn't hurt. It's never hurt him before—

This kingdom is not yours.

But it is. It is!

Another breath, then; another! He shall not let the sea conquer him. This is his birthright.

He is starting to float now, only the tips of his toes still brushing against the sand. When the waves envelop him, they will take him under, they will pull him to the palace beneath the waves, the throne that has been waiting for him since the moment he sprang from his mother.

Take me, he thinks.

His chest is getting tighter, heavier, as the water fills him; the world is starting to spin around him. To breathe only makes things worse and yet he continues, and yet he persists, certain that the waves will come for him like a chariot.

But it is not the waves that take him—only the darkness.

This kingdom is not yours.

As a candle extinguished, his consciousness.

When he wakes, the woman is there. She has her hands full of his robes and she is shaking him, pleading with him to get up. The salt of her tears mingles with the water that soaks him. His chest still aches, but she pushes into his stomach and he spits it out: the sea he once loved, pouring out of his mouth, darkening the sand.

"What were you thinking?" she says. Her voice is as shrill as ever. He does not want to hear her. "What if you'd died? What would we have done then?"

He wasn't going to die. He'd told her that. Why had she followed him? Can he not—is his helplessness so *pervasive*? Can he not even control the woman?

No.

No, he has lost the sea, but he will not lose *this*.

"You think that because you are a god, you can do what you like," she says to him. "But you do not remember your family or your people. You leave them directionless so you can—what? Do *this*?"

His chest is full again, but not with water. Anger now takes its place. She is so *loud,* and she cannot see the truth of the matter. The great crime of what his brother has done escapes her. She doesn't *know*.

Years, it's been. He is tired of trying to show her. What use was the promise he'd made, really? Words meant to bind him—nothing more. She was so stubborn, she was leaving him with no choice.

"What purpose does any of this serve? So your brother stole from you—"

"Don't speak of my brother," he says. He sputters, but there is strength left in him yet, strength left to show her the error of her ways. Near him, waiting like an offering bowl, is a conch shell.

He reaches for it.

"Don't speak of your brother," she says. "May as well not speak of the traitorous sun, Ya—"

"Don't," he says. The very tip of the shell is sharp as a dagger; he drives it into his thumb. A single drop of red wells up, and he smears this along the inside.

"Don't?" she repeats. "Do you expect me to stand here and not speak of it at all? If I hadn't found you, you'd be dead. And if you died—"

"I won't," he says. How tiresome, this argument. They've had it time and time again.

His head hurts. Where is his ink? Did it float away? No—the hand-sized box of writing supplies remained tucked in his robes.

A small miracle.

He reaches for it.

"You think that because you are a hero, your work is done," she says. "It isn't. It never is. You've caught the falling pot, but an arrow may still shatter it. This is your place now—to watch for the arrows."

He does not bother to grind the ink, only to break off a chunk of it. Heedless of the woman's rambling, he holds the shell out near the sea. Water rushes in, water devours the black.

So the sea would not heed him, and the woman would not heed him.

He dips his bleeding thumb into the ink, into the water, and he whispers to it with his mind as he has whispered to the others.

Serve me.

The water begins to bubble.

"What are you doing?" she asks him.

He does not need to answer her with words. So long he has known her that it is easy to reach for her mind, easy to whisper into her ear: *Drink.*

She does not want to at first. She fights him, tooth and nail she fights him, but he is a man who has been denied for far too long. The cuts along his face, the broken rib—these will not stop him.

What a warrior she is—but in her haste to save him, she left her sword behind. The gift the foreigner had given her.

He doesn't want to hurt her. Not really. Can't she see that? He's only trying to make her understand. To show her what he's lost.

To bring her into his kingdom.

She runs, and he catches her; he takes her by the hair and he pours the water, the ink, the blood into her mouth.

Listen: the waves crashing against the Father's Teeth. Listen: the beating of her heart, like a war drum. Listen: his pleased sigh as he drops the now-empty shell.

She falls to the ground, writhing, and he watches, for he can feel her mind opening up to him like an oyster, and he can see the pearls gleaming within. Stubbornness, pride, arrogance. She will not need them.

So he plucks them from her, and she stops, and she stares at him with glassy eyes that remind him so much of the moon upon the water. The whole of her soul is laid out before him now: he can see from the moment of her birth beneath the peach tree until the present. She honestly cared for him, didn't she? She honestly cared.

If only she hadn't been so *terrible* at showing it.

But that will be all right. Everything will be all right now, as he tells her which parts of herself she may keep, as he whittles her into something *new*. Someone he can trust to think for herself, now that he's removed all the parts that troubled him.

"Isn't that better?" he says.

BARSALAI SHEFALI

FIFTEEN

Breathe.

That is the first thought that comes to her as the waves recede, as she falls back into her own body. She needs to breathe. As she sucks in air, the scents of those around her come with it: peony, ink, perfume; old books and horses; delicate chrysanthemums and steel. She is not alone.

No matter what she has seen, she is not alone.

"Shefali?"

Her wife's voice is the first thing she hears; her wife's hands on her face the first thing she feels.

"My love, please tell me you've returned," she says. "Please."

Shefali—yes, that is her name—groans. It's the closest she can come to speaking when she is so nauseated, when the miasma of what she has seen still claws at her.

"That isn't Old Hokkaran," says someone else. Falling petals in the spring; a wry grin and a quick study. Sakura. "Maybe she's coming around?"

"Maybe," says a man. Shefali flinches at the sound of his voice; for a moment, she mistakes it for *his*. "Untie her—she isn't struggling anymore."

Ah, she feels it now—the thick rope binding her in place. Are those chains on her wrists? How worried had they been? She tries not to imagine what she must have looked like, tries not to imagine the things she must have said. Strangely, the bite of the metal into her skin reminds her that she is here—that all of this is real.

It does not wipe away the memory of the woman's throat beneath her hands. His hands. *He* was the one who'd hurt that woman, but—

Sky, she could feel it.

"Shefali?" says Shizuka again. She is the one who unties her, and Shefali wonders, vaguely, where she learned to undo knots. Do they teach you that in the army?

"I'm here," Shefali rasps. Speaking is like driving sand into her throat. She coughs, half-expecting water to come up. "I'm back."

Kenshiro lets out a sigh of relief, but it is Shizuka who throws her arms around her wife, who cradles her close. Shefali presses her nose to Shizuka's hair. The scent of her is like coming home.

But still—she cannot forget what she has seen.

"Are you all right?" Shizuka says. She is searching her face now, staring into the green eye and then the steel, as if the secrets of the vision will transmit themselves to her. No matter. Shefali would not let them.

"Yes," she says. "I saw—"

"We know," says Kenshiro. This is the gravest she's ever heard him. Now that her vision is settling, she can see him half-sitting on a chair. Sakura, next to him, has an open scroll she is scribbling characters onto with surprising haste. "You were speaking the whole time. Sakura recorded most of it."

Is it cowardly to admit she's relieved? That memory is a stain on her; she does not wish to speak of it. The look on the woman's face will haunt her, she thinks, for the rest of her days. It is one thing to kill a person and quite another to . . . to reach into their mind and shape them.

To change them, because you think they must be changed.

Vile. That is the word for it.

Shizuka is kissing her cheeks, her forehead. Shefali feels unworthy of such affection. She is not the one who hurt that woman, she thinks, and yet . . .

"It *was* helpful," says Kenshiro, "in the way that a knife is helpful to a dying man."

"What do you mean?" Shizuka says. She clutches Shefali to her chest, as if she is worried that she will float away.

Sakura answers her. "Ken-lun had a theory about how the blackblood worked, and he's right."

Shefali closes her eyes. She knows what he will say, even if Shizuka doesn't. She has seen it in the glassy gaze of the woman on the beach.

"It lets him control you," she says. It is best if Shizuka hears it from her. "It lets him change you into whatever he likes."

The pot, the arrow—Shizuka, Shefali. "What?" she says. "Shefali, are you saying . . ."

She nods. "He wants them to be monsters, so they are monsters."

Vile, her blood. Vile, the spirit lurking within it, trying with every passing moment to *shape* her. To make her more like him. If only she could bleed herself dry, if only that would save her.

Four months of peace.

What a naïve thing to wish for.

"The will of a god is a terrifying thing," says Kenshiro. "I saw you tear a man's head right off his shoulders once, Shefa-lun, and Shizu-lun's accomplishments speak for themselves. . . ."

"It's the reason you haven't died," adds Sakura. "The godhood. It's keeping you going, your will against his, all this time."

Her head aches. Shizuka, too, is in pain, though hers is not purely physical. She sits on her knees, slumped against her wife in the library. Shefali takes her hand. Their scars touch; once more the cold jolts her.

"But . . . the longer you carry his influence inside yourself, the easier it is for him to . . ."

Kenshiro covers his fist with his hand.

"There must be something we can do," Shizuka says. How quiet, the Sunfire Empress! "There must be some way . . ."

"What stopped it earlier?" Kenshiro says.

Shefali holds up their joined hands. As one, without having to speak about it, they show him their palms.

He lets out a low hum.

"And how did you get those?" he asks.

They should have known the question was coming. In spite of all that has happened—in spite of the filth still clinging to her—Shefali's cheeks go hot. To speak of the promise they made as children, their bloodbound oath, might deprive it of its magic. She glances to Shizuka. She, too, has gone a little red.

"We swore we'd face the Traitor together when we were children," she says. "Beneath a white birch tree."

"And you cut your hand open for that?" says Sakura. "Aren't you a calligrapher?"

"It healed," Shizuka says quickly, "and it was worth it."

Kenshiro rubs his chin. "Perhaps . . ."

". . . you let your blood mix," finishes Sakura. "So there's a bit of both of you in those scars, and when they touch—" She makes a gesture like fireworks exploding.

Kenshiro nods. "Not how I would have put it—but, yes. Perhaps when your scars meet, you can borrow some of Shizuka's divinity, and the two of you together can ward him off."

Shefali meets her wife's eyes. That the promise they'd made could shield her now—she wondered what her childhood self might say if she knew.

"This is good," Kenshiro says, "because it means that we have time to work out a plan, so long as the two of you are together."

"We don't have much time at all," Shizuka says. "Shefali says she will die on her next birthday, Kenshiro; what are we meant to do until then?"

Kenshiro palms his face. His stubble has grown out just enough to sound scratchy. His pale Qorin hair and the bags beneath his eyes lend him the look of a much older man. "I don't have the answers now," he says, "but I swear to you both—I will find them. I only . . . I need more time."

Shizuka is right—there isn't much left.

But if there is anyone she can trust with this—it is her brother. She knows that now. Who else would have put together what was going on? Who else could have gathered the resources he has; who else has shown such dedication? So he had betrayed her once—he was trying to make up for it now.

"Aaj is back in a month," says Shefali. "With the Qorin. Sanvaartains, too."

"They may know something," he says. "I'll write to them. Until then . . ."

"We wait," says Shizuka. She is not any happier to say it than Shefali is to think it—but displeasure will not change the truth of the matter.

"I wish I had better news," says Kenshiro. "But, yes. We wait. And you two—you stay together."

This brings something like a smile to Shefali's face. Nothing in the world is more certain than this: She will stay by Shizuka's side until the day she dies. That had always been the plan. That staying near her keeps the Traitor from attacking her is an added benefit—but it has not truly changed her plans.

"We will," says Shefali.

TOGETHER, THEY SWORE, and so it is. If Shefali felt awkward walking through the palace earlier, she feels an abomination now— but she clings to Shizuka's hand and she tells herself that this is only temporary. They will find some way to wrench the leech from her mind.

It was simple to believe such things when she was younger. Harder now, but that will only make it worthwhile. To triumph over the simple is no triumph at all.

You shall not rule me, she thinks to the Traitor.

With Shizuka's hand in hers, he is silent.

He is silent, too, when they reach their rooms, when they discuss in hushed tones their plans for the future. For the amount of future that remains to them. Shizuka asks her what she saw in the vision, and she recounts it as well as she can—it is like trying to recount a dream hours after waking. Certain things remain to her— the woman's eyes, the feel of her throat, the spray of the sea and the way it filled her lungs.

She cannot tell Shizuka of the sea—so she tells her of the woman instead. The story sickens her as much as it did Shefali. To see such disgust on her wife's face would be punishment enough.

"I will tear out his spine," Shizuka says.

That fire Shefali has grown to love—it reminds her, a little, of the fire in the woman's voice. There had been something of Shizuka about her.

Shefali holds her wife closer. In all the time it has taken them to walk to their rooms, she has not dropped Shizuka's hand. In truth, she is afraid to do so, afraid that if she lets go, *he* will come crashing down upon her like the waves, like the waves.

And she does not want him anywhere near Shizuka.

"When we made that oath, Shefali, I did not know what it was we were swearing to fight," she says. "I thought it would be a duel, like any other. That he was a man I could simply cut down."

"Maybe he is," Shefali says. She hopes he is. They might not be able to extract him from her body, but surely if they attack the man himself—surely manipulating minds will not help him then. Shizuka's will is as unshakeable as the Kyuuzen Mountains; he will not be able to sway her.

And Shefali? Well. She will be there, fighting one-handed if she needs to.

"Even if he is," says Shizuka. "He's beyond the Wall, months away. Shefali, what am I . . . How am I to face him without you?"

"We could leave," Shefali says. If they traveled by sea—across Peizhi Lake and up the western coasts—they might be able to make it over the Wall.

"I . . . ," Shizuka begins. "Not without giving Kenshiro his time. Not without seeing your family."

But if they wait until the Qorin arrive, it will be too late to travel, even by sea.

They know this. They both do.

Shizuka sighs. "With any luck, they'll arrive ahead of schedule, and Kenshiro will have his answers on the morrow," she says. "I have wandered into war without a plan too many times. We must know what we're up against. My uncle . . . I shall not be my uncle, Shefali. And I shall not deprive you of seeing your mother."

As the ragged edge of a shattered cup—Shizuka's voice. Shefali can only hold her tighter. Marching north—some part of her has always known it is a thing they *must* do. But north, to her, has always lived behind a veil of mist. Someday. Never today.

"I shall have to send word to the palace. Fujino will answer, of course, but Fuyutsuki may claim he has no soldiers left. He may not even be wrong about it," Shizuka continues. "Shiseiki can't muster. Shiratori is busy with the—"

She groans.

Shefali smooths her hair. "The attacks."

"It makes sense," says Shizuka. "You would *think* he'd been put in his proper place after the war, but he's growing bold again."

Shefali has heard only a little of the war; certainly nothing that might stay the Traitor's hand. There is something she does not know here, but she will not press Shizuka for it when they are both so exhausted.

"The mountains are the key," Shizuka continues. She's speaking more to herself than to Shefali. There is that little furrow between her brows, the one she gets when she's spent too much time fussing over which of her father's poems to write out in the morning. "We need to drive them back over. Whenever Kenshiro sends word—we must . . ."

"Sail," Shefali finishes. "Will you be all right?"

Shizuka's smile and laugh are sad and fleeting. "We are speaking of sending an army over the Tokuma Mountains to fight a god who can invade the minds of others, and you are asking if the water will frighten me?"

"I care about you," Shefali answers.

"And I am not the only woman in Hokkaro," Shizuka says. "Our lives have never been our own. I've forgotten that—you reminded me."

My life is not worth theirs, Shefali had said. The words feel bitter now, when all she wants to do is curl up with her wife and forget the world for a few hours. After so long apart, to be thrown once more into this maelstrom . . .

Shefali would ride beyond the Wall with her head held high, if only she had more *time*.

Shefali never heard a Tumenbayar story where the villain was time itself. She wonders what Tumenbayar would do, if she were in Shefali's stirrups, and decides it does not matter. When she dies—then she may become Grandmother Sky.

For now, let her be Barsalai.

For so long as her hand is in Shizuka's, let her mind be her own.

"Is there anything you want to do?" Shizuka asks her.

The question comes like a rock to the head. Is she not just planning out a war? "What?"

"Before we leave," Shizuka continues. "It was my idea to send us down here and my idea to leave. You should decide what we do in between. Given . . ."

She lifts their joined hands with a weak smile.

If there is one good thing to come of this, it is that no one will be able to tell them to stop holding hands.

It is difficult to think of more good things, but she tries. Shizuka indulging her like this—that is another.

"Let's race," she says.

"With our hands joined?" says Shizuka.

"Are you afraid of losing?" Shefali teases.

"Afraid of falling from my horse," she answers.

"No daughter of Burqila Alshara will fall from her horse," Shefali says, kissing the top of Shizuka's head. "But you *will* lose."

Shizuka chuckles. "All right," she says. "If you want to race, I'm hardly going to deny you. But that can't be all you want. Whatever it is, Shefali, whatever that comes to your mind—name it, and I will move the heavens for you."

A bear emerging from its cave on the first day of spring—Shefali allowing herself to dream, if only a little.

"A walk through the gardens with you," she says.

"I said something *you* wanted to do," says Shizuka.

"I like walking with you," Shefali says. "And the flowers are beautiful."

She has other dreams, too. A proper Qorin feast, where she can dance around the fire and sing the old songs with her family. Wrestling her cousin to the ground in front of the entire clan. (This is impossible, but she is talking of dreams.) Hunting the fabled white deer of Xian-Lun. Hearing Shizuka read her poetry, a new piece each night. Making a new deel for her mother. Finishing a bow that even Shizuka can use.

"I can fire a bow," says Shizuka, a little offended.

"A *Hokkaran* bow," Shefali says.

Shizuka is wise enough not to argue the point—only listen as Shefali thinks of more things she wants to do. Sixty-three days is such a short span of time, but there is so much she still wants to do.

Admittedly, half her little daydreams involve kissing Shizuka.

But she's spent eight years away from her wife—who would blame her?

Hours they speak of the things they will do together, until the sun sinks below the horizon again, and the room is once more painted in blue and violet. With how much the day has worn on them already, fulfilling these dreams will have to wait.

Shizuka falls asleep in Shefali's arms. Mid-sentence, it happens. "But how will we . . . ?"

She closes her eyes, takes a breath—and begins to snore.

The Empress of Hokkaro, snoring in her arms. The rise and fall of her breathing, the peace upon her face—yes, this, too, was one of her dreams.

She will indulge it so long as it lasts; she will lose herself in her wife's scent, in her heartbeat; the weight of her will keep her here, will make her real.

But—ah, how cruel!—this dream is not to last. Two hours, perhaps, that is all the rest Shizuka gets before the nightmares take her. Shefali holds her, as she has held her so often before, as she will hold her every remaining day of her life.

She is screaming about the waves.

When at last she has relaxed enough to speak, it is twenty minutes later. Red pinpricks beneath her eyes speak to her exhaustion; in the morning, they will be circles darker than even Kenshiro's. There are no tears—she does not cry anymore, Shefali's wife—but her voice is hoarse from the screaming, and she is a little dazed from the lack of sleep.

"Which one of us is in charge of dreams?" Shizuka rasps. "I'd like to have a word with them."

Shefali thinks of a woman she met once—a woman with skin of burnished copper, and hair of flame—and smirks. "Her name is Genovefa," she says.

"A foreigner?" says Shizuka. ". . . You met more of us?"

"I think so," says Shefali. "In Sur-Shar. Her and her wife."

"I didn't mean like us in *that* way," Shizuka says. "I meant more gods."

"They're both," says Shefali. She has not thought of Genovefa and her wife at all in the months since their parting. Where have they gone? Will she see them again? If the gods gather before cataclysms, she might.

But then, she didn't part on excellent terms with one of them.

Shizuka nuzzles against her. "If I had known there were so many women who loved other women as a child, I would have begged our parents to promise us when I was six."

"We made up for it," Shefali says.

Silence, then, though it is not really silence—outside, the night-jars have started to sing. In the markets, there is a festival going on; the drums carry all the way to the palace.

They are not alone, no matter how it might seem.

"Do you . . . do you want to hear the rest?" Shizuka says.

"The rest?"

"Of what happened during the war," she says. "I've not yet finished."

She thinks of this morning, an eternity ago, of the fear and the trembling. "Do you want to tell it?"

It is a while before Shizuka answers her. She looks over her shoulder, out the window. Shefali hears the fireworks going off, but cannot see them without turning around—and she cannot turn without letting go of her wife's hand. She watches the colors re-flected in Shizuka's eyes and counts that as celebration enough.

BARSALAI SHEFALI

SIXTEEN

They spend their days and nights together, as two pine needles, no matter what may come between them.

Which is not to say that very much *does* come between them. Xian-Lai is kind to them, as it has always been. How much of that stems from its relative isolation from the Empire and how much from Baozhai's benevolent interference remains to be seen. The end result is the same: They are rarely troubled. In the mornings, Shizuka is awakened by the gentle swell of music, and Shefali is roused from her whittling by the soft scent of fresh-cut flowers.

They break their fast alone in the room—the servants bring up a tray full of food for Shizuka and a cup of fragrant tea for Shefali. Shefali prepares her wife's ink as well as she can, and some mornings, Shizuka doesn't even tease her about the chunks remaining in the water. Shizuka writes her letters to the lords of Hokkaro, ordering them to muster their armies, and when she is done, she reads Shefali poems to pass the time. Some mornings, Shefali tells her Tumenbayar stories—but there's a maudlin color to those now that neither of them wants to address.

Their afternoons are spent outside. In the garden, at first, where they can enjoy the autumn flowers as they now begin to bloom. For centuries, the chrysanthemum has been the pride of Hokkaro, the Empress of Flowers, and so Shizuka is naturally excited to see them. She is unprepared—completely unprepared—to see the varieties Baozhai has planted for her: gold petals lined with red smile back at her. Shefali watches as she hurries from blossom to blossom, watches the flowers as they watch her wife.

Beautiful—all of it.

But the gardens do not consume all their time. Shefali asked for a race, and so a race she gets. One afternoon, the two of them mount their horses and race around the Bronze Palace, with Baoyi as their duly appointed judge. All Shizuka's fears about keeping their hands joined throughout dissolve the moment she mounts. Matsuda—her red—has never been in such a calm mood!

She loses, of course.

But it is a closer race than she imagined it might be, and if that is because Shefali spends half the time talking to both horses, well—that's a loss she's willing to accept.

Baoyi, too, occupies many of their afternoons. Shefali is determined to teach her as much of Qorin culture as she can before she and Shizuka must leave for the North. Thankfully, Kenshiro's done a fine enough job of the basics—she understands Qorin characters and a few common words. After their race is through, Shefali teaches her how to mount in the Qorin way, how to stand safely in the saddle. She *wants* to take her hunting, but Baozhai is firm: there will be no killing in the Bronze Palace. Shefali teaches her how to make a bow, instead.

In the evenings, before dinner, Shefali visits the stables. She is lucky—there are ten pregnant mares, and she has no one to compete with for milk. She milks them herself as her wife loudly wonders if there is not a better way to do this.

"It tastes better when you milk it yourself," Shefali says.

"But you can't even taste it," Shizuka says.

"One day I might," Shefali answers.

She makes ten more skins to hold her kumaq and ties them to the saddles of these horses. Baozhai is confused at first, when she hears about this request, but as it harms no one and matters so much to Shefali, she is quick to grant it.

And "grant" is the word—she is the Thorned-Blossom Queen now.

But at dinner, when they are all gathered together, she is simply Baozhai: simply a woman trying desperately to wring a pleasant dinner from her grieving family. What are they to talk about that will not inevitably lead to talk of Shefali's condition, or the mounting war? Poetry will lead surely to O-Itsuki, and O-Itsuki to his untimely death. They may talk of horses, but then Shefali might never stop talking at all. Flowers would do, and do on certain evenings, but you cannot always talk about flowers.

And so she tries, and fails, to keep the conversation from wandering too far into the dark.

Shefali appreciates the effort, even if it really is inevitable. Dinner is the only time she sees her brother. With every passing day, he grows more and more haggard—by the end of the second week, there's an ashen layer of white clinging desperately to his cheeks. His eyes are greener than ever, given the bags under them for contrast. Even Sakura is looking mussed—she's abandoned her complicated hairstyles in favor of leaving it unbound, and she hasn't worn makeup in days. They eat only palmfuls at a time.

How are you? Shefali wants to ask them, but she knows that if she does, he will not answer the question. Not really. As a wrestler redirecting his opponent's weight—her brother, sidestepping her questions.

He does ask her every night what she and Shizuka have been up to, and Shefali answers as well as she can. Many nights the answer is perfectly mundane, but Kenshiro listens intently all the same. What color were the flowers they saw? Ah, they'd heard birds—which ones?

It is Kenshiro who tells them of the festival, and Baozhai who encourages them to go. Every full moon there is a small one—vendors line the streets selling street food, mountebanks offer unwinnable games, the music swells even louder and more vivacious than usual. Hokkarans do this sort of thing only twice a year, and in truth, Shefali has never gone to one.

"What if someone recognizes us?" Shizuka says. "They won't be able to celebrate with me around."

"Is the mask I gave you so unsightly, Lady, that you refuse to wear it?" Baozhai counters. Was she the one who had given Shizuka the phoenix mask?

"Of course it is beautiful, Baozhai. You know how I treasure it! But if I wear that—surely everyone will know?"

"You are not the only woman to wear a phoenix," Baozhai counters. "We shall dress you both as guards, and no one will be the wiser."

Shefali smirks a little at the idea of her wife in a common guard's uniform. Do they make them that small?

They do. It is Shefali's uniform they have a little difficulty with; in the end, she borrows one of Kenshiro's shabbier suits of armor.

But the plan works just as Baozhai intended. The two of them are free to wander down the streets of Xian-Lai without interruption, without intrusion. How vibrant, this city! Everywhere

Shefali looks, there are more people gathered together. And it is not only the amount of them—it is what they are doing, as well. Here in Xian-Lai, no one shies away from affection. To see a married couple walking hand in hand in Hokkaro was the height of scandal.

And yet here there are couples of all kinds. Men and men, women and women, those who fit in neither category or both. The strict and rigid lines of Hokkaro are unknown here.

Shizuka demands they stop by one of the game stalls so that Shefali can win her a jar of festival candies. Shefali is, of course, happy to oblige her. Soon they are walking arm in arm as Shizuka munches on her hard-won treats. Later on, a quartet of musicians surrounds them, playing a lively melody Shefali has not heard and cheering at them in Xianese.

"They want us to dance," Shizuka says, laughing.

And Shefali smiles at her—this woman she has loved all her life— and takes her free hand. "Then let's dance."

Ah, Minami Shizuka, the Daughter of Heaven, the Light of Hokkaro—what a terrible dancer she is! Hopping from one foot to another, waving her arms around heedless of the rhythm—anyone who saw her would laugh. Shefali certainly does.

But it feels good to laugh. It feels *so good* to laugh.

Later, when Shizuka's feet grow tired, Shefali carries her on her shoulders.

No one stares at them for it.

It is a perfectly normal festival evening, full of perfectly normal moments of joy, and it is the only one they will have.

When Shefali cradles her wife to sleep that night, she tries to keep in mind only the dance, only the laughter, only the candies—and not the ache that arose between her shoulders, not the stiffness in her knees.

In the morning, the letters come.

Shefali is a little surprised at first. It has been so long since she wrote to anyone, or at least it feels as if it's been an eternity, that she cannot imagine why someone would write to her. But there they are: two letters with *Barsalai Shefali* written upon them in Qorin.

"Don't get too popular," teases Shizuka. "Someone will try to steal you away from me."

Shefali chuckles. "One of these is from Ren."

She expects Shizuka to stiffen. Instead—a coy grin. "Ah, so I was right."

Shefali rolls her eyes at her.

Pleased with herself, Shizuka turns toward her work once more. "I'll leave you be," she says. "I hope it's good news."

Their hands are still joined, as they have been for the past two weeks, when Shefali opens the letter. Ren's Qorin handwriting leaves a lot to be desired—but it is readable, and there's something a little delightful in making a Hokkaran write to her in Qorin.

> *To my darling Barsalai,*
>
> *Don't think I've forgiven you for running off to the South— but I cannot tease you too much for it when you're in such a state of worry. I hope this letter can comfort you even when I am so far away.*
>
> *You've asked me if it is the medicine that is causing you to have such a taste for blood. I will be honest with you, Barsalai: Those tonics are not so different from the ones I make to keep myself looking so devastatingly beautiful. I added a little to help with the pain and the stiffness you mentioned, but there's nothing in it that should inspire such a reaction. In fact—you mentioned that you hardly feel any pain at all when you've taken your dose, which is also a little*

strange. I'm good, but I'm not that good. I'm half inclined to
ask if there's anything else you'd like to tell me, but given
how that went the last time, I shall bite my proverbial
tongue.

If you were here, the two of us could experiment a
little—determine what it is exactly that's leading to all of
this.

But as you're so far, and as we don't have much time, all
I can say is this: The medicine was specifically made to help
you keep your shape. As I said before, it helps assert your will
over your flesh. For you to have had a reaction like that . . .
my instinct is that something greater than your sickness is
interfering.

I may not get the chance to write to you again. There is
much I want to say to you, but the better part of poetry is
silence. By the time you read this letter, you'll only have two
months left; I shall not burden you with an overwrought
declaration. You've more things in life to focus on. I hope,
truly, that you make the most of every day you're given—
and I hope that wife of yours is treating you well.

I'd try to steal you if we had the time.

Be well. Please. Be well, and be happy; that's all I've ever
asked of you.

You are a hero to me still, Barsalai.

Always yours,
Ren

Ah—what familiar pain it is, to hear from her. She lets the words
settle a little before reading the letter again, and again. Part of her
wishes it were longer, but . . . her relationship with Ren has always
lived in the things they've left unsaid. She will write to her, she thinks,

before she leaves with Shizuka. It is the least Ren deserves for helping her as much as she has.

Of course, that she hadn't intended for the medicine to work this
well is a little concerning. Surely her lack of pain isn't a result of the
Traitor's presence? If anything, he'd cause her more pain—she is
somehow sure of this.

Maybe Shizuka was right about the Xianese air lending her a bit
of peace.

She opens the next letter. Strange. This isn't Otgar's neat, if bom-
bastic, handwriting. This is . . .

Her heart is a washcloth, the letter the washerwoman wringing
it dry.

> For my daughter, Barsalai.
>
> I used to worry that keeping my mouth shut around you for
> so long meant you'd be as meek as a mouse. I was wrong—not
> because you're boisterous like your cousin, but because it was
> wrong of me to worry about you at all. I see now that there isn't
> anything beneath the Sky that could hope to get in between you
> and the things you want.
>
> Where do I begin with you? We don't get much opportunity
> to talk. You had the audacity to go home to your wife instead
> of coming to see us on your way back, and for that I should be
> furious with you—especially considering what you've told me
> about your health. I was furious with you, when your cousin
> told me what had happened. I thought of sending you a lamb's
> spine broken in two. Your cousin said that would be too
> dramatic, and your uncle wouldn't let me near any of his sheep
> besides.
>
> But reading your letter I realized that I would've done the
> same for Naisuran. I would've gone straight back to her.

Would've carried her the whole way home myself,
if I had to.

So I suppose I can't be too upset with you.

We're going to meet you in the South. We'll talk then, you
and I. Really.

But for now, know this: When I gave birth to you the
sanvaartain told me you were no normal child. Over and over
you have proved this to me, to your wife, to the world. All
along the Qorin roads your name is well known, my Shefa,
and well-praised. And you have earned this praise, wrested it
from the jaws of a foul evil that sought to overcome you. You
are a hero to more people than you know.

All mothers want to birth heroes, but none want to see their
child in danger. What fortunate misfortune I have—two
daughters, two heroes, two girls who treat danger like an
old playmate.

I thought I'd made my peace with it when you came to me
covered in blood at Imakane, but I was wrong.

I knew from the moment you both met that you'd go over the
Wall—and I've spent my life hoping that day would never
come. But now that it has, there is no finer reason that I can
think of.

I am proud of you, Shefali. Your people are proud of you.

And when you leave us to go beyond the Wall, we will
sing you the songs of Tumenbayar, and we will cast milk
on the roads, and we will watch each day for the return of
your mare.

May the Grandmother watch over you, my wanderer. I will
see you soon.

Burqila Alshara
Nadyyasar

She must read it again.

She must have read it wrong—there is no way . . .

The words do not change. Her mother is proud of her. She cannot remember the last time she heard those words from Otgar's mouth: to see them in her mother's handwriting is another thing altogether. A third time, and the words have yet to change on her.

"Are you all right?" Shizuka asks her.

For her eyes are wet with tears, for her hand is shaking, for her chest aches with a warmth she has not known in years.

"Shefali?" Shizuka sets aside her work, wraps an arm around her, wipes away the tears with her ink-stained fingers. "What's the matter?"

"Nothing, I . . . ," starts Shefali. She loses the rest to a sniffle. "It's my mother. She wrote to me."

Shizuka's eyes fall on the letter, on its blocky Qorin hand. To read it would be an invasion, wouldn't it? "Is she upset with you?"

"No," says Shefali. "Shizuka, she said she's proud."

And by the end of the month, she thinks, she will be able to hear it in person.

But it will be some time yet before then. They've more to endure, the two of them, not the least of which is their continued preparation for war. So far as Shefali is concerned, her preparations are simple: She must ensure that Shizuka is well, and must ensure that her horse is well, too. These—and the fermentation of kumaq—become her primary concerns.

Of course, there are many ways to ensure that someone is well.

If you ask the swordmasters of Hokkaro, they will tell you that it is best to act decisively: to wait until your opponent has raised his sword against you and, in a single strike, cut him down. In this way, you will know who your enemies are.

If you ask the Qorin, they will tell you it is best to keep your beloved warm and their belly full: to hunt for them and provide them with meat and fur alike. In this way, you will be strong enough to face the coming winters.

The answer for Shefali lies somewhere in between. They march, the two of them, to face their greatest enemy of all—he is already known to them. Yet there is no question in her mind that the two of them must act decisively, must arm themselves with the swords of their divinity, and strike at him before he can cut them down.

In the same way, it is true that Shefali must provide for her wife—but what use is hunting in the balmy South, where food and shelter are as plentiful as drops of rain in a monsoon? No—to provide for her now means to accompany her in all things, to lend her strength to Shizuka's, to be the fuel and the air for her all-consuming flames.

To encourage her to be the god that she has always been.

There are as many scrolls on swordsmanship and hunting as there are birds in the sky. Shefali is certain of this; there are few things Hokkarans like more than arguing over the correct way in which to live their lives.

There are no scrolls on godhood.

And so the only way to learn is to do, which is the most Qorin way to go about it.

At night, when the moon is high overhead and her wife has gone to bed, Shefali can practice. Pursuit of the cold in her veins is slow going, but she makes some progress. Kumaq appears to be essential to the process, or at least the scent of it—she cannot seem to summon the cold without the scent of fermented milk to guide her. It is a good thing, then, that she has requisitioned so much of it. Better still that she does this while Shizuka, who can't stand the smell, is asleep.

Her time in the Womb taught her little of this part of herself. She knows well how to shape herself, if the moment calls for it: how to conjure up an image and force her body to conform to it. It was the first of her divine aspects she truly mastered.

This business with the cold—it is aimless and vast. What can she do with it? What can she not do?

And so she fumbles in the dark, attempting to find out.

The first thing that she discovers—quite accidentally—is that when the cold is in her veins, her breath is as ice. One night as she feels it welling up inside her, she lets out a long breath, only to find the kumaq in the bowl has frozen over. She turns it over and shakes it, trying to keep the cold in her lungs as her own amusement threatens to melt it.

The kumaq does not drop out of the bowl. It remains frozen, little tendrils of vapor emerging from it.

This leads to further experimentation. Can she freeze anything, then, or only the kumaq? She reaches for the bowl Shizuka uses for her ink and fills it with water. Another breath. The vapor of her breath hits the water; pale fractals of ice form on the surface. She watches, entranced, as the water freezes over.

Her wife will be able to thaw that out in the morning. Probably.

(She does, although she is not happy about it. The fires come to her more easily than the cold comes to Shefali, and she wonders if it is because her wife often acts without thinking.)

Further practice yields further results: by focusing her attention on *expelling* the cold through her breath, she can coat nearly anything in a layer of frost. Her whittled wolves are her first victims—when she is done, they look as if they've spent the day romping through the snow. It is an adorable sight, almost distractingly so for Shefali, but an encouraging one. With more experimenting, she might be able to make something more useful of this—she begins to dream of freezing demons where they stand.

It's the sort of thing Tumenbayar might do.

The sort of thing she might do, given enough time.

But she isn't certain how much remains to them of this heady retreat. It is the thirtieth of Nanatsu already, nearly Shizuka's birthday; soon there will be no way to reach the North except by boat.

How much longer can they continue to ignore the wound of the North? How much longer can they allow it to fester before they must drive in the hot iron?

Shizuka receives the answer one morning in the form of three letters—each on fine Hokkaran paper, one of them perfumed. Shefali finds herself paying more attention to the bindings, after hearing Shizuka opine about the layers of meaning contained therein: one is bound with thin red string; one bound with a thick band of gold, attached to a fine lacquer box; one bound with common twine.

Shefali cannot read the letters, of course, but she can read her wife's expression and the subtle changes in her scent. She reaches for the red letter first: her heart swells with anticipation, her excitement as triumphant as its downfall is sudden. The moment she unrolls it, her spirits drop. When she sets the letter down, she does so carefully, carefully, an inscrutable look on her face.

"From Nishikomi?" Shefali asks.

Shizuka only shakes her head and moves on to the next letter— the twine. The contents of the red, it seems, are not worth sharing. If the first letter was a blow, this is the cut that severs something inside Shizuka. From the set of her jaw to the fury boiling up behind her eyes, it is clear she likes this even less than the first.

"Was *that* from Nishikomi?" Shefali asks again.

"From Shiratori," says Shizuka. "Three hundred li north of Nishikomi, there was a place called Sakawa Village. My mother used to send for their dried fish whenever she could—they have a way of smoking it that leaves it full of flavor even when it's been transported halfway across the Empire."

She pauses. Shefali sees her swallow, sees her sniff in the way she does when her eyes might have watered before.

"No one who ventured to Sakawa in the past three months returned. Lord Shiratori at last sent a full regiment to determine the cause. They found . . . the village was changed. Five hundred residents, their bodies twisted, all moving in perfect sync with one another . . ."

Five hundred. Even if Shiratori sent a thousand—it would be a difficult thing to overcome five hundred of the enemy clustered together. Shizuka's army succeeded only because they had a god with them.

This regiment did not.

One thousand lives likely lost. Impossible to imagine the horror of it; impossible to hold in your mind the truth of it all. A thousand grains of rice is not enough to fill a bowl; a thousand grains of sand barely enough to dust her palm.

But a thousand lives are not simply a thousand lives. Each of the dead have family and friends; no one is alone in the autumn. The man who sits every morning on the street corner eating dumplings may have no one to call his own—but the day he stops appearing, everyone who walked past him will know. And they will wonder: Who was that man? What led him to such a lonely existence? What blows did life rain down upon him, and how did he weather them? Was his loneliness a testament to the foul nature of his character, or was this his triumph in the face of adversity? Had he endured, or was he abandoned?

The answers will never come to them now.

One thousand lives, swallowed up in a day.

She thinks of Akane and her candles, of the lights so bright in the South and so dim in the North. How many remained?

"It's the farthest south we've seen them," Shizuka says. "If I'd left . . ."

Shefali's chest aches, and not because Shizuka is wrong. "We'll get there as soon as we can," she says. "We had to stay."

"A ruler's people are her hands and feet," Shizuka says. "If I cannot protect my own hands and feet, what use am I?"

She smells of shame, of regret, of bitter self-loathing. Her grip on Shefali's hand is tenuous at best. What is Shefali to say to ease her? If Shizuka had been speaking of her uncle, Shefali would've agreed with her. A ruler must protect their people.

And here they sit far from the front.

Yet if they leave . . . Shefali's eyes fall on her mother's letter, now worn from reading and rereading.

If they leave, there will not be time to meet with her family again. If they leave, Kenshiro will not have the time he needs for his research. Shefali would walk gladly into the afterlife holding her wife's hand—but if there is some way she might again stand under her own power, then it is better to find it, isn't it?

My life is not worth more than theirs, she'd said.

Did she mean that?

"I'm sorry," Shizuka says. Though her voice is quiet, the fury remains, buried like a body beneath a horsehair banner. "We've our reasons for staying. To dwell on it . . . the woman who dreams of hunting starves. That was how you put it, wasn't it?"

Yet they are both dreaming of hunting, aren't they? Shefali can only nod.

"Is there more news?" she says. Perhaps not all of it will be bad.

"The Axions claim they're seeing Hokkaran ships sailing toward them," says Shizuka. "Shiratori received a long letter about it engraved upon a sheet of bronze. It took ten messengers to carry it the whole way. I imagine there's some significance that merits the inconvenience of it all; significance beyond their displeasure with us."

Hokkaran ships sailing toward Axiot—unlikely, given the Father's Teeth and Mouth, but not impossible. In the days before the Wall was raised, when Iwa was the old capital, trade between the two was common.

But the Traitor seized Iwa as soon as he'd seized power, and the Three Nation Sea had suffered for it.

"You've met Axions, haven't you?" Shizuka says. "Can you imagine what it might mean—the bronze?"

Shefali shakes her head. "Silver for truth, gold for lies," she says. The knight wore silver-plated armor; she thought it kept her spirit pure. "Bronze—I don't know."

"There's a world between truth and lies," says Shizuka with a sigh. "We will have to write back to them on silver, then; it is a good thing Shiratori was the one to get it. . . ."

She writes a few characters down. A note to return to later, perhaps. When she opens the third letter—"acceptance" might be the best word for her resigned expression. As she reads it, the story changes. Has someone whispered a great secret to her? For her eyes are alight now, and when she reaches for the lacquer box, it is as if she is taking something from an altar. She holds the box up so that the light catches the gold inlay. Her mouth opens a little; her hand is shaking.

Shefali is almost afraid to ask what is in the box that might inspire such a reaction. To do so feels a little like trespassing upon a private moment. Marrying a woman means there are no secrets between you—but there is still privacy to be respected. It has been eight years, after all.

Shizuka does not open the box in front of her—only sets it down on her writing desk with the same reverence as when she picked it up.

A little later, the servants arrive with her breakfast. Shefali cannot remember the last time she saw her wife eat so heartily—she is taking big, openmouthed bites of her noodles and washing them down with equally large gulps of tea. Steamed eggs and a plate full of sweet-glazed pork await her once she is done. These, too, she eats to the last bite.

"You know you don't have to fight with me for food," Shefali teases. As a child, she and her cousins had often overloaded their bowls with food. If you were out with the horses when the stew was ready and didn't make it back to the ger in time, that was your own fault. You never knew when the next meal was coming—and no one wanted to share with a Hokkaran. To hear them tell it, she was going to die during the winter, anyway, so there was no point in her getting a full portion.

Otgar shared with her.

Sometimes.

"Never meet a head of state on an empty stomach," Shizuka says.

"Was that in Xianyu's lessons?" Shefali asks her. It sounds familiar.

Shizuka smirks. "Your mother's, actually," she says.

Shefali eyes the piles of food. There's a few bites left of noodles—mainly the ones that came in direct contact with shrimp. Shizuka's never been fond of shrimp. "Then maybe I should eat, too."

"You're excused," Shizuka says. She sets down her bowl at last, reaching now for a washcloth. "But you should prepare yourself. Our brother wants to speak to us."

Ah.

So the time has come, then.

To know an arrow is coming will not lessen the pain it causes.

She forces herself to have a little of the noodles.

They taste of ash.

BARSALAI SHEFALI

SEVENTEEN

The creatures on the doors to the library are scowling at her. Shefali isn't sure how she knows this, but she knows it, deep in her heart. Maybe they know what lies in wait for her. She wouldn't put it past them—they look clever, whatever they are. If Kenshiro's news is good, perhaps she will ask him what they're meant to represent.

They stand outside, hand in hand.

"Whatever it takes to free you from that man," Shizuka says to her, "know you have my sword."

She says "whatever it takes" as if she is certain there will be a solution. There may not be one at all. It may be that she is twice-cursed: to live with such a man in her mind, seeing through her eyes and touching through her skin; to die before she has done the things she has always wanted to do. The Traitor is not a tick; they cannot simply pinch him between their fingers.

Part of her has these thoughts.

And another part of her wants to hope.

"I know," she says to her wife—to the woman who has loved her in spite of her blood and birth. "Ready?"

Is that hesitation?

"Always," says Shizuka.

Again—she is the one who opens the doors.

Somehow, the library is in an even worse state than last time. It seems half the scrolls have been pulled from their places to form a fortress of knowledge—one that Kenshiro and Sakura man in the shadow of the old King's statue. The place smells of sweat and sadness. Shefali sees why: there are two cots set up on either side of the statue, each one little more than two blankets layered atop old books, with a block of wood for a pillow. Anyone who rested there would be miserable.

There are more trays of uneaten food, too—she counts at least five mostly full bowls of rice, two bowls of now-faded vegetables, three plates of spinach and peanuts, and even a particularly sad-looking roast duck left to go cold. It's hard to walk without stepping on an upturned teacup or an ancient manuscript.

Kenshiro and Sakura sit on their beds, each with a separate book in hand. Neither of them notices Shizuka and Shefali enter. Kenshiro's beard is so long now that he reminds Shefali a little of a goat; Sakura's hair is more nest than river of ink. She is the one with more scrolls piled up around her—Kenshiro seems to have done more of his own writing, judging from the smears on his fingertips and the calligraphy set within easy reach.

Seeing her brother in such a state is like seeing a horse with a broken leg. Shefali wonders if he's left the room at all. When was the last time he saw his daughter? She has not seen him with Baoyi the whole time he's been working. Sakura said he wanted to remember, but he'd sealed himself up inside this chamber instead.

"Ken," she calls. When he looks up at her, she sees that he is haggard, that his skin hangs a little loose around his cheeks. That he is surrounded by food only makes her feel worse about this.

"Shefali-lun," he says. His voice comes out a rasp. "How are you feeling? How was the festival?"

Shefali shares a glance with Shizuka. They need not speak to agree on what must be done. Shefali picks up the freshest-smelling tray of food, and Shizuka heats both meal and tea with a touch. They set this down between Kenshiro and Sakura, and then take their seats on the floor.

"You both need to eat before we discuss anything," says Shizuka. "You're lucky it's us finding you here and not your wife, Kenshiro-lun. Baozhai would sit you on her lap and shave you herself."

"Careful," says Sakura. She hasn't lost as much weight as Kenshiro has—when she reaches for the food, it seems more likely that she's forgotten to eat rather than she's made any attempt to refrain. "Talk like that, and you'll summon her."

Kenshiro makes a small affirmative sound as he gulps down some of his spinach.

"Different indeed," he says. Shefali wants to ask him what he means by this, but before she can, he speaks again. "You will excuse my appearance, I hope."

"But not the smell," Sakura says. "I've been trying to get him to bathe."

"There isn't time," he says, a little firmly. Shefali sniffs. Sakura has a point. "My wife will be joining us. I think it's best we wait for her, before we begin."

Shizuka stiffens. Confusion, anger, excitement—these things mingle in her scent, like flowers blending into a strange perfume. "Baozhai? Coming—why is she coming here?"

"Weeks of study have afforded me little insight, in truth," says

Kenshiro. "We made only minor discoveries. It wasn't until I spoke to Baozhai of our difficulties that the solution presented itself."

"Solution?" says Shefali. Hope springs in her breast.

Kenshiro nods, a smile tugging at his lips. "I believe we've got one."

A solution. Sky, she hadn't allowed herself to dream of one, not really. She should have known that nothing was impossible when it came to this family.

"Tell me," she says. "Please."

"It's best if she explains—"

"*Please*," Shefali repeats. She cannot remember the last time she's begged her brother, but she does it now, her voice soft and her head bowed.

Her brother—Kenshiro, the man of no nation—can only stare back at her. A hush falls over the three of them; four eyes settle on the sight before them.

There are years in this moment.

Low, he bows, low: his forehead touches the ground; some of his hair falls into the teacup, but he does not mind.

"Shefa-lun," he says. "It's not my solution to give."

A student, about to embark on a journey, petitions his master. Something is troubling his mind; he feels he cannot depart without voicing his concerns. In the morning, he visits his master and confesses to him: He is not certain this journey will enlighten him, and worse, he is not certain that he is worthy of it.

His master tells him to put one foot in front of the other—to focus on only this.

Two years later, the student returns, enlightened and worthy.

Shefali, the master; Kenshiro, the student.

Shefali is content, then, to let the moment fade into silence. When her brother rises again, they nod at one another. He continues eating and she continues to smell the kumaq, and next to her Shizuka runs her fingers over the phoenixes painted onto her robes.

When at last Baozhai arrives, the servants herald her again—this time as Lai Baozhai and not as the Thorned-Blossom Queen. Green and violet she wears still, though she has changed to a less ostentatious jacket and hairstyle. Her makeup hasn't changed at all—but the jacket and the hair are enough to lend her a softer look.

A softer look everywhere but her face. There is something of the Queen about her still, something unyielding in her bearing.

And yet when she lays eyes on Shizuka—then she truly becomes Lai Baozhai again. She does not hurry over—Lai Baozhai never hurries—but glides in a whisper of silk. To Shefali's surprise, she sits right on the floor next to them.

When her eyes fall on Kenshiro and the empty plate before him, she lets out a relieved sigh. But, as a hot sword becomes cold steel, so, too, does the relief in her voice cool. "Was that your doing?" she says. "You must tell me your secrets. My husband has flat-out refused to see me these past few days. My concern for his health could not overcome his concern for his studies, it seems."

Kenshiro shrinks a little. "I am sorry," he says. "I should have spoken to you of all this earlier."

"Yes," says Baozhai. "You should have."

The air between them is a bowstring. Shefali does not want to let it fire—not when they're on the precipice of a breakthrough. Perhaps it is selfish of her to want to move the conversation along, but how often has she indulged such urges? All her life, she has lived for Shizuka, or lived for the Qorin.

The Traitor in her head is there only because of the sacrifices she has made for others.

Is it so terrible to want him gone? Is it so terrible to focus on herself, if only for a single conversation?

"The solution?" she says. How ashamed of herself she feels! As if she has asked a dying woman for a favor, as if she is not the dying woman herself!

So sudden and forceful is her little utterance that Baozhai and Kenshiro alike raise a brow at her. Sakura smiles, which cannot mean anything good, and Shizuka squeezes her hand.

Now she is the one who feels like shrinking.

"Ah, there's the Kharsa's daughter," says Sakura. "Let's not keep her waiting."

Kenshiro nods, and Baozhai shifts over so that she is sitting next to him. The two of them say something to one another in quiet Xianese. When they speak, Baozhai's hand is in her husband's.

"What you are about to hear cannot, under any circumstances, leave this room," she says. "I'm risking the ire of my ancestors just speaking of it to any of you. For two thousand years, the Kings and Queens of Xian-Lai have kept this secret. When General Nozawa of the North led his conquering army to our gates, we bowed to him rather than divulge this. Am I understood?"

Shizuka smells a little of fear. Shefali wonders why. There is shame there, too, and disgust—mention of her ancestors often dredges up such feelings—but why the fear?

"Yes," says Shefali. Shizuka echoes her a moment later.

There is a flicker of uncertainty, of hesitation that crosses Baozhai before she continues. She must close her eyes to banish it. Shefali can smell the torment lurking beneath the mask Baozhai presents them.

Fear, shame, regret, determination. In some ways, she is so like Shizuka.

"I have often said that no one dies in the Bronze Palace," says Baozhai. "It is a common enough saying that you likely thought I was being facetious. That I was bragging, a little, about how well maintained my home is. I tell you now: that saying is true. No one dies in the Bronze Palace. No one has *ever* died in the Bronze Palace; not since the first King of Xian-Lai struck a deal with the Lady of Flowers some two thousand years ago."

She cannot be serious.

No one dies in the palace?

But that would mean . . . there is a question in her mind now for every blade of grass upon the steppes.

"Two thousand years?" says Shizuka. "Baozhai, you're saying *no one has assassinated a sovereign* in two thousand years? No one has tried? No arguments have broken out between your servants?"

Baozhai's face remains serene, but there is a flash of anger behind her eyes. "I choose my words carefully, Lady," she says. "I tell you again: no one dies in the Bronze Palace. No one."

"Xianese Kings and Queens were known for their longevity," says Sakura. "Before we happened to them, I mean. King Lai Xunyu lived to two hundred."

"That's only a story," says Shizuka. "Chen Luoyi was born on and died the same day he did; the man can't have been any older than ninety. A long life, to be sure, but—"

"Lady," says Baozhai. The only thing sharper than her tone is her glare. "You worked one year at the temple and you served three years among my people. For that we are grateful, truly—but twice-two years in the South do not make you a southerner. They do not entitle you to lecture a scholar on the history of her own nation."

Eight years ago, this would've caused an argument. Shefali half expects it to now—Shizuka's eyes go wide. The shame in her scent tells the true story: Shizuka only bows her head.

"You're right," she says. "My apologies. I spoke out of turn."

Shefali's heart swells with pride. That she'd apologize at all—this is not the girl she left behind; this is the woman she married.

The unadorned apology softens Baozhai's edge. She takes a breath before continuing.

"You're curious to the terms of the arrangement, and to its origins, I'm certain. You will not find them here; I must be spare with the details. Suffice it to say that my ancestor the Bronze King saved the Lady of Flowers one day. For this service, she granted him a boon. He asked that she never again enter his palace. The exact wording: 'May your shadow never fall upon the Bronze Palace.' In this way, he ensured we would still be able to birth heirs.

"The Lady of Flowers was not particularly pleased with the arrangement, but she did owe the man her life. She relented, on one condition: No one may spill the blood of another within the walls of the palace. She knew, of course, the quarrelsome nature of mortals, and expected that we'd break our oath within two generations.

"She underestimated my family's dedication.

"We pick our servants carefully, Lady, and we have always lived righteous lives. Even the more sinful members of my lineage knew what they would sacrifice if they allowed our oath to lapse— or, worse, what might happen if the truth concerning our life spans were to become common knowledge. In my estimation, you are the only two foreigners to have learned of this in at least two centuries.

"Thus, when *your* ancestor's army marched to the palace, we faced a dilemma. If we allowed you in, you would surely ransack the place. Your people are like toddlers loose in a glassmaker's shop: you leave everything you touch shattered and broken."

Shizuka, for her part, does not argue the point.

"Our options were to allow you inside, where you would paint the walls and floors with red ink, or to surrender to you and negotiate more favorable terms. My father chose to negotiate. The commoners hated him for it—but so long as we lived, we could watch over our people. That we retained much of the Bronze Army made negotiating easier, as well; your people were eager for victory, and did not truly want to face them. We retained what autonomy we could. If we waited long enough, your Empire would surely fall."

Shefali stifles a laugh. Somehow she never realized the Xianese hate the Empire as much as the Qorin do. Perhaps it comes from her age; in her grandmother's time, it is said the two nations were friends. Xianese merchants sailing across the Bay of Illusions often hire Qorin to escort them to Sur-Shar when they land. Deels resemble Xianese jackets more than they do Hokkaran robes, and Shefali is certain some of her uncle's recipes have their roots in Xianese ones, from the smell of them.

The Hokkarans did not kill more than half the Xianese, but then, the Xianese were very quick to surrender. It used to be the subject of Qorin jokes.

But Shefali sees the reason in it now. Alshara herself made a similar decision: to surrender a portion of her Qorin nature for the promise that the future would vindicate her decision.

Hm.

Who would have thought she'd ever compare Baozhai to her mother?

"There have been . . . brushes with destiny, over the years," Baozhai admits. "My mother. We've always given birth outside the palace, in case of any complications, but . . ."

For five hundred years, the Wall of Stone stood impregnable to the East, a testament to both Hokkaran engineering and close-mindedness. Five hundred years it weathered the slings and arrows of the Qorin; five hundred years it stood guard over a nation.

But Burqila Alshara brought it crumbling down with five wagons of Dragon's Fire.

It does not take five wagons of Dragon's Fire to shatter Baozhai's mask—only a memory. The anguish coming from her is so potent that Shefali cannot smell anything else—not even the still-open skin of kumaq within easy reach. She blames herself, doesn't she? It's impossible to ignore the images that paint themselves on Shefali's eyelids: Third and Fourth sisters laughing as they shove her into a thornbush; kneeling next to her father as he lights the incense on her mother's altar, the sadness like a veil upon him; wandering among the spiderlilies at the edge of the graveyard and wondering, wondering . . .

When Baozhai wipes away at her painted eyes, Shefali is kind enough to pretend she hasn't seen anything. Shizuka, though—her scent has gone sharp with concern.

"You needn't tell us any more than we need to know," she offers.

Baozhai sniffles. "Right," she says. "Well. You've what you need to know, then. So long as you stay within the palace walls, the Lady of Flowers won't come for you."

The Lady of Flowers—that is what they call the Mother in Xian-Lai, isn't it? Shefali thinks back to Akane, to her table full of candles. Had there been a black spot in Xian-Lai? She hadn't been paying attention at the time.

Kenshiro and Ren spoke of will, of power, of uniting two gods to counter one. If she stays here—where the weather is every day a dream, where the people do not stare at her, where the gardens are always in bloom, where she has her brother and her niece and her wife all at her side—then she might live.

Might.

It was Akane who told her of her death day, after all, and Akane who blessed this palace. It very well may be that nothing can keep her away.

But—does it not make sense? Does it not *feel* like it will work? For since she began staying here, her pain hardly troubles her; since she began staying here, she can move without fear of her joints betraying her. Isn't it already working?

Hope is a dangerous thing to nurture. You are never certain until it hatches whether it will be a bird in your breast or a serpent.

Let the serpent bite her, if that is what hatches; she does not want to die.

And yet . . . even as her mood soars, there is a cruel thought in her ear.

If she can never leave the palace walls, then what sort of Qorin will she be? Riding her gray around in circles, as if she were an Ikhthian leaper? Letting her brain sprout roots? How long can she bear such a life—how long before this palace becomes her cage?

Her gaze falls to Shizuka, who sits staring into her lap, deep in thought.

"It isn't a perfect solution," says Kenshiro. "I'm well aware of what you'd be giving up, staying in a place like this, but you'll find the palace is larger than you think. I hardly leave it myself."

That is less of an endorsement than he likely wants it to be. Their mother named him Halaagmod for a reason.

A life trapped between four walls. A life spent growing roots. A life with her family, a life with her friends.

A life she might spend with her wife, as they've always dreamed.

Is it truly so terrible?

Yet her death is somehow the least pressing issue. There is more to address, more that she hopes Kenshiro can answer.

"And the Traitor?" she says.

Kenshiro looks to Sakura, then looks down. From the way he slumps, Shefali knows she isn't going to like the answer.

"Nothing new, I'm afraid," he says. "But if you stay within the palace, we should have time enough to figure something out."

"And the sanbarteis are coming, with the Qorin," adds Sakura. At least she is attempting to pronounce it; so few Hokkarans try. "With our research and their secrets, there must be something we can do."

"You have our word—and that of the Thorned-Blossom Queen— that you may stay here as long as you wish," says Baozhai. "You will have your run of the grounds without restriction. So long as you do not spill blood, the Crown will not interfere with you, and whatever you request, within reason, will be brought to you."

No spilling blood.

No hunting.

She almost wants to laugh at that. So she is never going to teach Baoyi to hunt, is she? Someone has to. Maybe she can tell her the basics of it and let someone else do the real teaching. Otgar, if Otgar ever learned to shoot a bow as well as she can throw a man.

Thinking of her cousin leaves a bittersweet taste in her mouth. She will see her again soon, for better or for worse, and the two of them are going to have to talk about all that's come to light. What does it mean for the Qorin if Tumenbayar became Grandmother Sky? What does it mean for them to lose their two greatest heroes in one fell swoop?

"BELOVED," SAYS SHIZUKA. It has been so long since she's spoken that her voice is a little startling. "Is this what you'd like?"

How to answer her? Shefali's mouth feels dry, all of a sudden; she cannot think. "It's . . . safe," she says.

"But is it what you want?" Shizuka says. The air around her is shimmering; her eyes are more gold than amber. "To stay here in the Bronze Palace?"

To stay here, among the flowers, with her brother and sister and niece.

To stay here, in the South, where her family can visit.

To stay here, in the South, where she will never again behold the endless sea of silver, nor the mountain towering above it.

It is the scent of peony that persuades her, the promise of red silk, the light of an eternal fire, the heart beating in her own chest.

"Yes," Shefali says.

For she cannot imagine leaving this world while Shizuka is still in it.

As a war widow who sees her fallen husband in her son's smiling face—Minami Shizuka, smiling at her wife. "Well," she says. "Then it will be as you wish."

As she wishes? What is she . . . why is she speaking in such a way? This miasma settling over the five of them, this relief that is so like death—where did it come from?

"Shizuka?" Shefali says, for she knows—she knows—there is something amiss with her wife, some despair gnawing at her heart, and she cannot allow it to fester. "Are you all right?"

"I am," says Shizuka.

She is lying.

Shefali's brows come together. Why isn't she speaking to her about this? They're among friends, among family!

Perhaps Shizuka senses that her wife's concern will soon turn to anger—she kisses her between the eyes. "We shall speak of it later. So long as you are safe and happy, my love, there is little else that concerns me."

Again, she lies. But she is honest about wanting to speak of it later.

What can she possibly want to say that she cannot say in front of Baozhai? In front of Kenshiro, or Sakura?

"I will handle the preparations, then," says Baozhai. She kisses her husband, bows quickly to Shefali, and offers Shizuka only a nod. "I do hope the rest of this meeting goes well, but Baoyi's lessons will be over soon, and I must see to her. Don't be late for dinner."

"I'd never dream of it," says Shizuka. For this, at least, she is telling the truth.

"Just don't serve duck again," says Sakura.

"What was that?" says Baozhai. "You wanted hurt feelings? What an exotic meal, Minami-lao."

The back and forth between them soothes Shefali's temper a little—they bicker as Qorin do, and so she feels a little at home.

Even if Shizuka's lie is like a lash fallen in her eye.

Baozhai leaves them. The room seems less bright without her in it, though it is the middle of the day and one of them is a living flame. Shefali can never understand how that woman has such an effect.

It is Sakura, again, who breaks the silence. She's never been fond of them.

"We did have an idea about the other thing. The Traitor," she says. She picks up one of the scrolls at her side—it is about as thick as her wrist, and written on paper that would make Shizuka's skin crawl. "Well. I had the idea. Kenshiro sat there and nodded when I told him about it."

"This *is* her decision," Kenshiro says. "Whatever may come of it."

Sakura looks over the scroll in much the same way Shizuka looked at the black lacquer box this morning.

"My mother left me this," she says. "The one who gave birth to me, I mean. She left it with my real mother when I was a kid. Didn't even bother to come in and say hello to me."

Sakura sets the scroll down in front of Shefali—much to her surprise.

"I can't read Hokkaran," Shefali says. Part of her will always be a little ashamed of it, though it is no fault of her own.

"I know," says Sakura. "This isn't Hokkaran."

When she unravels the scroll, Shefali sees that she is right. The letters on that page aren't Hokkaran at all—nor are they Xianese, or Surian, or anything Shefali's ever seen before. A series of tightly packed circles makes up each word, with the circles filled in to varying degrees and in different ways—the top right quadrant filled here, two crossed lines there. Who would come up with such a system?

"Sakura, what *is* this?" says Shizuka. "You've never shown this to me before."

"It wasn't important," says Sakura. She waves it off, but Shizuka is frowning. "I told you I wanted to keep you company, and I did. But I also wanted to see if I could find someone to teach me how to read this letter, and you didn't really need to know about that."

"I could have helped," says Shizuka. Sorrow's turned to annoyance; she squeezes Shefali's hand more to vent her displeasure than to comfort her wife.

"You did," says Sakura. "You got Ken-lun to work with me. I already knew it wasn't Hokkaran or Xianese, since my old clients told me, but I thought that if anyone could figure it out, it'd be a White Leaf scholar. I just thought it would take longer to find one."

Kenshiro has the good sense not to look too proud of himself. Shizuka glares at him nonetheless. "You were supposed to teach her to read."

"I did," he says. "She reads quite well now."

"Better than you do," says Sakura. "Which is why this scroll's so puzzling. Every time I look back on it, the circles change on me—and it's the same for Kenshiro, the same for everybody I've ever shown this to."

The circles change? But Shefali looked up at Sakura while she was speaking, and the first five circles haven't changed at all in that time. Perhaps they will over time?

"So—I got to thinking maybe the reason I can't read it is because it's from over the Old Wall," she says. "My mom wasn't supposed to have come back. No one ever saw her again, after she went north, so if this is from her . . . maybe it isn't just from her. If that's the case, then maybe you could read it."

Maybe it isn't just from her.

Shefali swallows.

"You're free to refuse, if you aren't feeling ready," says Shizuka. "My *cousin* is being a bit demanding."

"I'm being demanding? *Me?*"

"Yes," says Shizuka. "You know Shefali has a lot on her mind, and you're asking her to do you a favor regardless."

That Shizuka cares so much about her well-being is endearing. That she so often starts arguments over it less so. Shefali traces an X on Shizuka's palm with one hand.

With the other, she picks up the scroll.

Like dancers kneeling at the end of their choreography—the letters, settling into place.

Her hand goes cold.

She begins to read.

> *Barsalai Shefali,*
>
> You don't know me, and to be honest, I don't know you. I know your mother, a little. As much as anyone can be said to know her when all she does is loom threateningly behind you at all hours. For months I traveled with her, and if she still lives, you may ask her about me.
>
> She might think that I died. I almost wish that I had. I think . . . after I am done writing this, there are options to consider.
>
> But I *must* write this. The words will knock against the inside of my skull until I get them onto the page. Maybe

when it's all set down in ink, I can begin to forget some of it.

My name is Maki Sayaka. I was born two hundred li north of Nishikomi, in the Year of the Brother. My parents must've taken that for an awful fortune; they shoved me into the arms of a passing merchant. The merchant left me at the Shrine of Jade Secrets in the city, and it was there that I spent my childhood. If you've heard of me—then you've heard of me as Spiderlily Sayaka: assassin for hire, master of the Spiderlily style, national hero.

I was one of the Sixteen Swords.

I never wanted to be one, mind, and I didn't want to go over the Wall.

Before I get into any of this, you need to know that. I didn't want to go; I only wanted the second-place prize money. Eight hundred ryo was more than enough to buy a plot of land in the capital and build a school. That was all I wanted—a school, where I could teach others this art I'd perfected. I don't know how long it's been, or how long it will be until you read this. Maybe you haven't heard of me at all. The Spiderlily style—my style—involves using razor-sharp wires as weapons. I got the idea from watching a spider weave in the corner of the Shrine. It took years before I'd made enough money to make a proper set of wires, and months even after that before I found a smith who could make them for me.

But the moment I first felt the heft of the wires against my arms, I knew. There's an art to it, you see. It isn't like using a dagger—you don't need to be close. It isn't like a sword—you aren't dueling them. Polearms are for killing the enemy.

This . . .

Waiting in just the right spot, for just the right
moment . . .

Yes. It was like a dance. It was *thrilling*, in ways that
nothing else was to me. You'll think it's strange that
I speak of killing in such a way. You have to understand, it
wasn't the killing itself that excited me. It was the anticipation of the thing. And even if I did enjoy it a little, is there
anything wrong with that? I never killed anyone who
didn't deserve it.

You've got to deserve it, if someone was willing to pay
my rates to see you dead.

Not that the money matters to me anymore, but it was
why I entered. For money. For enough to start a school,
for my style to spread, for people to light prayers to me
all across the Empire and beg me to do the work I so
enjoyed.

That was what drove me, not some misplaced sense
of duty to an Emperor who had just taken the throne.
To go over the Wall was to die. We all knew that, even
the ones who tried to claim otherwise. My plan was to
make it to the final match and take a dive. That way I'd
get the prize money and just enough fame for my first
few students. When everything was settled, I'd send
for my daughter and raise her in the capital as she
deserved.

My daughter—she's the one who's giving this letter to
you, or the reason you're reading it. I suppose I should tell
you a little about her. She'll want to know. Just—maybe
don't tell the Empress any of this. I assume she's Empress
by the time you're reading this; it's not like the Toad is

going to give us any heirs. What I mean is: This story isn't
kind to Minami Shizuru.

But my daughter will want to know it, so I'll write it
down.

When Minami Shizuru was young, she joined up with
the Shrine of Jade Secrets. I shouldn't need to tell you it
wasn't a shrine at all, but we called the women who
worked there shrine maidens. Minami-mor was what they
called a temple guard. At the time, I had just started
taking on my own contracts in Nishikomi, serving the
various gem lords in their petty squabbles. One of those
gem lords, Sumashi Taro, owned the shrine, and so I spent
an awful lot of time in her company without her realizing.
In my line of work, it was best if we remained mysteries.

And I was very good at remaining a mystery.

Until her brothers came to visit.

They'd heard what Shizuru-mor was doing, and not a
one of the three was pleased. They'd gotten it in their
heads to try to talk some sense to her—I just happened to
be at the shrine that day, keeping my eye on a future
target. It was impossible to miss what was going on,
Shizuru-mor being as unholy loud as she is, and her
brothers being no different. Apparently, the Minami name
meant nothing at all if its presumptive heir was working in
a pleasure house. Some of the clients were beginning to
filter out without requesting any private time just to get
away from the sound of them.

My target was one of them.

I waited fifty heartbeats before paying off my tab
and following him out—or trying to. Along the way, I
came face-to-face with all the Minami siblings at once.

Shizuru-mor, having spent two years by then in service to the shrine, now bore a tattoo to mark her; one of her brothers had torn her sleeve open to reveal it. Masaru— the eldest of them—stood with the sleeve in hand, screaming at her about their family honor. Goro—the middle—was torn between disgust and longing for the girls just beyond the door. Shizuru-mor was obviously not paying any attention to me; she was halfway to breaking Masaru's nose when I saw Keichi.

And more important, Keichi saw me.

I made such a habit of looking uninteresting that being seen was . . . frightening. If it weren't for the Minami family crest on his armor, I would've assumed he worked for my target, so intensely did he look at me. My skin tingling, I pulled down my hat and continued down the alleyway as Masaru hit the ground.

I lost track of my target that night.

Which meant I had to return the next.

I saw Keichi again, and again. The Minami siblings had resolved to stay in Nishikomi until their sister left of her own accord, you see, and so they had reason to stay and I had reason to bump into him. The only man who remembered my face no matter the disguise, the only man who recognized my voice no matter where he heard it. Twice he caught me while I was playing the part of a merchant—and each time, he told me where he'd be staying.

I won't waste your time with the details of it. He was a handsome man and a warrior besides; I fell into his bed and he caught me with little effort. Neither of us spoke of where we'd been or where we planned to go. At the end of

the season, Masaru's nose having been broken a whopping
five times by his own sister, they all left.

KEICHI LEFT MY life as quickly as he'd come into it,
and though he often sent letters, it was never quite the
same between us. When I realized I was pregnant, I didn't
see fit to tell him. I had *plans*, you understand, and a baby
wasn't part of them. Not for years yet.

So I left her with the Head Priestess at the shrine, with
a few of Keichi's things to prove her identity if the time
should ever come to it.

After that, it was straight to Fujino for me—she was
born on the last day of Emperor Yorihito's rule, and we
got word of the tournament nonsense shortly after he
passed.

So I went, and I fought, and I would have come right
back home if my final opponent hadn't decided to kill
herself in the ring. The tournament itself was a folly, she
argued. For some reason, she decided to enter regardless.
Honor, perhaps, or some gods-forsaken drive to make a
statement. Whatever it was—I wasn't quick enough to
stop her.

As she bled out onto the tile, I considered faking my
own death and returning to Nishikomi, but what good
would that do me? To do that, I'd have to abandon the
idea of my own school altogether—no one in the Empire
fights the way I do. What would I do for money? Become
a temple guard? But you see me: I'm a small woman, and
I always have been. My line of work hadn't left me with
many skills beyond the slow pursuit and murder of people
I did not know.

If I ran, I'd be giving up everything I'd worked so hard toward.

If I stayed, I was probably going to die.

But only probably—and that, in the end, tipped the merchant's scales. Even I had to admit the group we gathered was a fearsome one. Minami Shizuru, Keichi, three Hokkaran captains, General Kikkomura himself, and of course your mother, the Wall-Breaker. The idea itself was a farce—but if you asked me whom I'd take on a mission like this, I'd be hard-pressed to make a better list.

I wasn't happy about it, mind. Keichi's charm wore off by the next time I saw him—he'd spent too much time around his sister, and lost that shyness I treasured so much. I dragged my feet all the way up the Eight-Petal Road, but I'd resigned myself to this fate. Besides, if the worst really came to the worst and we encountered something we couldn't trounce—I knew well enough how to turn tail.

I ALMOST DID, one night.

I couldn't tell you if it was a dream or not. I had nightmares more often than not in those days. Maybe this was one, but I remember it even now with perfect clarity.

There was this sound. Like chopping wood, almost, only nowhere near so loud. *Chukk-chukk-chukk*— something like that. A normal sound if you'd heard it anywhere else—but who chops wood in the middle of the night? And we'd seen no other travelers for some time. No one in their right mind was going north.

Worse—everyone else was asleep.

Now, this sound wasn't very loud, but it was the sort that grinds against your ears. Even if you walked in a Jubilee crowd, you'd be able to hear it, on some level, making everything else unpleasant just by being there. That no one else had awoken told me something was wrong.

One by one, I tried to wake the others—and I mean really wake them. Some of them I even kicked, but it was no good. Not a one woke.

And I saw, then, that it was Captain Araya who stood near the tree. Captain Araya who, only a week before, had gotten a mouthful of demonic moss.

When you see a captain chopping at a tree in the middle of the night you get your weapons ready. I did, too, but in the end it didn't matter. I caught her in my snare, with my sharpest wires, and I pulled as hard as I could, thinking that I'd take her hands clean off.

I did—but not in the way I thought. Like rice paper they came away, bloodless, and thousands of insects poured out.

She told me then, as the insects ate away at me—she told me that Iwa was the queen of all cities, that Iwa was waiting for me.

And that's . . . That's where I got the idea.

You'll think it's strange that I listened to her in spite of the circumstances. The truth was, I'd had dreams of Iwa since I was a child. Dreams of a port city that was not Nishikomi, dreams of a place where everyone wore antiquated robes and women left their hair loose regardless of whether or not they were married. When I imagined my school, it wasn't in Nishikomi, it wasn't in Fujino. It was in this other place.

Iwa.

Everyone knows the stories. The Old Capital was the first to fall to the Traitor, the first to surrender to him. Minami Shiori personally escorted the Emperor from the ruins to Shiseiki, and later from Shiseiki to Fujino, fighting all manner of creature along the way. Supposedly she forged the Daybreak Blade in Iwa, with the Dawn-breaker Crucible. Seems every year someone else has found the thing. I can't tell you how many times I've seen one for sale in the Nishikomi night markets.

And it's not just the crucible people pretend to have. Lost scrolls turn up every day. On a monthly basis, you'll see some new ship with strange sails pull into port, proclaiming to everyone who will listen that they sailed to Nishikomi all the way from the Old Capital.

Now—I never believed any of these stories, but I wanted to. I was the fool stopping at each booth just to hear the supposed history of a shamisen from Iwa. Didn't I know Handa played it? Yes, that Handa! In the Cresting Wave Palace, he came up with his first tunes, and what do you mean he died only five years ago?

So—when I awoke in a cold sweat after this nightmare, with Iwa on my lips—something about it felt predestined.

We went over the Wall, the fifteen of us. Your mother probably told you all about that, and I won't reopen the wound. What I saw in the mist that day, I see still in the corners of my eyes. Even now, with you sitting here before me, glowing like a festival candle, I see them— their metal frames and the heads mounted on them.

That sort of thing stays with you. Stains your clothes like Nishikomi Blue.

When we were through it, on the other side of the Wall—Keichi-zun wasn't doing well. I knew the second I saw him what had happened, and so did your mother, but Minami-mor? She wasn't hearing it. Her brother would never get corrupted, she said, as if his blood isn't as red as yours or mine. As if he were any less human.

I . . .

It's hard to say this to you, since you're the Wall-Breaker's daughter. The fact that you're here before me means she must have gotten back, somehow, and there was no way Burqila was going to leave with Minami-mor. I don't know how either of them made it. Minami-mor had taken a nasty shoulder wound that was already starting to sour when I last saw her.

It was . . .

I'm not a bad person. Understand that, won't you? I didn't leave her for dead. It wasn't as if I saw her bleeding out before me and decided to take off for Iwa. She was safe enough. Burqila was with her, and the two children from Shiseiki.

I didn't leave her for dead.

It's only that I realized that I knew where I needed to go. The woman killing herself during her last match, my childhood dreams of the city, Araya's rattling words— they all pointed the same way.

And I was never going to have another chance to go there. All my life, I thought I'd be known for the webs I wove, for the style I'd perfected—but what if I was meant to be the woman who learned Iwa's forgotten secrets?

When I left your mother and Minami-mor, that was
what was on my mind. That was my thinking.

Of course—everyone says they can pluck a catfish
bare-handed, but it's another thing entirely to do it.

Forgive me, I know I'm wandering. It's just that my
time beyond the Wall has . . . it's broken everything into
little pieces, and I've got to try to put them all together
again. Indulge me a little longer. You need to know what
I saw.

The land beyond the Wall isn't like the land here. All of
it belongs to Him, and I do mean all of it. Blades of violet
grass sway without wind because *He* wills them to; orange
clouds roll across the sky because *He* wills them to; the
flowers all bloom out of season because *He* wants them to.
As if the land beyond the Wall is a great glass globe and
he sits above it. When he wriggles his fingers, all the
people dance.

And there were people. I knew better than to approach
them, but they were there—a few hundred along the way,
if I didn't miss my guess. I expected them to be as twisted
as the blackbloods, as the demons to the south. Looking
back on it, I think I might have preferred it if they were.
At least then you'd know what you were dealing with at
the outset.

Instead, each and every one of the Traitor's servants
was as pressed and pampered as any courtier. Silk, all of
them—the fisherwomen, the washermen, the farmers
leading their aurochs through their fields. All of them.
And I may not know much about color, but I do know that
only nobles wear more than two at a time, and never
colors from across the Empire. All of the women wore

eight proper robes, all of them! All of them had shaved
brows and blackened teeth, all of them bowed to me as
I passed and asked if I'd had my rice.

And not all of them were Hokkaran, mind you. Most of
them weren't. Do you have any idea how strange it is to
see a Qorin man with his pate shaved? To see Hokkaran
saddles on Qorin mares, to see women wearing old
Jeon-style braids in spite of their Hokkaran clothing? And
to hear them speak! The old men on the street creaking
their way through ancient plays—they sounded more
modern than these people. Qorin, Hokkaran, Jeon,
Doanese, or Xianese—it took me a while to realize it, but
they all sounded alike.

Because they spoke in the same voices, you understand.
Two voices for women (one younger, one older) and three
for men (young boy, warrior, and old man). No matter
where I went, no matter the shape they wore—the same
voices left their mouths each time.

It made my skin crawl.

But the worst thing was that they all moved at once.

Say I was walking along the riverbed and one of the
ones on a boat caught sight of me. The very moment he
caught sight of me, he'd turn to bow to me. So would his
companion. So would the woman ten horselengths away,
filling a vase with water. So would the people a li to the
north, little more than ants on the rolling hill—I saw
them stop and turn toward me, I saw them bow.

All at once.

"Have you had your rice?" they'd ask me.

So I don't think it's any surprise that I avoided them
from the second day on. Moving among the shadows is

the same no matter where you go. There were fewer of them beyond the Wall, but I found them all the same, and pressed myself into them for days at a time. Only when I saw no one near did I advance. In my childhood, I heard a song about Iwa—if you kept the Laughing Nobleman to your right at night, you'd find it in no time. Thankfully, the stars themselves had not changed.

I can't tell you how long I spent traveling. Until my feet cracked. Until my stomach threatened to eat itself, in hunger. Until my throat was dry as Rassat paper. Until taking a single step forward was as impossible as slaying the sun.

And with every step I took, I expected them to attack me.

They could see me, after all, even if I liked to pretend they couldn't. Though I clung to the shadows, I knew the trees were watching, knew the birds were listening, knew the water would swallow me whole if I went near it. Nothing in this place wanted me to be here.

But I was used to that. No one invites assassins to dinner. No one except Minami Keichi, rest his soul.

So—no eating, no drinking, none of that. Only the shadows and I.

By the time I saw Iwa rising up before me, I was so hungry, I thought I must be imagining it. Only twenty li before I thought I'd found someone selling starfruit, someone in a linen coat with his hair held back in a just barely proper horsetail. I was so weak that fetching coin from my purse took astronomical effort—my fingers weren't moving where I wanted them to, and in the end, I dumped two entire ryo in small coins onto his stand.

Or what I thought was his stand.

Instead, the coins clattered to the ground, where the
grass parted to reveal a mouth. That mouth swallowed the
last of my money and laughed.

I thought of lowering my neck above the mouth and
letting it eat me. I thought of using my own cords to
strangle myself, to end all this—but I'd made the decision
to go to Iwa, and I was going to see it if it was the last
thing I did.

It wasn't. But it might as well have been.

Here is what you must understand about Iwa: It is the
city of a madman. All the things I said before about the
residents of the land beyond the Wall are true of Iwa, as
well, but to an even higher degree. My first day there,
I was mystified by all of it: the silk-clad prisoners of the
Traitor going about their business, wandering up and
down alleyways that were almost but not quite like home;
the criers announcing the changing Bells with selections
of poetry I'd never heard before; the beggars, better
dressed than I was, with empty cups before them, thanking passersby for imagined donations.

A city is a living thing, Your Highness. It breathes in
dreams and breathes out wonder and greed; it sighs in
revolutions. A city without filth is like a woman with no
ornaments in her hair, like a man with no calluses. I tell
you now that Iwa was spotless. Gleaming, in places—the
houses that lined its streets were bright white, the thatch
of their roofs always new, no matter how many days had
passed.

But this is all telling you of the inside of the so-called
city, and nothing of how I came to enter it. I'm afraid
there is little to that story—there was an outcropping five

li from the gates, a statue of a man in robes with a massive sword standing atop it. When night fell, I threw my wires up around him and hauled myself up and over.

Now, there hadn't been anyone around to see me do this, but when I landed, I soon found myself surrounded by four Qorin in Hokkaran robes. Each one held a Hokkaran straight sword in hand, each one was smiling ear to ear at me. Three of them—the women—had blackened their teeth; the sole man let his fangs be seen without adornment.

And they were fangs, mind you. Serrated as a carpenter's blade.

As one, they bowed to me. They opened their mouths to speak—but I wanted nothing less than to hear them. With what little strength I had, I took off running, and behind me I heard them laughing.

"Enjoy your stay, Spiderlily," they said to me. "We've been so looking forward to it."

And that name died for me then, on the lips of those things that were not human.

Keichi had named me Spiderlily, you see. He thought it made me sound like the world's most dangerous blossom.

So often had I heard the words from his lips that I convinced myself he was with me so long as the name stuck. When the cheers went up in Fujino, when I caught wind of the gossip, the rumors about me—it was always about Spiderlily.

But these things spoke with the Traitor's voice, I was sure of it, and Spiderlily was what they called me.

The moment it left their lips, that part of me died.

But the rest of me would die, too, if I wasn't careful;

already I was near starving and delirious with thirst.
Where was I to find food? For in this city, I was surely the
only living woman. Blackbloods had no need to eat, and it
wasn't as if demons had a taste for fish rolls.

Fish rolls. Just the thought set my stomach rumbling—
but I would have taken anything you gave me at that
moment. If I'd come across a maggot-ridden carcass,
I would've brushed aside the wrigglers and helped myself
to the meat. I'm ashamed to say that I think I might have
even eaten another person if I'd seen them.

I didn't, of course. But I did see food. From my vantage
point up on the thatched roof of one of the largest houses
in town, I could see straight to the stalls, and in the stalls
I saw steaming lumps of what looked like meat served on
skewers. The so-called patrons of the establishment
mimed handing over coins, and the proprietor handed
over the skewers with a mechanical smile. I lay there for a
little while on the roof watching it all, for I could not
believe what I was seeing. What a simple thing—to buy
skewers from a vendor! And yet everyone involved now
knew the corruption of the Traitor, everyone involved
moved like animated dolls.

Would any of them even eat the things they'd
bought?

The answer was no. For one hundred breaths, I watched
them trail down the streets and not a one of them ate their
food. Instead they spoke to one another as they walked,
their mouths opening and closing as if on hinges, their
eyes flat and voices flatter. But what were they speaking
about?

I will tell you. As they passed by the thatched roof

house on which I rested, I heard them clear as temple bells.

"Magistrates over peasants, lords over magistrates, Emperor over lords, and the Eternal King over the Emperor. Everything in its place. Under Heaven, we are free."

Strange, I thought, but no stranger than the prayers I heard every so often back home. If anything, to praise the Traitor was almost more understandable—at least you could be certain he was alive, certain he was hearing you. I can't say the same for any of the old gods.

I told myself that this was normal enough. I told myself that if I got my hands on one of those skewers, if I ate—then I could explore the city and learn why I'd come. I told myself that this was not a mistake.

Mustering what little strength I had, I crossed the rooftops toward the stall—a feat made more difficult by the unfamiliar distance between the houses here. In Nishikomi, you stack everything together; it's called the Fish-Scale City for all the overlap. Here there was an alley between each pair of houses wide enough to drive two horses.

They weren't easy jumps to make, but I made them, and when I came to rest near the stall—well. I threw out a cord and brought back six skewers. Without stopping to study them, I gorged myself. Slimy meat met my tongue. Eel is my favorite sort of fish, I am no stranger to slimy meat: but this hardly tasted of meat at all. Sweet, it was, like overripe fruit, and yet when my teeth bit down, it had the same awful give as any other sort of flesh. Strips of sinew and muscle stuck between my teeth. Instead of tender, savory juices, my mouth now filled with a flavor at once too sour and too sweet.

Had I not been starving, I probably would have wondered what they'd killed to make such a thing, what sauces they'd used to settle those flavors. As it stood, my curiosity got the better of me for a moment, and I looked down into the stall from above. To the right of the vendor was a clay vat filled with murky black liquid, bubbling and broiling over as bits and bobs floated within. As a woman who has never in her life encountered such a thing as too much soy sauce—I was fine with this explanation.

Until I realized that it wasn't soy at all. The liquid was pure black, with none of that lovely brown around the edges; it smelled nothing like fish sauce or even molasses.

And, as I watched, I saw three human fingers floating among the shapeless lumps.

My stomach turned.

Have you ever gone hungry, Steel-Eye? Somehow I doubt it, so I'll tell you a little of it. When you get hungry, really hungry, you will tell yourself that you could eat a tiger if someone laid one in front of you. And you—you must be a rich woman. Let's say someone does put that tiger down in front of you, with a good sear on it, rubbed with herbs and covered with a creamy butter. The smell alone is feeding you by then. Ravenous, you dig in.

Two bites, maybe three. It's the most heavenly thing you've ever had, but your stomach's gotten used to not having anything in it. What's it going to do with all this meat? You've surprised your own body, and your body never takes well to surprises. Before you know it, you're not hungry. You're dizzy, in fact, lying down with one hand over your stomach, wondering why your flesh is buzzing.

Take one more bite. Force yourself to. I can guarantee you, you'll be vomiting within the hour.

When you've gone a long while without eating, you've got to start with small morsels and build your way up. I learned this when I was a child, but I'd forgotten it then, on the roof, and the sight of the fingers in the pot set me off. I rolled right over onto the edge and emptied my stomach. People, if you could call them people, walked right on beneath me. Not a single one bothered to change their path.

"Under Heaven, we are free," they said.

The stallkeeper was the one who called to me. "Spider-lily," he said, "you should have asked for food. The Eternal King provides for all his children."

The whole while he was rolling dough; he not once looked up to me.

"I don't belong to him," I creaked. "My blood's red."

"Everyone belongs to him," he said. "All children of the Empire. You have heard his voice all your life, you know, and have yet to heed him. What a spoiled child!"

I was trying to get to my feet by then, but my feet were buckling beneath me. Crawling farther up the roof was the best I could do—but even that, in the end, would not save me. After only sixteen heartbeats, the stallkeeper leaped right up there with me. I tried to skitter away, but he was always there, in the corner of my eye, with a bowl of noodles in his hands and that same grin on his face.

He shoved the bowl into my chest.

"Here in Iwa," he said, "we listen to our Father. He says to feed you, and so I have."

I could not let the bowl drop. No. Just the scent of it wiped away my nausea, just the scent of it had my mouth watering anew. When I took the bowl in hand, he produced a pair of chopsticks and a soup spoon, too. These he handed to me only when I'd sat down to eat.

He sat down with me, on the roof of that building, and no one thought to stare at us. No one so much as looked up.

My eyes met the noodles. Thick, served with cold broth and braised pork belly, it was. Shoots of bamboo added a bit of much-needed fiber, and a whole egg stood ready to add runny yolk to the mix. A finer meal than any I'd had since leaving the capital—that was to be sure. I wasn't certain the last time I'd even seen an egg.

Perhaps it was poisoned, but if it was my fate to eat poisoned noodles in the city of the Traitor god—well. There were worse ways to go.

This time I was more careful to pace myself. In the long spaces between bites, the stallkeeper took it upon himself to tell me of Iwa, of the city, of the Traitor.

"What you've heard beyond the Walls, none of it is true," he said. He was an older man from the look of him, though it is hard to tell with your people at times. The same warrior's voice I'd heard traveling north left his mouth, and yet it didn't seem to suit him. Too fiery, too brash. When he sat on the roof with me, his back was perfectly straight. Always, he smiled; never did it reach his flat eyes. Black colored his veins at the temples. "You know that. On some level, you have always known that.

The men who sit on the throne now—so little about them is divine."

I didn't care about Yoshimoto beyond hating him vaguely for sending me here; I hadn't cared about Yorihito at all.

"So far they have strayed from our teachings! Under Heaven, we are free—but they insist on imposing their own will onto the world. It isn't natural."

Nothing about this was natural, but I was too consumed by the soup to tell him so.

"The Eternal King is wise, Spiderlily, and he has always been so. When the Sun threatened to swallow the earth, it was the Eternal King who saved us."

Never in my life had I heard such a tale. The sun was one of the Grandmother's eyes. Everyone knew that, I thought.

"In payment, he asked to rule the seas—but when he saw how badly we were being governed on land, he abandoned his only love to preside over us. Humanity was a shattered pot, and he stitched us together with gold. Why should we not be grateful for him?"

So he spoke. So invested was I in my meal that I hardly paid him any mind. The bowl was the only thing that mattered to me. Only when I'd drained all of it, only when the last drops of broth fell onto my clothes, did I bother addressing him at all.

"Merchants all sound the same," I said. "Everyone is trying to sell something. But thank you for the soup."

He'd accost me again if I let him, I knew that much, and I was feeling a little heartier with the soup in me. I made my way to the edge of the roof and dropped down onto the ground.

I thought I'd be safe from him there, but I was wrong. He was in everyone.

The chant that left them—the bit about magistrates—fell away. All at once, everyone in the crowd turned to face me—even those far ahead of me had their heads turned like an owl's.

"Aren't you grateful for him?" they asked.

What I would have given then to be a bird. In the distance up ahead, I saw the towering masts of the wharf, and I thought to myself that perhaps I'd find a ship there. I'm no sailor, but I know a little here and there. Enough to hoist sail, enough about the stars to know which way to point the ship. To be the woman who genuinely brought back an ancient ship—was that why I'd longed to come here?

My feet carried me toward the ships.

"If he had not abandoned the depths for your forsaken people, Spiderlily, where would you be?" said the crowd.

Through them I walked, as if through the stalks of a bamboo forest. Not a one of them stayed still enough for me to bump into them. Always, they moved away at the last moment.

"If he had not taught the southerners to write," they said, "then where would you be?"

The alleys were giving way now to a common area, octagonal in shape, with eight statues at the center on a field of violet grass. The sky overhead changed from its usual eye-blistering colors to the pale orange of dawn. Shoulder to shoulder, the statues stood.

Eight of them, I said.

You'd think it was the Heavenly Family.

I did, too, until I studied them a little closer. In the
Son's place, I found a plump woman standing, her hands
raised and her hips caught in the motions of some foreign
dance. A plush red scarf around her waist was the only
thing about her not rendered in bronze—but the strange
thing is, I couldn't tell you much about it. Every time
I looked at it, the pattern changed—crashing waves,
needles, diamonds, stylized flowers, all of it I saw on that
scarf.

Who was this?

And she wasn't the only newcomer. Of the Heavenly
Family, only the Mother held her usual sickle and
cradle—and she was the only one who was entirely in
bronze. The rest of them each held something that clearly
hadn't been a part of their original statues. A Surian
woman surrounded by books and scrolls held a glimmering
crystal vial; a Qorin woman carried a bow so purely
silver, it made me long for snow; a Jeon man held a
still-beating heart in his outstretched hand.

Who were these people?

I hadn't realized that I'd stopped to look at them until
I heard the laugh.

Standing atop the eight statues was a woman, or
something like a woman. Her bottom half was that of a
spider's, her legs thick and covered in fur. Dark hair fell
across her face in brushstrokes, so that I could not see her
eyes—but she could not hide the pincers of her mouth
behind that veil. Over her top half, she wore a loose-tied
robe in Imperial Gold, of all things, decorated with maze
patterns. Sleeves concealed her human hands; she raised
one to her mouth to conceal her laugh.

"And where do you think you're going?" she said. That unnatural mouth meant the syllables came out with a strange rattle.

My hands were shaking, but I looped the threads around my fingers all the same. I had the sinking feeling that I wasn't going to make it to the docks with her in my way.

"Spiderlily," she cooed. I bit into my lip to keep from retching. "You haven't finished your work here."

I saw the gleaming webs between her spider legs a moment before she loosed them toward me. Unfortunately for her, I know a thing or two about webs—I whipped mine through the air in an arc, slicing through hers before they reached me. As the webs fell to the ground, I ran back the way I came.

Or I tried to, anyway.

The city's inhabitants got tired of me. They stood shoulder to shoulder, elbows linked, smiling back at me—a wall of them two score wide. Down the alley they went, too, so that looking out on them was like looking out on the reeds at low tide.

"Under Heaven, we are free," they said.

The woman was skittering behind me, laughing at me, and before me only this. My tongue stuck to the roof of my mouth. The only way to get out was to go over, then, and hope it would slow her down long enough that I could get away.

I flung my threads out for one of the roofs.

Two things happened then.

One: the stallkeeper appeared right where I was aiming—but he was different since I'd last seen him. His nose had gone all cucumber long and bumpy. More important, he held in his hands a chained sickle. The thing moved so quick, I hardly saw it, but I saw the result well enough—my threads were caught up in his chains now. If either of us pulled, we might knock the other out of place. I would have yanked at him if it weren't for the second thing.

See, if you've got yourself a magic sword made from sunlight, you can try to fight a general. You can hide, if you don't mind spending the rest of your life looking over your shoulder.

But you can't run from them. Especially not when you've run away in a straight line, like a gods-damned amateur. Nothing at all impaired the spider woman's shot—and I was so busy looking ahead at the stallkeeper that I did not think to look over my shoulder.

The web slammed into my ankles as heavy and hard as any chain. How disgusting it felt! Hot and thick, as if a massive tongue had caught hold of me. Unable to tear through the sticky film of it, I tripped and fell. I got my arm up just in time to keep my head from hitting the ground, but that was little help. By then, the spider woman's shadow was over me.

Panicking, I tried to draw back my threads, but the stallkeeper had dug his feet in like the Tokuma Mountains and would not yield. I might as well have tried to leash a pack of bulls. Instead he yanked as hard as he could, and I felt the cuts coming, braced myself for the pain—

I didn't get to feel it, in the end. The webs came for me first, a wad of them right at my head, covering my mouth and nose. You can hold your breath only so long before the waters take you. Screaming into the web took most of my breath. By the time my fingertips came off, I couldn't even feel them. I couldn't feel anything.

When I awoke, I was hanging upside down. My head was pounding, my eyes felt as if they'd pop right out of my skull. I wanted to scream, but my mouth was still covered; the best I could do was groan. From what I could see, I was suspended from a branch in the center of town. The citizens of Iwa stood beneath me, looking up at me, smiling. Again and again they repeated their little oath, until I no longer heard the words—only the sound.

And that sound . . .

When you stare at the sun too long, it burns. When you force yourself to look away, your vision swims with unnameable colors and shapes. So fascinating are these little blotches of color that it's tempting, at times, to stare at the sun a little longer. You start to see new things even as your vision fades.

So it was with these voices. As the words themselves faded into waves of sound, I heard a new word within.

A name.

Yamai.

The first Emperor—Yamai. These people, if you could call them people, *worshipped* him. The way they said his name! The way they swayed, their hands linked together, their eyes boring into mine; their smiles and the beating of their hearts!

All of this is for the Eternal King.

All of this is for Yamai.

Over, and over, that thought.

You will love him. He will teach you your place.

We are his kingdom.

Under Heaven, we are free.

I could not tell you if it was my thought. The voice in my head wasn't mine, but it was in *my head*. And I was sinking, sinking, into the eyes of those people, melting into them. . . .

I can't tell you if the first Emperor really was the Traitor; I'm not sure anyone can. If I were a false god, I'd tell everyone I'd founded the Empire, too. So I can't say, really, if it's true.

But I can tell you how they loved him. I can tell you how *I* loved him. I feel disgusting just talking about it, but I'll tell you: I loved that man more than I loved myself. I felt him like a caress on the back of my neck; when he turned his attention to me, I swore that I'd have swallowed poison and called it honey if he'd asked me to. I would have done anything for him. It was . . .

It was as if nothing mattered to me, except his attention. As if I wasn't alive when he was elsewhere.

I . . .

It's . . .

I should finish.

I got to know him more and more, the longer I hung there, the longer I became one with the citizens of Iwa. And I knew, truly, that his name was Yamai; that he had once been an Emperor; that he loved the sea.

But how is it that Emperor Yamai is the Traitor and there is no record? Every now and again, that thought bobbed up to the surface, when he was not paying attention to me and I could be more myself. How could this be? We remembered his name, if not the characters.

Surely someone would've remembered he became the Traitor.

But here in Iwa, the streets were clean, here no one went hungry, here money was never a concern. This city was his paradise.

And he wanted to bring it to the whole Empire. The blackblood—that's a blessing, to him. Something as sacred as shrine maiden wine.

You're wondering how I left that place. I've been holding back on answering because I know you won't like what you read. I don't know how long I hung there hearing that story, but I can tell you I was there more than a day. More than five, more than ten. I saw the sun rise and set so many times that it became a candle to me, with a singing girl waving her fan before it. I hung there until my head felt like an overripe grape about to burst; I hung there until I could not remember that I'd ever had a body to begin with.

And then one day, the story changed.

At the end of it, I heard music—a lively melody played on a flute. The sort of thing you'd hear at pleasure houses. I saw the stallkeeper sitting one of the statues before me, flute in hand.

When our eyes met, he set the flute down.

"We're sending you home," he said.

Where was home? I felt as if I'd always been in that place. As if I'd been born there, and the webs had grown with me. *Under Heaven, we are free* was the only language I spoke.

"Your daughter is waiting for you," he said. "You will give her a letter to carry, and you will address it to Barsalai Shefali. Do you understand?"

Barsalai Shefali? You'll forgive me. I didn't know your name then; I'd never heard of you. And what sort of name is Shefali? It isn't Qorin, is it? But I knew that I would do anything to leave that branch.

Perhaps, somehow, I was going to live through this.

"You will tell her that we will see her on the shores of Nishikomi. Do you understand? You will tell her that she may join us here. That she may have herself an army here, if she sees sense."

How was I meant to speak when I was gagged? At that moment, he might have said anything and I would have agreed, just to get away from the thousand eyes boring into me. I forced myself to nod.

"Good," he said. "We knew you were a good choice for this. We knew you would not disappoint us."

And then he put the flute to his lips again, and he began to play a song like a ship on rough waters. Louder and louder the sound of it, louder and louder—until the clouds themselves seemed to answer. I watched with my own two eyes as a cloud slowly descended from the sky and spread out beneath me.

"Tell her we are waiting," he said. He stood, then, and took from his robes the chained sickle. After a moment of winding it up, he loosed it at me—cutting through the webs and dropping me through the cloud.

Where I landed in Nishikomi.

I won't bore you with the rest of it. I've done my job. The world isn't as I remembered it, but it hasn't really changed. People don't change. I'll . . . I'll have to learn again, or I won't. It's a decision I've still got to make.

I don't know what year it is as I write this. I do know

the same woman runs the shrine. I've visited once or twice with my face wrapped up, hoping to catch sight of my daughter.

I haven't seen her. I'm not sure what I'll do if I *do* see her. When I speak these days, it isn't in Hokkaran or Qorin or anything like that.

It's in *his* language. I can feel it. I can feel him in the back of my mind, watching, feel his hand on mine even as I write this.

Tomorrow, I'm going to give the woman at the shrine this letter.

I'll decide then if I want to remain here. If I can make a life in this place again.

If you never hear from me again, if my daughter forgets who I am—please tell her I'll keep an eye on her. Tell her to light her prayers for me. Tell her that I'm sorry I wasn't strong enough to face her.

BARSALAI SHEFALI

EIGHTEEN

When she was seventeen years old, Barsalai Shefali tore a man's head off his shoulders bare-handed. At twenty, she was flinging boulders in a Surian fighting pit. By twenty-three, she was supporting the columns of Ikhtar with one hand.

No one could doubt her strength.

Why was it, then, that the scroll in her hand felt heavier than Gurkhan Khalsar?

She knows this weight. She's borne it before, in the depths of the Womb, when her mortal companions had looked to her for guidance, as if she knew any better than they did what awaited them. In the Womb, she had been the wolf among hunting dogs.

Now . . .

Now she was not so certain.

The contents of the letter slip down from her mind to settle like rotten food in her stomach. So much of this feels *wrong*. That it is addressed to her specifically, when Sakura claims to have had the letter since she was a child. Had Shefali even been born at the time? Sakura is older than she is, although Shefali's not certain by how much. How did she get this?

Why?

Why not address it to Shizuka?

Why leave this story—this awful story, this sickening vision—to Shefali?

She knows the answer, although she wishes she didn't.

This is my kingdom, the Traitor said in his vision.

You've always been the sensible one, the Traitor whispered to her.

He wanted her to know of the Qorin trapped behind the Wall. He wanted her to know what he'd done to them.

He wanted her to try to save them.

Shefali reaches for the kumaq. For the first time in years, she wishes she could drown her sorrows in it. The smell will have to do for now—the smell, and the comforting cold it brings, the winds of the steppes blowing in her lungs. *I am as much a god as he,* she thinks, *and one day, I will strike him down.*

"So . . . it doesn't seem like you read anything good."

Sakura. Always Sakura. The hope in her voice is as bitter as the letter itself. How many years had she wondered at this thing's contents? How many years had she imagined the words her mother must've left behind for her? And now Shefali is going to have to tell her the truth.

Is this funny to you? she thinks to the man hiding in her head. She cannot feel him anymore, not while she is so near to Shizuka, but she is certain he is there—certain he is listening some way or another.

"No," Shefali says. "Nothing good."

Shizuka is sitting closer to her now; she wraps an arm around Shefali's waist and clears away errant strands of hair. Shefali touches her forehead to her wife's. They do not need words then; to speak would rob this gesture of its comfort.

Except that she can look into Shizuka's eyes when she does this.

Her amber eyes, her Imperial eyes.

No—she will think of them only as her wife's eyes, as the honeyed glance she's fought to return to for so long. She *cannot* let him take Shizuka away—not that Shizuka would ever allow herself to be taken.

But she will have to know.

"I . . . ," begins Sakura. Shefali can smell her disappointment. "I thought . . . Was there anything about me?"

Shefali does not want to answer her—but it is her lot in life to do things she does not want to do.

"Sakura, please," says Shizuka. To Shefali's relief, she's kept her tone soft. "She needs a bit more time."

"It's all right," Shefali says. She trains her attention on Sakura: on her rumpled robes, on her brows as thick as Shizuka's, on the light that burns within her even when it should have gone out years ago.

This is going to hurt.

Well—it is not the Qorin way to leave someone suffering.

"Your mother wasn't well," Shefali says. "The things she saw changed her. Light your prayers for her; it is the only way she will hear you."

A warrior receives a fine sword as a gift from his master. Seeking to test its sharpness, he ventures into the bamboo forest. There he finds a stalk that speaks to him and falls into his stance. With a mighty shout, he slices at the bamboo—and yet when he has finished, he finds the stalk still stands before him. How is such a thing possible? For he knows he finished the cut. Mystified, he touches the stalk. Only then, when his fingertips brush against the hull, does the cut become obvious.

So it is with Sakura. At first, Shefali's words don't seem to affect her; she sits, as she has for the past hour, with a faint smile at Kenshiro's side. Nothing in her falters: not her gaze, not her breath, not the gentle rhythm of her heart. It is as if Shefali has told her about the weather.

But when she speaks! Ah, when she speaks, her voice splits like that shaft of bamboo; when she speaks, the tears roll from her eyes unbidden; when she speaks, she ends clutching her stomach in despair.

"Ah. I shouldn't have expected anything different. If someone wants to reach out to you, they'll find a way; if they don't, they'll find excuses. That's what . . . that's what my mother always t-told . . ."

Shefali's chest aches. It is not her fault—it was not she who sent the woman beyond the Wall—but she feels guilty all the same. Part of her wants to hug Sakura—but she isn't one of Shefali's cousins, she's Shizuka's; that contact might not be welcome.

Thankfully, Shizuka acts quickly. She flies to Sakura's side to comfort her, and Shefali follows, holding her wife's hand and trying her best not to intrude. Even Kenshiro joins in. Before long, Sakura is sobbing into Shizuka's hair as Kenshiro pats her on the back. Had this happened in court, there would be no end to the scandal, no end to the discussion, no end to the gossip. How dare a woman cry in front of others? How dare she so brazenly show emotion?

But they are not in court.

They are with family.

Shefali looks on them and longs for her mother's ger. Their aunts would've descended upon Sakura like birds. Someone would be playing the horsehead fiddle to try to liven the mood. Burqila would've put a bowl of stew in Sakura's lap, and Otgar would've signed that she should eat. You need to eat something hearty to get the salt back into you when you cry—that is Qorin thinking.

There is not enough stew in the world to fix this problem.

Sky, she's going to have to go north, isn't she? That must have been why Shizuka was so upset earlier—in her elation at the news of the palace, she'd forgotten the encroaching war.

Thousands of Qorin lay beyond the Wall, and she'd forgotten them.

Bitter—this thought.

Worse—part of her is *grateful* for Sakura's tears. In their wake, the others have forgotten her, have forgotten how long it took her to read the letter. They've no idea of the contents. For Kenshiro and Sakura, that is likely for the better: it would not do for Sakura to know the torture her mother endured beyond the Wall, and if Kenshiro heard what had become of their fallen ancestors, he'd saddle up and ride for the north himself.

It was best if they did not know.

For now.

And so Shefali watches as they comfort Sakura, and waits until she's recovered, and quietly suggests to Shizuka that she'd like to get some rest in their rooms. It is the Hour of the Father, hardly time to sleep. Shefali worries for a moment that Shizuka will ask her what is wrong right then and there, that she will make this a conversation for the four of them. She understands now that some things should remain between the two of them.

Thankfully, so does Shizuka. There is a glimmer of understanding in her eyes as she nods, but she does not press the issue. Instead, when Sakura can at last breathe normally and speak without hiccuping, she informs the others that Shefali isn't feeling well.

Kenshiro narrows his eyes at her. Her brother has always been clever—does he know? She braces herself for it, braces herself for exposing this new wound to the others.

But instead he only nods to her. "I hope the moon grants you peace," he says. "Will you be at dinner tonight?"

Shefali shakes her head. It's a good thing Kenshiro is the one asking; Baozhai could probably have shamed her into going.

"Well—I'll cover for you, Little Sister," he says. "And I'll see to your arrangements. We can make a ger, if you like, just for you and me and Baoyi."

What is a ger for if you do not fill it? Yes, her brother's head is full of more root than brain—but he is trying. What a shame that she will not be able to indulge him, even in this.

He throws his arms around her. She sniffs his cheeks and he sniffs hers, and she wonders if he can smell her betrayal the way she once smelled his. Sakura embraces her, too, and wishes her well.

Together, they leave the library.

Together, they wander the halls of the Bronze Palace, the weight of their destinies bowing their heads.

Shefali tries to remember the details of this place. If she is going to have to leave it behind, if she is going to face her death—then she would like to remember the paintings here, the flowers, the bright colors of the servants like the jeweled carapaces of Surian beetles.

She is happy here.

She *can* be happy here.

Sky, what agony it is—if she stays here, then she may live, but the Qorin beyond the Wall will suffer. If she goes, then she will surely die, but she may free her ancestors from the filthy grasp of the Traitor.

Wearing Hokkaran clothes, speaking Hokkaran, bound forever to a single damned city . . . can she truly ignore their suffering?

And yet if she leaves, she shall never again see her mother, never make amends with her cousin. If she leaves, she will never be able to practice Qorin with her niece.

If she leaves—she will die.

And no, she no longer feels at peace with that.

As the doors close behind them, as they enter once more their rooms, Shefali slumps against the wall. Her two minds have torn her soul down the middle; she is too exhausted to make it to the bed. Shizuka sits at her side. For long moments, she says nothing, for nothing needs to be said; she lays her head on Shefali's shoulder and traces the scar that joins them, and that is company enough.

Shefali must try to find the words.

How she tires of this.

At last she finds the strength to speak—and Shizuka places her finger on Shefali's lips.

"Before you begin . . . ," she says, and in spite of the situation, Shefali finds herself smiling a little. There's . . . is that hope, there, in Shizuka's eyes? Pride? Either way, it is infectious. In the darkest night, even a firefly can light the way.

"Yes?" Shefali says.

"I had an idea. While you were reading, I mean. Before that, I was quite cross with you," she says.

"I noticed," says Shefali. Yes—that is hope, and pride: an echo of her wife's cocky youth. How heartening it is to see her in such a way.

"Well, you'd forgotten all about the war," says Shizuka. "But anyway, it doesn't matter now. I've got everything sorted out."

Shizuka smiles at her—really smiles, the way she did when she suggested running off to stay in the hunting grounds for a night. Her scar is an echo of the crinkle she used to get across her nose; her cheeks are going red with excitement. All around her, the air is shimmering.

An assassin is hired to kill a minor gem lord in Shiratori. Wearing a servant's clothes, he slips into the gem lord's manse. No one who lays eyes on him thinks that anything is amiss—he is only sweeping the halls, only ensuring the manse is as clean as the lord likes it. He waits until the Hour of the Grandfather to strike. When he slides open the door, when he paws across the mats to the bed, when he unsheathes his knife—he does all of this in perfect silence. The only sounds in the room are the snores of the target's wife.

In the morning, when she wakes, there will be a moment where nothing is wrong. Groggy and half-asleep, she will tease her husband for being so cold. She will try to cover him with the sheets, and it is only then, when she gets close enough to smell him, that she will realize he is dead. How subtle the assassin's work! For there is not a mark upon him she can see, and with his eyes closed, he looks as if he is sleeping. No blood stains their sheets at all.

In the same way—Barsalai remembers the letter.

Joy dies in her heart.

"All our lives, we've lived in defiance of the gods," Shizuka says. "I see no reason to bow before them now, when so many of them are dead. The Mother claims that you will die on your twenty-sixth birthday. You cannot die while you are within the palace. I say: we show the Mother that she has no dominion over us. We stay in the palace until the second of Qurukai."

Shefali stares at her wife. This is her plan? This is what has so excited her? Well—it isn't *terrible*, but only because it is not much of anything, in truth. A gesture. A powerful one, perhaps, but only a gesture. When did Shizuka become a Surian merchant, looking to twist the words of her contracts however she could? The Mother's intent is clear.

"I don't think it's so simple," Shefali says.

"But it is," says Shizuka. "When Baozhai spoke of the deal her ancestor made, she was careful to give us the exact wording. The Mother's *shadow*, Shefali, and not her light: death, and not birth. When I was conjuring the New Wall, I knew instinctively which flowers I should and should not use—that, too, is a language. We must name the enemy before we can kill them, and name them *properly*. The language is important—I'm certain of it."

Hm.

Perhaps . . . perhaps this is less foolish than Shefali originally thought. She is right about naming, right about Baozhai's wording of her ancestor's oath. Flowers do have their own language, but it is not one Shefali speaks; she cannot say for sure how right Shizuka is about them.

But . . . Shefali thinks of her horse, of the language they shared.

And she realizes then that when the cold is in her—she is only ever thinking in Qorin.

"The Mother's laid claim to you, but only until the first. After that, my love, you are a free woman—and the two of us can go north to cut down the Traitor. To end all of this. My Wall cannot hold him forever."

A free woman with a fate she cannot avoid. Did Shizuka think that through before she said it? Shefali doubts it. Then again, that is Shizuka for you: absolute confidence that she is right, even when it flies in the face of reason.

How easy it is to believe impossible things when she is the one saying them.

We will cut down the Traitor.

We will go north to slay a god together.

We will slay a demon in Shiseiki, and the world will see us as heroes.

All the promises they made. What are they worth now?

Shefali closes her eyes. They aren't worth anything at all if she is not honest with Shizuka.

"I . . . Shizuka, there was something in the letter," Shefali says. If she is to speak, she must do it quickly; there must be no room for hesitation. She forces herself to continue before her guilt can stop her. "The First Emperor, Yamai—he is the Traitor."

If she'd wrapped these words in lamellar armor—if she set them among "I'm sorry" and "Please don't cry"—they would not have hit Shizuka any softer. Armor can turn aside a knife, but it cannot blunt a hammer. It is the hammer that meets Shizuka now, the hammer that shatters her, the hammer that leaves Shefali scrambling to pick up the pieces.

"What?" she says. A single syllable—and yet the torment within it! Shizuka stares down at her hands, at her wrists, as if in so doing, she will see him in her blood.

"I . . . In the letter," Shefali says. "Sakura's mother went all the way to Iwa. He has the Qorin there—thousands of them—and they all do as he commands. As if he's hollowed out their minds and poured himself in. They praised him by name. Yamai."

She does not know why she is speaking, only that she needs to get all of it out, only that Shizuka needs to hear it.

"He's hurt them, like he's hurt me," Shefali says. Sorrow cracks her voice. There is little comfort for her, even in her wife's embrace. "I have to save them. I have to."

And that is the truth of it: She cannot stay.

Not when the Traitor uses the bodies of her people as puppets.

Shefali slumps against Shizuka, and Shizuka slumps against her.

Who can truly say they know the silence of Heaven? As the stars move around one another in the sky, as the planets circle the gods' creation—who can say what sounds they make? The first gods, perhaps, knew something of that celestial music—but they are gone now, they are gone.

In a bedroom in Xian-Lai, two new gods come near to understanding that sound. It isn't silence, not truly: they have their heartbeats and their breathing, the distant cicadas and the music of the city. Outside, the servants gossip in Xianese; outside, a world of footsteps and laughter.

The servants cannot hear the faltering song of Shizuka's reality, the melody much older than she thought and the words false on her tongue.

The cicadas cannot sing Barsalai's sorrow, for they know not a song sad enough.

Outside, the world continues. Work continues. Dates are made and advances ignored; orders given and responsibilities abandoned.

The gods sit, their fingers joined, humming along with the silence. With their thoughts, with this weight thrust upon them.

To disturb it would be to disturb the bodies of Heaven—and they have done enough of that already.

How long do they remain there? How long does Shizuka stare at her hands, at the veins she was once convinced ran gold? What is that gold worth now—at what price did she come to own it?

Shefali cannot tell her. Her blood runs black, as it has for the past ten years. Fine ink can be more costly than gold—is that the case here? For this blood, for the power it lent her, she has given her life. Will it be enough to buy the freedom of her people?

Sky, Shefali is tired. More tired than she's been in years. When was the last time she slept? The past few days have worn her thin as old cloth. Perhaps it is the silence that allows her to feel it now, perhaps it is simply exhaustion. Her rage, her determination—the black in her blood eats away at them until there is nothing left but the heavy, heavy weight of sleep.

They say that if you fall asleep in the middle of the day, it is because you need to.

She had hoped that the first time she fell asleep with her wife would be in better spirits than this.

Barsalai Shefali holds her wife as long as she wants to be held, as long as she can hold her before she sinks into the sea of dreams. It is a long time—long enough for Shizuka to change. The soft, quiet sobbing that shakes her becomes something else. Quiet, quiet, wordless—the woman in her arms changes to steel. She no longer moves—only holds on tight to Shefali's deel. Her scent goes from peony to flame.

"He will pay," says the Phoenix Empress.

Shefali can barely hear her.

As the velvet dark comes for her, she reaches for the blazing inferno she married eight years ago.

But the fire does not answer.

Shefali sinks, and sinks, and the rest of it—the rest of it can wait.

ACKNOWLEDGMENTS

There's an awful lot of jokes I could make here about phoenixes and rising from the ashes—but in truth they'd all be unfair. *The Tiger's Daughter* was anything but ashen. So, instead, I'd like to thank a few of the people who've made it burn bright.

You can't have fire without fuel. Miriam Weinberg and Anita Okoye—my editor and her assistant on this book—provided it in abundance. Working on *Phoenix* has been a long and at times arduous journey, but with them in my corner I'm certain we've emerged triumphant. I'd also like to thank the entire Tor crew, who have made this experience as wonderful and surreal as I'd always imagined: Alexis, LJ, Patty, Irene, Diana, Devi, Jamie, Kirsten, and Tim. I couldn't have asked for a better debut year.

My agent, Sara Megibow, has been a guiding light. I wouldn't be here without her, and I can't imagine being anywhere else, either. Here's to one step closer to world domination.

For my squad—Rena, Harls, and Renee—I'm sorry I've become a

hermit working on this book, but I promise I'll go out into the sunlight soon. Until then, I'm always down to get drunk and play board games/delve further into the *secret alien truth*.

I've been told I can no longer refer to my D&D group as a D&D group, since we don't *actually* play D&D. For now, let's settle for tabletop gaming. So: thanks to Devin, Edward, Jace, Josh, Lee, Louis, Sergei, and Tyler, who have put up with me when I am too gay to function, too anxious to function, and everything in between. Thank you for indulging my parade of angry, gay, sword- and bat-wielding daughters.

Speaking of my gay daughters—I'd like to especially thank Kaleb Shulla and Matt Usher for making me cry about them every other day in the best possible ways. For all of the twelve-hour-long bits, the war orphans, the cute magic children, and the honest feedback: thank you.

For excellent music I listened to while drafting, I'd like to thank Ota Jun'ya, White Sea, Osamu Kitajima, Metric, Carly Rae Jepsen, and Lorde.

I'd like to thank my parents for plastering their room in *Tiger* promotional postcards. I'd be more embarrassed if they weren't so nice.

And Charlie—if you're reading this, I love you, ya big marshmallow.